Putting Down Roots

Roots Series
Book 1

Jenna Rogers

To the ones who are all too familiar with the suffocating grip of anxiety. To the ones who achieved what they thought they wanted, only to feel trapped by their own choices. And to the ones who believed they had to hide the storm inside their minds to protect those they love.

You are not alone. Change is possible, and you are worthy of love just as you are.

Content Warning

Putting Down Roots is a small town cowboy romance that focuses on finding yourself and building the courage to go after the things you want in life, regardless of what anyone else says. In order to tell this story, I made the choice to include topics that may be sensitive to some readers, including on-page panic attacks, discussions of therapy, alcohol consumption, and discussions centering around the loss of a loved one through an off-page car accident. Reader discretion is advised.

Putting Down Roots Playlist

I created this playlist to help me write *Putting Down Roots*, and I hope you can use it to enhance your reading experience. I have noted any songs that are paired well with specific chapters.

The Best Day - Taylor Swift (Ch. 1 and 32)
Up! - Red Version - Shania Twain
Unstoppable - Sia (Ch. 16)
Texas Cookin' - George Strait (Ch. 16)
180 (Lifestyle) - Morgan Wallen
Wanna Be Loved - The Red Clay Strays
Weeping Willow - Acoustic - Warren Zeiders
(Ch. 19)
Coal - Dylan Gossett (Ch. 19)
Any Man of Mine - Shania Twain (Ch. 24)
Man! I Feel Like A Woman! - Shania Twain
(Ch. 24)
I Don't Dance - Lee Brice (Ch. 25)
My Boots Miss Yours - Jake Owen (Ch. 28)
Lose Control - Teddy Swims

In My Head Again - Owen Riegling
Somethin' 'Bout A Woman - Thomas Rhett
Give a Cowboy a Kiss - Cody Johnson (Ch. 43)
Cowboy Back - Gabby Barrett
Something More - Sugarland
Love & Texas - Regan Stewart
When A Man Loves A Woman - Jackson Dean
Love Me Back - Max McNown
Ain't Nothing 'Bout You - Brooks & Dunn
On My Way to You - Cody Johnson
Fix What You Didn't Break - Nate Smith
It Just Comes Natural - George Strait
Carried Away - George Strait
There Goes My Everything - Kane Brown
Daylight - Taylor Swift
What's Mine is Yours - Kane Brown (Epilogue)

Chapter One

Olivia

THERE ARE A MILLION WAYS SOMEONE CAN GET INTO trouble at 2:30 in the morning. There's the usual sneaking out of the house, getting kicked out of a bar, or drunkenly throwing up in an Uber. Then there's my version of two am trouble, which is not sending a tax return up to my senior manager on time, despite my best efforts, on April 15th, aka Tax Day.

As a Teams message chimes… and another and another, the walls of my lungs close in until I'm gasping for air. Sweat coats my palms, and my heart pounds insistently in my chest until it's the only sound I can hear. My head spins as I scramble into the nearest empty room. I can't let someone else see me like this.

After closing the door behind me, I fling the window open, but the cool ocean breeze floating through does nothing to help me get more oxygen into my lungs.

Another Teams message dings. I don't need to read it to

know what it says. *Where is the return, Olivia? I'm waiting. This needs to be done.*

I've never failed to get something done on time, but this spring busy season has been awful. Everyone has been working more than seventy hours a week for over a month and a half. I'm tired. I'm not performing my best. Great, now I'm wheezing.

I slide down to the floor with my back supported by the wall. Tears slither down my cheeks as I pull my legs up into my chest and hold them tight. I'm in full-fledged panic, and I know from experience it'll take every fiber of my being to finally calm myself down again now that I've let myself spiral this far.

Come on. Pull yourself together. You don't have time for this.

I desperately want to call someone, to have someone rub a soothing palm on my back while I figure out how to breathe again, but there's no one to call. I'm alone, and it's way too early in the morning. My old college roommate, Anna, will be sound asleep until her fifth alarm finally gets her out of bed twenty minutes before she needs to leave for work. I know better than to mess with her sleep. Besides, I haven't done anything more than send her an occasional text or Instagram reel in the last few months. It's tax season, so I've been spending every day just trying to make it to the next. I've closed out the world because I've been so focused on filing tax returns for huge companies and millionaires that don't even know I exist. It feels unfair to call Anna after three months of near silence just because I need help.

You need to do this on your own. You have a deadline, and no one wants to see you like this.

Remembering what my mom first taught me freshman

year of college, when I couldn't think straight because I was so nervous about my final exam, I focus on my breathing.

Gradually, my pulse slows, and the sound of the wind zipping through the cracked window grounds me again. As my shoulders release the slightest bit, I think about what my mom would say if she were here. She'd probably tell me this is exactly why she didn't want to leave me here in California. She'd probably argue she should be here taking care of her daughter, to hell with finally getting to live her dream life with my dad in Texas, where he grew up.

There's a part of me that wishes she was still here, but there's also a part of me that knows my mom has made too many sacrifices for me in her life. It took me years to finally get my parents to loosen their grip on me enough to go live their own lives. I'm tempted to call Mom, and let her know that I love her, that I appreciate her. But it's 4:45 in the morning in Texas, and I have a return that needed to be sent to my senior manager about five hours ago.

I settle for a simple text, harmless.

ME

Just thinking of you. Love you

My love to dad too 🤍

With another swift breath out, I rise from my place on the ground, squiggling my finger across the mousepad to wake my computer back up. I just wasted fifteen minutes on a panic attack. I need to get back to work. I need to push this aside.

A wave of nausea rolls through my stomach as I swipe away my tears and type in my password on my laptop. *Focus. Focus. One thing at a time. I'm close. The deadline's today. I'm almost done.*

My thoughts are interrupted by the sound of "The Best Day" by Taylor Swift. It's Mom's ringtone. Furrowing my brows, I reach for my phone and hold the screen up to my face to check anyway. *Why the hell would she be awake before five in the morning?*

Frazzled, and a bit concerned, I swipe my thumb across the screen. "Hello?" My voice sounds like I just gargled with thumbtacks.

"Olivia, honey, are you okay? What's wrong?"

"I'm fine. I'm just trying to get some work done and thought it had been a little while since I'd sent a text."

"You don't sound fine. I *knew* something was off when I saw your text." Before I can argue with her, my phone is ringing again. It's the Facetime tone.

I accept the switch to video, hoping she won't notice my swollen red eyes or the dark, puffy bags that have made a permanent home underneath them over the last several months.

"Why are you up right now?"

"I'm always up early. I was up half an hour ago." She moves her face closer to the screen. "Ol, I need you to be honest with me. What's going on? You look like you've been run over by a truck. Twice."

Ignoring her questions, I mutter. "Gee, thanks."

I can't tell Mom about what just happened. She will freak out. Ever since I was little, any small thing that went wrong would send my mom into panic mode, whether it was a scrape on my knee or the hiccups. I can't exactly blame her after losing three babies before having me, but it doesn't change the weight it puts on me. It doesn't take away from the constant feeling that I need to protect both her *and* my dad from any of my darkness.

"You need some sleep. Whatever tax return you have to do can wait until the morning."

"No, it can't," my voice shakes. "This needed to be done *yesterday*. You don't understand the kind of pressure I'm under." Tears threaten the corners of my eyes. *No. No. No. Please, no.* "The tax deadline is today." I choke back a sob.

"Oh, honey! I'm so sorry! Everything is going to be okay. There's nothing you haven't made it through yet. You're incredible. Not only are you my little miracle child, but you are smart and *such* a hard worker. You'll get it done."

My heart squeezes at her words, and my lungs decide it will be fun to stop taking in oxygen again. I whimper as I try to get myself back under control. Mom's face contorts in horror. "What's going on? Whose ass do I need to kick? I'm getting on the next flight to San Francisco right n—"

"No! I'm just having a bad day... okay, a bad week." She pins me with a glare, but I don't dare let up again and tell her the truth. It's been a bad few months.

I bite my lower lip, trying to keep it from quivering. As much as I want to be comforted by my mom right now, I know I don't have the time for it, and I know telling her the truth about how I've been feeling lately won't get me the results I want. She'd give up the world to make sure I'm happy. She already has before, and I will never let her do it again.

"I really need to go, Mom. I have work to do."

"Oh, no you don't! I'm your mother. You're not fooling me. Have you been like this all night? All busy season?"

"No. Like I said, I really have to—"

"Olivia Parker! Don't you dare lie to me. I can see your face. I can hear your voice. You're my *daughter*. I know you're not okay. You had another episode, didn't you?"

Even when I was younger, my mom refused to put any

other kind of label on the panic attacks. I know it scares her when this happens. I know it makes her feel out of control, like she did something wrong when she was raising me. Sometimes it makes me feel like I failed her. She finally got her chance to have a kid, and she had me, this messy ball of anxiety that constantly makes her worry despite my best efforts to hide my troubles from her.

"When was the last time you had an episode?"

I shake my head, unwilling to answer. If she finds out, she is going to move back to California. I'm sure of it.

Her brows furrow and a deep crease appears on her forehead. I feel my resolve caving quickly as her anger smooths to concern. Her wide amber eyes have this little sparkle that gets me every time.

"It's been going on for the last couple months. It's just—"

"*Months?*" she explodes. "This job is obviously too much for you. This is not healthy. We need to do something about this."

"*We* aren't going to do anything about this. I'm twenty-four years old. I can take care of myself." I glance at the clock, watching precious seconds pass by. "I *have* to go. I can't argue with you about this right now."

"No. We are talking about this now. The deadline is today. Something needs to change. It's not healthy for you to be in this state for nearly six months out of the year." She pauses, thinking. "Maybe your dad and I need to come back. You obviously need a better support system. We could be there for you and help you better manage your anxiety."

"Absolutely not. You and Dad are so happy in Roots. I can't let you do that."

"I need to keep an eye on you though. I always worry

about you, but now that I know you're having episodes again, I'm going to worry twice as much."

I sigh, burying my head into my hands. "You're not coming back."

"Yes, I *am*," she insists.

"I can't—" I'm saved by the sound of barking on Mom's end of the phone.

"Rhett's here. Ugh, I need to go. We are going to discuss this more."

"I don't doubt it. Love you, Mom."

"I love you with my whole heart, Ol."

I stick my phone in my back pocket, swipe below my eyes one more time, and then slowly open the door, peeking out to see if anyone has noticed what just happened.

Feeling confident I wasn't caught, I slither out of the little room, taking several deep breaths as I move back to my desk. I make it a full three steps before I feel an arm tugging at me. I look up to find my career coach, who is also the senior manager on my return, looking down at me with pity in her eyes.

"Are you okay?"

My lip instantly quivers. *Why is it so emotional when someone asks if you're okay?*

"Yeah, I just needed to take a call from my mom in Texas. I'm getting right back on the return. I just need to do a self-review before I send it back up."

"Olivia, I saw you." Tears start to form in my eyes again. "Maybe you need to take some time off after the deadline, take a step back."

"What? No. I'm fine. I can't *leave*. I'm almost to senior. You *know* my goals."

"It'd just be a couple of months off so you can get the help you need and learn how to control your anxiety. You're one of our top staff. I'm certain the tax managing partner will allow you to take a leave of absence if it means keeping you around. You can probably even get promoted on time."

"No—"

She crosses her arms in a stern way that immediately makes me stop talking. "You haven't been producing the same quality of work I've come to expect from you over the last month or two, and someone needs to look out for you if you're not going to do it for yourself. I think you should start with three months off, and we can re-evaluate after that."

This is my worst nightmare.

Chapter Two

Rhett

THERE'S NOTHING I LOVE MORE THAN SPENDING Sunday mornings with Jack and Mandi Parker, but something feels off the moment I walk into the door this morning.

There's still the usual fresh fruit, scrambled eggs, bacon, and a full plate of pancakes already on the table while more cook on the griddle. Their two dogs, Daisy and Barley, greet me as usual with Daisy pawing at me and Barley nuzzling his snout into my hand until I pet him. But when Mandi wraps me up in a hug, it feels wrong. The joy that usually radiates off her is replaced by nerves that make the back of my neck prickle.

"Is everything okay?"

I watch her carefully, trying to get a read on the situation. Mandi and her husband, Jack, have become like family to me over the two years they've been in Roots. They've fed me, watched sports with me, and even invited me over for holidays. My own parents didn't care for me half as much as Jack and Mandi have, so, naturally, seeing the Parkers in any sign of distress immediately sends me into overprotective mode.

"Everything is great. Sit down, Rhett. Let's eat," Mandi insists, plating the last of the pancakes and handing them to Jack.

"They smell delicious, honey." He gives her a soft kiss on the cheek, and she graciously accepts. The sight settles me the slightest bit.

I follow them into the dining room and take my usual seat at the table. Instead of explaining to me why it feels like I'm at a funeral instead of Sunday morning breakfast, Jack grabs some pancakes, and Mandi hands me a bowl of fruit. I follow suit, pouring syrup over the top of my pancakes, but internally, I'm processing each possible thing that could make these wonderful humans seem so uneasy.

Then it hits me. *Olivia. What's she done now?* Last week, Mandi seemed to be upset over a phone call she had with her. That has to be it.

Jack sips his coffee before breaking the crippling silence. "I believe Mandi told you that Olivia was having some trouble at work?"

"Yeah. Is everything okay?"

Mandi straightens in her seat. "Our little Olivia has always been an anxious ball of perfection. Her anxiety works for her most of the time. It helped her work hard to get into a great college and earn her dream job after school. The issue is when her anxiety doesn't help her, and she has these... episodes."

"What do you mean by episodes?"

Looking frazzled, Mandi turns to her husband. Through a mouthful of pancake, Jack replies, "She means panic attacks."

"Jack!"

"Well, they are. She seemed to have her anxiety under control after college. That's what gave us the confidence to leave her on her own and move here, but I guess work has been very stressful lately. She works as a tax accountant, and they work really long hours with hard deadlines. I guess the episodes—" Jack looks to his wife, who nods along appreciatively. "The episodes have been coming back, and her coach at work suggested she take time off to get some help."

"That sounds very reasonable. I can watch the house and the animals if you two want to go to check on Olivia. I can't believe you'd think you'd even need to ask me. Go for however long you'd like. I know I work long days on the ranch, but I can talk to Austin and make it work."

Mandi grimaces. "That's not exactly what we were going to ask. Although we *do* appreciate the offer."

"I'm just trying to make up for all the things you've done for me," I insist. And I mean it. I've allowed very few people into my life since coming to Roots four years ago, but the Parkers are an exception.

Jack sets his fork down, beaming with pride. "Our little girl is a high achiever and she doesn't want to leave her job, but some time off to learn how to manage her anxiety will be good for her. She starts her leave of absence in about a week, and she'll be off for three months. Since she didn't want us to come to San Francisco, we convinced her to come to Roots. This way we can help support her, and she can enjoy the slower lifestyle Roots has to offer."

"You must be so excited to have her here."

"We are. The only problem is she doesn't want to live with us. She said the leave of absence is humiliation enough and living with her parents after being on her own for two years would apparently add to that. That's where we are hoping you could come in." Jack winces. "Would you be willing to rent out that little cabin you have on your property to her?"

"Absolutely! I'd do anything for you two."

"I think you'll really like having our girl around. She's beautiful and funny and so smart. You two could be great friends, or you know, more."

Jack nudges Mandi in the side. "Mandi! Don't make him feel uncomfortable."

After everything I've been through in my twenty-six years of life, an insinuation like that would normally make me want to run for the hills. I want nothing to do with love anymore. I'd hate to open my heart up one more time only to find it shattered... again. But I don't need to worry about falling in love with Olivia.

I've never met her, but the Parkers talk about her constantly and have shown me a million photos of her. She *is* gorgeous, but she has also refused to visit her parents for the entire two years they've been in Roots. Despite the way she keeps them at a distance, her parents still worship the very ground their daughter walks on. I could never love such a self-centered and cold-hearted person. I want nothing to do with her. In fact, I think the best solution is to just avoid her for the three months she's here.

Mandi speaks again, drawing me back. "In all seriousness, I think Olivia could use a friend here. Maybe you could just look out for her since you'll be so close."

Jack swoops in. "Yeah, a friend could be just what she needs to make this easier. Olivia is having a hard time taking the leave of absence. She's career-minded like her father, and she's got her sights set on that senior promotion this fall."

Part of me is inclined to say no. We are in the tail end of

calving season at the ranch, and quite frankly, I want nothing to do with Olivia, even if I did have the time for her. But then there's the part of me that is desperate not to mess things up with the Parkers, the part of me that is grateful to have them in my life, to have them care for me, even if it's the littlest bit. That part wins out.

"I'll have a lot going on this summer with the ranch, but I will keep an eye out for her."

"Thank you!" Mandi bursts from her seat at the table and huddles me into her arms.

"Yes, thank you, Rhett. Again, I know we ask a lot. We just look at you like a son," Jack adds.

How can I say no to that?

"When is she coming?"

"She will be here in about a week. She has to get all her affairs in order with work and her apartment and then she's going to drive over."

"I can't wait!" I fake a smile while I mentally tally up the things I need to do over the next week to prepare the dingy old cottage for Olivia. There's no way it'll be ready in time, but I have to find a way to make it work because she's sure as hell not going to wind up staying in my house.

Chapter Three

Olivia

Veering off the highway, I'm welcomed by a swarm of red and yellow wildflowers and field after field of tall grass. I've been pleasantly surprised at how green the area surrounding Roots is as I've driven in. I always pictured Texas to be desert-like, with cacti and tumbleweeds, but instead, it's luscious green fields and lots of leafy trees.

I turn right, following my GPS, and find a large white sign with italic font reading, "Welcome to Roots, Texas, where everyone wants to put down roots." Cheesy. More dainty wildflowers make their home at the base of the sign. They truly are beautiful.

I still can't believe my parents have been so supportive of me taking time off from work. They've always been so proud of me for doing so well in school and for getting a job at the Big Four. They bragged to all their friends about how smart their daughter is and how hard I work. My dad has walked a little straighter over the last two years knowing his daughter is going to fulfill the career aspirations he never could, but now that I'm so close to promotion, so close to the dream my dad and I have shared since I was a freshman in college, they decide some time off would do me some good. I don't know what to make of that.

My GPS tells me to take a left at the light, but the little gas station on the corner is calling my name. I'm not ready to get to the cabin and start my life for the next three months. *Three months!* It'll probably feel like three years out here.

I step out of the car and tap my card on the pump. The gas begins glugging slowly, and it promptly stops after only a minute. To be fair, I did just fill up half an hour ago.

I purse my lips. So much for stalling. A flashing sign in the window of the gas station shop catches my eye, and I suddenly have a strong urge to use the restroom. There's no way I'll make it to the cabin without going now. I whip out my phone to check how long the drive is. Four minutes. Yeah, I *definitely* can't wait that long.

I step through the door with my nose still in my phone and bump into a human brick wall. Disoriented, I slip my phone into my back pocket and look up to find a towering man in Wrangler jeans, a backwards hat, and cowboy boots standing in front of me. My cheeks flood with heat as I take him in. He looks to be about my age, with shaggy, chestnut brown hair curling out the sides of his hat. Stubble covers his jaw, and as I meet his striking emerald green eyes, I swear he can see into my soul.

"You're Jack and Mandi's daughter, aren't you?"

I smile sheepishly. I did *not* expect the whole Texas cowboy look to work for me, but apparently, it is. Even with the questionable stains on his jeans and a smattering of dirt crusted on his cheek, I still feel a pull to this man.

Pinching myself with the hopes of urging my mind back to working capacity, I stammer, "Yeah, I—I am."

"Welcome to Roots. It's so good you were finally able to come visit. Your parents have created quite the life for themselves here. Everyone loves them, and they seem to be really happy."

My insides warm the slightest at that knowledge. My parents had talked about getting out of the rat race while I was in high school, but they didn't leave California until after I graduated college because of me. *We don't want to pull Olivia from school now. We can't leave Olivia in the state alone when her anxiety is this bad.* Now, they have the slower lifestyle they wanted, and apparently, they're thriving. It's nice to hear. I just wish I wasn't threatening to get in the way of that again, but I guess I was stuck between a rock and a hard place because I could either come here or let them uproot their lives to come to me.

"I'm glad to hear they're happy. It sounds like you already know, but I'm Olivia." I offer my hand to him.

He wraps my palm in his, and his warm touch releases a swarm of butterflies in my stomach. When I gently pull away, I look to him to see if he felt it too. There's no reading his stoic face.

"I'm Rhett Lawson, the one that's renting out my cabin to you. It's a pleasure to finally meet you." His charming smile is back.

"Cool. Yeah. You too." *Oh my god! I'm so lame.* Then it hits me. "Wait, *you're* my parents' friend that I'm renting the cabin from?"

"Yeah." He shrugs as if I should've expected my parents' friend to be this masterpiece of a human instead of some middle-aged man my dad plays poker with. He continues, clearly not as in shock by our situation as I am right now. "I know I said I would leave the key under the mat, but since everything lined up for us, I can lead you to the house and let you in myself."

"Oh, that really won't be necessary."

"I insist I help you settle in. It's not out of my way, and your parents would kill me if I willingly let you take care of everything yourself." His laughter that follows is soothing, and it silences all the noise around us.

"You're right. They probably would. Well, let me run to the restroom real quick, and then we can go."

"Not a problem, I promised your dad I'd bring him some scotch for dinner tonight."

"Dinner tonight?"

"Yeah, your parents invited both of us over for dinner." He flashes his pearly whites at me, and I swear they sparkle like we're in a cartoon.

Everything about this interaction has been overwhelming. I don't feel in control of anything that's happening in my life. Leaving work wasn't my choice, and I only came to Roots to keep my parents from abandoning their lives. Now, I'm getting caught off guard by some handsome cowboy who is apparently super close with my parents. Plus, on my first night here, I'm expected to be at dinner with my parents and this man who makes me so nervous that I can feel my own tongue in my mouth.

I turn to the clerk at the counter. "Where are your bathrooms?"

He thrusts his thumb in the direction behind him, hardly looking up from what appears to be a game of Sudoku. I suppose it's refreshing to be ignored for a piece of paper instead of a screen for once.

I head for the ladies' room, and as soon as the door is closed, I let out a deep breath.

Roots was never part of my plan, but about a week after the dust settled from spring busy season, I set my ego aside long enough to realize this break could be good for me. Not only am I completely alone in San Francisco, but I don't know what I'm doing with my life. I've been working so hard that I haven't had a moment to breathe and actually take care of myself. My panic attacks are completely out of control. I don't know what makes me happy anymore. I don't have hobbies. I haven't spoken to Anna in months, and I apparently don't know what's going on in my parents' lives either. As much as this break terrifies me, I think it can be what I need to reset and launch back into my career stronger than before, a moment of weakness for a lifetime of strength. I will make sure that I can turn this around and still make my parents proud.

Staring at my reflection in the mirror, I realize how much of a mess I must've looked like to Rhett. This is the first time he's meeting me, and there's a crease in my otherwise stick-straight brown hair that makes it more than clear I spent the last couple of nights sleeping in my car. My face has an oily sheen, and there are dark circles under my eyes that haven't left, even after busy season ended.

I pat a paper towel on my shiny face and rustle around in my purse to find cover up, quickly using it to hide the circles beneath my eyes. I pull a tin of lip balm from my purse to add a shiny coat to my dry lips and quickly run my fingers through my hair. Better.

As I make my way back down the hallway, Rhett's gaze falls on me, and I have to try incredibly hard not to let his attention turn me beet red. I'm pretty sure that only makes me blush more.

"What're you up to tonight?" the clerk asks Rhett as he

approaches the counter. He pronounces the word 'to' more like 'ter.'

"I have dinner tonight with the Parkers. Naturally, I had to pick up a bottle of Jack's favorite scotch beforehand."

Rhett crouches down to grab a bottle of way-too-expensive-looking-to-be-sold-at-a-gas-station scotch, and I take a moment to enjoy the view. His Wrangler jeans hug his butt in just the right way, and I'm suddenly understanding what everyone's obsession is with *Yellowstone* and all things cowboys.

Rhett pays the clerk at the counter and brings his attention back to me. "Are you ready?"

"Just give me one more minute. You can go ahead. I'll meet you."

The second the door closes behind him, I pounce on the poor clerk. "What do you know about Rhett?"

"Everyone loves Rhett. He's always helping people out around town. He moved here a few years ago, maybe a year or two before your parents, and now he works as a cowboy over at Copper Hill."

"What's Copper Hill?"

"It's only the biggest ranch in the entire county. We're talking a couple thousand acres. It's no Four Sixes, but it's pretty sizeable for around here."

"Four Sixes?"

"The biggest ranch in Texas. You seriously don't know about the Four Sixes?"

"I'm from San Francisco," I deadpan.

"Well, anyway, he's a really nice guy. I'm sure you'll figure that out soon considering he's practically a son to your parents. You'll probably be spending a lot of time with him."

"Practically a son to them?"

"Oh yeah! I heard Rhett and your dad like to watch football and baseball games together, and he's helped them with their animals. Your dad has that Texas blood in him, but your mom was no country girl when she got here." He laughs fondly.

What the hell? I can't believe I haven't heard about any of this. I don't even know who my parents are anymore. I would've expected them to tell me about someone so close to them.

This nagging little voice in my head chimes in. *Why would they tell you? When was the last time you asked your parents anything about their lives?* Touché.

"Are you coming?" Rhett calls from where he's leaning against his truck.

Ignoring the churning feeling in my gut, I nod and push through the doors of the gas station shop.

Chapter Four

Rhett

Turning my keys in the ignition, I finally let out a deep sigh and curse under my breath. The second I saw her I knew I was in trouble. Olivia Parker is gorgeous. With her big amber eyes and her long, thick lashes, I could hardly look away. She carries the weight of the world in her eyes, and seeing that hurt only made me think of myself four years ago. Maybe she's more than the ice-cold woman I thought she was.

I glance in my rearview mirror at Olivia following closely behind me. God, even from here I can see how plump her lips are and how kissable they must be. Her high cheekbones, with a smattering of freckles across them, and her shy smile race through my mind. I can't get the images to stop, and it freaks me out. *Where is my self-control?*

As I wind down the gravel drive and find the rustic white cottage waiting in front of me, I'm pulled back into reality. I park in the driveway of my house and quickly step out of my truck, motioning to show Olivia where to park.

She gives me a curt little salute and drives past me. I can't help the smile that crosses my face. *What was that?* I don't even care. It was adorable.

My smile falters as I shake my head vigorously, trying to snap myself out of whatever trance she has put me in. I can't have these feelings. Not for Olivia, not for any woman. My situation is way too complicated, and I know better than to believe this attraction could lead to anything but hurt.

I bite my lip as I walk toward where Olivia parked her car. I open her rear door and reach in to grab her two suitcases. I can't believe this is all she brought with her when she's supposed to be here for three months. I guess she's really set on not making this permanent.

"Oh, you don't need to take those." She reaches out to me, trying to pull the bags from my grip.

"I insist."

She drops her hands to her sides looking defeated. "Are all cowboys this stubborn? I can do things for myself."

A bark of laughter escapes my chest. "I know you can do it for yourself, but I wanted to be a good host. If it bothers you, you can carry your own bags."

"It doesn't *bother* me," she mumbles under her breath, crossing her arms.

"Okay then." I grab her bags and carry them toward the cottage, knowing better than to try and roll them across the rocky gravel.

I set them down on the porch and snag the key from under the mat, fitting it into the lock and jiggling up and down as I pull the door toward me and to the right before it finally creaks open.

"Here we are, your home for the next few months."

She takes in her surroundings silently, and I can't help but wonder what she thinks of the place. It's just a one-bedroom with one and a half bathrooms, but I spent many sleepless nights cleaning it up for her over the last week.

"I'm not sure what you're used to in San Francisco. This doesn't exactly have an ocean view, but there's a creek that runs through the property, the wildflowers are running rampant this time of year, and all the back windows face the sunsets every night. It's really not a bad place to slow down a little."

Her cheeks flush the slightest as if she's embarrassed to be here, to be forced to slow down. "I'm sure it'll be great. Thanks for letting me stay here."

"No problem. I'd do anything for your parents."

She winces and then stares down at her feet, clearly not sure what else to do or say at this point. Her phone starts buzzing, and some upbeat song slips from its speakers, but she quickly pulls it out and silences it.

"Well, thanks." She looks at me expectantly as if to say *you can go now*.

I nod. "I can, uh, drive you to dinner tonight. I'll come back in about an hour and a half?"

"Sounds great."

I swivel on my heel and hightail it out of there, desperate to escape this awkwardness. The second I pass through her front door, my phone buzzes in my pocket. I pull it out to reveal Mandi on the caller ID. I'm surprised she hasn't called me sooner.

"Hey, Mandi! How's it going? Have you heard from Olivia yet?"

"She texted that she was at the gas station a little bit ago, but that's it. Has she made it to the house yet?"

"Yeah, I actually just helped bring her stuff in."

"Aw, thank you! I tried calling her just now, but I guess she must be busy unpacking." I opt not to tell Mandi that her precious daughter just sent her mom to voicemail without a second thought. "I appreciate you agreeing to let her stay over there. I wish she would've swallowed her pride to stay with Jack and me, but I guess this is the best I can get."

"Ouch," I tease as I jimmy my front door open and slip inside.

"Oh, you know what I mean! I wouldn't trust her with anyone else. You know that."

"I do. What big plans do you have for tonight when you see her?"

"Just dinner. We figure she'll be tired from driving, but we broke out some of the good steaks for her." She pauses and then excitedly blurts, "You're still coming, right?"

"Only if you want me to. I don't want to impose on your first family meal in two years."

"No, you wouldn't be imposing at all. You're practically family, and I think you being there would help Olivia feel like there isn't so much heat on her. She's been closed off since the morning we spoke on the phone. I know I've been a bit much, but I can't help that I worry so much."

"There's nothing wrong with caring about the people you love. Hold her tight while you have her." I quickly clamp my mouth shut, wondering if I said too much. *Will Mandi hear the soft hurt blanketing my words? Will she finally see the underbelly of all the secrets I've been trying to keep buried since coming to Roots?* If she notices, she doesn't say anything.

Quick to change the subject, I ask, "What time is dinner, and what can I bring?"

"Go ahead and come on over any time after six."

"Can I bring dessert? It sounds like I have some time to kill while Olivia unpacks."

"Oh, you should bring your chocolate lava cakes! Olivia will love them." She shrieks with glee. "I see how you work, Rhett. Trying to wiggle your way into my daughter's heart with food. I have to say, that's probably your best bet. She won't see you coming that way."

"I, uh—"

"I'm just teasing you, honey. But I want you to find some happiness too. I appreciate all you've done for Jack and me over the last two years. I know you keep yourself busy, but you can see where that landed Olivia." Affection coats her voice as she adds, "Don't fall into the same trap, please."

"I won't. I'll see you tonight."

Slipping my phone back into my pocket, I pull out the ingredients for lava cakes. As my hands work on autopilot, my mind wanders to Olivia and the way she sent her mom to voicemail without so much as a look of regret.

I can't believe the unconditional love Mandi has for her daughter. Even when Olivia has completely shut her parents out, refusing to come home to visit, Mandi still holds her in such high regard. It irks me that Olivia takes her parents' love and support for granted the way she does. Not everyone is fortunate enough to have that kind of love in one's life. Some of us had that kind of love and lost it.

Chapter Five

Olivia

After swirling my dark brown locks into a claw clip, I glance at the clock on the nightstand. I still have a few minutes before Rhett is supposed to come pick me up for dinner. This is the calm before the storm.

I bound down the narrow staircase into the living room. The house is tiny and old, but it has everything I need if I'm only going to be here for a few months. The living room hosts a loveseat and a small green couch, facing a TV. I can already see myself plopped on the couch binge-watching *Dexter* till two am.

Glancing out the windows to the back porch, I note the lovely view of all the wildflowers I've already grown to love. There's nothing but the gentle sound of the creek trickling past and the occasional song of a bird drifting through the air. It makes me feel oddly at peace in comparison to the constant sound of traffic and sirens I always hear from my apartment in San Francisco. Visions of me sitting on the peaceful porch editing content for my Instagram account silently dance in my head, triggering me to slide the door open and pull my phone from my back pocket. I *do* have some time while I wait for Rhett.

The humidity instantly wraps me up in a warm, damp hug, squeezing perhaps a little too tight, but then a gentle breeze sweeps through the air, and it feels incredible.

I settle in on the patio furniture, scrolling through Instagram and checking the DMs on the account I made back in college. @Dog_Central_ started as just a fun way to get a little dopamine rush from seeing pictures and videos of animals, but editing media I collected from the people in my dorm turned into a full-blown account with nearly fifty-thousand followers. It's not exactly stardom, but it's something.

I've always had an interest in social media and marketing, but pairing it with another passion of mine took it to a whole new level. I've learned through lots of trial and error about how to capture people's attention and sync audio satisfactorily in a video. It's been a fun challenge outside of work, and has very little demand. During busy season, I'd make a couple of videos on Sunday evenings, save them as drafts, and post them throughout the week.

The sound of crunching gravel interrupts me mid-edit. I look up to find Rhett smirking at me as he hovers over my shoulder and asks, "What're you working on?"

"Nothing. Just a silly hobby of mine." I quickly tuck my phone into my back pocket. "Ready to go?"

A dimple on his right cheek comes out to play, and I have to look away to keep from blushing as I nod.

I rush in his direction as he leads the way toward his black Ford F-250. He scrambles to beat me to the passenger side of the truck, so he can open the door for me with a soft smile.

"Thanks."

When he leaps into the driver's seat and puts the truck in reverse, I can't help but ask, "So, you live here all the time?" I lift my hand to gesture to the bigger house nestled about a hundred feet away from the cottage.

"Yup. It's pretty nice, huh? I don't spend all that much time here between working on the ranch and helping people in town with various projects, but that might change with you around." The way he says it isn't sleazy or even flirty. It's more like a protective *I'll be looking out for you* kind of way. I hold my breath as I try to tamp down the image of an overprotective Rhett. Oh god, I don't think I could take being more attracted to him.

"Your parents are going to be so excited to see you."

"How did you meet them?" I pry, still trying to get a read on him and why my parents love him enough to invite him to dinner on my first night in Texas.

"I helped your mom with a flat tire one day on the way home from work. She's so kind. I immediately knew I liked her. We got to talking, and she said I'd probably hit it off with your dad, which I did. When I found out that she and your dad were starting to get some animals on their property, I offered to help out just a bit in the evenings, and the rest is history. I think they're really happy now that they've had some time to settle in. They've said they're living their dream life."

"I bet they call you their dream kid too," I murmur.

He doesn't seem to hear me as he flips his blinker on, completely clueless.

"Did you grow up in Roots?"

"No, I moved here about four years ago, and now it's my home."

I purse my lips. He's hiding something. "Why'd you

move here? You must've been right out of college when you came to town, right? What kind of person graduates from college and moves to a small town like this?"

"I grew up in Texas but went to college in New York. After graduation, I quickly realized the city life and a corporate job weren't for me. I wanted some community and a fresh start, so I found Roots."

"I'm still not sure I get it."

"You will soon. There's just something about Roots that makes people want to stay here."

I raise my eyebrows in amusement. "Yeah, right. The heat alone is enough to send me packing ASAP."

He just laughs. "What about you? What brings you here?"

"Haven't my parents already told you?"

"Yeah, but I figured I'd ask for your side."

I consider that for a moment. I respect him for wanting to hear what I have to say. I'd like to think my version is a little less dramatic, but at the end of the day, I'm sure the facts are all the same.

"I—" I haven't exactly shared my story out loud yet. I'm not sure what to say.

Rhett just continues driving, waiting expectantly.

He turns off the main road onto a gravel driveway with a red-painted mailbox that reads Parker in white swirly stencil letters.

The gravel road winds down to a large home with a sprawling green lawn that looks straight out of one of my mom's Better Homes & Gardens magazines. Chickens roam freely in the front yard, and if I hadn't just seen my last name on the mailbox, I wouldn't believe my parents live here. My mom was always terrified of birds.

"Saved by the bell, I guess," Rhett notes. "You can tell me on the way home."

"Can't wait." I grimace.

As we pull up, my dad rolls out from underneath an old green truck. He must've been tinkering with the engine. He's always liked cars and motorsports, but when we lived in California, he only ever watched shows about them on television. Now, he appears to have started a collection of old trucks. It feels different from the dad I grew up with, but maybe he's just getting back in touch with his Texas roots. He grew up not too far from here.

My mom rises from her position crouched in the lawn, plucking weeds. Her hair is swirled in a messy bun, and there's dirt all over her knees. She too has changed a lot from the woman who used to get bi-monthly manicures and wouldn't be caught dead in public without a full face of makeup.

Two dogs come running toward us, both headed for Rhett, whimpering and practically begging him to pet them. I always wanted a dog, but my parents wouldn't let me have one growing up. We didn't have the space. My parents' lives have changed so much in just a couple of years, and I haven't been around to see any of it. *Do I even know them anymore?*

They move toward me quickly, smiles on their faces, along with dirt and grease. Dad reaches me first, giving me a tight squeeze. "There's my girl! We've missed you so much."

"I've missed you too."

Mom quickly inserts herself, grabbing onto my shoulders with tears in her eyes, and pulling me into her. Despite my mom's ability to be a bit overbearing, her hug affects me. I feel myself melting into her the slightest bit. It's as if the last several years never happened. I'm back in college, and my mom is my best friend again.

My heart falls out of my chest and shatters at the thought of what once was.

"I've missed you so much, Ol. Your dad and I have been so worried about you. We're never going to let you out of our sight again." She gives me a teasing smile, but I know she isn't really joking. "I hope you brought an appetite. This is a special occasion, and we are treating it like one. We brought out all the stops, fresh veggies from the garden, steak from Copper Hill, and—did you bring them, Rhett?"

Rhett pulls the back door of his truck open and slides out a white catering box with pride. "Of course I did!"

"Oh my gosh! I can't wait to get my paws on those chocolate miracles. Your lava cakes are the best dessert I've ever had." Mom turns to me. "Rhett makes them completely from scratch."

I jerk my head back and blink at my mom. I've never in my life seen her eat dessert, and now she's eating Rhett's lava cakes? Let's not glaze over the fact that this man apparently bakes excellent chocolate desserts. I just don't know what to make of anyone or anything anymore.

Rhett beams with pride as he opens the box for me to see. Every muscle on his upper body is on display in the tight white t-shirt he's wearing, so it's impossible to miss the way his biceps flex as he holds the box. Any negative feelings I had toward him go out the window as I swoon slightly and think *I'd eat his molten lava cakes any day.*

This is getting ridiculous. I do *not* like Rhett! Something about him just feels... *off.* He's too nice and too close with my parents. That can't be genuine, right? I have my reasons for not being as close with my parents, but it still really stings to watch them practically replace me with Rhett.

Besides, I'm supposed to be in and out of this town. I need to focus on learning how to manage my anxiety so I can go back to work and get promoted. I don't need any distractions, especially not in the form of handsome cowboys in tight t-shirts.

"We'd better head inside. I don't think I'll be able to wait too long to break into these." Mom nudges Rhett as she takes the box from him. He responds by tossing back a smirk.

As my mom leads the way to the front door, she turns to me. "These cakes might be enough to make you want to stay in Texas, Ol. I swear there's nothing better."

I bite my tongue as I try to tamp down the frustration rising inside me. She's already making comments about me staying here, as if that's a possibility. I have a feeling all hell is going to break loose tonight.

Chapter Six

Rhett

All through dinner, I've been carefully assessing Olivia. I cannot figure her out. She has moments of warmth, but she can also be a bit callous. I'm not sure what it is about her parents that makes her want to keep them at such a distance. After everything she's been through, I would think she'd understand that she needs some support.

The cherry on top of it all is that despite the qualities that make me want to just implode on her, I still have this strange feeling in my gut when I'm around her. She ignites something in me that I haven't allowed myself to feel in more than four years. It feels simultaneously amazing and terrifying.

I pour Jack another glass of Scotch as Olivia helps her mom wash dishes. Mandi rambles on about all the things she's excited to do with her daughter in Roots, and Olivia just stands there, drying a dish silently and staring at a spot on the wall.

What is going on with her? Her parents are amazing! They're the parents *I wish* I had, and she doesn't even appreciate them. She has parents that love and support her no matter what. I would *love* to have that.

"You and Rhett should definitely hang out while you're in town. He knows Roots better than any local. He can show you all the cool places," Mandi insists with a smile.

I can see Olivia's defenses immediately rising again. She's on guard, eyeing me and wondering what the catch is.

"I'm sure Rhett has much better things to do than show me around town. Besides, I was thinking I should find a job around here. It'd be good to make a little money and have something to do. As long as I don't work for a competitor of my firm, I can still work during my leave of absence."

"Just because you *can* work doesn't mean you *should*. Don't you think you should be taking it easy? Maybe this would be a good time to see a therapist and work through your episodes."

"You know counseling isn't a good fit for me, and even if I got help, I'm not going to spend my entire three months in therapy. You promised you wouldn't do this, Mom. I said I was going to figure out how to handle my anxiety on my own. You don't need to make it your problem. That was the *one* condition I gave you when I agreed to come here."

"I know, honey, but I can't help being worried. I didn't hear from you for weeks and then when I finally talked to you, I found out you've been having your episodes again. Do you know what that does to a mother?"

"And a father!" Jack chimes in.

"And a father," Mandi amends. "All any parent wants is to see their child grow up and thrive. I can take not hearing from you for a while if it's because you're out there doing wonderful things that make you happy, but instead, you were just pummeling yourself into the ground, working seventy-hour weeks and having episodes the whole way through. I think it'd be smart for you to take this as a break, and get some professional help while you work on your mental health. You haven't taken a breath in two years. When else will you get this opportunity again?"

Olivia visibly swallows as if she's trying to tamp down whatever words she was about to unleash on her mom.

"I get where you're coming from, but the reason I'm here is to show you that I'm *fine*. I had a low point, but I'm past it. You don't need to worry about me."

"Now hang on a minute. We all know your panic attacks haven't been a one-time thing," Jack interjects harshly. "Maybe the job is just too much for you."

Olivia's eyes go round, and anger seeps out of her pores as her face turns bright red. I feel uncomfortable being here to witness all of this.

"The job is *not* too much for me! You *know* this has been our dream for a long time, Dad. I'm doing things the way you wanted. I got my CPA license. I made it to the Big Four. This isn't too much."

I can't tell whether she's trying to convince her dad or herself at this point.

Determined to extricate myself from this private matter without making it awkward, I start grabbing some forks for the lava cakes. Just as I turn toward the dining room, Jack throws an arm out to stop me.

"I know, but things change."

"You two are making way too big a deal out of this. Maybe I had a few other panic attacks before that, but they were minor. I haven't had one since. It's not worth giving up my future for."

"Well of course you haven't had more! You haven't been

back to your job since then." Mandi is shaking now.

"I think it's time for me to leave."

"No, don't go. We still haven't had dessert." Mandi's eyes are pleading, but Olivia is already marching furiously toward the front door.

"Are you going to give me a ride, Golden Boy, or should I start walking?"

I raise my eyebrows. "Golden Boy?"

"Yes, Mr. Perfect."

"We haven't had dessert yet. I think we should stay, and you can all sort this out," I offer, trying to keep the peace.

Her eyes shoot daggers at me, and I finally understand where the phrase comes from because I can *feel* the pain of her sharp gaze on me. I look to Mandi and Jack for some sort of support or guidance. This is their daughter. They should know what to do with her. I certainly don't.

Mandi bites her lip but nods her head the slightest bit toward the door, indicating I should follow her. I nod and head that way but pause briefly. "What do I do?"

"I'm not sure what she needs these days." Mandi sighs, looking defeated. "I just want my happy baby girl back. She used to be my best friend, but now she won't open up to me. I want to help her so badly, but nothing I do is working."

I rub Mandi's back gently, trying to ignore the squeezing feeling in my chest on her behalf. She just wants to love her daughter. I know it's not my place. I shouldn't get involved, but I can't stand seeing Mandi like this. She deserves to have a daughter that reciprocates her mother's love. Maybe I can help.

Mandi doesn't meet my gaze as she turns to the counter and grabs the box of cakes I brought. "Make sure she tries one. She's going to love them."

I take them and trudge out the door to find Olivia

leaning against my truck, fuming, but her attitude doesn't deter me. I'm going to fix this.

Chapter Seven

Olivia

RHETT MEETS ME OUT AT THE TRUCK, STILL determined to make peace. "You know your parents just want the best for you. You haven't exactly let them help you at all. Maybe if you'd stop—"

"I forgot you're the expert on *my* parents now. Please tell me exactly what I need to do to fix my relationship with my parents."

"Fine. If that's how it's going to be..." He swings my door open for me. "Do you want a ride home or not?"

I leap into the passenger seat, buckling up and crossing my arms. I'm fully aware of the fact that I am acting like a five-year-old right now, but Rhett, with his high and mighty perfect near-son-to-my-parents act, pisses me off beyond reason.

He throws the truck in reverse, and we drive in silence the whole way home. I can't help but wonder what he's thinking. I haven't come to visit my parents in the entire two years they've lived in Roots, and I've insisted they don't come visit for holidays because of work or being sick. Now I'm storming off like some brat after they fed me dinner and showed concern for me. I must look like an awful human being, but I'm keeping them away for a reason. The second I validate their concern, they'll drop everything to take care of me. I can't be responsible for one of them giving up their happiness for me again. I want better for them.

We pull into the driveway, and Rhett wordlessly pulls the key from the ignition. I slither out of the truck, trying to silently rush back to the cottage for some peace and quiet, but Rhett gently grabs me by the arm. His eyes are serious as he grumbles, "We should talk."

I want to argue, to just scuttle off alone to the cottage where I can pretend this whole day hasn't happened and figure out how to let my parents in without becoming a burden to them, but his sharp gaze convinces me to follow him to the front door.

Once we are inside, he gestures toward the couch. "Sit."

Arms still crossed, defeat in my voice, I say, "I just want to go home. I've had a long day."

"I wanted to sit and enjoy those delicious lava cakes with your parents, but I guess we both aren't going to get what we want today."

Feeling a little guilty, I slowly move closer to the couch, sitting with just one butt cheek on the cushion.

"What do you want to talk about?"

"I just want to understand why you're being so rude to your parents. All they're doing is loving and supporting you. All they've ever wanted is to be a part of your life. What reason could you possibly have for keeping them at a distance?"

There's a fiercely protective look in his eyes, and his

face is growing red. *Have I really made him that angry in just a few hours?*

"You know your parents started contacting realtors to look at selling their house in Roots the day your mom found out you're still having panic attacks? They were ready to uproot their whole life, this life that they've spent two years building and growing very fond of, just to be with you in San Francisco and make sure you get the support you need. You're being ungrateful and selfish."

"That's *exactly* why I keep them at a distance!" My sharp tone shocks even me. "My parents' world has revolved around me since long before I was even born. My mom, especially, has always hovered and worried about me since the moment she knew she was pregnant. You just don't understand the pressure that puts on me. I feel like I have to be perfect to keep them happy. Any time something goes wrong in my life, they make it their problem to solve instead of mine. I *refuse* to let my parents spend one more second letting their own lives slip away worrying about me. *That's* why I keep them at a distance."

With a sigh, I stand from the couch and start pacing. "I love my parents so much. There was a time when my mom and I were *so* close, but she completely lost herself in me. Every time I have another episode, I swear I'm killing a small piece of her. I hate it. I can't seem to get these panic attacks under control, so at least if I keep my parents at a distance, I'm less of a burden. It's harder for them to see me fail. They can live in peace. Look at everything they've done in the two years since I started closing myself off from them."

Silence falls over us. It's as if my explanation has shattered the picture he had of me. I'm sure he thought I was spoiled, entitled, ice cold, but I'm only motivated by a desire to let my parents live a happy life. He can't fault me for that, can he?

"Have you ever considered seeing someone about your anxiety to help you get it under control? If you're so worried about how it impacts your parents, then why don't you try to do something about it?"

Instantly, I stiffen. "I did try. In college. The counselor just wanted to diagnose me and put me in this box. She made it all feel so sterile, like I had a sickness that needed to be cured, and she did nothing to actually teach me how to manage my anxiety."

"Obviously that counselor wasn't right for you, but there are so many others out there. You have to try. You're so lucky to have parents like yours. You can't waste that. God, what I'd give to have someone love me the way your parents love you."

He steps closer to me, the heat of his body radiating off of him. I catch a faint whiff of his cologne, and now I feel like a stampede of elephants has been unleashed in my chest.

My eyes soften as I take him in. Maybe Rhett has his motivations for being as prickly as he is toward me. He turns away from my gaze, but it doesn't stop my mind from running rampant, wondering *who hurt him? Who left him? Why is he so desperate for someone to love him like my parents love me?*

"I'm not just going to sit here and not make a change. There are other ways to deal with anxiety, like meditation or journaling. If one of those doesn't work, I'll come up with something else, but I need to keep my parents away while I figure it all out."

I take another step toward him, curious about what it'd

feel like to be just a little closer. The gentle heat of his body turns to a flickering flame.

Frustration grows on his face, but even so, there's a crackle of electricity in the air between us, and it's paralyzing. Looking into his eyes, a tiny part of me believes he feels it too. I hardly know Rhett, and he boils my blood, but now I can't stop picturing what it'd be like to touch him and be cared for by him in the same fiercely protective way he cares for my parents.

That daydream quickly ends when he snarls at me. "You're clueless."

"Excuse me?"

"I said you're clueless! You shouldn't just push your parents away to help them live a happy life. Clearly, it isn't working because despite your best efforts, they still almost gave up everything for you. They will still give up everything for you if you screw something up here. Go ahead and try something besides therapy if that's a better fit, but you need to find a way to have a better relationship with your parents. You need to try. You're breaking their hearts."

"Everything would've been fine if I hadn't slipped up and let my mom in again. I had one small moment of weakness. I just missed her, but then I ended up in this whole mess."

I subtly wipe at the corner of my eye as tears form. *Am I really going to cry in front of him?* Shit.

Nervous laughter escapes me as I try to cover my embarrassment. "I can't believe I'm crying in front of the Tin Man."

"Tin Man?"

"Yes, I'm implying you have no heart," I croak.

"I'm only arguing with you because I want what's best

for your parents. I'm upset because I care so much for them."

"But you also just yelled at someone you only met today."

"Touché." He bites his lower lip as remorse fills his face. "I'm sorry."

"Listen, Rhett, I appreciate that you care for my parents so much. I'm sure you're the child they always wished they had, but that doesn't make this your business. You're acting like you know what's going on, but you don't. I've had a very long day, and all I want to do is be alone right now, so if you'll excuse me, I'm going to head home."

I let myself out his front door, and once I'm back inside the cottage, I head straight for the bathroom to start getting ready for bed. I turn on the sink to wash my face, but no water comes out. *Great.*

Swiveling to the shower, I turn the handle to see if that works. The stupid thing greets me with a groan. Slowly, the groan is exchanged with the sound of water rushing through the walls. But when the water finally spurts out, it's accompanied by a loud popping sound, and then water is everywhere. It's spilling out of the shower and trickling into the hallway outside the bathroom. It's seeping into the floors.

I don't think this day could get any worse.

Chapter Eight

Rhett

I can't stop thinking about Olivia and the way we left things. My heart practically fell out of my chest when I saw tears in her eyes. I wanted to pull her to me and apologize. I was supposed to help her see the error in her ways, not attack her. I don't understand what has gotten into me. I'm normally much more even-keel, but I guess when it comes to the Parkers, some of the few people left on earth that I know care about me, I will always fight hard to defend them. Even so, I messed up.

I sit down on the chair with a huff. I need to find a way to fix this. After a whole two minutes of coming up with nothing, I pull my phone out to look up @Dog_Central_ . I saw the Instagram page on Olivia's phone before we left for dinner earlier, and I'm curious.

As I scroll through her feed, I'm instantly hooked. The page is a gold mine for dog lovers. I've never considered myself one. Not that I don't like dogs, but I don't *love* them. After looking at Olivia's page, I'm starting to think maybe

I'm becoming a dog lover. How could you look at these videos, displaying their sweet faces and goofy personalities, and not fall in love?

What's really shaken my world though is not only the time and effort put into the page, but the care. Olivia blatantly lied to me when she said it was nothing. She has been doing affiliate marketing for different dog products on her page, so she advertises for a type of dog food or a dog bed and gets a portion of the sales whenever someone buys a product with her link. According to her page, all the proceeds she's made go straight to the Humane Society and other local shelters in San Francisco. Turns out the ice queen does have a heart, a big one at that, especially for dogs. An idea begins to bloom in my mind, but I hardly have a chance to flesh it out before there's a pounding on my door.

I swing the front door open to reveal Olivia, sopping wet from head to toe. There's tears and panic in her eyes.

"What happened?"

Her lip quivers before she finally opens her mouth. "A pipe burst in the cottage. Everything is flooded. I'm so sorry."

Without thinking, I pull her into me to calm her down. I rub a gentle hand on her back for a moment until my shirt starts to soak through, and I realize what I'm doing. I draw back, going into problem-solving mode.

"Let's go take a look."

She leads the way, and as soon as the door of the cottage is opened, I know there's no way she will be able to stay here anymore. The damage will take weeks to fix, maybe even a couple of months in a place as laid back as Roots.

She silently helps me clean up the water, and when we are finally done, I turn to her. "You can stay in my guest bedroom until we get this sorted out, but it's going to be a while."

The look of horror on her face makes it more than clear this situation is going to be extremely uncomfortable unless I can fix what I did tonight.

———

When I get home from work, Olivia is in her bedroom with the door closed, so I knock gently.

The door cracks open, and her auburn eyes peer out. "What's up?"

"I wanted to apologize again for last night."

"Me too. I'll pay to fix the damages."

"I'm not talking about that. Don't worry about the cottage. It's as old as Roots. I'm talking about the way I spoke to you."

She flushes. "Me too. I guess we need to be a little nicer to one another if I'm going to be here for a little while, huh?""I guess so. I want to make it up to you. I have a surprise."

"What is it?"

"Can you just trust me?"

"Why would I?" *Okay, that's fair.* "Rhett, I appreciate you coming to apologize and trying to surprise me with something, but I'm not really sure what to make of you. I just moved into a new town where I'm supposed to stay for three whole months. I currently have no income. My relationship with my parents is on the rocks, and to be honest, I don't know what the hell I'm doing with my life right now, so I'm sorry, but I don't have the energy for another rocky relationship that's going to constantly keep me on my toes."

"I'm not trying to be another rocky relationship. I'm

trying to be an ally. I actually want to listen to your side of the story and try to understand. If you're going to live in my house and stay in this town for three months, then we should at least be able to tolerate one another, maybe even learn to be friends."

"Let me get this straight. Yesterday, you were *fuming* with me and calling me clueless. Now, you want to be my friend?"

"That about sums it up."

She purses her lips, but after a beat, she asks, "What should I wear for this surprise?"

"You don't need to dress up. Just wear some comfy clothes you don't mind getting a little dirty."

"Give me thirty seconds."

When she comes out of her room, her hair is thrown into a bun. She's got on a USF t-shirt that's way too big for her, and a pair of athletic shorts. I lead her to my truck, opening the door for her, and ask, "Have you spoken with your parents at all since our dinner last night?"

"Yeah, I went over this morning. We talked things out a little bit, and they helped me find a counselor. I'm supposed to start seeing her in about three weeks."

I try to hide my smug smile. I can't help but think maybe I had something to do with that. "What made you change your mind?"

"I was thinking about what you said last night, that I need to be better. I really *want* to be better for my parents, and if I want to get back to work at the end of my three months, I don't have time to mess around with different solutions. I think seeing someone who knows what they're doing will help me a lot. My dad knows a counselor in the area who specializes in anxiety and panic attacks. I agreed to give her a shot."

"What about your bad experience?"

"I trust my dad. Plus, if I don't like her, my parents agreed to stop pressing me about going again." She gives me a satisfied smile. I can't help but note the way she looks just a little bit lighter than when she first came into town. *Is it possible for that to happen so quickly?*

"I don't have anything to lose at this point. I've already hit rock bottom. It made my parents happy that I'm going to try therapy again, and if it does work, then I'm making myself less of a burden to them."

I nod, trying not to push too far, despite all the questions swirling in my mind. I understand that her parents had to go through a lot to finally have a child, but I don't understand exactly why Olivia thinks she's such a burden to her parents.

I don't get to ask her about it because we've already gone three miles down the road. I flip my blinker on, announcing, "We're here."

Chapter Nine

Olivia

As we turn into a gravel driveway, the arch overhead greeting us reads, "Welcome to Resilient Paws Animal Rescue."

Biting my lip in an effort to contain my excitement, I turn to Rhett. "What are we doing here?"

"I know how much you love dogs, so I thought you might like to come meet Carol and some of the rescues she has here."

"Carol? Is there only one woman who runs this whole rescue?"

"Yeah, pretty much. She lives with her sister, but I don't think Aimee gets involved much. Carol does amazing work here though, even on her own. There are a lot of dogs that would not be alive if it weren't for her. The shelters in Dallas are getting overcrowded, and Texas isn't a no-kill shelter state. Carol has helped take in some of those dogs that wouldn't otherwise have a place to go."

"That warms my heart to hear there's people who care, even in this tiny town."

"Roots is a lot more than just a small town."

As we pull the truck up to the house at the end of the driveway, a woman with graying hair swept into a bun appears almost out of nowhere. She rushes over to us and wraps Rhett up in a hug. "Look what the cat dragged in. I haven't seen you in ages."

"I haven't been hiding."

"I know. You're just a busy man. I get it. Who's your friend?" She wiggles her eyebrows at Rhett with a not-so-subtle smile. I try to hold back my laughter before she turns to me and gives me a hug.

"I'm Olivia Parker. My parents are Jack and Mandi Parker."

"Of course! I know your parents. They adopted their dog Daisy from me. I'm Carol, by the way." She shakes my hand. "Well, come on, let me show you around. If there is any piece of you that loves dogs, then this place will be both your heaven and hell." The smile on Carol's face is bittersweet.

"These poor animals. I can't believe how cruel people can be. I admire people like you. I wish I could do something more like this with my life."

"I always need helping hands. You should come help out."

"That would be incredible!"

Rhett steps in close, grabbing my arm and leaning in to whisper in my ear. His soft lips brush against my skin, igniting me. "Do you think you should be volunteering at the rescue right now? I thought you wanted to work on your mental health and your relationship with your parents? You don't need to overwhelm yourself with too many commitments."

I bat my eyes at him and give him a plastic smile. "Thanks, *Mom*. I'll be fine. All kinds of studies show dogs are actually great for reducing anxiety and improving mental health." I lower my voice, adding, "I have been *miserable* for the last two years. I have felt helpless and broken. *I am* these dogs. Maybe I can help these innocent animals find homes and find pieces of myself along the way. I don't see any harm in that, do you?"

"No," Rhett sputters, looking stunned. I get an odd sense of satisfaction in making him a little off-kilter. "You're right. I was butting in when it's not my place. I think this could be good for you. I mean it."

"I think it could be too. This is something I *really* want to do."

"Then let's do it."

"Let's?"

"I mean, you will be the one coming back to help out. That can be your thing, but let's go meet the dogs now and make sure you're up for it."

I nod, bouncing up and down in excitement.

Carol unlocks the gate to her backyard. "Let's go see some pooches, shall we? You two came at the perfect time. I like to let all the dogs wander the property as much as I can, but the best time to see them playing is early in the morning and then later in the evening when it's not so hot for them."

Carol makes sure to lock the gate properly behind us and then gestures to the several acres of land in front of us, completely enclosed with high fences. "Here we are."

A large Husky rushes up to greet us, followed quickly by a black Pitbull-looking dog. Their tails wag rapidly, and they both look as happy as ever to see new people. My heart cracks in two as I immediately crouch down to pet one with each hand, speaking to them in a high-pitched voice. *This is where I belong.*

Carol places two fingers into her mouth and whistles, which instantly attracts the attention of the rest of the dogs wandering around the grassy yard. In an instant, about fifty dogs are rushing toward us. Behind them, the expansive Texas sky is highlighted in orange and red hues as the sun slowly starts to sink below the horizon. The sight makes my *soul* happy. I've never seen so many happy dogs in one place.

I quickly capture a video of it and then glance up at Rhett, ready to thank him for bringing me here, but I find his attention is already on me, his eyes looking softer than I've ever seen them. Trying to distract myself from the fluttering in my stomach, I turn to the chocolate lab in front of me.

Her whole butt wiggles and her tongue lolls out of her mouth as she slips under my palm and then finds her way to Rhett. She nuzzles her face right into his hand until he starts petting her.

"Looks like you found yourself a friend," I say, trying not to let the image of Rhett loving on a dog melt me right here and now.

"That's Hope. She's fairly new to the rescue. She's only about six months old, but she's a perfect angel," Carol explains.

Rhett gently scritches the soft patch of fur behind the dog's ears. "Hi, Hope." I can tell he's trying not to get attached to the sweet pooch, but I think he's failing.

More dogs continue to come up to us, and all of them gravitate toward me, making me feel whole. It's like they know I need their love. Or maybe they need what I have to give. I'd like to think it's a mixture of both.

I pull out my phone to take a video of all the dogs for @Dog_Central_. This content would be great for the rescue's social media too.

I start to ask Carol about her marketing plan, but I quickly become distracted when a German Shepherd comes up and sets his snout on my shoulder. Suddenly the smile that hasn't come off my face in the past twenty minutes wavers, and tears threaten the corners of my eyes.

"What's wrong?" Rhett instantly goes into protective mode.

"Look at him! He's practically giving me a hug. This is just what I needed today. Thank you for bringing me here." I turn to Carol, sniffling. "I just want to take him home. I want to take *all* of these dogs home. It's just not fair. How do you do this?"

"It's not easy. Most days suck. But when I find a good home for these animals, it's an amazing feeling. It's a lot to take care of so many dogs, but it beats the alternative. I'll keep hundreds of dogs here with me if it means they get a shot at a good life. I just do my best every day. That's all I can do."

The German Shepherd has moved from giving me a makeshift hug to basically sitting in my lap, even though he must easily weigh at least ninety pounds. Man, he knows how to wiggle into a woman's heart.

"I haven't seen him like this," Carol notes. "He came to the shelter a week ago, and he's been so skittish. He must really like you."

I stroke his back and kiss his cheeks. "I think I'm in love."

"You should take him home," Rhett says.

"I can't."

"Why not?" His tone is a little accusatory, so he softens it and asks, "Wouldn't it make you happy?"

"More than anything in the world, but I can't take him home. I'm only here for three months, and, in case you've forgotten, I'm living in your house indefinitely."

"I'd allow a dog in my house if it'd help you."

"But I'm going back to living in a high-rise apartment in the concrete jungle at the end of all this. I don't know if you've ever been to San Francisco, but that city legitimately has no grass. I can't have a dog like this there."

"I always need more fosters," Carol interjects.

I chew on my lip, looking into the eyes of the dopey dog who is clearly just as much in love with me as I am with him. I want a good reason to say no to this, but the only one I can come up with is that I'll get attached. That's a fairly weak argument considering I'm already attached.

Sensing my hesitation, she adds, "You can co-foster. It's perfect! You two live at Rhett's place together now, right? You can share responsibility for him, so you can still enjoy your time here. Plus, this way, when Olivia has to go home in three months he won't have to be sent back to the rescue, and he will be staying with someone familiar."

"That sounds an awful lot like adoption," Rhett interjects. "I don't know how to take care of a dog."

"Call it whatever you want," Carol says with a smirk.

"I'll do most of the work for the first three months, Rhett," I jump in. "I'm sure Carol could give you some tips too."

Carol nods eagerly at Rhett as she strokes the top of the dog's head. "This guy would love to go to Copper Hill with you too. Besides, you normally live all alone on that big property. You could use a friend just as much as he could."

"He's just a puppy. He needs to be trained."

"He's almost a year old. He's already potty and crate-trained. Plus, he does well on a leash," Carol explains.

I turn back to the scruffy dog in my lap, knowing this might just be the nail in the coffin. "I'm sorry, buddy. I won't be able to take you home today, but I'll come back to play with you real soon." I place a kiss on his forehead right between his eyes.

"Fine. I'll do it."

I swoop the dog into my arms for a hug and then leap from the ground into Rhett's arms. He stumbles back, stunned by the force, but he still manages to wrap me up. Having his arms around me might just be the greatest feeling in the world. He places his hand over the top of my head and smoothes it down gently. At the motion, a small sound of satisfaction slips from my lips, and I have to cough to cover it as I go rigid and pull back.

"I guess we're doing this."

Rhett looks at the sweet dog watching us with wonder and hope in his eyes, then back to me. As if he's too weak to say no to the two of us, he says, "I guess we are. What am I getting myself into?"

Chapter Ten

Rhett

"How should we split responsibility for him?" Olivia asks as she pets the puppy, who's peeking his head between our two seats. We've decided to call him Maverick.

"I don't know. I figured he'd kind of be like your dog while you're here."

"Rhett, we can't do that to him. He's a rescue. He needs stability, and if I'm going to leave, I can't become his primary person. He needs you too. That's the only reason this was supposed to work."

"Okay, then what do you suggest?"

"Could you bring him into work like Carol mentioned?"

"That depends on how well-behaved he is and if Austin, my boss, says it's okay."

She nods, but looking at her eyes, I can tell she's only halfway here with me. The other half is off plotting the rest of this dog's life.

"Will we let him up on the furniture?"

"Absolutely not. He's a beast. He doesn't belong on the furniture."

She immediately covers Maverick's ears while her mouth hangs open. "You take that back. He's an angel. I think he should be allowed to sleep on the bed with one of us."

"First of all, letting him sleep with you isn't going to help make it any easier when you leave. Second of all, if I'm going to be the one keeping him in three months, then I make the rules. He doesn't go on the beds, the couch, or any other furniture in the house."

"Fine, Tin Man."

"Okay, we aren't going to make that a thing."

"I don't know. I kind of like it. It has a nice ring to it." She smirks devilishly.

I want to be annoyed right now, but my body is betraying me. My heart is pounding just a little faster in my chest, and a smile is blooming on my face. *Stop that.*

I pull into the driveway and help Olivia and Maverick out of the car. He doesn't budge when I grab his leash, staring at the house like it's a monster.

Olivia crouches down to him. "I know it's scary to come to a new place, but this is going to be your home now. We're going to take good care of you." She presses a kiss to his forehead and gets up, patting her side. Just like that, the dog starts trotting toward the front door. I guess I'm not the only one Olivia has an impact on.

As the three of us walk into the house, it feels like we are part of a family, but we are so far from it, it's not even funny. I hate that a part of me wants something like this, and I *really* hate that a part of me is picturing it with Olivia of all people. I know better.

Clearing my throat, I say, "Well, it's getting late. I should head to bed."

"You're not going to hang out with him for a bit? We should let him explore his new home before sending him to bed."

"He'll be fine."

"Would you be fine if you were abandoned and left alone with no one to care for you? Then, imagine you get taken in by someone who seems safe, but you're quickly thrown into the home of strangers. Would you still feel safe?"

"Fine." She gives me a satisfied smile. "What do I need to do?"

"We should set up his space and then give him time to explore the house. We just need to show that we are safe people, I guess. I don't have all the answers."

I pull his bed from where I set it by the front door and move it to the corner of the living room. Olivia helps me set up the kennel near the kitchen. When I go to fill a Tupperware container with water for Maverick, my eyes snag on the big catering box on my counter. The lava cakes. *Mandi asked me to give Olivia lava cakes.*

I pick up the box, turning toward Olivia. "Do you want some cake?"

Her eyes light up. "Is this still your way of apologizing to me?"

"Sort of."

"I like this. You should keep messing up, so you always have to apologize."

I roll my eyes as I reheat the cakes. When they're warm, we take them out onto the back porch. At this time of year, the humidity keeps the seventy-degree temperatures from being too cold, and the lack of sun keeps the humidity from feeling too hot.

Olivia hooks Maverick up onto a long leash Carol gave us so he can roam around outside. I don't know why she bothers with the leash. The dog is completely infatuated with her, making his home at her feet.

Silence falls over us as we dive into the chocolatey, spongey delights.

Finally, without lifting her eyes from her plate, Olivia notes, "These are fantastic. Where'd you learn to bake?"

"My friend Callie helped me learn."

"Wow, I want to meet her. She must be a damn good baker."

"She is. I can introduce you sometime."

More silence. This is so awkward. *Why is it awkward?* We just spent a few hours together and got along well, but it feels like there's something hanging over us. I guess I don't truly know Olivia, and she certainly doesn't know me.

I take another couple of bites, basking in the silence for a moment longer before breaking it.

"What happened between you and your parents that makes you so insistent on keeping your distance? I've been wondering since you showed up in town... actually probably before that."

She stiffens, spooning a bite of lava cake. "We're going to start there?"

"When I apologized, I said I'd listen to your full story. Help me understand."

She sighs. "I wasn't always this distant with my parents. My dad worked a fair amount when I was growing up, but my mom was my biggest cheerleader and, really, my best friend. I just felt like she understood me on a soul-deep level, and she was there for me when my friends at school weren't. Throughout middle school and into high school, we used to have movie nights together. She encouraged me to go after everything I wanted in life, and she made me believe that I could have the world.

"I've always had anxiety, but I don't think I realized what it was in high school. I didn't have a name for it at least. I knew I stressed more than most of my friends about getting good grades and getting into a good school. Maybe I shut some of my friends out a bit because of how focused I was on succeeding. But it wasn't until I got to college that I realized there was a name for what I was feeling or that it was maybe a little irregular to feel so anxious about everything all the time. And it got worse. I started making myself nauseous from the stress and had my first panic attack my freshman year."

I grab her hand without hesitation. Her vulnerability is kind of shocking me. I *did* only meet her yesterday, and it's not like we got off on the right foot. Maybe I won some points by agreeing to take Maverick home.

"Long story short, I felt like I needed help, and when my mom learned what was happening, she freaked out. I think she's always had this insecurity after the miscarriages, like it was her fault she couldn't have a baby right away. When she saw me struggling, I think it dug up those old feelings, and she felt like she did something wrong when she raised me. Except now she actually had a chance to do something about it, so she did everything she could to step in and help me."

I'm hanging on the edge of my seat. I thought Olivia was a monster, but each time she opens her mouth, she proves me wrong. Now, I just want to know the whole story so I can understand her motivations.

She scans my face like she's debating exactly how much

she wants to let me in, and I can't help but hope I look trustworthy enough as I ask, "Why are you hesitating?"

"I've told you a lot about me, but I know nothing about you. Maybe you could share something. That'd make me feel better."

"Okay." I pause as I try to think of what I could tell her that doesn't get too deep into the past I've been trying to carefully hide. "My favorite color is red. When I was little, I wanted to be a cowboy because I loved the idea of getting paid to be outside and get dirty. Let's see... oh, and my favorite TV show is *Friends*."

"What are you a twenty-year-old girl?" She giggles.

"What are you talking about?"

"Your favorite TV show is *Friends*?"

My cheeks flush. "What's wrong with *Friends*? It's a timeless classic!"

"There's nothing wrong with it, but I wouldn't expect some gruff cowboy like you to enjoy it."

"It's funny, and I have a special attachment to it."

She cocks her head. "You mean you actually have a sense of humor?"

I'm trying to act unamused, but I kind of like her sass.

"What's your special attachment to it?"

My smile from moments earlier is swept off my face, and I immediately close down. We weren't supposed to get into this territory. I'm not trying to talk with her about my life before Roots. I don't mean to, but I wind up growling out my response. "A friend of mine introduced me to it in college. That's all."

She assesses me for a moment but doesn't dig further. "Lame."

"*You're* lame."

"Oh, good come back. I never would've thought of that."

"Okay, okay. We're getting off track. It's your turn. What's your favorite color? What'd you want to be when you grew up, and what's your favorite TV show?"

"Okay, um my favorite color is green. I wanted to market for animal shelters because I liked social media and animals, and my favorite TV show is *Dexter*."

"*My* turn to judge *you*. Isn't that the TV show where the guy is addicted to murdering people?"

"Yeah, but he only kills bad guys."

"That show is one of the most depraved shows to ever exist! Do you seriously watch that? For fun?"

Her jaw falls to the floor. "Are you kidding me? Depraved? He kills bad guys! That's a *good* thing. It's such a great show. Have you even seen it?"

"I don't need to see it to know how messed up it is. The main character is literally a psychopath, but the writers get you to root for him. That's messed up."

She turns to me, fully invested in defending *Dexter*'s honor. "The show is a masterpiece! The fact that they can get you to care so much for someone who has very few human emotions and has the urge to murder people is what makes it so great."

"Did you hit your head at some point today?"

Laughter slips from her lips, and it sounds like music. "I assure you I did *not* hit my head. You just don't have good taste I guess."

"I have excellent taste. You're the one who likes dark, deranged shows." A swirl of something mixes in my chest. When I woke up this morning, I wasn't expecting today to go this way. I didn't anticipate bringing a dog home or enjoying a conversation with Olivia. This needs to stop. I'm getting off track from my goal for the day. I need to steer this conversation toward the original topic.

"Back to what we were talking about earlier. What was wrong with your mom stepping in to help you?"

"It—got out of hand." She's still holding back. "Plus, it made me feel helpless. I felt like I had to start hiding my anxiety from her because it wasn't getting better, and I could tell that it was killing her every time she saw me that way. I finally figured out the balance to let my parents go on living their lives after I got out of college, and I was proud of myself. Being responsible for another person's happiness is a big weight to hold on a person's shoulders." Her face turns somber. "I never wanted to push them away, but I didn't know what else to do."

My heart melts for her. Olivia isn't a bad person, and she's not ungrateful either. She is truly driven by a love for her parents, even if it's misguided.

Ready to be done with this conversation, I pick up our plates and bring them into the dining room. "I need to get to bed. Tomorrow morning is going to be hell."

———

When I wake up at four-thirty in the morning, Maverick is nowhere to be found. There's a sinking feeling in my chest as I imagine Olivia's reaction when she wakes up to find out we already lost the dog. She'll be crushed.

As I move quietly throughout the house, whispering his name, it hits me there's one place I haven't checked. I crack the door open to the guest bedroom and find Maverick sprawled out on Olivia's bed. The two of them are practically spooning.

She's already broken the only rules we had. Rule number one: don't let him up on the furniture. Rule number two: don't get too attached.

That dog is in love with her already, and the feeling is obviously mutual. There's no way she's going to be able to say goodbye to him without breaking both of their hearts. As for me, I definitely won't let him up on the furniture, but it feels too late to avoid breaking rule number two. I hate to admit it, but I'm quickly realizing that rule actually has nothing to do with Maverick.

Chapter Eleven

Olivia

"WHAT DO YOU HAVE PLANNED FOR THE REST OF THE day?" Mom asks as she takes the dirty dishes into the kitchen.

"Maybe I could just hang around here and play with the dogs? I can take all three of them on a nice long walk and tire them out for you."

Hanging out with dogs sounds a lot better than hanging out with humans. Besides, Rhett has the day off today, so it feels a little weird to hang around his house. We've gone a whole week and a half living together without killing each other, and I don't feel like breaking that streak.

Our schedules haven't exactly aligned too much since he gets up before the sun, and I'm not even close to a morning person, but we usually eat dinner together. Then we sit in the living room so we can be in the same place at once for Maverick's sake. Usually, I watch Dexter on the floor, so I can pet Maverick without breaking Rhett's stupid rule, and Rhett does research for the ranch or pretends to read a book. I say pretend because it's more than clear he's getting sucked into *Dexter,* which gives me an immense amount of satisfaction.

"It's Saturday. You should be hanging out with friends or something," Mom says, pulling me from my thoughts.

"I don't have any friends here." *Granted, I now live and co-own a dog with Rhett. Is that the kind of thing friends do together?*

"Maybe it's time you made some."

"Does Maverick count?" I point to the dog at my feet, but Mom looks incredibly unamused, even though she thought he was one of the cutest things she'd ever seen when I first brought him over. He's still warming up to her and my dad, staying at my feet constantly.

"No, he doesn't count." She flicks me playfully with a towel. "Have you spoken with Anna since you got here?"

"Yeah, we've talked twice."

Dad walks into the kitchen at that moment, asking, "How's she doing?"

"Good, but she's unreasonably worried about me because of the whole leave of absence thing."

"She isn't being unreasonable," Mom murmurs.

"Mom—"

"It'd be easier not to worry if you had friends here."

"But—"

"Oh, you know what would be a great idea?" Mom turns to Dad, beaming. The look in her eyes makes me a little nervous. "We should call Rhett and have him take her out. He has the day off, remember? Plus, he knows this place like the back of his hand. I'm sure he could show you all the ins and outs of the town and all the cool places for you twenty-somethings to go."

"I didn't think there were any cool places to go in Roots," I tease.

Mom returns my remark with a displeased frown.

"I know you want me to feel like I fit in here, but I don't think it's necessary to force Rhett to spend time with me. Besides, Rhett and I have nothing in common. I don't think we could spend a whole day together." I still haven't told her about the flood in the cottage. Telling her we are co-fostering a dog was plenty. I don't want to hear how excited she'd be when she finds out I'm *living* with Rhett.

"Come on! You guys have tons in common. I'm sure of it. Right, Jack?"

My dad glances up from his mug of coffee. "Oh yeah, tons."

"Like what?"

"For starters, neither one of you grew up around here. He only came here four years ago. I'm sure Rhett can totally relate to you." Mom turns to Dad again for help. "What else?"

"You're both very hard workers," Dad offers. "Rhett may not work in an office like you, but he works long hours, and his work can be very grueling."

I nod, pursing my lips. I didn't think they'd accept the challenge, and I don't like where this is going.

"Oh, and—"

"If I agree to hang out with Rhett for a day, will you stop trying to convince me he's so great?"

"Absolutely! That's a promise. Right, Jack?" Mom gives Dad a nudge in the side with her elbow.

Trying to hide a smile, he remarks, "I wouldn't trust her as far as I could throw her, Ol. I say run. Run far away from here and save yourself. Your mom is never going to leave you alone about anything, ever."

My mom's mouth drops open, but she's smiling as she swats his shoulder. "Jack!"

Watching the two of them tease one another makes my heart float. I miss this. It almost makes me angry with them for welcoming me back in with open arms after I've done so much to screw up their lives. I'm not worthy of their love.

"I'm only teasing, honey." Dad wraps Mom in a hug.

She reciprocates but quickly turns back to me, as if she's worried I'll change my mind. "I'll call Rhett right now."

———

"I can't believe you agreed to this," I mutter as Rhett, Maverick, and I walk out to the truck.

"Why?" Rhett gives me a brief puzzled glance before opening the passenger side door and helping Maverick and me in.

"I know we are living together, but I still figured you wouldn't jump on the opportunity to spend a whole day with me. The first time we were alone together, you yelled at me. The second time, I made you agree to co-owning a dog. Who knows what kind of trouble I could get you into next?"

His lips quirk the slightest bit, and he arches a brow. "See, I would be worried if I wasn't in complete control right now."

"What makes you think you're the one in control?"

"For starters, you're in *my* town, and *I* get to plan the day. The ball's in my court." He shrugs casually before flipping the truck in reverse.

"Great, so we are going to spend all day chasing cattle on horseback? No offense, Rhett, but I don't feel like smelling the way you do when you come home from work."

I plug my nose, earning me a frown, but I keep going. "Oh wait, you're going to make me watch a *Friends* marathon, aren't you? I'm sorry my mom forced you to hang out with me. I'll do anything to make it up to you. Just please don't make me watch *Friends!*" I grab his shoulder and lean into him, trying to emphasize the drama.

"Are you done?"

"I think I have one more in me." I fluff my hair. "*Please* don't make me watch *Friends*! I can't stand to watch that dreadful show!"

"Have you ever seen it?" he asks coolly.

"I've seen an episode or two. I *did* go to college."

"An episode or two? That's what's wrong with you! Maybe we *will* need to cancel our plans today."

I ignore the twitch of my heart at the thought of getting to lie in bed with Rhett watching TV all day.

"In all seriousness, what's your plan for today? What kind of fun things could there possibly be to do around here?"

"You'd be surprised."

"Okay, the whole cryptic act isn't all that fun. Spill your guts."

He turns on the radio. "What do you want to listen to?"

"You're avoiding my question."

"I'm just trying to be a good tour guide. Have you seen downtown yet?"

As he pulls onto Roots Road, he points over the dash. I don't dare admit that I've sort of become a hermit since moving here. Instead, I just silently take in the town for the first time since I rolled into Roots.

Most of the buildings are made of brick, and judging by the architecture, they look like they could be one hundred years old, but they're well maintained and host charming splashes of color ranging from lilac-painted window trim to double doors painted a soft robin's egg color. Lights are strung over the sidewalks, and banners with the town name line the street lights. I'm certain this place looks magical at night-time.

We pass a barbecue joint and a bar, then a bank and a nail salon. Rhett pulls into a spot right in front of the local café. It's rustic, with dark wood covering the top half of the building and shiny tin covering the bottom half. Wildflowers that match the ones along the highway when I came into town, grow in the flowerbeds in front of the building, and the name "Cup of Sunshine" is written in curly letters on the yellow awning above the window.

Rhett steps out of the truck, rushing over to swing my door open and help me out. I hand him Maverick's leash before I step down.

"You like coffee, right?" he asks.

"Does a bear poop in the woods?"

"Uh, yeah, I guess so?"

"Yes. The answer is yes. I love coffee. Good idea stopping here. I could use some more caffeine. I've only had one cup today."

"I might've had another reason for bringing you here." He opens the front door for me, and we are welcomed by the musical chime of a bell overhead. Before I have the chance to swivel around and ask him what he's talking about, a tall redhead barrels in our direction.

"Oh my god! Oh my god! Oh my god!" As she approaches me, I immediately notice her bold green eyes and the way freckles coat her cheeks and her arms. "You must be Olivia! I'm so excited to meet you."

Her drawl is quite possibly the best thing I've heard in my entire life. She is clearly a Texas native, and something about her accent makes me immediately feel a sense of warmth toward her. I go to take her hand, both startled and delighted by her energy, but before I have a chance, she opts for wrapping me up in a hug instead.

"Your parents are the absolute best. They just adore you. I'm so excited you came in here." She grabs my hand and drags me to a nearby table, indicating for me to sit.

Watching her with wide eyes, I silently obey. She takes me in for half a second and then bolts up from her spot at the table. "You need caffeine, don't you? How do you like your coffee?"

I rub my eyes. "Black, please."

"Oh, you're bold! I like it!" She rushes behind the counter. "Do you want anything, Rhett?"

"Oh, you *did* notice I was here?" His words drip with sarcasm. "I'm good. Thanks."

"No need to be jealous. You haven't been replaced... yet." She winks. Then she notices Maverick at Rhett's feet. "Oh my god! Who is this little fellow?"

"This is Maverick. We're fostering him."

"You two?" She points between Rhett and me, a look of pure delight on her face. "That's so sweet! How'd that happen?"

Rhett pinches his fingers at the bridge of his nose. "I'd rather not get into it."

When she reaches out to stroke Maverick, he moves behind Rhett's legs, and she takes the hint, not forcing herself on him. "How about you take Maverick outside so he doesn't have to feel so afraid and us girls can chat for a bit?"

"How about you introduce yourself first? Right now, you're just coming off as some crazy person who wants to get Olivia alone. She probably thinks you're a murderer or something."

"Don't be ridiculous." She turns to me. "I'm so sorry! I just got excited to see you. I'm Callie Fletcher, the other owner of this place."

"Other?"

"Yeah, Rhett and I co-own it."

I look back at him, and he just shakes his head.

I want to ask Callie about it, but she's already buzzing around the café to point out all of her favorite features. A staircase goes up to the second floor that overlooks the shop and hosts a couple of tables as well as a bar and barstools along the black railing. There are plants everywhere, hanging from the ceiling, decorating the shelves, and even on either side of the front door. Delectable pastries fill the glass case near the register, and it reminds me that Callie was the one who taught Rhett how to bake.

"This place is amazing. I love it."

"Thank you. I decorated it myself." She beams with pride.

Rhett stands off to the side, still holding Maverick's leash and looking a little unhappy about being left out. "You forgot one important part of your introduction."

"Oh yes, I also pride myself on being the number one pain in Rhett's ass."

"I might be giving you a run for your money," I stage-whisper to her.

"I hope you are."

Yup, I definitely like this woman.

"Last I checked, it wasn't a competition to see who could annoy me more, and that's not what I was referring to. I meant you forgot to mention you were born and raised in

Roots." He turns to me. "Callie grew up here. She might be the best one to show you around town."

"That too." Callie sets a ginormous mug of coffee down in front of me. The cup is big enough to fit a puppy.

Embarrassment rushes in, coloring my cheeks red. "I totally get it if you want to bail, Rhett. You don't have to show me around on your day off just because my mom asked you to."

"I didn't mean it like that. Of course I'll show you around today. I just thought Callie might be more fun for you to hang out with. She's also the best proof I have that Roots isn't so bad."

"Aww!" Callie tosses her hand humbly at Rhett before totally switching gears. "Okay, let us ladies chat. I want to get to know Olivia."

"Gladly. I think Maverick could use a walk anyway."

He storms out of the café, but it's impossible to miss the hint of a dimple that's starting to show before he rolls his eyes and turns away.

Callie joins me at the table. "Hurry. I don't know how long we have until he comes back, but we've got a lot of ground to cover."

Chapter Twelve

Olivia

CALLIE GIVES ME A MOMENT TO TAKE A SIP OF MY gargantuan coffee before ambushing me again with her chattery excitement. "I have to say, the rumors swirling around town about you are ridiculous."

My stomach sinks. *Rumors? About me?* Memories from high school come flooding back. I'm going to be sick. "None of those are true!" I blurt, even though I don't even know what she's heard.

"Of course they aren't. The rumors in Roots never are. They're just how people in this small town entertain themselves." She scoots her chair closer to the table. "You have to hear how ridiculous these rumors are. I've heard you're here because you're on the run from the law. I've heard you came here because you realized your true calling is in country music. That one doesn't even make much sense to me. I'd think you'd go to Nashville if that were the case." She gives a soft smile. "I promise, no one actually believes the nonsense that gets spread around town. I think people just like to see how crazy of a story they can come up with."

I take another gulp of my coffee. It's not kicking in fast enough to keep up with Callie's energy and the bomb she just dropped on me. I don't like that people are spreading rumors, even if Callie claims everyone knows they're nonsense.

"Sorry." She grimaces. "I realize I can come on a little strong. I'm just so excited to have someone new in Roots. I've been *dying* for a friend."

"I could use a friend too."

Laughter bubbles out of her as the corners of her eyes crinkle. I like her energy. There's just something about her that makes me immediately feel comfortable around her.

"So, what do you think of Rhett?"

I nearly choke on the sip of coffee I just took, sputtering and coughing in a manner that certainly seems incriminating. "You just jump right into things, don't you?"

"I was going to ask you why you're really in Roots. Which would you rather start with?"

I shake my head but accept her offer to start on a lighter note. "I don't know what to think of Rhett just yet. I think we are starting to warm up to one another, but he's a bit closed off whenever I ask him anything personal." I glance up at her. "He mentioned you two are friends. What did it take? I should at least try to be his friend since he's so close with my parents."

"Rhett is kind of like a pineapple. He's a little prickly on the outside, but if you slice him open, you'll realize just how sweet he can be. Give him a chance. You two would be a pretty cute couple." She nudges my arm from across the table with a smirk. Then she goes serious again. "You're not alone in how you feel, but you just need to learn to be stubborn like everyone else in Roots. We are all insistent on seeing the best parts of a person, and we aren't all that okay with just being another face to each other. We *want* to be friendly. We *want* to live in a town full of people who will drop everything to help each other out. You'll get through to him eventually. I'm sure of it."

"Wow. I guess I'm not in San Francisco anymore."

"No, you're not, Dorothy. So, have you seen Rhett in a backwards hat yet? If you think he looks good with his hat on forward, you have another thing coming."

I burst into a fit of laughter. "He was wearing one the first day I met him."

"Oh, then he didn't even give you a chance of not falling for him!" She giggles. "You stick with me, and I'll look out for you. I can give you all the tips to thrive in Roots. I'm a professional after all."

"Noted. Thank you."

"So, what really brought you to Roots?"

I hesitate. She *did* just tell me how crazy the rumors here are, so obviously she's involved in the gossip somehow. I don't need the whole town talking about how much of a mess I am, but something in me is telling me to be honest with her anyway. I think I can trust her.

"I, uh, work in a pretty demanding job. I spend more than half the year working sixty-plus hour weeks, and it's pretty stressful. We have a lot of strict deadlines, and no matter how far I plan ahead or how much I prioritize things, there's always something that pops up. I have always dealt with anxiety, but it started getting out of hand again over the last couple months. When my coach at work found out, she insisted I get away from things for a while. My parents were really worried about me, so I came here to show them I'm okay."

"How did you get into a job like that? That sounds so stressful."

There she goes again, cutting straight to the chase.

"It's been my dream to be a tax accountant at a Big Four ever since my freshman year of college."

"Before you go any further, you're going to have to tell me what the Big Four is."

"It's just what we call the four largest accounting firms in the world."

"Okay, you may proceed."

"I needed a sturdy job, and I've always been good with math and numbers, so accounting was a no-brainer. My dad was a CPA too, but he had to leave his job before he even made it to senior because of some family complications. He's always talked about how he wishes he could've stayed longer to further his career. Between my dad's experience and the way my school's accounting program pushed it, the obvious choice was to work for one of the Big Four. You're supposed to be able to work there for several years and then go work anywhere you want in the accounting world."

"I don't think you once said that you actually enjoyed the job."

"I—" I'm speechless.

Acting as if she didn't just stump me, she asks, "So, how are you going to spend your time here in Roots? You don't have to work, right?"

"I don't need to work while I'm here, but I'm not exactly used to having free time." I take a sip of my coffee, stalling. "Maybe I will pick up a part-time job to give me something to do. I could use the money after all. They don't exactly pay me to take time off work."

"You could work here!" She must see the look of uncertainty on my face because she adds, "It's a great job. I'll give you flexible hours, and you can work with me most of the time. I could use some help with the baking and whatnot."

"Okay." Somehow her smile grows wider. "Where do I fill out an application?"

She tosses her hand at me. "You don't need to fill out an application. Consider the last fifteen minutes your interview. You did great. When do you want to start?"

"That's it? You're going to hire me without an application or anything?"

"Yup. When do you want to start?" she repeats.

"When do you need me?"

"How about you take the next week to get settled." She pulls out her cell phone. "Give me your number, and I'll call you to figure out more details about your schedule."

I type my phone number into her phone. When I hand it back to her, she quickly presses a few buttons. "There, I just texted you my name, so you can add me to your contacts too. Welcome to Roots."

"Thank you." Hearing the rumble of Rhett's truck outside, I say, "I guess it's time for me to go, but it was great meeting you. Thank you for the job. I think this will be good for me."

"No problem."

I close the door gently behind me and turn to find Rhett loading Maverick into the truck. His skin shimmers with sweat from walking around in the hot sun. Once Maverick gets situated, he sticks his head out the open window, and Rhett gently scratches behind Maverick's ears. Despite what he says, I can tell he already really likes this dog.

At the sound of my footsteps, he turns to me. "Are you two done gabbing?"

"We weren't gabbing, you grump. She was just welcoming me to Roots. I like her. I can see why you would've hit it off with her so quickly." I'm not sure what I'm hoping for when the next words slip from my mouth, but they escape me anyway. "She's pretty too."

"Yeah, Callie's great." His facial features don't give away a morsel of anything. "Should we head to our next adventure?"

Chapter Thirteen

Rhett

AFTER DRIVING UP AND DOWN ROOTS ROAD TO POINT out all the businesses and stopping for lunch at PorkScrew Barbecue, we finally pull into Copper Hill's gravel driveway. A large copper gate at the front with the letters "CH" in the center welcomes us as I punch in the code.

Olivia takes in the scenery around us. The entry to Copper Hill looks incredibly rural. You can't see the barn or the main house from the road. It's just sprawling green fields on either side.

"Where are we? What are we doing here? Did you take me here to murder me?" Olivia's eyes go round in fake horror. "This must be where you keep the supplies and dump the bodies! I knew something was off with you."

I pull up to my usual parking spot near the barn. "No, I didn't bring you here to murder you. If I was going to do that, I would've brought you way further from town, and I would've left Maverick at home." I give her a sly smirk as horror crosses her face. "You've been watching too much

Dexter. I just thought I'd help you see the beauty of Roots."

"And this barn is where it's all hiding?"

"Stop being a smartass and come see what I mean."

I leap out and open the truck door for her and Maverick, leading them toward the barn while I remind myself that it doesn't matter how much I enjoy her witty remarks or the beautiful smile on her face whenever she catches me off guard. Nothing will ever happen between us. These feelings I have are only temporary. Love doesn't exist, at least not for me. It doesn't matter how hard I try, I can never be good enough to keep love in my life, so my best option is to keep today about doing a favor to Jack and Mandi. That's all this is. That's all anything has been with Olivia since she came to town.

"Where are we?" Olivia asks

I slide the giant barn door open and try not to let it go to my head as I catch her ogling me out of the corner of my eye. *Nothing will ever happen between you two. Stop caring.*

"This is Copper Hill, the largest ranch in Roots, and the whole county. This is where I work and where your parents got the steaks for your welcome dinner."

She nods, silently taking it all in and eagerly peering past me inside the barn. Maverick follows her every move, his nose to the ground sniffing like it's his job.

"Have you ever ridden a horse?"

"A couple times when we would visit my grandma and grandpa, but it's been ages since I've been on one. I wish I'd had the chance to do it more. I think you've learned by now that I love pretty much anything with fur," Olivia says as she strokes the top of Maverick's head.

"We can get you set up on Maggie. She's the sweetest, most mellow horse you'll ever meet. She won't take off on you, and she obeys orders better than any horse I know. We teach all the beginners how to ride on her. I want to take you out on the trails around here, and we can't take my truck up them, so we have to go by horse. There's a— you know what, I'll let that be a surprise."

"What is it with you and surprises? Just tell me what it is now."

"Can you please just let this be a surprise? I promise it'll be worth it. It's not like I let you down with the last surprise I had for you."

I walk to the far-left stall in the barn and lead Maggie out. I washed her beautiful tan coat and brushed her blonde mane yesterday, so this is a perfect day to take Olivia out on her. She gives me a gentle whinny in greeting as I stroke the crooked white line down her snout and hook her lead to get her tacked up.

"Olivia, come say hi to Maggie."

Olivia's eyes light up, but I can sense a little hesitation. I slowly lead Maggie to her, tying her lead up, and showing Olivia how to approach her. The second Olivia strokes her snout, I can tell she's in love.

I grab my horse, Archie, a dark Appaloosa with a white rump hosting dark speckles. Once both the horses are tacked up, I help Olivia get into the stirrups and onto Maggie. She's a complete natural on a horse, needing very little instruction on how to sit or how to hold the reins. She looks like she was born to be on a ranch. I guess her visits to her grandma and grandpa couldn't have been too long ago.

To my surprise, Maverick also looks like a seasoned vet on the ranch, gently sniffing Maggie and Archie before leaving them alone.

I lead Olivia and Maggie around the arena out back until Olivia's comfortable giving Maggie commands on her own. Then, I grab Archie and lead us toward the trails, whistling for Maverick to follow.

The trail we take winds up around the hillside. It's shady but hosts a beautiful view of the ranch below. Olivia takes it all in with awe.

"It's incredible, huh? The Rhodes family has owned Copper Hill for five generations."

"Wow. That's insane! I can't even imagine growing up here. That seems like a lot of pressure to keep it in the family after all this time."

"That's probably why their son, Charlie, left a few years ago. At least that's my guess."

"You mean people actually *do* leave Roots? I thought no one ever leaves." She smirks.

"When you've grown up here, there are usually two paths. Either you never want to leave, or you spend your whole life plotting how to get out. There's no in-between."

She takes in the beautiful green fields flecked with cattle. I wonder if this is giving her a new appreciation for Roots or if she's thinking about how much she misses the ocean back home.

"Was this Charlie Rhodes guy supposed to inherit the ranch?"

"Yeah, the ranch has been passed down to the first male of the family for generations. It's going to his younger sister, Lauren, now. She stayed in Roots and is getting married soon. Her fiancé, Austin, seems really interested in the business. He's always going to other ranches to see how processes are done in other places and trying to improve operations here."

"I guess even small towns have scandals and secrets."

"I'm not sure I'd call it a scandal that Copper Hill is going to someone besides the first-born son for once."

"Yeah, but I'm sure it was a big deal at the time when Charlie left. I'll have to ask Callie about that. She seems to be in on all the town gossip."

At her statement, I grow rigid. I'm sure Callie hasn't said a word to Olivia about my past, but the thought of Olivia knowing still makes my stomach churn.

The first thing I did when I moved to Roots was make Callie promise to never tell a soul about where I came from and why. I made some mistakes that still haunt me, and I'm doing the best I can to move on from them, but it'd be a lot harder to move on if the people of Roots knew. They'd look at me differently in more ways than one. There'd be some who take pity on me and others who'd blame me. I like the way things are right now.

"You two seem close," Olivia notes, snapping me out of my thoughts.

"Who?"

"You and Callie."

"She was one of the first people to accept me in Roots. She's like a garter snake. She seems harmless, but she will just slither right into your life. It's impossible to keep her at a distance."

Olivia roars in laughter. "Callie's not a garter snake! Snakes freak me out. She's more like a happy little puppy you want to have by your side all the time, like Maverick." She gestures to Maverick, who is trotting alongside Maggie, a mushy look in his eyes as he looks up at Olivia.

"Yeah, I guess so."

"You don't seem too keen on letting people into your life, or even dogs for that matter. Is there a reason for that?" she asks slowly.

I flinch. We are creeping into dangerous territory.

"I could say the same for you. You won't even let your parents into your life."

"This isn't about me, Rhett, and you know I'm trying to get help. I'm asking about *you*."

"It's hard to let people in sometimes. We all have our own darkness, I guess, that keeps us from letting people in, from letting people love us. Not all of us have been so lucky to find unconditional love that lasts."

"Who didn't give you unconditional love that lasts?"

"It doesn't matter."

She looks disappointed, but she simply sighs and says, "I'm sorry you haven't been loved the way you deserve. I can tell my parents love you though... a lot. It's annoying."

"They love you a lot too."

"Yeah, I know."

"You have so much going for you. You have a family that knows your darkness and wants to love you anyway. Don't waste that. Going to therapy doesn't mean you're making an effort with your parents. It's actually the opposite, since I know you're just doing it so they'll stop worrying about you. You should spend some more time with them while you're here."

"I just had breakfast with them this morning. What more do you want?"

"For you to talk to them about your life, to accept their love and their help. You don't have to be on your own, but you're choosing to be. I don't get it."

"I don't know. It sounds like a good idea when you put it that way, but I haven't been happy in a while, and everything I've done in my life up to this point has been to satisfy them. I'd hate for them to see that their love led me to such a dark place."

I meet her gaze, hoping I can get through to her. "You

wouldn't be ungrateful if you told your parents you want to change directions in life. You're young. You're not supposed to know what you want to do with your life now, let alone two years ago when you graduated college. You still have so much life experience to gain. That lost feeling you have right now, that feeling of hopelessness, it'll change. You just need to give yourself some time and some grace. Your parents will help you figure things out if you let them. They won't be mad that you're unhappy. They'll probably be upset that you've kept it from them, but they would never be upset with you for feeling that way."

"I don't know. It feels too late to change my mind. This was my dad's dream for me, and I spent all this time and money on degrees and licenses..."

"None of that should matter. It's in the past. You just need to look at how you're going to move forward."

"That seems a little ironic coming from the man who just told me some bad past experiences make you unworthy of love. Look at you now. People in Roots love you. One bad experience shouldn't overshadow all the good you have now."

Instinctively, my guard goes up. "It wasn't just one bad experience. It was my parents and then—it wasn't just one bad experience."

"You're a good guy, Rhett. You're *worthy* of love. You can't—"

"We're about to reach the surprise. Let me help you down from Maggie so you can take it in."

I want to sink into the comfort of her words, but I know better. I've had this conversation before. I let myself be convinced things were a fluke, but it was all taken away from me. I'm not making that mistake again.

As I help Olivia slide off of Maggie, my hand meets the

bare skin of her waist. It makes it impossible to think straight. If this small touch causes such a big impact, I wonder what it would feel like to be able to touch other parts of her, to caress her face and kiss her lips, to—*snap out of it.*

We reach the end of the trail, and everything opens up. "Look!" I point toward the horizon. The landscape is flat, so you can see not only Copper Hill, but Roots Road, the glistening river that winds through town, and even my property. At this time of year, everything is green and vibrant, but we can also see patches of red and yellow that mark the beautiful wildflowers that grow around here. It's my favorite view in the entire world, but today, as I watch Olivia's eyes sparkle with amusement, the sun shining on her face and illuminating the tiny freckles on her cheekbones, all I can focus on is her.

"It's incredible up here. You can see everything." She bites her lower lip as if she's trying to tame her reaction to all of this. *God, she's beautiful.* And stubborn but brave and devoted. And infuriating but magnetic. Except none of that matters because I can't have her.

Chapter Fourteen

Olivia

Bringing home a one-year-old German Shepherd a little over two weeks ago has already been providing its challenges. For starters, Maverick still needs stuff to call his own. Carol graciously sent us home with a few days' worth of kibble along with a kennel and a bed for him, but I'd still like to get him toys and some bowls to eat and drink out of that are actually meant for a dog instead of the mismatched Tupperware from Rhett's kitchen.

However, that minor inconvenience pales in comparison to the excitement of finally having a dog in my life. I woke up early to the sun shining and the birds chirping and got to take him for a walk before the heat settled in for the day. Between the exercise and having a dog in my presence, I felt so content. When we got back, I fed him and then he laid with his head in my lap for a solid half an hour while I worked on a couple of posts for @Dog_Central_.

I settle back down on the couch with my laptop in hand, while Maverick watches me lazily. The tan patches of fur above his eyes look like eyebrows, and right now I'm convinced he's raising them at me.

"What are you looking at?" I giggle. "I have a whole list of to-dos today that don't just involve taking you on walks. First, I need to check the schedule Callie sent over to me this morning. Then, I want to create a rough draft of a marketing plan for Carol. I think she could boost her funding for the rescue if she plays her cards right. After that, I need to figure out what to do with the rest of my day while my parents are working. That's where you come in again." I give him a wink.

He just sets his head down on the floor and huffs a deep sigh, as if the fact that I have other plans for the day is a deep inconvenience to him.

"At least I didn't leave you here while I went to work, like Rhett."

He doesn't look amused.

I pull open my email, and instead of a schedule from Callie sitting at the top, I have a message from my coach. *Why would she send something to my personal email?*

Olivia,

I hope you're doing well and getting some time to rest up on your time off. We will be ready for you in the full swing of fall busy season by the time you come back.

I wanted to check in with you regarding promotions. I know it was your goal to make senior and that you were concerned your leave of absence might affect this. I spoke with the tax managing partner at the firm,

and he seems to still be open to promoting you in October with the rest of your start class if we can build a strong portfolio for all the things you've contributed to the firm. These portfolios will need to be submitted by the middle of August, which will only give us two weeks after you return to pull something together. If you have anything you'd like to submit now to stay ahead of the game, please let me know. You're a superstar!

Best,
Madeline

Lowering my laptop screen, I take in a deep breath. I hate that this email is getting to me as much as it is, but I can't stop the large pit from forming in my stomach. This should be a good thing. I *want* to get promoted, but I'm not ready to think about going back to work just yet. I'm just getting started here in Roots, and I kind of like the life I've been building. I have my first therapy appointment tomorrow, and after the immense amount of research I've done on her, I'm hopeful this counselor will teach me some tools for how to manage my anxiety. I have Maverick now, who has been such a joy to have in my life. I'm starting to actually like Rhett, and I'm excited about helping out at the rescue *and* working with Callie at Cup of Sunshine.

A tiny part of me wants to see where all of this could go, but then it hits me how close I am to my goals. I need to refocus on what I came here for. I'm supposed to help settle my parents, work on my anxiety, and then I need to get back to my job. That's always been the plan. That's what's always been expected of me, but maybe things could change. I can't shake this nagging feeling in my gut.

"The Best Day" by Taylor Swift trickles through the speaker of my phone, indicating a call from my mom. I take one more deep breath, trying to recenter myself, and then answer.

"Hi, sweetie! I just wanted to check in with you. We're still on for dinner tomorrow night after your appointment, right?"

"Yup."

"Okay, great. I think I'll invite Rhett too."

"Sure, sounds great!" I wince. The words came out a little too eager. I hope she didn't notice.

"What are you up to right now? Is everything going okay? I'm sure you must be bored with your dad and I both being at work, and then I have my church group meeting tonight. I'm sorry."

"No, it's fine. Um, I just got an email from Madeline, my coach."

"Oh, why is she emailing you when you're on leave? Isn't there some sort of policy against sending you emails?"

I shrug as if she can see me. "I don't know. I don't remember seeing anything in the paperwork. It's not like she was asking me to come back early or do taxes."

"Then what did she want?"

I quickly fill her in on the email, bringing back that nagging weight.

"Oh, that's wonderful, Ol! You can still make it to senior! Your dad will be *so* proud. You know how bummed he was that he had to leave his firm just before promotion."

"Yes, I remember the story. I'm excited about it." I try to force my tone to sound light, hiding the way my mind is currently swirling with overwhelm. "Aren't you supposed to be working right now, Mom? I can let you go."

"Yes, I am, but that's okay. You know what, I can blow off my meeting this afternoon and come hang out with you. We could go shopping and get some ice cream or something. Oh, that'd be so fun!"

"What meeting?" Panic inflates in my chest. "No, don't blow off your meeting for me. I promise I can entertain myself."

"It's no big deal at all."

The panic continues to rise, and I desperately try to breathe through my nose to keep from going over the edge. She's not going to blow off something important for me again. I won't allow it.

"Don't leave work early! I'm fine. Just stay there, and I'll see you tomorrow. You have your life now. I'm okay with that. You don't need to change all your plans for me. *I'm fine.*"

"Okay, okay. I get the message. I'll text you later and see you tomorrow then. Kisses!"

"Bye."

I hang up the phone and toss it on the couch as my mind spirals out of control. I'm overwhelmed. First, I had these feelings of wanting to explore my life in Roots and not go back to my job. Then, Mom has to go and remind me exactly why I can't give up what I've built over the last few years. She nearly bailed on her meeting just to make sure I'm not *bored.* She's relentless. I don't know what more I could do to keep her happy and make sure she and my dad are living their own lives.

Figuring I just need to distract myself, I force myself into the kitchen, grabbing a loaf of bread and the jars of peanut butter and jelly. *I'm making a sandwich. I'm focused on the sandwich.* I grab a knife from the drawer and stick it into the jar of peanut butter, taking out a heaping glob.

I'm making a sandwich. I'm making a sandwich. It almost works, until my thoughts completely take over again.

I just don't know what to do with my parents anymore. It's like everything I do is for nothing. All my hard work to keep them happy is a waste. I'm making myself miserable, and it's still not working. I need to try harder. As my thoughts grow further and further out of control, so does my breathing.

I know what comes next. Tears slither down my cheeks, and my palms grow clammy. The jar of jelly in my hand slips from my grip and shatters on the floor. Maverick leaps up to his feet at the sound. I want to apologize and comfort him, but instead, I gasp for air and crawl to the guest bedroom, where I curl into a ball, wanting this pain and all my spiraling thoughts to just stop.

Maverick comes over to me and lays his head in my lap. I thank God he's shown no interest in human food since he came home, considering the mess I just made.

My ragged breaths continue as I curl tighter into a ball. I don't know what to do.

Chapter Fifteen

Rhett

I GOT OFF WORK A LITTLE EARLY TODAY, AND I CAN'T shake my excitement over the fact that I'll get to spend more time with Olivia. Most nights when I get home, we cook a late dinner and head to bed maybe an hour later. Today, we should have more time together.

I swing the front door open, half expecting to find Maverick and Olivia running around the house together or sitting on the couch watching *Dexter,* but instead, I'm met with deafening silence.

I scan the kitchen and find crusty jelly on the floor. An open jar of peanut butter still sits on the counter. I've only known Olivia for about two and a half weeks, but I'm pretty confident she wouldn't just abandon a mess like this.

I peer into the guest bedroom, which still has the door open, and find Olivia, crumpled in a ball and covered in both a blanket and a protective German Shepherd.

I rush toward her and am met with a curled lip from Maverick. Doing my best to ignore him, instead of making him feel challenged, I drop to my knees by Olivia's side. When I sweep my hand gently over Olivia's forehead, he backs off.

I scoop her into my arms, noting her shallow breathing. My touch seems to draw her out of her cocoon. When she looks up at me with those amber orbs I've already become so fond of, they're stained with tears. I've never seen someone have a panic attack before, but I imagine this must be it.

I rub my hand gently on her back. "It's me. It's Rhett. It's okay now. I'm here."

She goes stiff when realization hits her. "Rhett? What... are you... doing... here?" She's still gasping.

"I came to check on you."

"Please... go... away."

"No, I'm going to stay right here with you until it's over. What can I do for you?"

"Just... hold me... please."

I lift her onto her bed, wrapping my arms around her with firm but gentle pressure, letting her know I'm here without restricting her ability to take in air. "I'm here. I've got you."

As her breathing slowly starts to sound regular again, I remain silent, allowing her to have whatever space she needs to calm herself down. Just when I think we have made it out, she takes a sharp inhale, wheezing again. Without even thinking, I hold her tighter and nuzzle into the crook of her neck, whispering. "It's okay. You're safe. I'm here. I've got you. Breathe." The words come out sounding confident, but inside I'm a wreck. I hate seeing the strong and fierce woman I know be torn down by her thoughts.

I take one hand and smooth it gently over her hair,

sweeping it away from her face as her breathing begins to slow again. I don't relax until she finally says, "Thank you."

"You're welcome," I whisper against her ear, afraid to shatter the calm that has finally settled upon us.

We sit there quietly for all of thirty seconds until she regains her bearings and realizes she is practically sitting in my lap. She scrambles from my arms, eyes wide.

"Can I do anything for you? Do you want some water?" I ask, trying to look nonchalant after what just happened. I don't want her to feel judged. I just want to make sure she's okay.

"You have done plenty already. Thank you." After a pause, she admits, "Water does sound nice though. I can grab us some glasses."

As she attempts to rise from the bed, I yank her back down, wrapping her up tightly in my arms. "Olivia Parker! It's okay to be vulnerable once in a while. Let me take care of you. When was the last time you let someone take care of you without fighting it?"

She keeps her mouth clamped shut, which is all the answer I need to suggest she has no recollection of a time that she accepted help from someone else.

"That's what I thought." I slowly release her from my grip and get up from the bed, slipping into the kitchen. I pull out a single glass and fill it with water, narrowly avoiding the jelly mess still on the floor.

I wipe it up with a paper towel, and as I come back into the room, I ask, "Maverick didn't try to eat this?"

"No, he is the least food-driven dog I've ever seen. I can drop whatever I want on the floor, and he won't touch it. I guess you need to spend more time with him if you don't know that yet."

"Or I'm just not as messy as you."

"No way! Have you seen the dirt you track through the house from your cowboy boots? Don't even get me started on the way you smell right now."

A smile slips onto my face. My fierce girl is back. I mean not my girl. Definitely not mine. Even so, I sit back down on the bed extra close to her. I'm worried. I knew she was struggling, but it's one thing to know it and another to see it.

"Here," I say, handing her the glass of water.

"Thank you." She takes a sip. "You know, it was just a panic attack. It doesn't mean I can't get myself water. I deal with these alone all the time."

"I'm sorry you have had to go through these alone." I know what it's like to do hard things with no one to support you. My heart aches for her. "I hope you know you don't *need* to be alone. Your parents would be there for you if you let them, and you wouldn't be a burden to them. It'd probably actually help make them feel like they're still needed. I —I could be there for you while you're here... if you ever need it again. I don't have much experience with panic attacks, so I'm not sure the right way to help, but I can learn to be better—"

"Rhett, you don't need to be better. You were great. I was very thankful to have you here."

A hesitant smile crosses my lips. "I did okay then?"

"You did more than okay."

I give her a nod and try to hide the satisfied smirk that's tugging at the corners of my mouth. "Can I ask what happened? Or do you not want to talk about it?"

"I don't think I'm ready yet. If I talk about it now, I'll just spiral right back to where I was a few minutes ago."

"Okay, then how do we help you get to a place where you can talk about it without panicking again?"

She chews on her lower lip. "Could you just talk to me

about other stuff? Tell me about you." The look on my face must show my hesitation and dread because she adds, "You don't have to tell me all your deepest, darkest secrets but tell me something about you. I don't know much. Where'd you grow up?"

"I grew up in a small town outside of Austin."

"Did you have siblings?"

"No, I was an only child like you."

"Were you close with your parents?"

"No," I say simply.

"Well damn."

I furrow my brows. "What?"

"I just can't seem to get anything out of you. Why weren't you close with your parents?"

"Do you want more water?" I quickly stand from the bed again, causing Maverick's ears to perk up.

"No, I'm fine. Rhett, please. This is helping me."

I sigh and sit back down. "My parents got divorced when I was ten. Their relationship was rocky for as long as I could remember though. They always put me in the middle of their stupid fights, which made it pretty hard to bond with them over anything else."

"Did it ever get better though? Do you still talk with your parents?"

"I think it only got worse. I was relieved when they split, but it turned out they were holding themselves back when they lived together. Once they had a taste of being apart, it was impossible for them to be in the same room together. Growing up around that, it makes it hard to believe in love, you know? Then I had to go and make some decisions that only drove a bigger wedge between me and my parents." I stop, not willing to go any further. I've already said more than I ever planned to tell Olivia. *How'd she do that?*

She reaches out to me, gently tracing her finger across the top of my hand, over and over. Somehow the action relaxes me. "Is that why you said you haven't been so lucky to have unconditional love that lasts... because your parents couldn't set aside their differences to stay together?"

I open my mouth and then quickly clamp it shut, casting my gaze down to my lap. "Yeah, for starters."

"What else?"

"I don't want to talk about it."

Silence falls over us like a wet blanket. It quickly becomes too much for me to handle. Clapping my hands together, I say, "Okay, well that's enough of that Debbie-downer shit. Is there a different way I can help you?"

"Will you watch *Dexter* with me?"

"Really? That show?" Any other time I might agree because I'm slowly getting sucked into the show, but I'm worried it won't help her. "We should watch *Friends*. That'll get you laughing and help your anxiety. *Dexter* will just get you amped up."

She tosses her hand out as if to say *duh*. "But it'll get me amped up in a *different* way than before."

I bark out in laughter and roll my eyes, the shadow of a smile gracing my lips. "How about we try one episode of *Friends*? It's just twenty minutes of your time. After that, if you don't feel better or still want to watch *Dexter*, we can do that."

She crosses her arms. "I thought I got to choose what was going to help me."

"Not anymore." I sweep her off her bed, throwing her over my shoulder like a sack of potatoes and carrying her up the stairs to my bedroom. That's where the good TV is.

"Rhett! Put me down!" She wails, batting her palms against my back. Maverick starts barking at me.

"Stop resisting! Just let me take care of you for a little bit longer. It'll all be over soon."

"Thank God!" she says as I set her down. Our gazes meet, and there's something there. I can feel it. I know she can feel it too. This is not just about how beautiful Olivia is or what it feels like to touch her. I actually care for Olivia as a human being. I want to protect her. I want to make her laugh. I want to protect myself from these feelings, but we've both knocked down some of our walls today, and I'm scared to death that without those walls, I'm beyond saving.

Chapter Sixteen

Rhett

Curled up in a ball, breathing heavily with her head on my chest, Olivia looks like a dream. She made it through maybe one and a half episodes of *Friends* before she dozed off, but the feeling of her asleep on my chest, tucked under my left arm is nothing short of incredible.

I take her in as she lays there peacefully. She has a smattering of freckles that fleck the tops of her cheeks, and a small mole on the left side of her neck that I desperately want to press my lips to. Her rhythmic breathing grounds me.

Another episode begins on the TV, and the theme song blasts way louder than the rest of the show. Olivia instantly stirs, and as she realizes she's wrapped around me like a koala on a tree, horror fills her face.

She shoots up, startling Maverick who was comfortably sprawled at her feet.

"Sorry," she says to Maverick and then to me.

"Don't be sorry. You needed rest."

"How long was I asleep?"

"Couldn't have been long. Maybe two episodes?"

"Oh." She directs her attention to Maverick, scratching behind his ears after he settles back down with his head in her lap.

"I should probably get off your bed now." She looks at me, obviously seeing the concern in my eyes because she adds, "I'll be okay. I promise."

She's closing down. She's going to hide away in her room until Maverick needs something, but I still really want to be with her.

"Are you hungry? I can cook some burgers for us."

"I could go for a burger."

My lips quirk. *God, why am I so desperate to be around her?* I know I can't have her, and yet I can't stay away.

———

Pulling the burgers off the grill, I turn to Olivia. "No way. Your mom turned your wheelchair into a carriage for Halloween? I didn't realize she was crafty."

"I don't think she is." She laughs. "That's the only time I've ever seen her creative side come out, and she spent two whole weeks on it."

I pass her a burger and a bun so she can add toppings. When we settle into the chairs on the back porch, the humidity swaddles us, and the sound of birds playfully chirping fills the air. It's peaceful. I figured it'd be exactly what Olivia could use after the day she's had.

"Do you want to see the costume? I'm pretty sure I have a picture."

"Hell yeah, I want to see it."

She scrolls through her phone for a few moments, her

face screwed in concentration, before she finally hands it over to me. Five-year-old Olivia is perched in a wheelchair with her brown hair cascading over her shoulders, topped with a sparkly crown. I can just barely see her baby blue Cinderella dress over the top of the elaborate carriage Mandi created from cardboard and a lot of duct tape.

"Your mom really cares for you."

"I know. She did stuff like this all the time. In high school, I failed an English test and she stayed up all night with me before the next test to help me study. My dad has done some above and beyond things for me too."

"Like what?"

She pauses. "Are you sure it doesn't bother you to hear all these stories about my parents... given your relationship with yours?"

"I've moved on, and I enjoy hearing stories about your parents."

"Just tell me if it bothers you, and I'll shut up."

"No way. I want to hear it all, starting with something cool your dad did for you."

"He used to volunteer to announce at my track meets in high school. He'd announce all the events, and he even snuck in music before my races to help pump me up. There was this one song, 'Unstoppable' by Sia, that would always get me ready for a race."

"You ran track in high school?"

"I used to run the mile and two-mile."

"And who's Sia?"

"She was popular in the early to mid-2010s. Her music is way better than all that George Strait and grassroots country you listen to."

"You take that back! You haven't even heard my music."

"Yes, I have. We spent a couple hours driving around

town together that day you took me to Cup of Sunshine and Copper Hill. Besides, I hear the music you play in the morning when you're cooking your breakfast before work."

"You hear that?"

"Yeah, my bedroom is right next to the kitchen."

"Sorry. Why haven't you said anything?"

"I didn't want to tell you how much I hate your taste in music." A devilish smile paints her lips.

"Okay, that's it. We can't be friends anymore."

"Oh, we're friends now?"

"I don't know what to call you." A twinge of hope and fear swirls inside of me. I don't want to put myself in the friend zone, but I don't want to let this go too far. I don't know what I'm doing when it comes to Olivia. It's like I'm not even in control of myself when I'm around her.

"That makes two of us." She smirks, and now my heart is soaring. So much for not letting this go too far.

Her smile falls quickly, and she pulls out her phone, putting on a song with a funky beat.

"What are you doing?"

"Playing 'Unstoppable' for you."

I sit next to her in silence, imagining Olivia listening to this song in high school. It's about putting on a brave face, pretending you're okay, and pushing forward to succeed. No wonder Olivia is constantly smiling for everyone else's sake.

When the song ends, I shrug, saying, "Eh, it's all right. I'll show you real music."

I take her phone and play "Texas Cookin'" by George Strait.

Immediately I start tapping my foot, which turns into moving my shoulders from side to side until I'm out of my chair, taking her hand and spinning her around. She tilts her head back, laughing, and I wish I could hear the sound of her laughter every day for the rest of my life. I tell myself I'm only spinning her around again because she had a hard day and deserves to laugh, but when I pull her into me and feel the warmth of her whole body pressed against me, I snap out of it, letting her go and sitting back down. *What am I doing?*

The last minute of the song plays as we sit there, staring at each other, both our chests heaving as we process what just happened.

When the song finishes, I take advantage of this opportunity to change the subject.

"What triggered your panic attack today?"

"Do we have to talk about this?"

"I think it could be good for you. Plus, I want to know if there's a way I can help."

She leans back in her chair, crinkling her nose and pressing her lips together. It's so darn cute. "I guess a couple things piled up and sent me spiraling. My coach emailed me today and said I could still get promoted to senior this fall. I should've been happy because that's always been my goal, but a part of me doesn't care about being promoted anymore."

"It's okay to realize you don't want the same things you used to."

"No, I *have* to stay until senior."

"Why? You don't seem to enjoy your job. It clearly makes you very anxious."

"My dad worked for a smaller public accounting firm when he was my age, and he loved it. He had to quit to come home and help take care of my grandma, and he's always wished things could've been different. When I ended up in accounting, my dad immediately showed me the right path. This is how I get ahead in my career. This is how I make all the hard work of the difficult undergraduate degree, the Master's degree, and taking the CPA exam worth it. Making it to senior opens up a lot more doors in my career than if I left now."

"Did you even want to be an accountant and work for the Big Four?"

She glances down at the ground, breaking eye contact. "When I started school, I wanted to go into marketing. I always loved social media and creating content, and I liked the idea of using that for a good cause like helping non-profits raise money, but by the end of my freshman year of college, my parents helped me realize there are more steady careers and better uses of my intelligence and work ethic, so I found my way to accounting. I'm good at it, and it's a very secure job. It pays well. There's lots of opportunities. After working at the Big Four, I can go onto other jobs that could lead to a career as a CFO or Controller—"

She's rambling now, and I see right through her. "But that's not what you want."

"It is to a degree. I've always wanted a secure job, something to make my parents proud. This is it. It's hard work, but you don't get ahead if you don't work hard."

"But it's killing you."

"Rhett, I don't want to argue with you. You asked me what triggered me, and I'm telling you. I can stop."

I sigh heavily. "Go ahead. What else caused you to start spiraling?"

"My mom called, and she wanted to leave work to hang out with me."

"That's sweet. Why did that upset you?"

"Because she's always giving things up for me! I don't understand why she keeps worrying about me. I'm going to see a counselor tomorrow, just like she and my dad asked me to. I'm trying to give them everything they want."

"I don't think she's giving anything up by leaving work a little early."

"She was going to skip out on a meeting. Knowing her, it was probably some important meeting that she shouldn't miss."

"It sounds to me like your mom has her priorities in line, and you're at the top of the list. Maybe you should take note. Screw this job that you don't even want. Who cares about being secure and looking good to other people?"

"Actually, a lot of people care about that," she grumbles. "This isn't the first time she's blown off something important for me. In college, she skipped out on a super important work meeting, and I still can't forgive myself for letting her do that."

"Whatever happened, I'm sure it couldn't have been that bad. Your mom is happy now. She's thriving."

"Yeah, but I still wonder how things would be different if I hadn't gotten in the way."

The irony isn't lost on me as the next words come out of my mouth. "You can't let all the what-ifs drown you. Life goes on. It's what you do with the rest of it. Do you learn lessons from the past? That's what matters."

"I'm going to therapy. What else can I do?"

"Let your parents in a little."

"That's what has started every mess I've ever been in."

"Then let's figure out how to let them in without messing it up this time."

"Let's?"

I grab onto her hand, looking into her eyes and giving her the only thing I can ever give her. "You're not in this alone."

Chapter Seventeen

Olivia

I'm just starting to lock Rhett's front door when my mom steps out of her car, watching me. *Crap.*

She stands there, clutching a baby blue box and wearing the same look on her face as when something juicy happens in one of her soap operas. "I just wanted to bring you a cinnamon roll from the diner as a little good luck charm for your first day."

She's trying, but failing, to pretend she's not interested in what I'm doing with a key to Rhett's place. As soon as I take the box from her and lead us inside the house, she asks, "What're you doing here? Is Rhett home?"

She knows for a fact Rhett is working. I wish I could think of something else to tell her instead of giving her the satisfaction of knowing I've been living with Rhett, but since I can't, I opt for the truth and hope she won't bother me about how great Rhett is and how she knew I'd like him. That's the last thing I need. I haven't been able to get him off my mind all morning, which is rather useless when I can't do anything about it.

"I knew you two would like each other. He's so kind, and he's handsome too."

Taking a lesson from Rhett, I redirect her. "This cinnamon roll looks delicious." It's almost as big as my head and covered in a thick layer of cream cheese frosting. I put it in the fridge as I say, "Thank you."

"What'd you end up doing yesterday?"

I pause, unsure how to answer. *Oh, I just had a panic attack, and then Rhett showed up to comfort me, cook for me, cuddle with me, and make me confess all my secrets.* Yeah, that's exactly what I should tell her.

"Rhett got off work early, so we hung out."

A smile bigger than the size of Texas spreads across her face.

"Don't get too excited. We just watched some TV, and he cooked dinner. It's hard not to acknowledge each other's presence when you live in the same house."

"But he clearly likes you or he wouldn't be sharing his house with you."

"He's only sharing because he has to. The cottage won't be ready for me to live in for a while. It worked out well for Maverick to have us in the same household too."

I scratch Maverick's ears.

"You're getting pretty fond of the little guy, huh?"

"I'm just fostering him while I'm here. I can't take him back to San Francisco. Rhett is going to take over when I leave, remember?"

"If you don't go back, you won't have to say goodbye."

Again, I ignore her comment. "It's great that you're here, Mom. I have to leave in a few minutes to drop Maverick off at Copper Hill. He's going to spend the day with Rhett because I have my counseling appointment after my shift at the café, but I wanted to talk with you."

"Is everything okay?"

"Yeah, it's great." I join her on the couch. "I was just thinking that maybe while I'm here, we could reinstate movie nights."

"Oh, yes! That'd be wonderful! You just name the time and place. I'm pretty flexible, but it sounds like you've made yourself busy here already." She grabs my hand. "I hope you're letting yourself take a little break still. You should rest some while you're here. Lord knows you'll be busy again once you get back."

I wave her off. "That's part of what movie nights are for. They'll be a good way to relax while spending time with you."

She pats my hand. "I will take any time I can get with you. Maybe we could do this weekend? Oh, wait, I said you could pick. You just pick the day and call or text me, and I'll make myself available."

I glance at the time on my phone. "I need to leave now, but let's plan on movie night this weekend."

Mom pulls me in for a tight hug, and I allow myself to sink into it for a brief moment before I pull away. "I'll talk to you later, okay?"

"Okay, have a good shift. And say hi to Rhett for me." She winks, something I swear she's never done in her life.

"Oh god! Please don't do that."

She snickers. "It's just that your time together seems to be about more than just Maverick."

"I really need to go, Mom."

"Okay. Okay. I'll take the hint." She kisses me on the cheek and rushes out the door.

———

The moment the bell over the front door jingles, Callie leaps from her spot behind the counter of the café to wrap me in a hug. "I can't tell you how excited I am that you're here! It's been so slow this morning. I need the company."

She pulls back and returns to her spot behind the counter, ducking down and plucking a blueberry muffin from the glass display. She sets it on a plate. "I just baked a fresh batch of muffins this morning. Want to split one?"

"Did you just hire me to hang out with you or am I actually going to help you with work?"

"Would you be mad if I said I mostly wanted the company?"

"Not really."

"Good." She sits down at the same table we sat in when I first met her. "There are some chores I could use help with sometimes, but things don't get too crazy around here since Roots is such a small town."

I join her at the table, and she instantly pounces on me. "Tell me all about your day with Rhett."

"What?"

"I'm dying to know what you two did all day together! I know Rhett pretty well compared to most people in this town, but even I don't hang out with him. I want to know what he's like in the wild." She sets her elbows on the table cradling her chin in her palms, looking at me intently.

"That was a week ago. Are you serious?"

"Dead serious. Tell me what you two did."

I take a moment to compose myself, carefully masking my excitement. "We got lunch at the barbecue joint in town. Best barbecue ever! Oh my god!"

"I know. Texas does a lot of things right, but the barbecue is definitely at the top of the list."

"Can we also take a second to talk about the name? I don't know whether it's cute or disturbing."

She chuckles as she tears a chunk off the muffin. "Pork-Screw? It's meant to be a pun, like corkscrew. If you knew the owner, Ray, you'd understand. He's just the most wholesome old man you'll ever meet."

I eagerly take another piece of the muffin and take satisfaction in the feeling of a warm blueberry bursting when I bite down on it. "We also went to Copper Hill and rode horses. There's this trail with an incredible view at the top."

"Oh yeah, I know about it."

"You do? How?"

Her guard seems to go up as she crosses her arms and says, "I know about everything in this town, which leads me to my next point: You and Rhett have been living together since before I met you. Why didn't I know that sooner?"

"I haven't exactly felt the need to broadcast that knowledge to people in town. My mom only found out this morning. How did you hear about it?"

"Rhett told me."

"He did? When?"

"I don't know, earlier this week when he came by. Anyway, how did this happen? Rhett wouldn't tell me much."

"It's just because a pipe burst in the cottage."

"You could've just stayed with your parents though, right? Did Rhett even suggest that?"

I open my mouth to tell her he did, but then I realize that was never something that was brought up. "To be fair, he knew I didn't want to stay with my parents. That's why I was supposed to stay in the cottage."

"But letting you stay in a separate house on his property is a lot different than letting you stay in his guest bedroom. Who knew Rhett had a soft side to him anymore."

"Soft side?"

"Yeah, he's turned into mush since you came to town, adopting a dog and letting you move in with him."

Then it hits me. "What do you mean 'who knew he had a soft side *anymore?*'"

My heart is pounding in my chest. Callie knows something I don't. I can tell. I don't understand why Rhett has been so secretive, and it bothers me to know I can't get past those layers but Callie can.

"Rhett hasn't dated anyone since he moved to Roots. He's never even shown interest. I was beginning to think he is incapable of love, but maybe he just needed the right girl to come along."

"Whoa, I think you're getting a little ahead of yourself. My relationship with Rhett is not even remotely romantic." I shove a chunk of muffin in my mouth, trying not to think about the way he gently caressed me yesterday while I came down from my panic attack or the way he draped his arm around me while I laid my head on his chest. *That's totally platonic, right?*

She gives me a knowing look. "He took you to the animal rescue on your second day in town just because he knew you love dogs. That takes planning and care. It even kind of sounds like a date to me."

"He only did that because he wanted to apologize to me. We'd only known each other for a day and didn't even like each other."

"A simple 'sorry' would've been good enough, but that's not what he did. What else have your interactions been like around Rhett? I'll bet this isn't the only time he did something nice for you."

I blush as I think about the past week. He's been making me coffee every morning. Between seeing Rhett and getting coffee, I'm suddenly a morning person. Two nights ago, he brought home a bundle of wildflowers for me to put in my room because he knows I like them. He said I should be able to make the guest room feel like my own space while I'm there.

"I'll take that silence as all the answer I need. Tell me what else he did. I'm so intrigued!"

A little sunshiny ray of warmth lights up my chest. I haven't had a good friend since college. I adore Anna, but we've drifted apart the last couple of years as life and work got in the way. I stopped making an effort. I stopped letting people in. I forgot how rewarding it can be to share your ups and downs with someone who genuinely cares. I make a mental note to call Anna tonight.

Giving Callie a shy smile, I fill her in on every little thing Rhett has done for me over the past week.

"*Shut up!* Okay, Olivia, you are going to have to start giving me daily updates on your relationship."

"Nothing is going on. You better not go around telling people any of this. The last thing I need is the town to start spreading more untrue things about me." I also don't need things getting back to Rhett. Who knows how easily he'd get scared off?

She swallows her bite of muffin and wraps her hand gently around mine. "I promise I would never play a part in telling people about your personal life, whether it's true or untrue. I really like you. I think we could actually be friends."

"I'd like that."

"Great! Let's be friends then. We should hang out soon! Next Friday, the Callahan sisters are playing at the Long Neck. I can take you out and then you can spend the night at my place."

"The Long Neck?"

"That's the bar in town. It's actually called Long Neck Bottle, but all the locals just call it the Long Neck. On Fridays, all women get half off drinks."

"Oh, that sounds great. I'd love that."

As if I needed another reason to like this town, now I have a new friend and plans to look forward to. I plaster on a smile for the rest of my shift despite the thought that continues to linger in my mind: *I have to leave everything I'm building here in just a couple of months.*

Chapter Eighteen

Olivia

"Hey, Carol? My accountant brain is going crazy wondering how you're able to keep the rescue afloat. You have so many dogs, and a lot of them have special needs…" I trail off as I scoop food into bowls for the first group of dogs to eat.

"It's been hard the last couple years. It's already difficult enough to care for so many dogs, but figuring out how to provide for all of them financially gets to be overwhelming. Even after several years, I haven't effectively figured out how to navigate it. Thankfully, local businesses and people around town have made a lot of donations over the years.

"I have a social media page where I share the dogs' journeys. When I get dogs that need medical procedures, I'm able to fundraise through social media too, but creating content is exhausting. I hate doing it, and I don't have the time to spend on it when fifty-something dogs are depending on me to take care of them."

"I could help with the social media. I love creating

content. I already have all kinds of pictures and videos that would be great for your page."

"You'd do that?"

"Of course! I enjoy making content, and I'd love to help you. I've actually sort of been working on a marketing plan since I first came to the rescue."

"Thank you."

As I grab a bag of food, a shaggy white dog comes charging into the room. His ribs are protruding unhealthily, and he hobbles on three legs.

"What happened to him?" I gasp.

"This is Nate. He came to me earlier this week. We think he was neglected by his owner and finally escaped or was intentionally let loose. Then he got hit by a car and lost his leg."

I stoop down as Nate approaches me and reach my hand out quietly, turning my head away from him so he doesn't feel threatened. He sniffs it and steps away before slowly coming back to me. "Oh, the poor thing! I want to do more to help. I feel like coming here a couple times a week and helping with the social media isn't enough. There has to be more I can do for these dogs."

"If you have any ideas, I'm all ears."

Pursing my lips, I admit, "I don't have any ideas yet, but I'm not going to sleep tonight until I have something."

"Please don't lose sleep over this," she says, rubbing my arm up and down with a gentle smile. "Let's finish prepping group one's food, and then you can go outside to play with some of the group two and three dogs."

Carol splits the dogs into groups based on the amount of food they eat and rotates through feeding time to make it less overwhelming. It's truly brilliant.

I dig the scoop back into the bag and pour food into the

bowl in front of me, but my mind is already going one hundred miles a minute as I plan.

Once the last bowl is filled, I look to Carol for approval. When she nods, I grab the handle of the sliding door and draw it back. The dogs from group one noisily pour in from the kennel we corralled them into earlier.

"I'll keep an eye on them. Why don't you go find Maverick and play with the other groups?"

I silently exit the room, entering the sticky Texas humidity. I'm astounded by how warm it is here even though it's later in the day and still only late May. Not a single one of the dogs seems fazed by the heat as they rough house with one another and chase each other around the edges of the enclosure.

Maverick rushes to my side the second he sees me, joyfully circling me with his tongue out. Soon his playmate joins him, and then another dog and another, until I'm swarmed with pooches. I accept the love, choosing to just sit in the grass while they all encircle me, eagerly trying to get some attention. I grab my phone and capture a video, doing a full 360 as nearly twenty dogs crowd around me.

Without thinking, I send the video to Rhett. He *is* the one who showed me the shelter. I'm sure he'll be happy to see I'm enjoying my time volunteering.

ME

Just another day hard at work

RHETT

Looks like you're working really hard there

I did just help Carol feed one of the megaesophagus pups. Those high chair-type things are not my friend

Mega-what?

Don't tell me you don't know what that means!

Do you even know what it means?

It's a condition that affects the dogs' esophagus and makes it difficult for him to eat his food without sitting upright.

I'm glad to see you've been enjoying your time there and learning new things. I know Carol appreciates the help

I wish I could do more

My phone vibrates in my palm with a call from Rhett. "Hello?"

"If you want to do more for these dogs, then let's figure out how to do more."

"What do you mean?"

"What are you doing after you finish up at the rescue?"

"I was going to cook myself a late dinner and then lie awake for hours while I try to think of something to help the dogs."

"Not anymore. I'll help you come up with something."

I swallow, trying to ease my dry throat. "You'll help me?"

"Duh."

My cheeks are definitely tomato-red now. "I'll be another thirty minutes, and I need to grab dinner on the way home." I pull my phone from my ear to check the time. It's already seven thirty.

"I'll make us something while you finish up. I've been waiting so we could eat together."

"You didn't need to wait."

"I wanted to." My heart soars, and I bite back a smile. "Text me when you leave."

———

When I walk in the front door, my nose is immediately filled with the smell of cocoa. "Oh my god! It smells incredible! Are the brownies our dinner?" I wouldn't complain if they were.

Rhett leads Maverick and me to the back door, answering my question by pulling off two steaks from the grill. "The brownies in the oven are just to celebrate when we come up with a genius idea on how to help Carol and the dogs."

"You're a saint." I take a plate from him and sit down at the dining room table.

Maverick rushes to follow, looking up at us with hopeful eyes as we begin cutting into our steaks. Doing my best to ignore his begging, I explain to Rhett the current method of fundraising at the rescue. "I was thinking we could host a fundraising event for Resilient Paws that could be done a few times a year."

Rhett's lips slip into a smirk. "You haven't stopped thinking about this since the idea popped into your head, huh?"

"Of course not! That's just not how my brain works. I think of something, and I hyperfocus on it until I have a solution. Why do you think I have such bad anxiety?"

"That doesn't sound healthy."

"That's what counseling is for, right?"

He snorts. "I guess so. How's that going?"

"I've only had one appointment, so we haven't gotten

into a whole lot. It's mostly been explaining my background so far, but I already like her better than the therapist I saw in college, and she gave me one small tip for managing my anxiety at the end of our session."

"That's good."

Eager to get back on track, I clap my hands together. "Okay, so I just need to come up with an idea that will attract a lot of people for the fundraiser. It needs to be something great to bring in lots of money."

"You don't need to put so much pressure on yourself to figure everything out. I'm here to help too."

I barrel on. "Maybe we could host some sort of event here in Roots. We could get the café involved, but I think we need more businesses too."

He pulls my plate away from me, grabbing my attention. "I'm all for helping you with this fundraiser, but you need to promise me you're not going to let this consume you. You came here to get away from stress, not to create more for yourself."

"But—"

"Promise me, or I won't help you. I fully support your mission to help Carol, but not at the expense of your mental health."

"Fine, but I might need a little help. I don't know how to shut my brain off."

He smirks, sliding my plate back to me. "I know. We'll work on it together."

"Thank you."

Dismissing my praise, he says, "I think getting the café involved could be great. Did you have anything in mind?"

"That's where I'm a little stumped. I want to host a farmer's market of sorts that would attract people from outside of Roots. I think there's a lot of money to be found in the outskirts of Dallas that I'd love to bring in, but I'm not sure how to put all this together. I'm a tax accountant, not an event planner."

He takes a few bites of his steak, chewing pensively. "That could work. We can get some more businesses in town involved, and maybe some smaller businesses from around Dallas would be interested in joining. We can pose it as a marketing opportunity for the businesses so that they have an incentive to join. Not everyone feels the need to help other people like you do."

Excitement builds in me as I pull my phone out of my pocket.

"What are you doing?"

"I'm looking up small businesses in the Dallas-Forth Worth area. I'll compile a list tonight and call them tomorrow before my shift at the café starts."

"There's no stopping you when you put your mind to something, huh?"

"Nope."

There go his beautiful dimples.

He takes both our plates into the kitchen and says over his shoulder, "How can I help you slow down a little?"

"I already told you. I don't know how to shut my brain off."

He sets the plates down, crosses the kitchen back over to me, and scoops me up into his arms with a smile. Laughter slips from my lungs, and I catch myself wondering when the last time was that I laughed like this. It's been gradual, but as I've been removed from my life in San Francisco over the last three and half weeks, I've started to feel lighter and lighter.

"I think I can find a way to help."

Chapter Nineteen

Rhett

OLIVIA HOVERS OVER ME AS I PULL THE BROWNIES OUT of the oven. Her warmth simultaneously comforts me and makes me uneasy.

I don't know how I ended up cooking her dinner and baking her brownies. I've *never* done anything like this for another human being, let alone a woman who isn't even my girlfriend. Our whole relationship feels like it's quickly getting out of hand. The more I try to wrangle things back in, the more things slip out of my control. It's exhausting trying to keep my feelings in check, and my resolve to remain "just friends" is wearing thinner by the day.

Something changed that day we spent together after her panic attack. We both let each other in just a little bit, and I think we both realized it felt good. As much as I hate to admit it, Olivia's presence lights me up, and damn it, I love the feeling. I can't get enough of it, of her. Even if I should stay away, I can't. Somehow that logic makes me feel better. This is all out of my control. Whatever might happen between us isn't my fault. It isn't me naively giving in to love again. It's me making the best of the cards I've been dealt.

"I don't know how you were blessed with the beautiful gift of being an expert baker, but I'm not complaining. Can we dig in now? The smell is killing me!"

I push her back with a smile. "These need to set for twenty minutes, or they're going to be a mess."

"That's okay. I like my brownies to be like my life, a hot, gooey mess."

"Your life is gooey?" I scrunch up my nose in disgust.

"I don't know. It sounded better in my head." She brushes past me to look in my freezer. "Do you have ice cream? Brownies need ice cream."

I step in closer, pushing the freezer closed and ignoring the way her closeness makes my heart pound out of my chest. "You're getting way too comfortable around here, but yes, I have ice cream. You can't have brownies without it in my opinion."

"I agree." She returns to the table and picks up her phone, rattling off a list of businesses. "Do you think this is enough? I'm guessing there will be a few people who say no when I call, so I want to make sure we have a big enough list."

"I think that will be perfect. We don't want to over-whelm ourselves. We only have a few weeks to get this planned if we are going to do everything before you go back to San Francisco." The words make my stomach drop, and I swear they have the same effect on Olivia because the deter-mined spark in her eyes fades.

"Right, of course. I still have a little over two months left here though." I'm pretty sure she's talking more to herself than anyone at this point. "Do you think six weeks is enough time to plan everything?"

"I think that will work."

"Then it's settled. I'll call everyone tomorrow and keep you updated. I can talk to Callie during my shift tomorrow too. I'm sure she'll want to be involved, and we will probably need her help baking and prepping for the café's part of the event."

She sits down in her chair at the table with a huff. "Is it time to eat the brownies yet?"

"Let's just sit for a little bit. We have at least fifteen more minutes until we can cut into the brownies."

She pouts, and she looks so dang cute doing it that I can't help myself as I reach out to her, pulling her from her chair and into my arms. "What are you doing?" She giggles. Her laughter is more intoxicating than any drug.

"Let's go outside. You need to stop thinking about every little thing, and you could clearly use a distraction while we wait for the brownies."

"I don't think going outside is going to be enough to quiet my mind."

"Just trust me."

Surprisingly, she doesn't pepper me with questions as I set her and Maverick out on the back porch with nothing but the porch lights and the soft setting sun. Moments later, I return, guitar in hand.

Her eyes grow round. "You play guitar?"

"I do."

She bites her lip as if she's refraining from saying anything more, but the dark look in her eyes makes me shift nervously. If I think too hard about it, I'm going to take that look as more than it surely is.

I put my whole focus into tuning the guitar carefully. "It's been a while since I've played. Life has been a little hectic over the last few weeks since I got this new roommate." I give her a small smile, and she returns it with a look of pure glee. "Do you have any requests?"

"What can you play?"

"A lot. I've been playing since I was twelve years old. My guitar playing is much better than my baking in my opinion."

She presses both of her palms to her cheeks and slowly drags them down her face. "Rhett!"

"What?"

"How are you so perfect?"

"I'm not." I feel the shadows rolling in at her words, but I do my best to shake them off.

Thinking for a moment, I finally offer, "How about some Warren Zeiders?"

"You mean you listen to music that isn't by George Strait?"

I roll my eyes. "Of course I do. I'll play you the song on the guitar first and then I'll show you the real song. I don't need you judging my rusty guitar skills after you've heard the real thing."

"Okay, but you have to tell me the name of the song first or I'm never going to be the country music aficionado you want me to be."

"'Weeping Willow.'"

As I begin strumming gently, I let the music take me to another place. I'm no longer sitting on this back porch. I'm a part of the music. My foot taps along involuntarily. I don't realize it until I see Olivia's look of shock, but I'm singing along to the song.

She gives me an eager nod of assurance. "Keep going," she whispers, barely audible.

Her words encourage me, so I keep going, keeping my eyes on Olivia, strumming vigorously, and singing about how the woman in the song is so incredible that she could even make a weeping willow smile. As I play the closing chords, it hits me how perfectly this song fits Olivia. She's brought color to my life and made me smile when I had fallen into this stale routine I never planned on getting out of.

Her eyes remain closed till the end like she's completely absorbed in what I'm playing for her. I can't help but think maybe I did a good job. Perhaps I really did get her out of her head for those three minutes.

When I stop, her eyes shoot open. "Play another. Please."

I begin strumming again, this time playing a more upbeat tune. "This one is 'Coal' by Dylan Gossett."

I lose myself in the song as I recall the lyrics that talk about a man's struggles through life, wondering how those struggles and all the weight they've brought with them haven't turned him from coal into a diamond. I have always related deeply to those lyrics, but I can't help but feel just a little bit lighter this time playing the song with Olivia's adoring gaze on me.

As I wind down the song again, she admits, "I don't want to hear the original versions of the songs. I like yours." The words are a whisper, as if she's afraid they'll take us out of this moment. "I never want you to stop playing. It just brings me so much peace. I know you're not going to like hearing this, but you're *so* good."

"I've had a lot of practice." I brush her off, pulling my hat down to hopefully hide the way my face is turning an aggressive shade of red. "I've written a few of my own songs, without lyrics of course. Would you like to hear one?"

Her face splits into a huge grin, and I don't even have to wait for her response to strike the first chord. I'm not sure what compelled me to make this offer. I only started writing songs five years ago. Inspiration came from some of the best and then some of the most difficult times in my life, and I haven't been able to write music since. Writing music helped me get through a tough time of unrelenting grief and guilt, and then it was over. I was done. The songs were never meant to be shared with a soul. Yet here I am.

Less than thirty seconds in, Olivia is closing her eyes again as she gently sways her body to the melody, completely enraptured. There's a moment where I consider telling her everything, where this song came from, and why I am who I am today. It should be a betrayal to share this song with her. It was written for someone else after all, but it doesn't feel wrong. When I glance up at her and see her soft amber eyes set on me, it makes all this feel right. That look makes me feel like a good man. It makes me feel worthy of love and adoration, but I know better.

I know if I tell her the truth, she won't look at me like that again, so instead of telling her everything, I keep quiet as I continue to play her a song that I wrote after I lost my fiancée four years ago.

Chapter Twenty

Olivia

Rhett's beautiful melody is interrupted by the timer on his phone. The brownies are ready. A wave of disappointment washes over me. I didn't expect to be upset about an interruption that leads to delicious dessert, but here I am, feeling mopey we have to go eat brownies right now.

He rises from his chair and reaches out a shaky hand to me. As I zero in on his face, I think I see tears prick in his eyes, but he tilts his hat down subtly before leading me back to the kitchen.

Pulling two bowls from the cabinet and a knife from the drawer, he hands them to me. "I'll let you do the honors."

"Are you sure? I might just cut you a crumb and give myself the rest."

He rolls his eyes. "No, you won't. Just don't give me too big of a piece."

I glare at him. I have yet to see what's underneath that t-shirt, but it fits his form well enough to suggest I would very much like what's underneath. "Rhett, shut up! You could eat all of the brownies and the whole pint of ice cream and still have the body of a god. I'll give you however much I please." I cut him a slightly bigger piece than mine just to prove a point and slip it into his bowl.

"Thanks."

I give him a nod as I take my piece. Something has shifted between us in the last five minutes. Maybe it was the fact that he willingly played guitar for me, or the fact that he offered to play a song he created. It was beautiful and vulnerable. He didn't sing with this song, and he didn't give me any backstory, but watching him play that song made me want to weep. I could see the muscles in Rhett's jaw working as he played, suggesting that maybe the song evoked some deep emotions in him.

Seeing that vulnerable side of him made me want to absolutely melt, and now the air feels charged with electricity as if lightning is about to strike.

Rhett silently scoops us each a ball of ice cream and places it on top of the gooey chocolate brownies.

"Do you want to sit outside again? It's a nice evening."

"Yeah, I'd like that."

We each take a spot in one of his patio chairs, and Maverick lazily follows us outside, quickly settling down in the grass off the edge of the patio. We sit in silence for several minutes, enjoying the mix of still-warm brownies juxtaposed with the smooth, cool ice cream.

Something about that song makes me think there's so much more to Rhett than I realized hanging below the surface. Feeling desperate to learn more about him, I cut through the silence. "You didn't tell me the name of the last song you played."

"It doesn't have a name."

"What's it about?"

"There aren't any words." He quickly fills his mouth with a heaping spoonful of brownie and ice cream.

"But you must've had something that inspired the song, right?"

"I guess so."

"What was it?"

"It was about the moment I finally gave up on ever having love in my life."

Silence falls over us instantly. I don't know what to say to that. I want to encourage him not to give up. I want to hold him and make everything better. I want to do *some-thing* to fix this, but I don't know what to do or say.

Instead of pressing him further, I try a new strategy. Maybe if I stop holding back with him, he'll stop holding back with me. "Can I tell you something personal?"

"Yeah, you can tell me anything." He takes a bite of brownie, savoring it before furrowing his brow and adding, "But why?"

"I held back a bit after my panic attack, and I thought maybe it was time I tell you the full story."

"Okay, what's up?" He looks like one of the new dogs at the rescue, ready to bolt at any second.

"I mentioned my anxiety started to get worse during my freshman year of college. I think the peak was second semester. It was finals week, and I had this one class that I was struggling with. I realize now how ridiculous that sounds because I still had an A in the class, but I was on the cusp of a B, and the perfectionist in me was horrified. I was always *very* focused on my grades, even before I started pursuing a career path in the Big Four. It was just an expec-tation, set by both me *and* my parents, that I'd earn good grades and succeed.

"The final exam was a big chunk of our grade. I don't even remember how much, but it was enough to easily change my A to a B. I studied so hard for that test. I started prepping way ahead of time, but the morning of the test, I was going over my flashcards again, and it was like everything I had studied just fell out of my brain. I couldn't remember the answers to anything."

I pause to take in Rhett's expression. He's leaned in toward me, completely invested in every word I have to say.

"Looking back on it, I'm sure it was just a combination of nerves and the fact I didn't sleep much the night before, but either way, the knowledge wasn't there, and I began to panic." Even though this story is from about five years ago, my shoulders are slowly rising closer to my ears.

"I spiraled pretty quickly into one of the worst panic attacks I've ever had, and at the time, they were still relatively new. I didn't have any tools to handle them, so it only made me freak out even more. I couldn't breathe, and I was absolutely sobbing, so I did the only thing I could think to do. I called my mom."

Noticing the way my whole body is reacting to the story, Rhett reaches out to me, pulling me from my seat and into his arms. As I melt against him and allow his warm, strong arms, to surround me, I feel as if this is where I'm meant to spend the rest of my life. I feel safe. I feel comforted.

Maverick noses his way between us, growing jealous of the fact that he's not being included in the affection being given between his two favorite people. His wet nose against my bare thigh snaps me out of my lazily comforted state. "I'm not done. It gets worse."

Rhett nods his head above mine, not allowing me to pull

away. "You can keep talking, but you're staying here while you do. I can't take seeing you like this."

What did I ever do to deserve being wrapped up in Rhett's caring arms?

I take a deep sigh and summon the courage to continue. "My mom, being the amazing mom and woman that she is, answered the phone right away, even though she was about to go into one of the most important meetings of her life. She had been going through the motions in her career for years and had recently joined a start-up working on this big ocean conservation project a few months before all this. It was her dream come true. The meeting was supposed to be a pitch for the company that could clinch millions of dollars from key investors to fund the project. She had been preparing since the day she started, and the pitch was entirely riding on her. She had done all the research. She had created the presentation. I *knew* it was that day. I *knew* what time it was, but I was so stressed about my exam that I called her in tears without even thinking about the fact that she had her meeting right then.

"When I told her what was going on, she became so worried about me that she dropped everything to come to me. The office was only about ten minutes from campus, which of course felt like a lifetime to me. She held me and talked me through my breathing. Never once did she say a word about the meeting. I later found out she accidentally took the thumb drive with the presentation on it when she left the office, and she missed ten phone calls from her coworkers while she was with me. Without that drive, the company couldn't do the presentation. They missed out on millions and were almost forced to shut down the project because of that incident, so they fired my mom. To this day, she still hasn't said anything about it. She never blamed me.

She just gave up her dream to help her pathetic, hyperventilating daughter, and she didn't once complain about it or ever show that she held it against me.

"I carry around the guilt of knowing that my mom gave up her dreams for me, and I am determined to *never* let her, *or* my dad, do something like that again. I know parents are supposed to look out for their kids, to love them, to care for them, but this is another level. I can never forgive myself for that, and I know neither one of my parents would hesitate to do it again, so I need to protect them from me. I'm trying hard to let them back in now, but I'm still so terrified that I'm going to drag them down again someday."

He strokes his hand gently over my head, smoothing my hair down. Then he laces his fingers in mine. I'm completely stunned by this display of affection. It's amazing, and I'm terrified of doing something to make it stop.

"Thank you for sharing with me. I know that was hard, and I can tell it still tears you apart." He pulls away slightly to look me in the eye. "I think you should talk with your mom about it. I know it wouldn't be the easiest thing to do, but I think clearing the air will help you feel better. Your well-being is more important than any dream or any job, and I know your mom would agree with me. I guarantee she doesn't resent you for that missed opportunity. She seems very happy here in Roots. Her life has turned out great even without that job."

"Yeah, but she only came to Roots because I pushed her away. If I didn't give her that space, she would still be in California, and I know she was never completely happy there."

"You don't know that. One thing we *do* know is that you called your mom because you needed her. I guarantee you'll show up in the same way for your own kid someday. You can't change the past. Trust me, I know firsthand. But you can try to be better moving forward, and your mom is still around to repair that relationship. Tell her you're sorry for the role you played in getting her fired but recognize she's an adult and she made the decision to be there for you because she wanted to. Don't cut her out. That's not fair either."

His words swirl around in my head, and I feel a little overwhelmed. Everything he says makes sense, but it's still so hard to accept it as the truth when my reality for years has been that everything was my fault, that my mom had been silently miserable because of me.

"You're right. I need to talk with my mom."

He smirks as he glances at the dark sky and then his phone. "You're not going to do that now. It's almost ten. Get some rest tonight, and you can talk with your mom tomorrow, or the next day. Or the one after that. You don't need to rush it, but I think you will feel better when you talk with her."

"How'd you get to be so wise?"

"Years of making mistakes." He smiles, but I don't miss the small wince in his eyes.

"Well, thanks for screwing up so much so that you could help me." I chuckle, trying to lighten the mood.

I watch him as a hint of something crosses his face. He opens and closes his mouth, and I swear he's going to finally share something with me too. *Did my own vulnerability finally crack Rhett open?*

When he opens his mouth again, he simply says, "Happy to help."

Chapter Twenty-One

Olivia

I take one final deep breath before knocking on the door. I hate that I'm so nervous right now. I used to love movie nights with Mom. They became a tradition long ago when I needed a friend the most. They were something I looked forward to each week, a reward for making it through a long five days of stressful school assignments and mean kids at school. Now, I'm just hoping I can make it through the night. I *do* want to be here. I *do* want to bond with my mom, but it's been so long that I'm terrified things won't be the same anymore.

The door swings open, and I'm immediately dragged into Mom's arms for a tight hug, her lips curved into the biggest smile I've ever seen on her. "I'm so excited for our movie night. I pulled out a few of the classics for you, and I stocked up on some Blue Bell ice cream. I know we used to get Ben & Jerry's, but I thought you might like to try a Texas brand."

She swiftly moves toward the freezer and pulls the

drawer open to reveal three pints of ice cream. "I wasn't sure what you would want, so I got a classic Dutch Chocolate, some Cookie Two Step, and Cookies 'N Cream Cone because it sounded fun."

I try to tamp down the anxiety rising inside of me and ignore the urge to immediately put my guard up. I remember what Rhett and I talked about, how lucky I am to have someone who cares so deeply for me, even if it is a little overwhelming. *I wonder how my counselor would guide me through a situation like this.* I'm oddly excited to go back and dig into how to manage all of the raging emotions that are constantly swirling in my mind. She hasn't tried to put me into a box or made me feel like something is wrong with me. She's instead taken an approach that we are a team working toward a common goal of helping me learn how to manage my anxiety effectively.

"Thanks, Mom. You didn't need to get me ice cream. I just want to spend time with you." I inspect the pints. "They all sound delicious."

I must've done something right because I watch her inflate with pride. "I'm just so happy you're here for movie night again! I can't believe it."

Dad walks into the room, wearing a Ranger's jersey. "Can't believe what?"

"That she's here."

"Me either." He turns to me. "I heard your coach said you can still make senior this fall, even after your time off. That's great!"

"Yeah." I fake a smile, trying not to let anxiety rise inside of me at the mention of work.

"I'm just so proud of you for sticking with this job, even when all these challenges have been thrown in your path.

You will *not* regret staying this long. The things this will do to launch your career—"

Mom interrupts, looking irritated. "Don't you have to go? I thought the game started in ten minutes. You're barely going to make it to the Long Neck in time for the first pitch."

I breathe a sigh of relief as Mom starts pushing him toward the door.

"Oh, is it 6:45 already? I guess I better get going. You two have fun tonight." He presses a kiss to my cheek and rushes out the door.

Mom turns her attention back to me. "Are you hungry? Do you want anything to eat besides ice cream?"

"No, I'm okay. Rhett smoked brisket a couple days ago, and we've been living off the leftovers." I can't help it as a smile spreads across my face at the thought of Rhett. I'm disappointed he didn't open up to me about the meaning of the song he played last night, but the thought of him playing the guitar for me still makes me giddy whenever I think about it.

"You two seem to be getting along well now. Do you want to tell me what's actually going on between you two? I don't buy that a smile like that would be on your face over someone who's just a friend."

"It's nothing, Mom. He's just polite to me because he cares for you and Dad. Plus, we share a pretty needy dog, so we have to be friendly with one another."

"If you say so. He's just so handsome and so kind. He's the kind of man I always pictured you with."

"Mom! I am *not* talking about this with you."

"We used to talk about boys all the time on movie nights. Remember when you had that massive crush on that Nathan boy? You used to tell me about all the little details, even if it was just that he asked you for a piece of gum in the hallway."

The memory causes the smallest flutter of warmth in my chest. "Yeah, I did. I don't know, though. Rhett is nothing more than a friend."

As much as I want to repair my relationship with my mom, it still feels difficult to share details of my life with her. What if I share something with her and it has repercussions? Maybe she'd think a crush on a boy would be enough to keep me here in Roots. I don't want her to be disappointed when I leave.

Her face grows serious, and she reaches out for my hand. "Whether I was in California or Texas, I was always there for you. I don't know your reasoning for keeping me at a distance over the last couple years, but I never stopped being your mom, and I was always willing to move mountains to be there for you and give you whatever you wanted or needed. I still am. I love you."

"I love you too, Mom. I'm sorry. I hate what's happened to our relationship over the last couple years. It's just complicated."

She nods. "I'll take what I can get. I'm happy you're here now."

I open my mouth but quickly clamp it shut as my mind starts swirling. I know in my heart I should try to let her in, but there's still that part of me that has blocked out everyone for so long. That's not going to go away overnight.

So instead of telling her about that tiny, okay fine, all-consuming, spark I feel with Rhett, I say, "Let's see what movies you have."

Two hours later, the credits of the movie roll while we each dish up a second bowl of ice cream. "Which flavor was your favorite?"

"Oh, I think the Cookies N' Cream Cone may have won me over," I say as I pull the top off the carton. "Which one was yours? Have you already tried these flavors before?"

"Actually, I've only tried a couple here and there. I think I was partial to the Cookie Two Step myself."

"I *knew* it! You're such a sucker for cookie dough."

"Can you blame me?"

"No. What'd you think of that ending?"

"It was cute, but I think he should've ended up with the other girl."

"Right? I get that Shawna was pretty, and she helped him through the death of his brother, but Ashley has been there for him since they were little. The movie could've been ten times better if they had gone with the friends-to-lovers trope."

"I agree. We should make our own movie. We could do better than Hollywood."

"Totally!" I burst into laughter, becoming aware of the fact that I'm actually having a good time. It's already 9:30, and I know I should head home, but I don't want to. It feels so nice to have a sense of normalcy with my mom again.

"I've missed this," Mom says casually as she scoops her bowl of ice cream.

It hits me then how much it must've hurt my mom to keep her at a distance. All this time, I thought I was helping her, but maybe I don't know what I'm doing. Maybe I don't know what's best for her, or even what's best for me. Obviously, I've made a lot of mistakes, or I wouldn't have ended up in Roots with my life in shambles. At least I still have the chance to make things better. Like Rhett said, I have people who love me no matter what. It's clear to me that my mom has always been, and always will be, there for me. I owe it to her to try to be better.

"Mom, you were right—about Rhett earlier. I can't help but feel like maybe there is a *little* bit of a mutual attraction."

"I *knew* it!" She does a little dance before grabbing me by the hand and dragging me back to the couch. "Your dad should be out for another hour at the Long Neck with his buddies. Tell me everything."

"I didn't like him at first if I'm being honest. It bothered me how close he is with you, and it still bothers me how he won't open up much about his life before he came to Roots. Doesn't that bother you?"

"Everyone is hiding something."

"You're serious?"

"Of course! You've kept your father and I at a distance for several years, but you've never said why. You're hiding something. I never told my mother-in-law that it was me who broke her favorite vase at her sixty-fifth birthday party. I will take that secret to my grave. Now you will too!" She gives me a pointed look.

"That was *you*? Grandma was pissed about that."

"To your grave, you hear me?"

I draw an x over my chest, my lips quirking. "Cross my heart."

"My point is that everyone has something they're not proud of. Rhett seems like a genuinely good guy, and if there is something he's hiding, maybe it's just because he isn't proud of that version of himself. I suspect he came to Roots for a fresh start, and he's done an excellent job at that.

Don't hold his potential secrets against him. You should go for it."

"Are you just saying that because you think it will get me to stay in Roots?"

"Of course not. I just want to see you happy, and I adore Rhett. I'd like to see him happy too. Plus, he'd be a great son-in-law."

"Okay, you're moving a little too quickly there. All I said was I think he's attractive."

"Tell me about your interactions with him. Has he given you any signs he might be interested?"

"I don't know. He started watching *Dexter* with me in the evenings even though he called the show depraved when we first met. He sends me songs he thinks I'd like and sends me pictures of Maverick because he knows it makes me happy." I shrug as I add, "I just don't know what to make of him because every time I think I'm making progress with him, he closes down."

"How about I tell you this, and that will be the last I say on the matter."

"I doubt it."

"Okay, maybe not the last thing ever, but the last thing for tonight. I have never seen Rhett enjoy the company of a woman like this. He's always very polite to everyone in town and more than willing to help them out, just like a Roots native, but I've never seen him care for someone the way he seems to care for you. If he's watching a show he wasn't interested in and taking the time to send you things that he knows will make you happy, then I can't help but think that makes you a very special person in his eyes. You just need to be patient, and I guarantee you things will happen between you two."

"We already knew I was special," I tease, trying to mask my embarrassment.

"You are. I know that. Your father knows that. It seems like Rhett knows that too."

"We'll see. It's not worth digging into. I'm not here to fall in love. I'm here to spend some time with you guys so you know I'm okay, and then I'm headed back to California."

Remorse washes over me as my mom's soft smile fades. I want to take back what I said, but I can't. It's the truth. I'm not here to stay. That was never the plan. Just because I'm starting to build a good relationship with my mom again doesn't mean I'm going to suddenly stay. And no hot, broody cowboy is going to change that either, even if he's slowly creeping into my heart.

Chapter Twenty-Two

Olivia

Glancing down at my cut-off shorts and yet another oversized t-shirt, I groan, "I look ridiculous, huh? I didn't know what to wear for Ladies' Night. I'm not sure how casual the bar is, but I don't own any going-out clothes. In San Francisco, most of the outfits I'd wear in public were work clothes, and that just didn't seem like the vibe for the Long Neck."

She sticks her tongue out and makes a disgusted face. "No, it most certainly is *not*! We can take a cruise through my closet to find something for you to wear tonight if you want."

She marches down the hallway just off the living room, and I follow, realizing I could feel embarrassed about not having anything to wear, but Callie is just so warm. It's impossible to feel bad about myself in her presence.

I reach the doorway to Callie's room and stop, awkwardly lingering. Maverick catches up to me and walks right past me, sniffing all over the room. He must smell

Callie's cat, who is currently hiding in the other bedroom. I told her I could just leave Maverick with Rhett today, that he'd enjoy going to the ranch this morning, but she insisted she wanted to see the little guy again.

"You can come in, you know. You don't have to stay outside."

I slip through her doorway and find her room is just as vibrant as she is. The walls are coated in a beautiful sage color, and the bedding is a mix of blues, purples, and greens. It's oddly the perfect mix of juvenile and mature. Even though I've only known her for a couple of weeks, the whole room strikes me as perfectly fitting for Callie.

A signed Shania Twain poster hangs on the wall, and a slew of picture frames cover her dresser and nightstand. I pick one up and take in an image of teenage Callie with a girl who looks exactly like her, just a couple of years older. They have their arms thrown around each other, and they're laughing.

"This is a cute photo. Who is this?"

She peers out from her closet, her grin whooshing off her face as if she's seen a ghost. "Oh, that's my sister."

"I didn't know you have a sister. Does she live in Roots?"

She steps out of the closet, a pair of brown cowgirl boots in one hand and a silky red tank top in the other. "Try these on. They'll look great with your shorts."

I nod and follow her orders, waiting patiently for her to answer my question.

She sits down on the edge of her bed next to me as I slip the boots on. "Her name was Isabel. She was my older sister. She left Roots to go to college in New York, but she wanted to come back here someday."

"Was?"

"Yeah, she passed away a few years ago."

It feels like all the air has been sucked out of the room. I don't know how to react. I don't know what to say. I've had my share of challenges in life, but I still don't know the right thing to say in a situation like this.

"What happened?" I nudge gently, reaching out for her hand. It's comforting when Rhett or my mom does it for me, so hopefully it helps her too.

"She was out at a party with friends one night, and her Uber was t-boned on the drive home."

"Oh my gosh! I'm so sorry!" I remove my hand, reaching out to wrap her in a hug. "I'm sorry I asked. We don't have to talk about this. You hardly know me."

"It's okay. I don't mind talking about it. It's been several years. I wouldn't say I'm over it, but it's gotten easier with time." She winces. "Stop looking at me like that. See, I liked it when you were new and clueless."

"Is that why you wanted to hang out with me?"

"Duh! It definitely couldn't be anything to do with your great personality." She nudges my shoulder with a wide grin.

"I'm still really sorry. I can't even imagine what that must've been like. How old were you?"

"I was twenty. It was sort of weird because I was away at school when it happened. I just got this phone call, and that was it. It didn't feel real."

"That must've been so..."

"It was hard. That's why I came home from school."

"I didn't know you did that."

"Yeah. Roots was always my home. I needed the support of the people I cared about, and all of those people were in Roots. My parents were here, but so many other people got me through that hard time. Ms. Easton, my next-door neighbor, used to babysit me when I was too little to talk. I used to go over to her house to pet her cat and do puzzles with her, and now we go out for Sangria together. She was there for me when Isabel was gone. She checked in on me to make sure I was eating and showering every day because my parents were too distraught to do it. She was amazing. Then there's Benny. He owns this little taco truck in town that I went to all the time in high school. He gave me a job when I came back to town and taught me everything he knew about running a small business. I don't think I'd have had the courage to open the café without him."

"Sounds like you had a great support system." I pick at a string on her bedding, unable to push my curiosity aside. *What would it be like to not care about everyone else's expectations of you and just do what you needed to do to let yourself be happy?*

"Were your parents upset when you came home instead of finishing up school?"

"I think they were a little disappointed. I never quite fit the mold they had for me, but they were too busy grieving to give me a hard time about it. I think they just gave up on me. Isabel was always their favorite, and they moved to Florida shortly after her death. That's why I love Roots. Even when my parents were gone, I still had a family here that loved and accepted me for me. They helped me realize I just had to do what was best for me at that time, and it turns out what was best for me was coming back to Roots and opening the café. Isabel and I dreamt of doing it since we were little."

"That's so sweet. You're brave for chasing your dreams like that."

I wish I could be more like her. I wish I didn't *need* the stability of a sturdy job or that I had the bravery to chase a dream without letting fear hold me back. I wish I knew exactly what it was that I needed to fix the things that feel off in my life. The craziest part of it all is that she's gone through so much and only come out stronger, always smiling and making an effort to make people feel loved. I want to be like that.

"You could chase your dreams too, you know. It just takes a little bit of courage, literally just a few seconds here and there to get started."

"I don't even know what my dreams are. I mean, yes, I have interests like marketing and dogs, but those aren't the kinds of things you make a career out of."

"Sure they are! Have you ever heard of an influencer? The world is full of more possibilities now than ever. Ninety percent of the journey is just knowing who you want to be and then wanting it badly enough to go after it."

Starting to feel uncomfortable, I search for a way to change the subject. "How did Rhett get involved with the café? He's kind of like a silent partner, right?"

"Yeah, he just happened to come to town at the right time." She pauses, thinking for a bit. "I forced him to be my friend, kind of like I'm doing to you. He didn't have any choice but to spend some time with me, and he understood the importance of what I was doing."

"Aww, I love that for you."

"Yeah, Rhett's pretty great." A mischievous look crosses her face. "Speaking of how great Rhett is, we should invite him to come out with us tonight. It could be fun. It'd be good for you two to get out of the house and hang out in a low-key environment. Let loose. Do a little dancing." She shimmies her shoulders as she leans in toward me.

"No way! You and I are supposed to hang out."

"I don't mind third-wheeling for a good cause."

"Callie!" My face must be as red as the top she gave me.

"I just want you two to get together already."

"That's not going to happen."

"Why not?"

"I'm leaving in a couple months. I don't want a relationship. I don't think Rhett wants one either."

"Trust me, he's just saying that. That man is a sucker for love."

"How do you know?"

"I mean it's obvious if you know Rhett. He's always doing kind things for people. It's clear he just wants someone to see him for who he truly is and love him for that."

"I hate to see the way he's closed himself off so much. He's helped push me to reconnect with my parents and to see a counselor for my anxiety. He's even been there when I had a panic attack. I'm not saying I'm magically healed now. I still have a lot of work to do, but he helped me get started. I just wish I could do the same for him."

"Then we should definitely invite him out. It'd be good for him to just hang out and have a good time. I promise I don't mind. Now try the top on! I'm dying to see the full look on you."

I slip my oversized t-shirt off and slide the tank top on. It fits nicely. It's slightly cropped, so it sits just perfectly at the waist of my high-rise shorts, and the neck swoops just enough to be flattering without giving away anything. The boots Callie gave me make me look like I actually belong in Roots. I kind of like the sight.

"Damn, you look hot!"

I blush. "I've always wanted to have cuter clothes, but when all you do is work or sleep, there's no sense in buying a top like this."

"Why not? You could wear this to work!"

"No way! I have to look professional, not draw everyone's attention to me."

She purses her lips. "Well, I can assure you, there will be nothing professional about tonight, and everyone's attention will be on you, especially Rhett's." She gives me a once over again before her eyes light up. "Oh, I have this eyeshadow that will make those beautiful eyes of yours *pop*! Let me see if I can find it."

Chapter Twenty-Three

Rhett

I hear Callie and Olivia the second they pull into the driveway. It shouldn't come as a shock to me. Nothing about Callie is subtle, from the rumbling red pickup truck she drives to her shining personality, she was born to stand out.

"I'll just wait out here while you go inside to drop Maverick off," Callie says from her spot in the driver's seat.

"Okay, I'll be right out."

"Don't hurry back."

Oh my god. Is she trying to play matchmaker? She's unbelievable.

Olivia hardly has time to knock on the door before I've swung it open. She takes a step back, looking a bit surprised.

"I heard you two coming from a mile away," I explain.

"Oh, okay." She blinks, revealing the soft pink shimmer coating her eyelids. It makes those amber eyes I've grown so fond of nearly impossible to look away from.

As she steps in, Maverick in tow, the cowgirl boots she's

wearing click on the tile. She's still wearing her signature high-rise shorts that accent her curves and make her legs look a mile long, but she's traded in her usual oversized t-shirt for a form-fitting red top that looks incredible on her. I want nothing more than to just stare at her in awe, but I'm cut off when she asks, "What are you two going to do tonight?"

I force my attention from her pouty pink lips to Maverick, the safest place my eyes can be considering the knockout woman in front of me right now. "I don't know. Guy stuff? Most days on the ranch we bond over chasing cattle and peeing outside."

"Gross. I'm glad I'll be gone then."

I glance out the window at Callie waiting in her truck, music blasting. With my front window open, I can hear Miranda Lambert's voice all the way from here. "How are you getting home? I hope Callie isn't planning on driving you after she has a couple drinks."

"Of course not. We'll just get an Uber or something."

"Roots doesn't have Uber."

"Oh, well, uh, we can walk home if we need to. Roots is small enough." She laughs, clearly proud of her own joke.

My phone vibrates in my pocket. Ignoring it, I offer, "Do you need a ride?"

"No, that's okay. You enjoy your guys' night. I was just joking about walking. We will figure it out. I think Callie may have mentioned something about a friend who works at the bar. Jax or Dax? I don't remember. I think we might catch a ride with him though."

Jealousy rips through me. I know Jax. He has a reputation for being the biggest flirt in Roots, maybe in all of Texas. And it's a *big* state. No part of me feels comfortable with that womanizer hanging around Olivia.

My phone vibrates in my pocket yet again. And again. And again. I huff and glance out the window, knowing full well the only person who would text me this many times in a row is Callie. She's sitting in the truck, pointing insistently at her phone, a bright and innocent smile on her face.

"Give me a second." I sigh, pulling my phone from my pocket.

CALLIE

Want to come out with us tonight?

Okay I can tell from here that you two are totally flirting

Just give into it already

You want to come out with us. I know you do.

You will have a veryyy good time

Rhett stop being a stick in the mud and come with us!!

Please

Olivia wants you there too!

Knowing she won't stop texting me until I acknowledge her, I groan and type out a quick message.

ME

We aren't flirting. We are talking about how you're getting home. I can't come tonight. There'd be no one to watch Maverick

He can be on his own for a little bit

"Sorry, am I interrupting? I can just go. Callie is waiting outside."

"No, sorry. It's just my boss being an asshole like usual," I quickly cover. "So, you're a real cowgirl now, huh?"

"What?"

"The boots."

"Oh, these old things?" She sticks one of the brown boots out for me to see properly. "I've always had these."

"Yeah, I'm sure you got a lot of use out of them in San Francisco."

"Okay, fine, Sherlock Holmes. They're Callie's."

"I knew that."

"Really? Do I look like that much of a fraud?"

"No, you look beautiful. You'll fit right in tonight. It's just a different look for you," I hurry to correct myself. "I like it though."

"Thanks." She glances down at her boots, blushing, before looking back at me with sweet eyes. "Do you want to come out with us tonight? I know you have Maverick, but he'd be okay for an hour or two on his own. Plus, you could use a little fun. Leave your annoying boss behind and come hang out with us. I heard some band is playing there tonight. Callie is excited about it."

How the hell am I supposed to say no to those pleading eyes? I want to say yes. I want to go dance with Olivia and end the night by finally kissing her, but I've already said yes too many times where Olivia is concerned. I'm headed down the wrong path, and I need to reel things back in.

Forcing myself to buck up and do the right thing, I step back from her, trying to pry myself out of her elusive aura. "I don't really go to bars." Her shoulders visibly sag, and it crushes me. "You make an enticing offer, though."

She gives me a small smile, the slightest bit of hope in her eyes. She leans in toward me, grabbing onto my arm and looking up at me with big doe eyes. Her touch is electric, and my resolve is rapidly crumbling.

"Please come out with us tonight. Callie is the one who suggested it, so I know it's okay with her. Plus, I'm a little nervous about being alone with her all night."

Again, I have to put some space between us before I can tell her no. "You'll be fine. You and Callie have been getting along really well. This will be good for you."

"I'm sorry. Did you just say this will be good for me?"

"I may not enjoy bars all that much myself, but I think Callie is great and the two of you could become good friends. It'd be nice for you to have a friend here. You need someone to hang out with besides a grumpy cowboy." The traces of a smile line my lips.

"Are you making a joke right now?"

"Maybe."

She narrows her eyes. "Didn't you once tell me Callie and I are trouble together?"

"You need to listen a little less to everything I have to say. I'm allowed to change my mind every once in a while."

"Okay, but don't do it too often. It's freaking me out."

"Trust me, I try not to." The irony isn't lost on me because I know it's going to take every fiber of my being to keep from changing my mind, accepting her invitation tonight, and letting myself completely fall for her.

Chapter Twenty-Four

Olivia

The Long Neck is filled with an exorbitant amount of people. The rumbling of voices paired with pounding music on the speakers is almost overwhelming. I didn't even know Roots had this many people, but here's the proof that I was wrong. The bar is packed to the brim with chattering Roots residents. There are tons of men dressed just like Rhett in cowboy boots, well-fitting Wrangler jeans, and hats. *Maybe Texas isn't so bad after all.*

Everything, and everyone, is bathed in neon lights, and the walls are covered in pictures of either long-neck bottles or people drinking beer from a long-neck bottle. *Very clever.*

There's a stage at the front of the bar and a doorway to the right-hand side of it that leads to an outdoor patio, which is really just a small fenced-in patch of dirt where string lights are hung overhead and tables have benches made out of tailgates.

Callie grabs my hand and leads me toward the bar, heading directly toward a bartender who looks to be about our age. He has sandy blonde waves sticking out of his ball cap and a perfect coat of stubble across his jaw line.

He leans onto the bar with both his elbows. "Hey, Cal!" His beautiful blue eyes catch on me as he asks with a smirk, "Who's your friend?"

"This is Olivia," she says with pride. "Olivia, this is Jax. We went to school together for years and became friends in high school."

Jax reaches his hand out to shake mine. "Nice to meet you, Olivia. You wouldn't happen to be Olivia Parker, would you?"

My stomach sinks. "How does everyone in this town know who I am?"

"It's a small town. Don't worry. I've only heard good things." His perky smile and magnetic charm draw me in immediately and help me forget my nerves over the fact that people in this town are talking about me. "What brings you to town?"

"I'm just visiting my parents for a bit. My job is pretty demanding, so I'm taking some time off to reconnect with family."

"Roots is the best place you could come to slow down a little. It doesn't look like it now, but I promise you, this place is usually far more quiet when the Callahan sisters aren't coming to play. Plus, I make some of the best drinks you'll ever taste." He leans back on the bar. "Speaking of, what can I get you to drink? I already know Callie wants a Ranch Water."

"Don't forget the lime!"

He rolls his eyes. "You remind me every time. I couldn't possibly forget. I have nightmares about forgetting your limes."

Callie eases back in her seat with a smug smile on her face. "Good."

"I'll take an Old Fashioned," I say.

Callie's jaw falls to the floor. "Olivia! You badass! I like the energy. Tonight is going to be *fun.*"

Jax gives me an approving nod as he turns to make our drinks.

"So, did you ask Rhett to come out with us?" She wiggles her brows.

"I may have mentioned it, but he said no, just like I expected."

"Text him. Tell him I want him to come. It's not too late."

"No, that's okay. I want to hang out with *you* tonight."

"That's so sweet, but I'm having a real dry spell with men these days, and I *really* want to live through you right now."

"Why don't *you* dance with Rhett then? Or Jax? Jax is super cute." I lower my voice. "Did you see his eyes? And you two seem to have some sort of banter going."

Jax swivels around and sets our drinks down on the bar. "Here you go, ladies. Should I just go ahead and open a tab?"

Callie slides her credit card across the counter. "Yes, please. Olivia, we can square up later."

Jax takes the card. "I hope I'll see you two later," he says, giving me a smirk before he rushes off to help another pack of thirsty Roots customers.

"Sorry, you were saying I should go for Jax while he was busy flirting with you?" Callie teases.

"What? No, I—"

"I'm kidding."

"Why haven't you gone for Rhett or Jax? They're two of the most beautiful men I've ever seen."

Callie grabs her straw, swirling the lime in her drink around distractedly. "I wouldn't touch Rhett with a thirty-nine-and-a-half-foot pole, but *you can.* As for Jax, he *is* cute, but he and I are just friends. He's been my buddy since sophomore year of high school, and I've never looked at him as anything more."

"What's wrong with Rhett that would keep you away from him? That doesn't exactly instill confidence in me to go after him."

"Don't worry! There's nothing wrong with him. He's actually quite perfect. He does have a tendency to be closed off, but I think you could get through to him. I haven't been very successful in the whole four years he's been here, but you seem to have some sort of effect on him. Besides, Rhett is like a brother to me at this point."

I purse my lips as I consider her response. "Do you think that's all he needs? Someone who can open him up?"

"Yes, he's needed that from the moment he stepped foot in Roots. He just has a lot of things lurking in the shadows, but I think you might know a thing or two about that." She pins me with a meaningful look. "Yet, look how you're already thriving here! I think you could help him."

I want to. I open my mouth to tell her that, but the lights on the stage come on, and everyone in the crowd begins to cheer. There are whistles and howls. I've never felt so much energy in one place.

Callie's eyes light up, and she grabs my hand to drag me off my bar stool. The band comes out first and starts playing a lively tune while the two beautiful brunettes saunter out on stage in tiny denim shorts, cowgirl boots, and almost identical lacey cream tops. The taller one grabs the mic first and sings the opening line.

Immediately, Callie starts wiggling around to the beat. I'm impressed by her ability to time her movements to the tune of the music. She looks hot. Meanwhile, I'm pretty sure I'm tone-deaf because whenever I try to move to music like that, I look like a fish out of water.

I sip my drink and let the sweet tang of the whiskey coat my tongue, quickly warming my insides and making me feel tingly with just a sip. It's been way too long since I've had alcohol. I'm going to take it nice and easy tonight.

The second sister steps forward and belts out a rich, growly note that coats my arms in chills. Damn, she's good.

Leaning into Callie's ear, I ask, "Did you go to school with them too?"

"Who haven't I gone to school with in this town?"

"I was thinking the same thing, but I wasn't going to say it out loud."

Shrugging, she says, "It's okay. I don't take offense to it. Most people who have stayed in Roots after high school have come to embrace how small the town is. I'm proud to live here."

"San Francisco is better, but this place isn't half bad."

The smile on her face is immediately wiped clean. "Olivia, I haven't been to San Francisco, but I can *still* tell you it doesn't compare to Roots. No big city like that could ever compare to Roots. This is the place people come to make a *home*."

"Some people like the big cities."

"Do you?"

I shrug. "I thought I did."

She doesn't say anything in response. She just nods

quietly, but as soon as the next song starts, she begins jumping up and down and whooping.

I take another sip of my Old Fashioned and then cheer with her. I might as well make the most of tonight.

———

I'm on my second drink now, and as the next song begins, Callie turns to me. "Please tell me you know Shania Twain's music."

I wince. "I'm more of a Taylor Swift girl."

She tilts her head from side to side as if she's weighing the merit of my answer. "Shania Twain is kind of like the Taylor Swift of country music... except not. She was my idol growing up. I guess we have some work to do while you're here."

"Sounds good." I laugh easily. The warmth of the whiskey is already coursing through my veins. "How about we start with the name of this song?"

"Oh dear, you have so much to learn. This is 'Any Man of Mine,' which is just one of the many anthems of all women everywhere that Shania sings." She grabs my hand and tugs me toward the lines of people that are forming on the dance floor in front of the stage. "Follow my lead." She begins to tap her boots on the hardwood floors, still holding her drink casually in one hand.

My focus lasers in on Callie's feet as she continues to tap the toes of her boots on the floor. *Okay, this isn't bad. Maybe this is the one kind of dancing I can actually do.* Then she starts moving backward, and I scramble to keep up with the perfectly timed steps, which is difficult when I don't know the tune of the song *at all!* Callie bumps into me as she does some sort of grapevine with her feet. She laughs lightly. "We are going to do the same thing in the other direction," she instructs, but she's already moving that way.

The second she finishes her other grapevine, she does a weird step where her hips seem to just follow her flinging feet until we are facing another wall. She repeats the toe-tapping, and I follow along, the movement already feeling slightly familiar. This time, I match maybe half of her steps as she steps backward, and I manage to avoid slamming into anyone during the grapevine. I wouldn't say my feet are weaving perfectly as I step from side to side, but I at least know when to move right and when to move left.

The chaotic spinning step comes again, and I stumble over my own feet, blushing a little as everyone else seems to perform the dance flawlessly. "It takes a while to pick up the box step. Don't worry about it," Callie says. "I've been doing this since I was eight years old. My sister used to drag my family out to lessons every Wednesday night, so I'm a professional at teaching it now if you want me to show you how to do it later."

We complete the third sequence, and I'm smiling now because I'm starting to get the dance with the exception of the stupid box step, but then I catch a glimpse of a smirking Rhett leaning against the back wall with his arms crossed. I meet his gaze for the tiniest second before I stumble over myself and try to scramble back in line with everyone else.

"You okay?" Callie asks.

"What is he doing here? I thought he didn't do bars."

She smiles. "He just couldn't stay away. I have never in my life seen Rhett enter this bar. You may not have cracked him open the way you expect to just yet, but you're doing something to him just the same."

The music cuts, and everyone disburses as the next song starts up, a slower one.

"You think so?"

"I've known him for a long time. I'm pretty confident on this one. Go talk to him. See if he will dance with you. I guarantee he won't be able to say no."

I swallow the last of my drink and set it down on the edge of the bar. I walk toward him with a new determination and liquid courage flowing through my veins.

Chapter Twenty-Five

Rhett

I haven't been able to take my eyes off Olivia since I walked into this bar. As she makes her way toward me, I can't remember why I'm here or why I'm supposed to keep her at a distance. Those amber eyes have a beautiful light in them that makes me want to give her my whole heart, and something about her makes me believe that if I did, my past would be erased.

When she gets closer, I can see the shiny look in her eyes that indicates she is clearly feeling the booze.

"Hey, hotshot! What are you doing hiding out in the corner?"

"Hotshot?" I arch a brow.

"I don't know. You looked a little too-cool-for-school standing here by yourself while everyone was out there dancing."

"I told you. I don't do bars, and I definitely don't dance." At least not with her. That sounds like a recipe for disaster.

"I just came to make sure you two had a ride home. Maverick was asleep already anyway."

"Too much cattle chasing and peeing in the yard?"

"Yup." I chuckle.

"Please dance with me, Rhett."

"Not happening."

"Why don't you dance? Are you afraid of being bad? You can't tell me you didn't see me out there making a fool of myself. I still did it anyway."

"I can dance, but I don't dance."

"That's even worse. Come dance with me, please." She draws out the e. "Show me how it's done." She grabs one of my hands and begins dragging me toward the dance floor.

All of my instincts are screaming *no*. I already let things go too far the other night. I opened up more than I ever intended to, and I know better than to do it again, but her soft touch plays tricks on my heart, and now my feet are shuffling after her. When we make it to the edge of the dance floor, she begins to smile, and I swear that smile could light up the entire bar. God knows it's lighting up every dark corner inside of me.

I eye her carefully. "What're you smiling about?"

"I just really wanted to dance with you. Callie told me you wouldn't say no if I asked, and I guess she was right."

Damn it, Callie. We are going to have a talk about her interfering in my love life after this. Not that this is my love life. I don't love Olivia, and I never will. I'll just keep saying that until I know it's true.

Callie catches sight of me and waves joyfully from her spot on the edge of one of the picnic tables to the side of the dance floor. I give her my best scowl, but the second Olivia looks up at me like I put the stars in the sky, that frown is erased, leaving no trace of it behind.

"Rhett, can I ask you something?"

"Sure."

"I'm just trying to understand why you've never come to the bar before, but you're here now."

"That's not a question."

"But it's not entirely a statement either."

I grimace. I don't want to talk about this. When she peers back up at me with those softly shining amber eyes, some of the walls inside of me start to crumble. *Maybe she won't even remember this conversation tomorrow.* Wishful thinking, I realize considering she doesn't seem much more than buzzed.

I inhale sharply, and then the words tumble out. "There was a time when I did drink and go to bars, back in college. My senior year, I made a big mistake that I can never take back, so I decided from that point forward to stay away from parties and alcohol. Nothing good comes from it."

Pity creeps into her face, but she promptly pushes it away, and I'm grateful. "I understand. It doesn't bother me if you choose not to drink or go to bars." She pauses, clearly still thinking. Then she adds, "I just can't figure out how to put together all the puzzle pieces I have of you. I'm still missing something."

"I told you not to try. I probably shouldn't even be here. I just wanted you two to be safe. A responsible person makes sure the people he cares about make it home safely."

Something flickers in her eyes but silence washes over us for a while as we just sway to the music. I'm certain she's just willing this dance to be over with. I've said too much. I've probably scared her away now that she's caught a glimpse of the darkness inside of me. I guess that's a good thing. That's what I need if I'm going to keep us apart.

But as the song winds down, she doesn't immediately

pull away. Instead, she moves in a little closer and leans her cheek into my chest. I feel my hard exterior melt a little, and it's terrifying. "Thank you," she whispers.

"For what?"

"For sharing with me, even if it was a little tiny sliver of the whole complex puzzle that makes you up. I'm starting to realize you aren't too keen on sharing much about your life with people, so I'll take whatever I can get."

"Don't get used to it."

"I'm going to crack you all the way open someday. Just you wait and see."

"Trust me, you don't want to do that."

"You told me I'm lucky to have people who accept me and love me with all my flaws. You said you'd give anything to have that, but you won't let anyone in and give them the chance to love and accept you. I hope to get that chance someday."

My stomach does a somersault or two, and I'm rendered speechless. I stand there staring blankly at her, and I can feel the tension building between us as the song ends. *Did I upset her?*

When she draws away from me, she grimaces and says, "I'm sorry, but I really have to pee!" Spinning on her heel, she dashes off to the bathroom before I can even process what she said.

Only a minute after Olivia has pulled from my grip, Callie rushes up to me. "What're you doing here? I saw you two dancing. Did it go well?"

I roll my eyes. "We just danced. It's no big deal."

"It *is* a big deal, Rhett. I saw the way you were looking at her."

"It doesn't mean anything." It can't.

"What's your problem? Why can't you open yourself up to anyone?"

"I want to. I just can't."

"Why not?"

I want to tell her everything that's been plaguing me since the moment Olivia walked into my life, the burning desire not only for love, but love with this wonderful woman I've grown to enjoy spending time with, the fear that I'll never be worthy of love, the fear of losing yet another person I hold close to me, but in true Rhett-fashion, I quickly dodge her question.

"Shouldn't Olivia be back by now?"

"I'm sure she's fine."

"No, it shouldn't take her this long to go to the bathroom."

"There was probably a line. You wouldn't understand this, but as women, we like to go to the bathroom in packs, so we usually have to wait in line to pee."

"Why didn't you go with her?"

"I didn't know she was going. She didn't ask me to come with her."

"She could be getting into any kind of trouble alone right now. She was clearly not sober."

Callie reaches out to me, grabbing onto both of my arms. "Olivia only had a little buzz. She can still take care of herself."

I'm no longer listening as I tear away from her grip and surge toward the bathroom. I'm about to walk in when Callie catches up to me again. "I'll go check to see if she's in there. Chill."

When she comes back out and shrugs, I begin to panic. This is why I had to come here tonight, to make sure they were being safe. *Oh god, could she have left the bar on her own? She wouldn't do that, would she? Was she upset with me for not being more open with her?*

Again, Callie grabs onto me. "I see what you're doing. Slow down that brain of yours. I'm sure Olivia is still here and perfectly safe. Something bad doesn't happen every time someone drinks. I promise." She draws back. "I'll go check the dance floor and the patio in case she just needed some air. How about you check the bar?"

I nod, taking a calming breath. This isn't like me to feel anxious, but all of this seems just a little too familiar.

I reach the bar, scanning the barstools for her beautiful brown hair or bright red top reflecting in the neon lights. I don't see her. *Deep breath. I'm sure she's fine.* It's a lot easier to say it in my mind than to actually believe it. *Why would she just disappear like that?*

"She's definitely not outside or on the dance floor, but I'm certain she wouldn't just leave." Callie stops, her eyes trained on something behind me. A lopsided grin slowly grows on her face, and she points to what she's looking at. "Found her."

Chapter Twenty-Six

Olivia

"What on earth are you doing back here?" Callie calls, dragging my attention from Jax who is showing me how to make a Mai Tai.

I rush up to the counter where Callie is leaning over, beaming. Rhett lurks behind her, looking a whole lot of things, none of which are happy.

"Sorry! I wanted a glass of water after I went to the bathroom, and then I was going to come back and find you, but Jax was showing me how to mix drinks and telling me about how he's going to buy part of the bar. I guess I just got distracted."

Jax hands me a cup of water, and I take it before walking around to the other side of the bar. Rhett immediately pulls me toward him, wrapping me up in a hug. "You can't just take off like that."

"I'm sorry. I just wanted water and got distracted."

"Are you upset with me?"

I narrow my brows. "For what?"

"For not telling you more about my life."

"I mean I want to know more, but I'm not angry with you for it."

"You're sure?"

"Yeah." I smile at him, but it slowly falls. "Are you okay?"

He nods, shirking me off and muttering something about waiting for us out in his truck.

———

Ever since Rhett retreated from the bar, I've been distracted, trying to figure out what happened tonight. What would make him so closed off? What would put that panic in his eyes at the idea of not knowing where I was?

Something traumatic must've happened to Rhett at a bar, maybe involving someone he loves. That would maybe explain why he won't open up to anyone or why he doesn't believe in love anymore. He's afraid of growing attached to someone again because he's afraid of losing them. Knowing what motivates him makes me feel a little more confident that I can help him and return the favors he's done for me.

"Hey, are you okay?" Callie draws me out of my head.

I give her a nod and the best smile I can, which she thankfully seems to accept.

Despite being distracted, I've still managed to have a great night with Callie. She has a zest for life and this way of making me feel so loved and welcomed. I wish I could wrap her up and take her back to San Francisco with me. I could use someone like her in my life on a daily basis.

The Callahan sisters played three more Shania Twain songs. I unfortunately only remember the name of one, "Man! I Feel Like A Woman!" because, one, the title is funny; two, Callie informed me it is another one of her female anthem songs; and three, I enjoyed the beat but had to stand off to the side looking like a chump during the line dance because it involved a lot more footwork and spinning than "Any Man of Mine."

When Callie and I approach the bar to say goodbye to Jax and close out our tab, he gives me a firm handshake before saying, "Screw it," and pulling me in for a quick squeeze. "It was nice to meet you. I hope I'll be seeing more of you real soon." The meaningful look he gives me as he says it makes me feel a little uneasy. Maybe Callie was right. I think he *is* flirting. "Ya'll get home safe."

"Don't worry, Rhett has been sitting in the parking lot for the past hour waiting on us." Callie laughs.

"Oh, wow. Sounds like Rhett has taken a liking to the new girl, huh?"

I give him a soft smile, but Callie says, "Oh yeah, he has, so back off." *What?!* Kissing him on the cheek, as if she didn't just say that, she cheers, "Goodnight, Jax!"

Swiveling around, she leans into my ear. "Damn, girl! You better be careful. You're going to have this whole town falling for you. First Rhett and now Jax seems to be taking a liking to you too."

"I'm sure he was just being friendly."

"Jax is known as the biggest flirt in all of Texas. I don't think he knows how to just be friendly, but we can use this to our advantage. Watch this." She winks at me as we approach Rhett's truck.

Rhett gets out to open his rear door for us and grabs Callie's hand to help her in. She takes it and turns back to me. "Jax is known for being flirty, but, man, he seemed genuinely interested in you."

Rhett places his other hand out in front of her, pausing her from getting into the truck. "What's going on with Jax?"

She doesn't miss a beat. "Jax seemed interested in Olivia. I think she should go for it because I *love* Jax. What do you think?"

I give her a skeptical look as Rhett offers me his hand. Rage swirls in his eyes, and he presses his lips together. I have to admit, it feels damn good. That look right there inflates me with hope.

"I think she should stay away from Jax." He's talking to Callie, but his eyes don't come off me. "He has a reputation for a reason. I wouldn't trust him as far as I can throw him."

"His reputation is for being a big flirt, and I hear a pretty good hookup. Maybe that's what you need to complete your Roots experience, Olivia. It's perfect! What with you leaving and all, Jax is exactly the kind of guy to go for. It's uncomplicated. No strings."

"Is that really what you want though? A fling?" Rhett gets into the driver's seat, meeting my gaze in the rearview mirror. I give him a soft, perhaps slightly cocky smile, as I shrug.

"Your parents asked me to keep an eye out for you, and I don't think they'd be too happy if they found out I just stood by and let you get involved with Jax."

"She's a big girl and can look out for herself. It's not your place to get involved in her love life."

I'm starting to feel uncomfortable with all of this, but I can't help the smile that crosses my face when I swear I hear him murmur, "Maybe it is."

He pulls out of his parking spot, but when he reaches the exit, he asks, "Where am I taking you two? Callie's?"

"Yup, the plan still hasn't changed. Can you be a dear

and connect my Bluetooth? I need to play more Shania Twain for Olivia."

Reluctantly, he presses a couple of buttons on his dash.

Callie swipes and taps a few times on her phone until her phone starts playing one of the songs from the bar earlier. "Can you turn it up? I'm going to be singing along, and either you turn it up, or you have to listen to my horrible voice."

Rhett huffs but turns up the volume more than just a few notches. In the rearview mirror, I see the hint of a smile, which only fills my heart with adoration for this man. From that simple gesture, I am reinvigorated with my determination to crack Rhett open, even if it means putting myself out there too. Whatever darkness he thinks he holds inside of himself is worthy of love, and despite knowing that I'm leaving in a couple of months, I *need* to give him a chance to see that.

———

With the smell of whiskey on my breath now replaced by fresh mint, I draw back the comforter on Callie's queen-size bed, murmuring, "Thank you."

"For what?"

"For taking me out for a fun night and for making me feel so welcome here. My parents are great. Rhett is great. Really everyone in Roots is great, but I don't think I'd enjoy my time here half as much if it weren't for you. You just have this way of making me feel so... loved, and worthy of that love."

She gives me a soft smile, and I can see hints of pain and warmth in her eyes. "That means a lot to me."

"How did you get to be so vibrant?" I prod, amazement still filling me.

"Stop! You're making this a bigger deal than it is." She swats at me. "My whole life, my parents always picked my sister first. I never really questioned it. In fact, I understood. She was kind and brilliant and funny. But at the end of the day, it definitely made me feel like I wasn't good enough. With time, people like Ms. Easton and Benny swooped in and made me feel loved. It made me realize the profound impact one person can have on another, and I wanted to be that person for someone else. Then after high school, I went through a tough breakup that made me feel like I wasn't someone's first choice again, and my sister passed away a year later, proving how quickly life can be snatched away from you. Since all that, I've made it my mission to live a positive life and to help others to hopefully never feel like they're someone's last choice, at least not in my presence."

"I admire that. And for what it's worth, I think you do a hell of a job at it. I'm sorry you've felt that way in life. You deserve better. If I can help it, I'm going to do my best to be a good friend to you who never makes you feel that way."

"Thanks, Olivia." She pauses. "Can I ask you something?"

"Sure."

"Why don't you want to stay in Roots? I know you have your life in San Francisco, and I don't know a ton about what that looked like, but it seems to me like you're building something great here. And again, I can't speak for San Francisco, but I know you have a lot of people here who already adore you and want to put you first. I guess I'm just thinking if I had that as an option at some point in my life, I'd choose it."

Her words sting. They remind me a little of what Rhett

has said about how I have people who care so much for me, but I push them away. "It hadn't occurred to me that I actually could stay."

"Why not? I'm sure your parents have been begging you to the moment you got here."

"I've spent the last couple years trying to keep my parents at a distance because I felt like my anxiety was ruining their lives. The idea of staying here and letting them be a regular part of my life again has never felt like it's an option. Beyond that, I guess Roots just doesn't seem to fit into my goals for life. I've always wanted to make senior at my job, and I've worked so hard to get here. I can't just give all that up. My job, my apartment, my—" I trail off because quite frankly I'm not sure what else. "They're all in San Francisco, and I don't know how to make a good life here in Roots."

"It seems to me like you've already started. You've got a job. You've got family and friends, and a potential love interest." She wiggles her eyebrows. "You've got an adorable dog who loves you to pieces, and you've even gotten involved with the local animal shelter. That seems like a beautiful life to me. Just saying."

"But that life doesn't pay my bills. It doesn't build my resume, and it doesn't help me get the job title I've been striving for since I was in college. I can't stay in Rhett's house with extremely discounted rent forever, and I can't live off of part-time wages from the café. Besides, I have a Master's degree and my CPA license. I worked so hard for those. I need to put them to use."

"That education, that license, they're both impressive, but they don't mean anything if you're not happy. Considering the circumstances that brought you here, I think it's safe to say that you weren't all that happy in San Francisco. I'd like to see you create a life that brings you joy."

I nod silently, not sure what else to say. She is so right, but I feel stuck. It's not like I have the experience to jump into the things I want to do in life. My anxious self craves stability, and I can't imagine getting that from pursuing some sort of career related to social media or non-profits. *And what about my dad?* He'd be horrified to see me give up my career just before I make it to senior the same way he had to when he was younger. It's a nice thought, staying in Roots and living like this all the time, but it's not practical, which breaks my heart.

Chapter Twenty-Seven

Rhett

I'd like to say it's a happy accident that Olivia is still in the café when I get there for my check-in with Callie, but I was definitely very intentional when I scheduled our meeting for right when Olivia's shift is over, and even more intentional when I decided I might as well pop in twenty minutes early to see how things are going.

I haven't been able to stop thinking about the panic in my chest when we couldn't find her in the bar last week. It's had me making her breakfast on my day off and making sure she always has a fresh vase of wildflowers for her room. No matter how hard I fight my feelings, I always fail. It doesn't help that I can't get the image of her with Jax out of my head, and I'm starting to feel a little possessive. It's unfair of me to want her away from him if I can't commit to her, but I'm stuck between a rock and a hard place. I can't take the thought of losing her, and yet I know that's what will happen if I open my heart up to her. That's how it's always gone in my life, and I'd be insane to give love one more try with someone who is leaving in a couple of months.

The bell on the door overhead rings cheerily, and before I can even step both feet through the door I'm immediately greeted with a simple, "Hi, Rhett!" Her voice is soothing and warm, and her dazzling smile melts me like butter. She crouches down to the ground, cooing at Maverick as he pulls on his leash until I finally release it in time for him to bound across the café into her arms, licking her face frantically as if he hadn't seen her in much longer than the six hours it's actually been.

"Hey! How's your day going? Is your shift almost over?" I play innocent as I place my elbows on the counter and lean into her because that's the only way I can respond to her magnetism. I catch the faintest whiff of her lavender scent and want to wrap myself up in it.

Callie barges in, already interrupting us as she exits the kitchen, brushing her hands together. "You're early. I told you when her shift ended. That's why we planned on meeting at two."

"I've got a lot going on. I can't keep track of everyone's schedules and remember every little detail," I growl. Turning back to Olivia, I ask, "What're your plans for the rest of the day?"

"My Mom and I are going out to some fancy restaurant in Fort Worth."

"How have things been going between you two? Have you talked with her about the—" I glimpse at Callie standing three feet away, "—the incident?"

"I know I should, but I don't know if I'm ready yet. I've been trying for over a week to recite the conversation we would have in my head, and every time I chicken out. If I can't even do it in my head, how am I supposed to do it in real life?"

"You can totally do this! I believe in you. You know you'll feel better once you do." I lean onto the counter. "Focus on what it will feel like to have that weight lifted. Because it will lift. I know your mom. If you talk with her about things, you're going to feel better, and you're going to come away with a stronger relationship with her. I think it'd be good for you."

She nods in acceptance. "You're right. I hate that you're right." She scrunches up her nose in fake annoyance at me, and it's the cutest thing I've ever seen.

"I don't know why you're acting surprised. I'm always right."

"Don't go getting a full head there."

"Too late. Hmmm... should I use this superpower for good or for evil?"

"Stop it! You're being so ridiculous." She giggles and shoves my shoulder. Her laughter makes me wish I was cleverer and funnier because I want to keep making her laugh forever, but I'm out of things to say now.

I look up to find Callie still standing there quietly, her arms crossed and the most ridiculous smirk on her face. "Are you two done flirting yet? I need Olivia for one more thing before her shift is over."

Olivia's eyes go wide and her face flushes, turning the same color as the vibrant curtains Callie insisted on putting on the windows when we first bought the café. She recovers quickly though, making my stomach sink as she says, "Don't be ridiculous! I would never flirt with him. He's completely intolerable what with his big head and all." She turns to me and gives me a quick wink, making my stomach somersault. I'm so confused. *Am I upset? Am I happy? Is she flirting? Is she not?* I can't figure it out.

"What do you need help with? I need to leave right at two if my mom and I are going to make it into Fort Worth and back today."

Callie grabs her by the arm and drags her off into the kitchen, leaving me in the dining area with Maverick. I pick up his leash, settle into a chair at one of the tables, and open up the notebook I brought with me that holds everything I need for business with the café. Maverick sits staring at where Olivia and Callie just left, whimpering.

"I get it, buddy. She'll be back."

I stare intently at the numbers from last month, trying to rid my mind of Olivia with her earth-shattering smile and the contagious joy that has seemed to overcome her in the last couple of weeks as she's settled into Roots. I've been so impressed with her ability to turn things around from how she started here. She was angry at the world and afraid of letting anyone in. She was anxious and stubborn. She's still a little anxious sometimes and still definitely stubborn most times, but I love dealing with her stubbornness now, and I definitely didn't when she first got here. Maybe *I'm* the one who's changed.

Okay, I'm horrible at keeping her off my mind.

She steps back out from the kitchen, and I can feel her presence before I even see her. That's what she does to me. It's all-consuming, and it's terrifying.

"Okay, I have to run. Ladies' Night this weekend, right, Callie?"

"Of course."

"I'm so excited! They better play 'Any Man of Mine.' I've been practicing my dancing."

"You remembered the name. I'm so proud! I can personally guarantee you they'll play that song. If they don't, I'll take it up with Jax myself. Now get out of here! You said you had to leave right at two, and it's 2:02 now."

"Shoot! You're right." She calls goodbye to all of us, pressing a kiss between Maverick's eyes.

I hardly have time to get out the first syllable of my goodbye before she's rushing out the door, taking with her that warm and fuzzy feeling that was once filling the room.

At the slam of the door, Callie focuses on me, her hands on her hips. "So, care to tell me what's going on?"

I sigh in exasperation. "We talked about this on the phone last night. I want to run through the numbers for the month, and I figure we might as well touch base on the fundraiser. I'm sure Olivia got you all up to speed on things today, but—"

"I'm not talking about that. I'm talking about you and Olivia."

I blink at her dumbly. "There's nothing to discuss. She's staying in my guest bedroom, and she's Jack and Mandi's daughter, so of course I'm friendly with her. We spend a lot of time together, but it's mostly because of Maverick."

"Yeah, the dog. Mmhmm." She backhands my shoulder.

"Ow!" I instinctively start rubbing the spot she smacked. "What was that for?"

"I was hoping it'd help you be less of an idiot. Even some random person off the street would be able to see the sparks flying between you two. I haven't seen you like this in a long time." She pauses briefly as the weight of that statement settles over us, leaving me feeling nothing but guilt, but she catches me off guard with her next sentence. "It's nice, really nice actually. It's like watching my brother fall in love."

I frown. She shouldn't be happy for me. She has every

right to be upset with me for feeling something for anyone besides her sister. "I don't like Olivia in that way." The words are not even remotely convincing.

"I know it might feel weird to talk with me about this, but I think I'm one of the people you need to hear it from the most. Isabel is gone. She's been gone for four years. I know she was your fiancée, but I also know you're not still in love with her, so why won't you let yourself move on? What's holding you back?"

"It's complicated."

"Then uncomplicate it, Rhett. You don't owe Isabel anything but to allow yourself to move on and be happy. If Olivia is the one who is going to make you happy, then please, for the love of God, go after her."

"You don't understand. This isn't just about Isabel. I mean it sort of is. It's just that, I didn't believe in love before your sister. She changed all of that, but now she's gone, and I screwed things up before she died. Maybe love does exist for other people, but her death was proof that *I* will never be worthy of love."

"What are you talking about?"

"I didn't believe in love when I met Isabel. My parents didn't give me a good example of it. They treated each other with such hatred both before and after they were divorced, so love always seemed like more of a fleeting feeling than anything to me, something shiny and exciting for the beginning of a relationship that turns dark after a while. I wanted nothing to do with it. Isabel came along and refused to let me believe that. She broke through my hard exterior, and I fell in love with her. Things were good for a while, but then we had the biggest fight of our relationship, and she died the same night.

"That's when it started to click that maybe love just

doesn't work when I'm involved. My parents' marriage fell apart after they had me. They disowned me and stopped loving me after I got engaged to Isabel. Then I argue with my fiancé, and she dies. There's one common denominator in all those things I just told you. Me. I'm just not meant to have love in my life. I've accepted it."

Callie furrows her brow, reaching out to me. "You know that you're not out of chances when it comes to love, right? Just because your family fell apart and you lost your fiancé... okay, that does sound bad, but it's not the end for you. You have to get back up and keep trying. If you let every bad thing in your life knock you down—"

"Callie, please don't."

"No, you need to hear this."

"Even if everything you're saying is true, I don't trust myself anymore. I just seem to hurt the people I love."

I push out from the table, grabbing Maverick's leash and giving it a gentle tug so he'll follow me out.

As I storm toward the door, I can hear Callie still talking to me. It isn't until she grabs my arm that I finally stop and register what she's saying. "Olivia lights you up in a way I've *never* seen, not even with my sister. You're an amazing guy, Rhett. You're worthy of love. You made my sister *so* happy, and one poorly timed fight doesn't change the three years of happiness you gave her."

I slip my arm from hers gently and to even my surprise, I pull her in for a hug. "Thank you. I know you're just looking out for me, and I appreciate it. I just can't let love in that easily. Something didn't just break inside me that day I lost Isabel, something shattered. It'll never be fixed. It's not just that I don't believe in love anymore. I don't trust myself to keep it if it ever comes my way again. Isabel was my one shot at starting over and giving love another chance, but I ruined things with her beyond repair. I'm terrified of what I might do to anyone else."

"It wasn't your fault." Her words are barely above a whisper, but they hit me hard. "You treated her like a queen. If she can't have that love anymore, then someone else should. Call me crazy, but I think that someone could be Olivia. I've heard the way she talks about you, and I hear all about the incredibly sweet things you do for her. You are constantly proving that you are still more than capable of loving deeply and treating someone right. Trust me, I know a thing or two about people that make you feel unloved or unworthy, and you are not one of them. Don't let that self-doubt creep in."

"I should go." I finally say. I am barely holding myself together right now, and I don't want Callie to see the spiraling that's about to commence as I question my whole world for the past four years.

"Rhett, wait!" I stop and glance over my shoulder at her. "Please just promise me you'll think about what I said. You deserve to be happy. That's all I want for you. It's what Isabel would've wanted too."

"I'll think about it. Now leave me alone. You're driving me crazy."

She smirks. "But nothing compared to the way Olivia drives you wild, right?"

"Shut up," I growl as I storm out the door, trying to keep the corners of my mouth from turning up.

Chapter Twenty-Eight

Rhett

I'M A SWEATY MESS, BUT NONETHELESS, A WAVE OF satisfaction rolls over me. I woke hours before the sun was up for the past week and a half, working closely with Austin, the soon-to-be owner of Copper Hill. Calving season ended in May, but breeding season is May through August. Plus, the cattle are grazing this time of year, so we are moving them to different pastures sometimes three times a day.

Even though we've been busy, something about working on the ranch brings me peace, and I've needed some peace after my conversation with Callie.

"Hey, you two! Glad you finally came back," Lauren remarks as Austin and I enter the barn. She leans in to give her fiancé a quick kiss. "Are you two wrapped up yet?"

"Actually, I have one more project if you're up for it, Rhett."

Glancing at my watch, I note it's 9:30 pm. I've been going home later than this for the past week, but I'm exhausted. "I think I should head home now. I'll see you tomorrow though."

Austin gives me a smile and a firm handshake. As I head toward my truck, I hear the happy couple murmuring to one another. They don't sound so happy. I guess wedding planning can be stressful. Turning my key in the ignition, my lights flicker on just in time to illuminate Lauren marching out of the barn with her arms crossed and a frown on her face.

The sight reminds me of my stupid fight with Callie. I must've looked like such a child for marching out of the café like that, but she caught me off guard. I thought I was doing a better job of hiding my feelings for Olivia than I apparently am.

It's just so complicated. It's not like I'm still hung up on Isabel. I will always love her, but four years has been enough time for me to recognize that I have room in my heart for someone else. I want to love again. I do, but I also don't trust myself, and I'm terrified of losing someone.

I could open up my heart to Olivia, but it would only get crushed in a matter of time. I'd mess it up, or she'd be taken away from me, perhaps sooner than later considering her time in Roots has an expiration date.

Pulling into the driveway at home, the soft yellow glow of the living room light catches my eye. She's still awake. I've avoided Olivia for a full ten days, getting up before her and coming home after she's gone to bed. I'm not sure if I have the clarity I need yet, and I don't think I'll get it by being with her, but seeing the light on in the living room makes me suddenly aware of the dull ache that's settled upon me since I've last seen her. Living without her feels like trying to get somewhere with no map. I might be able to continue like this. I might get where I need to go eventually, but it's painful and unnecessary.

I lock my truck and walk toward the house, not moving my eyes away from that beckoning light, and the ache turns sharper by the second. I need to see her, so badly that I think I'm seeing things. I could've sworn I just saw her amber eyes and dark brown hair popping over the window ledge.

When I get to the front porch, the door swings open, and Olivia runs at me with a frying pan in her hands and a wild look in her eyes.

I leap back, holding my hands in front of my face. "Woah! What the hell are you doing?"

"Rhett?" She drops the pan, looking surprised. "You scared the crap out of me! What are you doing home this early?"

A pang of guilt hits me in the chest as I take her in. Her hair is tossed up into a messy bun. Little strands of wispy hair outline her face. She's wearing a wrinkly USF t-shirt and sweatpants. Her freckles have come in since when she first got here, the sun doing wonders to bring out her natural beauty. I don't think she's ever looked more beautiful.

"I'm sorry I've been coming home so late." I close and lock the door behind me. "Is this how you protect yourself in case of an intruder? Run at him with a frying pan?"

"Sorry, I don't know where you keep your baseball bats."

"You don't need a bat or a frying pan. Nothing bad ever happens in Roots. Even if it did, you should know you can call me."

"You haven't been around though. I was starting to think you were avoiding me."

"I—" I stop dead in my tracks. I don't know what I'm doing. I didn't plan on seeing her tonight. My heart brought me here without giving my head any say in the matter. "I've been really busy helping out at Copper Hill for the past week and a half. This is our busiest time of year."

"Do you like your job?" She pats the cushion on the couch, waiting for me to join her. I settle down just on the other side of Maverick.

"I love it. Austin isn't the greatest boss in town, but I love the work. Plus, Lauren has been helping out a good amount over the last year since she got out of college, and I like working with her. She's sweet and quiet, but she has this sassy, sarcastic side that will come out every now and then, and it's always fun."

"Who are Lauren and Austin?"

"Oh yeah, I guess I forgot you don't know this town like the back of your hand just yet." I chuckle softly. "Remember I told you Charlie Rhodes left Roots and his little sister's fiancé is in line to take over Copper Hill?" She nods. "Lauren is Charlie's little sister, and Austin is her fiancé."

"Lauren and Austin. Got it. It's locked in now." She touches her pointer finger to her temple, a look of laser focus on her face.

Silence falls over us, and I'm forced to consider what my intentions are now that we are finally face to face again. I'm no longer naïve enough to believe I can ignore my feelings for Olivia, but I'm not sure what to do about them. She's leaving soon, and I have demons I need to deal with. This relationship would be doomed before it even began. I feel like a fool. I should've taken more time.

Picking at her nails, Olivia glances up at me, breaking the silence. "I've been revamping the social media for Resilient Paws. I made a post the other day, and it just took off." She reaches over Maverick to hand me her phone, leaning in to watch over my shoulder as I take a look at the screen.

"Eight hundred thousand views? This is incredible! How did you manage that?"

She tries to humbly hide the smile growing on her face, but it slips through anyway. "I'm not exactly sure what I did. The audio I used was trending and I synced up the music to the video well. I think that helped. I'm confident the rest was just the dogs being their wonderful selves."

"I think it had a little bit to do with the person behind the camera being her wonderful self too."

She blushes. "I guess it pays to be authentic. I had this idea in my head for a couple weeks, but I couldn't figure out how I wanted to do it. I finally decided to just post it, and here we are. Resilient Paws got over one hundred new followers out of all the attention, and I think it's going to help me promote the fundraiser."

"This is amazing. You have a gift. I can't stop watching the video. It's no wonder it went viral."

"I wouldn't call that viral. It's not like it had millions of views or anything." She reaches to take the phone back, but I pull it in toward my chest.

"I'm not done watching it. I'm serious. I can't stop."

She laughs. "You're making way too big of a deal out of this. Anyone can get this kind of activity on one post. I need to be able to continuously repeat this sort of attention if I want to make a difference. They say the amount of followers that actually see your posts is miniscule, something like ten percent. So, by that logic, of those one hundred followers I got for the account, only ten of those people will see anything else I post about the fundraiser or a new dog in the shelter that needs a home."

I grab her hand, watching the overwhelm rise in her by

the second. "I can tell you care about the dogs. Maybe it is true only ten percent of your followers see your content, but that still means ten more people are going to see what you post." I scroll through the feed, clicking through the photos and videos she's added over the last couple of weeks. "This is all very powerful. Just getting one more person to see it is going to make a change because then that person will show someone who will show someone and so on."

A soft smile lights up her face. "Thanks, Rhett. I just really care about these dogs."

"I know." Still holding her hand, I say, "Don't put too much pressure on yourself. Try to let yourself enjoy being with the dogs, creating content, and planning the fundraiser. I don't want to see this tear you up and make you anxious."

"I maybe get a little anxious about it, but it's a different kind of anxiety from what I experience when I have a panic attack. Anxiety with work is debilitating, but this anxiety is subtler, and it drives me to keep going. Actually, according to my counselor, my anxiety can be a good thing when it's managed well. It's part of how I have been able to achieve so much all my life. I just need to work on preventing the debilitating part of it."

"That sounds like a good start."

Realizing I'm still holding her hand, I slowly release it, but our faces are so close that I can feel her breath on my lips. It's warm and gentle, just like the rest of her. Unable to control myself any longer, I move slightly closer, catching her familiar and comforting scent of lavender. She doesn't move away, and her eyes bob briefly down to my lips.

It makes me wonder what it'd be like to kiss Olivia. *Would her lips be as soft as they look? Would her skin feel smooth as I run my palms over her curves? Would she melt into my kiss? Would it be slow and passionate or rushed and desperate?*

Exhaling, I move in closer, but Maverick picks that moment to leap up barking at what appears to be nothing. His big head is in Olivia's lap one moment and smashing into her nose the next. My heart sinks as she lets out a shriek of pain.

Chapter Twenty-Nine

Olivia

It's been nearly forty-eight hours since Rhett and I almost kissed. Have we talked about it? Nope.

Rhett scampered off pretty quickly after my nose stopped bleeding with some excuse about needing to be up early for work the next day. Now it's been almost two whole days, but we still haven't had a chance to talk about it. Between the fundraiser, the café, and the ranch, it's felt like we're two ships passing in the night. Maybe I should be grateful for the time to think. I know in my heart what I want, but my brain is telling me something else entirely, and I'd really like the two to agree. Realistically, the time has only given me the space to come up with every reason why that almost kiss didn't mean anything.

"What's going through that beautiful head of yours, Ol?" Dad narrows his eyes at me as we sit on the couch after dinner.

It's been a great night with incredible food and good conversation, but try as I might, I can't keep my mind from swirling with thoughts of Rhett or the realization that I'm only here for another month and a half. *Where has all the time gone?* And inevitably, that leads me to the fact that I don't want to go back to my job after all this, and I don't want to leave Roots.

"Nothing. I'm fine."

I have to be. It'd be selfish of me to leave my job at the Big Four. It'd be impractical. I just can't help the fact that I'm enjoying my time here, and I want to explore all these new relationships—with my parents, with Callie, and, of course, with Rhett, even if we haven't had the chance to discuss what that almost kiss means.

Wringing my hands together in my lap, I look up at Dad. His eyes have returned to the TV as two announcers analyze the upcoming Rangers matchup.

"Actually, can I ask you something?"

"What's up?"

"Why does it bother you so much that you left public accounting early?"

He mutes the TV and turns toward me with even more concern on his face than earlier. "I guess it felt a bit like a failure to me. In school, the standard was always to *at least* make it to senior, and I couldn't even do that." His sorrow-coated voice quickly takes on a new tune as he adds, "But my little girl is going to do better than her dad ever did. I mean, look at you! You're taking time off and getting the help you need. I have no doubt you'll come back stronger than ever and get that promotion this fall like we always dreamed, right?"

Like we always dreamed. How the hell am I supposed to tell him that it's only ever been his dream? How do I tell him that I think this career has been what's driving my anxiety? I can't tell him the truth. It would kill him. I have to stick it out. I have to stay in San Francisco and make it to senior, regardless of whatever I may want.

Mom comes back into the room. "What time is Rhett coming over?"

"Should be any minute. The game starts in twenty."

"Rhett is coming over?" Despite my best efforts to sound nonchalant, the words come out extremely high-pitched.

"Yeah, he always comes over to watch the Rangers play. He didn't mention it to you? I thought you two were living in the same house now."

"We are, but he's been so busy with work, I've hardly spoken to him lately."

"Is something going on with you two? You can tell me."

"It's nothing."

Oddly enough, I don't want to keep my mom out of the loop just to keep her at a distance. I'm opting for silence because I'm embarrassed. I've replayed the events of the other night over and over again in my head, trying to convince myself Rhett wasn't going to kiss me, but there's no other explanation. If Maverick hadn't popped up, it would've happened, and I'm certain it would've been incredible. Except, when we were interrupted, I swear he looked relieved and ashamed, like he would've regretted it.

Even so, I can't seem to tamp down that flicker of hope that still blazes inside of me, that piece of me that hangs onto that little something I saw in his eyes that makes me believe whatever made Rhett scurry off the other night had nothing to do with me.

I should be excited about the opportunity to finally see him again, but the last thing I want is to be stuck hanging out with him for the evening while my parents hover over us and watch our every move. I want to address the elephant in the room, not just pretend it isn't there.

A knock at the door makes my stomach somersault.

"I've got it!" Dad calls. His excitement over Rhett's presence is kind of cute.

When my dad and Rhett walk into the room, Rhett's eyes immediately catch on mine. I can see a whole storm swirling inside of them, and it gives me even more hope. I'm not the problem. I *know* it.

I awkwardly bring my hand up to give him a half-hearted wave and smile, which he returns with a lopsided grin of his own.

"First pitch should be any second." My dad hands Rhett a glass of water.

"Ol, have I shown you the new paint swatches for the living room yet?" Mom grabs me by the hand and drags me off as I give Rhett one more glance over my shoulder.

———

"Well, this game is basically settled then," Mom notes. "What do y'all want to play after?"

"Please don't make me play anymore card games, babe," Dad groans. "You know I love you, but I'm all card gamed out."

"Even poker?"

"Even poker."

"Damn." Mom brings her pointer finger up to her mouth in thought. "What about pool?"

"Oh, pool could be interesting. What do you think, Rhett?"

"Pool sounds great as long as you're ready to lose."

I toss a hand on my hip. "What am I, chopped liver?"

"Of course not, honey, but you're not our guest."

"I don't live here. Shouldn't that make me a guest?"

"You're our daughter. That means you don't count."

My mouth falls open, and Dad chuckles. "I'm just teasing you, Ol. You know what I mean. You always count."

The Astros get three outs in only five pitches, ending the game abruptly, and we all head into the spare room for a game of pool.

"What do you think of men versus women?" Dad suggests.

"But Mom sucks, and I'm rustier than that truck you have sitting out in the driveway."

"You take that back!" Dad shouts, a smile still on his face. "That thing is my baby, and it'll run someday. I swear."

"Your dad has been giving me lessons." Mom's eyes flit to dad for support. "I might surprise you."

"I'm sorry, Mandi. You still suck. We can do you and me versus Olivia and Rhett."

I glance at Rhett and catch him wincing. *Jeez, what did I do to him to make him so upset with me?*

"Go ahead and break, Jack."

Dad sets up and nails the ball perfectly, managing to send two solids into the pocket.

Rhett grabs a cue and walks around the table, assessing the balls carefully before setting up. As he places one hand down on the table to hold the pole steady and pulls his other arm back, his triceps flex, on full display for my enjoyment. He stabs the cue ball and sends two balls in opposite directions, somehow pocketing both. *Of course he's good at pool! It wasn't enough for him just to look good while doing it.*

In line with my expectations, Mom takes her turn and completely misses the ball. I'd say she didn't even try to aim, except that she spent a solid two minutes lining up the ball, closing one eye and sticking her tongue out before striking the cue ball.

When it's my turn, I waltz around the table, determining the best move to make. I can feel Rhett's gaze on me, but I try not to let it distract me. I strike the ball, and when I just barely miss, I throw my head back, groaning.

Dad just chuckles as he quickly sneaks in and knocks two more balls in. Rhett counters with one, and my mom once again does very little to contribute to her team. We go around the rotation a couple times until we are down to one ball for Mom and Dad and two for Rhett and me.

I rub some chalk on the end of the cue and start to line up. Before I can go, Rhett places both hands on my waist, tugging me gently back. I swivel around to look at him. When I come chest to chest with him, my breath catches, and I can't help but wonder if my parents can also feel the crackling electricity in the air between us right now.

"What're you doing?" I whisper.

"I wouldn't go for that one." He tilts his head as he moves to the other end of the table and points to a purple-striped ball. "This is the one."

"Are you sure?"

"Definitely. Line it up and see for yourself."

I do as he says, and again, he stops me before I can hit the ball. "You look off-center."

"What do you mean? How can you tell?"

"Line up again."

As I do, he leans over me from behind, guiding me to adjust my setup slightly to the left. I'd like to say I can feel the difference in what he's showing me, but all I'm aware of right now is the way his whole body is wrapping me up and setting me on fire.

"Now go," he whispers in my ear, covering my arms in goosebumps before he pulls back from me.

I hit the cue ball, and it stops immediately when it strikes the ball I'm aiming for. The ball shoots into the pocket, and I jump up and down hollering. "I did it!"

I twirl around to Rhett, and he's absolutely beaming, sending me into a melted puddle on the floor. We move in close to one another, and I have to quickly draw back, realizing the way his magnetism just seemed to pull me right in. I settle for giving him a high five before asking him to help me set up for the next one, claiming, "We have a chance. We have to beat my parents."

"You'd take us down after we fed you and clothed you all these years?"

"Yes," I deadpan, narrowing my eyes playfully at Dad.

Rhett sidles up next to me again, setting me up, and once again the ball goes in with ease. I leap into his arms, and he accepts me, holding me tight until our gazes meet and time stops. We sit there like that for a beat longer until we realize where we are and break apart.

He clears his throat and scratches the back of his head. "That was good."

"I couldn't have done it without your help."

He nods, and the tension is finally broken when Mom announces, "We need to switch teams! I want Rhett on my team. Your dad is apparently a really crappy teacher."

———

I tuck a strand of stray hair behind my ear as we walk out the door together and get our first moment alone for the night.

"Is there anything you aren't good at?" I tease.

"Of course."

"Really? It doesn't seem like it to me. You play guitar. You cook. You bake. What can't you do?"

"I can't whistle. Every time I try, I sound like a dying cat." He demonstrates, and I can't help but laugh. He *does* suck at it. "I'm also terrible at golf. I took lessons one summer when I was thirteen, and I'm pretty sure I'm single-handedly responsible for the instructor's retirement that fall. And worst of all, I'm terrible at staying away from you."

My mouth goes dry, and my head immediately spins with all kinds of thoughts, but before I can jump to conclusions, I ask, "Why do you need to stay away?"

"I don't do love."

"But why not?"

"I told you about my parents."

"There has to be more to it than that. You can't let your parents' bad relationship stop you from having one."

"Okay, well answer me this. Are you planning on staying in Roots?"

"I—no. I mean, part of me wants to, but it's not practical."

"Then you and I don't make sense, right? If I have been hurt by love before, why would I want to start a relationship that is guaranteed to end and hurt me again?"

My stomach sinks. He's right.

"What if you didn't have to commit to love? Then would you let me in?"

"What do you mean?"

"I don't know. I don't have an answer. I just know that I was disappointed when we didn't get to kiss the other night."

"Me too." He steps closer, and I instantly feel the heat radiating off his body. My breath hitches, and I can feel my heart pounding out of my chest. He snakes one arm around my waist, pulling me into him and pressing his forehead against mine. "I don't think I can do casual with you. You're not the kind of girl someone keeps things casual with."

"But what else can we do about this?" I press my pointer finger from my chest to his and back. "We just have to pretend we aren't attracted to one another, that we don't care for one another? I don't think I can do that. I'm still here for over a month. We're still living together. The cottage won't be ready for at least another two weeks."

"I don't want to do that either." He kisses the crown of my forehead, and I become increasingly aware of how hot it is outside tonight. He slowly brings his face closer to mine, and I stand on my tiptoes. The herd of elephants is back, stampeding through my chest when the porch light flickers on. Mom barges out the front door, and the two of us leap apart.

"Rhett, don't forget your—" She stops, furrowing her brows as she takes us in. "Did I interrupt something? I can go back inside."

"You didn't interrupt anything. I was just saying goodnight." Rhett turns back to me. "I think I have a solution to our problem. Will you come with me to Copper Hill tomorrow?"

Chapter Thirty

Rhett

Olivia pulls up to Copper Hill in her Volkswagen, looking completely out of place on this ranch. She steps out of her car, dressed in jeans, cowgirl boots, and a plain white scoop-neck tank top. She looks incredible, and seeing her here makes my nerves tangle in my stomach.

My reaction to her presence is terrifying, but I need today. It's become obvious over the last couple of weeks that Olivia is torn between being the overachieving, always-on-the-right-path person that she is and following her heart. I can tell she doesn't want to go back to her life in San Francisco. I just need to figure out how to convince her to stay. I want to give love one more chance, but if Olivia won't allow herself to be happy and stay here then there's no point in opening up to her.

"Where'd you get your outfit from? I *know* this hasn't been sitting in the back of your closet in San Francisco," I tease.

"I came straight from Callie's. She was helping me with

some fundraiser details this morning, and she insisted she help me dress properly for the occasion."

"I like it."

She gives me a little nod. "I like the cowboy hat and boots look on you too. Not too shabby." She gives me a sly smile as her cheeks rouge.

"So, what're we going to do today? Am I just going to be your shadow?"

She's looking up at me as if I make the sun shine, a genuine eagerness filling her eyes. We might as well just go all in now. I want her, and for some reason, I fully believe we could make this work, but I refrain from sweeping her off her feet and kissing her, instead opting for a simple, "I already helped Austin with a few projects early this morning. I'm not going to make you do any physical labor in the sun with this insane heat wave we're having, so I thought maybe you could help me clean out the horse stalls today."

She rolls her eyes. "I am fully capable of doing physical labor, even if it is hotter than Hell out here."

"So you don't want to hang out with Maggie today?"

Crossing her arms and pressing her lips into a line, she mumbles, "I didn't say that."

I lead her toward the barn while she follows closely behind. After I drag the giant barn door open and turn back to her, she's just standing there, her head slightly cocked and a small smile on her face.

"You have a little drool there." I point to the corner of my mouth.

Her jaw drops open, but her lips quickly quirk into a smile. "I was just admiring the barn. Look at all the accents and details in here, like this." She drags her hands against the wrought iron stall doors.

"Uh-huh."

"I *do* love this barn. I've always liked the rustic look in a home, kind of like in your house."

"There's a lot of rustic buildings in Roots. You could have a place of your own with this exact aesthetic if you stayed past your three months." I shrug, trying to act nonchalant, but I am definitely failing.

"I've thought about it."

"Where have those thoughts led you?"

"Nowhere really. Like I said last night, I don't see a practical way to stay here. As much as I've loved my time in this little bubble of perfection the last couple months, I recognize this isn't real life. I don't have the stress of regular bills to pay here, and I don't have a full-time job. I'll be twenty-five in the fall. I don't want to just rely on my parents' connections to get me sweet deals on housing, and I certainly can't keep working part-time like I am now. There just aren't many job opportunities in this tiny town."

"Is that all you think I am? Your parents' connection?" I try to hide the hurt in my voice. I know Olivia is just trying to convince herself this isn't the right option for her because she's scared, but it still stings.

"Of course not. You've become—more." Her brows knit together as she busies herself with picking at her nails. "I can't keep getting handouts. If I moved here, I'd need to find my own place and pay for it like a real adult."

"Paying rent doesn't make you an adult."

I unlatch the first stall, slipping into it and hooking a lead to Maggie's bridle.

"I don't know, Rhett. It's just so complicated to stay here. It wouldn't make any sense."

"You're just scared of what your life could be like if you stayed here. You may not like your life in San Francisco, but at least it's familiar. Here, there's a whole new realm of possibilities for you, and I think that scares you."

"No! It's not just that. You're not the first one to ask me why I don't stay here. Callie has said things about me staying too, but I talked with my dad yesterday, and it just reaffirmed that no matter what I want, I can't give up everything in San Francisco to stay here."

I tie the mare up to the rail outside of the stall. "Do you want to stay out here and pet Maggie or do you want to clean her stall?"

She looks back and forth between me, a pitchfork in hand, and Maggie, who is calmly watching the two of us banter.

"Both? I can get dirty too."

I chuckle. "Here, you can watch my technique while you pet Maggie for a bit, and I'll let you finish the stall."

She nods eagerly.

"So, what happened during your talk with your dad?"

"He reaffirmed the fact that I have to make it to senior. He'd be so disappointed in me if I left now, just like he had to do."

"Did he say that?"

"No, but it was heavily implied."

"You can't honestly tell me you want to go back to that job after all the hell it's put you through." The sharpness in my voice causes both Olivia and Maggie to stir uncomfortably.

"I don't know. I'm just so scared. My relationship with my parents has been great. I've made friends here. The work I'm doing at the rescue makes me excited, but I'm not so naïve to think that staying in Roots would make all of this permanent. Leaving my job before becoming senior could ruin my relationship with my dad. Being around my parents so much could ruin my relationship with them too. Maybe I'd realize helping out at the shelter feels like too much pressure and causes me just as much anxiety as my job does now. Maybe this is just how I'm meant to be, and there's nothing better for me out there." She takes in a sharp breath. "Oh my god! I'm sorry. My counselor would tell me I'm spiraling and need to recenter. I didn't mean to dump all of this on you like that."

"Don't apologize." I set the pitchfork down and march toward her, pulling her into my chest tightly. "I'm not sure what led you to believe everyone else's expectations of you are more important than your happiness, but it's just not true. You are amazing, Olivia. You deserve to be happy.

"You are brave and intelligent. You have this wonderful light inside of you that I've had the privilege of seeing shine since you came to Roots. When you first rolled into town, there was no sign of that light, but then you came in and made friends. You started helping out at the shelter and taking matters into your own hands to do something that you care about, and you became the brightest ray of light I've ever seen."

Now that I've started, I can't stop. "I'm telling you right now, the job you are in is not meant for you. I think you've always known you wanted to do something bigger with your life, but you settled for something safe that would please everyone else around you. *That's* probably why you've been having so many panic attacks in San Francisco and why they've dwindled since you've been here. Your body was telling you that something was off. It's *begging* you to let yourself be happy and do the things that you know in your heart you are meant to do."

A muffled sniffle escapes from against my chest. "Damn it. Did I make you cry?"

"Kind of." She pulls away from me, swiping at a tear. "It's okay. It's not a bad thing. You're just being so nice to me, and you're making a lot of sense and I—I can't just leave my old life behind, Rhett."

Seeing her doubt herself fuels me with anger, sadness, and love all at once.

"I get that you're afraid, but that doesn't mean you shouldn't try to find a way to be happy again." That's the place I'm desperately trying to get to, letting myself be happy again, even if I'm afraid.

Crap. Am I going to let myself try to love again? I can't. Can I?

She nods, clinging to my every word. Then she buries herself back into my chest so that her *thank you* is barely audible. Having her wrapped up in my arms feels so right. I want to hold her here forever. There's no way I could possibly ignore the feeling I have when I'm with her.

Olivia steps back from me, swiping a final tear, her face filled with determination. "My turn to clean the stalls."

I stand back and let her, processing everything that just happened. It's amazing how she can go from crying moments ago to cleaning out a horse stall as if nothing happened. I recognize mucking a stall doesn't require a superb amount of brain power, but still, she's amazing.

She finishes up, setting the fork aside and dusting her hands off with a look of satisfaction. "On to the next one?"

"Actually, how do you feel about ditching this place?"

"I just got here. It hasn't even been an hour. You need to put me to work! Plus, if you want me to stay here, I might need a job, and mucking horse stalls could be the only work available. I need to learn."

"You'll find something better than mucking horse stalls.

I know it was my idea to bring you here, but now I have a better idea."

"What do you have in mind?"

I grab her by the hand, filled with renewed energy. "Come with me."

Chapter Thirty-One

Olivia

I follow behind Rhett, feeling slightly giddy, but that feeling quickly fades when the barn door slams shut, rattling the whole building. A tall woman with beautifully full golden waves rushes into the barn, tears staining her cheeks. She wipes her palms across her face and peers up to see Rhett and I staring at her.

Her hazel eyes go round, and she looks horrified to see us standing here. "Oh, Rhett! You scared me. I didn't know you'd be here."

She plasters on a smile, but I don't miss the pain in her eyes before that smile reaches her lips. It breaks my heart to see. I am all too familiar with the burden she's clearly carrying, thinking she has to deal with her pain alone. I just want to wrap her up in a hug.

Awkward silence falls over us, so I swoop in. "I'm Olivia. I don't think we've met yet. It's kind of crazy to think there are still people in Roots I haven't met considering how small this town seems to be."

"Oh, sorry! I don't know where my manners have gone. I'm Lauren Rhodes. My family owns the ranch. It's nice to finally meet you. I've heard so much about you."

I blush, and she quickly corrects herself, trying to make me feel better. "I've heard you're putting on a fundraiser for Resilient Paws. That's incredible! It's about time Carol and those dogs get some real support. If there's anything Copper Hill can do to help out, let me know. Maybe Austin and I could set up a booth to sell some tallow and steaks. I'd be willing to donate all the proceeds for such a good cause."

"You would do that? That'd be amazing!"

"Of course. I'm more than happy to help out."

"Thank you so much."

"Well, I just came to—" She glances around desperately, "—to check the barn for my hat. I can't seem to find it anywhere. Guess it's not here."

She rushes off, and I want to call her back, give her a hug, and ask her to tell me everything that she's dealing with, but I don't know this girl. She clearly didn't want to be around us, so it's best to just leave her by herself.

Rhett seems completely unaware of what just happened as he leads me out to our cars. I grab him by the wrist, stopping him in his tracks. "How old is Lauren?"

He scrunches his face as he thinks. "Umm, twenty-three I think? She's a year younger than Charlie and Callie."

I nod. "I'm surprised Callie hasn't ever mentioned her before. She seems super nice."

"Callie has always been pretty averse to associating with anything related to Copper Hill. I've learned not to press it. We all have things we prefer to keep buried in the past."

Man, I want to ask Callie about that.

"So, what's your big plan?"

Rhett presses his lips together as he realizes we both have our cars here. "How about we drop your car off? Then we can pick up Maverick and grab swimsuits."

"Where are we going that we need swimsuits?"

"You'll see."

"Don't make me wait to find out what we're doing. The curiosity already killed the cat, don't let it kill me too."

"A little mystery won't kill you. Just follow me home, and we can go from there."

———

Thirty minutes later, we pull to a stop in Rhett's truck. Maverick nearly leaps from his spot in the back seat into my lap as his excitement grows to be too much for him to contain.

"Mav!" I giggle. "You need to calm down." Turning to Rhett, I say, "Curiosity is going to kill the dog too."

"You're so dramatic." He rolls his eyes, but a smile is spreading across his lips.

I take in our surroundings. We drove down a gravel road for the last five minutes, and it has reached a dead end that doesn't appear to lead anywhere.

"You just dragged me out into the middle of nowhere. I think it's more than fair to ask what we're doing here."

"We aren't in the middle of nowhere. You could throw a rock and hit the center of town." He grabs my door handle and swings the door open for me.

"Are you ready to go?"

"I guess. Let's see what Texas has to offer."

He leads the way to a trailhead that's nearly hidden amongst the overgrown grass and dainty wildflowers. "I didn't know Texas had so many wildflowers. I'm obsessed."

"Yeah, they're pretty."

"They're more than pretty. They're *gorgeous*, and yet simple. They're one of the first things I noticed when I was driving into town. I love that they can grow all on their own wherever they're planted and thrive."

"That reminds me of someone else I know, Wildflower." Heat rushes to my cheeks. "They *are* pretty, but not the best sight in Roots."

"What is?"

Rhett glances down at his feet. "I think you know."

I bite my lip, letting it pass, even though I want to hear the words from his mouth.

The open landscape that welcomed us at the beginning of the trail is now engulfed with trees. I'm thankful for the small relief their shade provides from the beating Texas sun. Paired with the humidity, this heat is borderline intolerable. "San Francisco never gets this hot. No one prepared me for this kind of torture when I came to Texas."

"It's not usually *this* hot in June, but you get used to the heat."

He pushes aside a branch and waits for me to catch up to him, still holding it aside. I move in next to him to see a waterfall trickling down the rocks. It's not huge, but it's still magnificent, and the pool of water sitting at the bottom is calling out to me.

I stand there in awe, just looking at the water flowing.

"What do you think? Are you in love with Roots yet?"

"It's beautiful, but it's going to take a bit more than a little waterfall to convince me to stay here."

Rhett gives a curt nod and then crouches down to rifle through the backpack he's been carrying. He pulls out two rolled-up beach towels. "What if I told you we could swim in the water to help get you out of this heat?"

"I'd say I like *you* a little better now."

He smirks as he begins tugging off his shirt. Suddenly all I can focus on is shirtless Rhett. He's all hard edges of sculpted muscle. I suppose doing manual labor at the ranch every day pays off for him.

Glancing back at me with a smirk, he asks, "Are you going to join me or just stand there?"

I open my mouth and close it again, desperately trying to pull my attention away from his perfect six-pack. Maverick barks with joy as he meanders down to the water's edge. When he bounds in, the splash of the cool water on the backs of my legs is enough to snap me out of my thoughts.

Rhett dives in gracefully and rises quickly back up gasping and shouting, "It feels amazing! Hurry up and get in."

"Okay, okay, I'm coming! Don't get your panties in a wad."

Something about that grin on his face, and the adorable dimple in his cheek, makes me practically delirious.

"I'm not getting my panties in a wad, I just want you to experience—" He stops mid-sentence as I tug my t-shirt over my head and shimmy my shorts over my hips, moving closer to the water's edge. Now it's him who's there with his mouth open. I'm not going to lie, it feels good.

"You better scooch back. You're right in my diving spot."

He doesn't budge, so I shrug and instead opt for a cannonball, landing right in front of him. When I come up for air, he's still right there, wiping water from his eyes. "You did that on purpose!"

A giggle slips from my lips. "Only because I asked you to move, and you didn't."

"You're dead." He narrows his eyes and pushes off a rock to lunge at me. When he reaches me, he circles his big arms around me and pulls me toward him. The feeling of his skin on mine is electric. His face is so close to mine. All I have to do is make one small movement and our lips would be touching. I'm no fool. I know he feels this too. Whatever is going on between us isn't just physical, and we both know it.

Chapter Thirty-Two

Rhett

I wasn't thinking when I pulled her in close to me. It seemed like a fun and playful thing to do, but now that our faces are only an inch apart, I can't even think straight. I'm still not where I want to be with Olivia before I kiss her. I want that certainty. I want to *know* I can go all in with her.

A pebbled wet nose nudges into my arm, and claws drag from the top of my ribs down to my hips. I let go of Olivia and turn to find Maverick trying to wedge himself between Olivia and me. The adorably obsessed rascal protectively inserts himself between the two of us, trying to corral Olivia back toward the shore, glancing over his shoulder, giving me the eye as he does so.

"I'm okay, Maverick. It's okay." Olivia's gaze flickers back up to me, and there's something in her eyes that makes it clear her mind is spinning just as much as mine. I wish I could fix that, solve all of her problems, and try to put her mind at ease. I guess that's what today is for.

She climbs out of the water, cooing to Maverick. "Should we get you a stick to chase?" She plucks one from the shore, letting Maverick sniff it and approve.

When the stick launches over my head, and I hear her splash back into the water, I finally look back her way. "So, what do you think?"

"This spot is great! How'd you find it?"

"According to Callie, she grew up coming out here. They'd come here to drink as teenagers, swim in the summertime, and do just about every stupid thing you could think of. I think the kids found a new spot nowadays. I'm not quite sure."

"Hmm, well I like this spot. Thanks for bringing me here. And for taking me to Copper Hill. It was cool to see where you work and visit my friend Maggie again. I think maybe in another life, I could live on a ranch and just be out in the fields working with my hands around animals every day."

"It doesn't have to be in another life. That's what I've been trying to tell you."

"Even if I stayed here, I'm not going to work on a ranch."

"Why not?"

"It's just not who Olivia Parker is."

"Then who is she?"

She purses her lips. "That's a good question. I think I'm still figuring that out."

"That's okay. I think I'm still figuring out who Rhett Lawson is too, and I have a two-year head start on you."

She gives me an appreciative smile. "We can figure it out together."

Maverick comes swimming back toward me panting with the stick still in his mouth. Olivia takes it gently from

Maverick and throws it again for him. He rushes off after it with excitement.

"Maverick is quite the fish, huh?"

"Yeah, I guess so. It doesn't surprise me. You've said he's perfectly at home on the ranch. I think he likes having a purpose. It's in his blood." She glances at him lovingly as he determinedly makes his way back to where Olivia is treading water. When he reaches her, she takes the stick and chucks it before saying, "And I guess he loves the water, so there's no stopping him now."

"We'll have to come back again."

"I think he'd like that."

"What about you?"

"Yeah, I'd like it too."

———

Sitting on her rumpled towel, leaning against me, Olivia happily munches on the apple chips I packed. Maverick dozes to her side with his whole back pressed up against her outstretched leg, and she looks at peace. I don't want to speak, don't want to move, don't even want to breathe too loudly out of fear that I will ruin this perfect moment that I'm trying to engrain in my memory right now.

But Olivia finally breaks the silence. "I love it out here. I could get used to this. We've got snacks and look at this view. It's just breathtaking."

I follow her gaze to the scene set in front of us. The swimming hole shimmers in the sun. The live oaks that surround us in a canopy open up about ten feet behind us to create a small plain of long grass and wildflowers that blow in the gentle breeze. Birds chase each other overhead, singing a cheerful tune. It's stunning, but the only sight I care about right now is the kind-hearted woman by my side, with freckles dusting her cheeks and her oversized t-shirt hanging off her shoulder in typical Olivia fashion as she gently sinks her fingers into the thick tufts of fur on Maverick's back.

"Yeah, it's pretty great," I say, keeping my eyes steady on her.

Her cheeks flush when she catches my gaze on her, and she quickly busies herself with rolling up the bag of apple chips. When I snatch my hat from the ground and place it on backward, the blush on her cheeks grows brighter.

Olivia's lips curve into a slight smirk before she leans back against her palms and sighs contentedly. "I know you didn't grow up in Roots, but were your summers still spent like this when you were younger?"

"Yeah, my summers were pretty similar to this. Granted I didn't usually hang out with beautiful women." She looks down at the ground, clearly uncomfortable with taking the compliment. "I spent most of my summers with a couple of buddies that lived on my street. We got into all kinds of trouble."

"I would've liked to see teenage Rhett and all the shenanigans he got into."

"My parents let me get away with probably too much. That was back when they liked me." I laugh, trying to keep the mood light. "That's probably why I connected so well with your parents. I never really had people in my life who were strong and loving parental figures."

"My parents think of you like a son. My dad particularly loves having you around. I know he loves me, but I also know he would've loved to have a child who he could teach about trucks and watch sports with. Now he has that with you." After a beat, she adds, "I'm sorry about your parents.

I'm willing to share mine, but you can't have them *all* to yourself."

"I still had a pretty great childhood. I had good friends, and we had lots of adventures."

"Tell me a story. I want to hear about some of your adventures."

"Hmmm." I lean back, letting the hot sun beat down on my face as I think. "My freshman year of high school, I went dirt bike riding with a couple of my friends. I'm not sure how familiar you are with riding a dirt bike, but the throttle is on the handlebars, so you have to grab it like this." I make a fist with my hand and show her the motion of grabbing onto a handle and then pulling my knuckles toward me to throttle. She nods along in fascination. "We had been going for a little over an hour, and I was starting to feel confident when I accidentally grabbed a handful of the throttle on my way up a jump. I flew through the air, and when I landed, my front tire hit the dirt at the wrong angle. I got tossed from the bike and broke my collar bone."

"Oh my god!"

"It didn't hurt that bad." She narrows her eyes at me. "Okay, it hurt like a bitch, but it was actually pretty great because the accident helped my parents stop fighting for a little bit while they focused on taking care of me."

"They fought even after they divorced?"

I nod. "All the time, probably even more than before they got divorced. It was like the divorce allowed them to openly hate each other."

"How long did they stop fighting?"

"Maybe a week, but it was the best week of my life. My mom made me breakfast in bed. My dad would come and watch old movies with me. Sometimes my mom even joined."

"Do you talk to either of them much anymore?"

I shake my head, and she must recognize that I'm reaching my limits for how much I'm willing to share because instead of asking why, she asks me for another story.

"You have to tell me something about you first. It's only fair."

She nods in agreement, pursing her lips as she thinks. It's funny because I'm used to asking people about themselves as a way to deflect, to move the attention away from me and keep my past hidden, but this time, I genuinely want to know more about Olivia. I want to learn every little detail about her. I want to know the basics like her favorite color and her favorite season, but I also want to know the deeper things like how she got that scar along her right shin and what makes her think she doesn't deserve a life free of stress and full of joy.

"I don't think I have any stories that are as funny as yours."

"That's okay. It doesn't have to be funny. I just want to hear something about you from before we met. Tell me a favorite memory of yours or a least favorite. I don't care. I just want something."

She sits up a little straighter, turning to face me straight on. "I don't know if I can definitively say this is my favorite memory because it's a little bittersweet, but it's one that sticks out to me." I nod along encouragingly, keeping my mouth shut so as not to interrupt her. "When I was a freshman in high school, my best friend since first grade started dating some jock, and she started to fall in with the cool kid crowd. This went on for a few months. We still hung out outside of school, but she would practically ignore me during school hours and it stung. It got way worse when rumors started going around the school about me, and she didn't do anything to stop the rumors from flying."

She must see the pity on my face because she smiles at me, patting my knee, and says, "I promise the story gets better, but it's going to get just a smidge worse before it comes back around. Stick with me."

I chuckle, feeling oddly protective over her even though this was years ago, and I can see her smiling about it now.

"I came home one day absolutely bawling because I had just found out my friend, Natasha, had been the one to spread a particularly nasty rumor about me, and it just felt like the world was ending. When I got home, my mom took one look at my face, grabbed her purse, and dragged me right back out the door. She took me into town for ice cream, and we wandered around these little shops near the beach that were about half an hour away. I loved those shops. It was my perfect day, if you ignore the whole best-friend-betrayal that started it off, but it was a very special moment with my mom. We'd always been close, but I think that's when I started to see her as my best friend, not just my mom." She glances down at her towel, finding a loose thread. "You know how much I love Taylor Swift, right?"

"Do I? Everyone in town must know by now with the way you blast her music in your Volkswagen."

"Well, my favorite song is actually one of her older ones. It's called 'The Best Day,' and it's sung from the daughter's perspective to her mom, talking about how her mom is always there for her and like her best friend. It speaks to my *soul*. It's one of my all-time favorite songs, and I don't think many people know that or the meaning of the song for me."

She continues picking at the thread on her towel, focusing hard on it.

"I love how close you are with your mom. Things were a

lot more forced when you first got here because she was desperate to connect with you, but it seems to me like you two have found a good balance. You've gotten back to that friendship you used to have."

"Yeah, it's been a little terrifying to let her in again, but I love my mom so much. I missed having that closeness."

Silence settles over us for a beat before I ask, "Can you play the song for me? I want to hear it."

"Sure!" She eagerly plucks her phone off the grass and presses a few buttons before a joyful tune slips through the speaker. I try to focus on the words, picturing a younger Olivia with her mom. Having this new piece of Olivia makes me fall just a little bit more for her.

The song ends, and I watch her face change as she begins chewing on her lip. She places all her focus on scratching behind Maverick's ears, and I give her the space she needs after this moment of vulnerability.

Finally, she says, "I don't want this day to end."

"I can't do anything about the sun eventually going down, but I can cook us dinner and then we can find one more Roots adventure before midnight if you're up for it."

Chapter Thirty-Three

Olivia

THIS DAY HAS BEEN PERFECT. EVEN THE INSANE HEAT and humidity bearing down on us all day hasn't deterred my euphoria. I don't remember the last time I felt this way about someone. Yes, Rhett is an extremely attractive man, but he also has this beautiful golden core when you take the time to dig into him.

I feel like I can tell him anything, and there's no judgment, only curiosity and eagerness to learn more. He makes me laugh, and being in his presence fills me with this giddy, sunshiny warmth. I don't know what to do with all these feelings. I want to let myself explore them, but I also know I was never planning on staying here. I've already determined it can't be an option for me, but Rhett and this whole life I'm building in Roots make me want to change that.

After putting our dishes in the dishwasher, I turn to Rhett for guidance. "So, what did you have planned for the rest of our never-ending day?"

"Follow me."

He grabs my hand, intertwining his fingers with mine. Between the smile he gifts me and the gentle look in his eyes as they land on me, I feel so adored. I've never experienced that with anyone before. I've never been able to physically see the love someone has for me.

He grabs a blanket in the other hand and whistles for Maverick to follow as we rush out through the back door. When we step out into the evening air, the humidity settles upon me, wrapping me up like a warm hug. Frogs croak and cicadas chirp. The sky is dusted with a beautiful blanket of shining stars, but all I can focus on is how natural it feels to hold Rhett's hand, like I should've been holding it my whole life.

We reach the line where his perfectly manicured lawn meets the wild grass of the Texas plains. Instead of taking the path we usually take down to the river when we walk Maverick, he leads me to yet another trail. I don't know how I never noticed this one before. I guess I've been so busy with the shelter, the café, and my parents that I haven't spent much time exploring Rhett's property.

Getting jealous of my attention being on Rhett, Maverick makes his way through the tall grass and then presses himself into my side, nearly tripping me. I release my grip from Rhett's to stabilize myself. "Aw, Mav, I'm right here. I'm still paying attention to you."

"He needs to learn to share," Rhett remarks, watching me crouch down to give Maverick the affection he deserves.

"You're just jealous because he likes me better."

"I don't understand why he would. I'm the one who gives him steak juice on his food, and he liked sleeping on my bed when you stayed the night at Callie's. We cuddled."

"Rhett Lawson! I thought you said you didn't want him on the furniture."

"That was before he spent a night with just me and gave me the puppy dog eyes. He's such a good cuddler. I know he weighs ninety pounds, but that dog is a lap dog through and through."

"This makes me feel so much better because I sleep with him every night."

"Did you honestly think I didn't already know that? I see the dog hair all over your bedding. Come to think of it, I've *seen* him on your bed dozens of times."

"Can you blame me? It's impossible to say no to this little face," I say as I crouch down and press my hands to Maverick's plush cheeks.

Rhett's boots stop marching, and he grabs the blanket that was tucked under his arm, laying it on the ground.

I look around us. We are in the middle of nowhere. There are no lights from the cottage or Rhett's house to be seen, no sound of rushing cars or blaring sirens that I've become so accustomed to in San Francisco. It's quiet, and it's dark.

"What are we doing here?" The words come out as a whisper, as if raising my voice would shatter our delicate surroundings.

Rhett sits down on the blanket, grabbing my hand gently and pulling me toward him. Once I'm sitting on the blanket next to him, he wordlessly lies on his back, and I follow. I take in the faint hint of twinkling lights overhead.

"Have you ever stargazed before, like, real stargazing? Looking up at a sky polluted with city lights doesn't count."

"No."

"Then you're in for a treat. Next time you're anxious, you and I can come sit out here in the silence with nothing but the stars to light our way, and it'll be impossible for you to feel anxious anymore. It's just so peaceful. I thought it was important for you to get to experience this part of Roots before you go… or you could just stay and enjoy it every day."

I open my mouth to tell him once again that I can't, but I don't feel like arguing. I don't want to ruin the moment. So instead, I lie on my back in silence, taking in the stars and letting my surroundings ground me. He's right. With tiny twinkling stars overhead, nothing but the gentle sound of cicadas in the air, and Rhett pressed against my side, a wave of peace floods my soul.

Rhett slowly reaches over and laces his fingers with mine, making me feel so whole and loved. I bask in the feeling of this moment for several more minutes before breaking the silence.

"What did you mean earlier when you said that was when your parents still liked you?"

"Wow, you just dive right into things, don't you?"

"I learned it from Callie. I just want to get to know you. You've helped me so much since I've been here in Roots, and I want to do the same for you, but I can't help you if I don't understand you."

"I know." He tugs Maverick's sleepy body toward him so that his spine is pressed against his side. "I'm afraid that if I tell you about my past, you'll think less of me."

"In case you haven't noticed, I've grown quite fond of you. I went from wanting to avoid you to choosing to hang out with you because I like the person you are."

"You also had to live with me because of the flood in the cottage."

"We could've figured out another arrangement, but we didn't."

"True. I just think you like the person you believe I am, but you don't know who I was or who I truly am."

"So tell me. Give me a chance to show you that the past won't change things. I have a hard time believing you could've done something so terrible that it would change the way I feel about you."

Anticipation fills me as the silence extends. Maybe I asked for too much. We haven't made any kind of commitment to one another, but here I am trying to get him to open up to me, telling him I'll still care for him after. Even though I believe the words with every fiber of my being, I recognize this is still a lot to ask of him given our circumstances.

"How about another question?"

"It's not going to be any better."

He frowns.

"Why did you look so panicked when you and Callie couldn't find me at the bar?"

"For the same reason I've avoided bars before that night. I had a bad experience one time, and it's been hard to shake."

"That was... vague."

A smile breaks out on his face, and I feel relieved. "My turn to ask you a question."

"What? No! That doesn't even count! You only gave me half an answer."

He shrugs. "Guess you should've picked a better question. I gave you a second chance."

"You're so frustrating."

"That's what everyone keeps telling me. I don't know why." He smirks, turning toward me eagerly. "Okay, my question is... what's the most embarrassing thing to happen to you?"

"No way! Veto! If you're not going to answer my first question and give me a bullshit answer for the second, then I don't have to answer your question."

"Fine. Then I get another question." I shake my head, but he asks anyway. "Has today convinced you to stay in Roots?"

"You don't deserve an answer to your question after you dodged mine."

"Oh, come on. Tell me!" He leans in closer, starting to tickle me.

"Never!" I huff out in between squeals. I roll away from him, trying to get relief, but he follows me closely. Again, I try to turn away from him and slip out of his grasp, but immediately his hands are on my hips, and he drags me into him. Then we both stop. Our gazes lock. My breath hitches, and my heart stops as I wait for him to make that first slow movement toward me, the anticipation of the sparks that are about to fly between us building with each second.

Something about the way he's looking at me floods me with fear. *What're we doing? Why am I playing with both our hearts when I know I can't stay here?*

Instead of leaning into him like I desperately want to, I draw back and finally answer, "Today hasn't changed anything."

Chapter Thirty-Four

Rhett

Her words were barely above a whisper, but every syllable echoes in my head.

Today didn't change anything. My heart stops beating. I pull back, releasing my grip from her waist and rolling onto my back in disbelief.

Hurt and confusion mix with anger. How dare I let myself start to feel something for someone again when I *know* better. She's going to leave me behind like everyone else. I've always known I couldn't have love in my life. *Why did I think this time would be any different? How did I let this happen?*

I sit up abruptly. "It's getting pretty late. I know we said this day wouldn't end, but I think it's time that it did."

She nods, pain swirling in her beautiful amber eyes. I want nothing more than to hug her tight to me. I never want to be the one responsible for hurting her. I want to be the one who makes her feel loved, who helps make her problems easier to handle. Instead of saying anything, I stand, offering her my hand to help her up too.

"Thanks for bringing me out here. It really is beautiful. Roots is more than I thought it was when I first came here."

I give her a soft smile, trying to hold back my own emotions. I'm not mad at her. She did nothing wrong. "I'm glad you had fun today. I guess even if you can't stay, maybe you gained some appreciation for this little town."

"Yeah, I did. I guess it's better we head back now. I have to work an early shift at the café tomorrow."

She helps me fold the blanket up and then leads the way down the path. She's acting nonchalant, but I just know she's feeling the same sense of sorrow and regret I'm feeling too. I wish things were simpler, but I have some things I still need to work on, and she has a whole other life waiting for her in San Francisco.

———

Less than twenty minutes later, I'm pounding on Callie's door. She swings the door open wielding a spatula, a messy mop of hair on her head, and a wild look in her eye.

"What the hell are you going to do with that?" I chuckle. "Were you planning on murdering me with a Cutco? At least get a sturdy frying pan like Olivia."

She narrows her eyes, dropping the spatula to her side as I brush past her. "What the hell are you doing showing up at my door right now? It's almost midnight!"

"We need to talk."

She closes the door behind her and swivels toward me with her arms crossed. "Awfully bold of you to come pounding on my door late at night considering you stormed out on me the last time we saw each other."

"Yeah, well I stormed out because I came there to talk about finances, but instead you ambushed me about Olivia."

"Touché."

"Damn right." I huff. Realizing my arms are crossed, I release them. I need to cool things off between us, or we aren't going to get anywhere. "I'm sorry for storming out."

"I'm listening."

"I know you had my best interest in mind, and I've spent a lot of time thinking about what you said. I can't deny my feelings for Olivia, and I've even tried to give things a go with her. We almost kissed a few days ago, but we were interrupted. Then we spent the whole day together today, and it was amazing."

"That's great! Why'd you have to come tell me at midnight? It couldn't wait?"

"No, it couldn't, because I'm not finished. It was amazing, but then it ended with us almost kissing again, and this time we chose not to."

"Why not?"

"It can't work between us. She's going to leave."

"You don't know that."

"Actually, I do. I spent the whole day showing her how great Roots is, and she told me it didn't change a thing. She's still going back to San Francisco and that terrible job. I just don't get it." I hang my head in my hands. "I knew this was coming. I shouldn't be this disappointed. I thought things could be different, but this proves I don't deserve love. I picked the wrong person."

She takes a few steps toward me, reaching out to pull me into a hug. I allow her to wrap her arms around me and hesitantly wrap an arm around her. It does feel good to have someone who knows about all my flaws here to comfort me.

When she draws back, she makes a point of looking me

in the eye. "Rhett, I never want to hear you say those words ever again. You're an incredible man who deserves to be happy. I wish you'd recognize that. Olivia looks at you like you put the stars in the sky. I've seen it. You don't have to change a thing for her to continue to fall for you. The real issue lies in whether or not you can allow yourself to believe you're worthy of her love. Otherwise, you will just keep closing yourself off before you even get the chance to explore something amazing with her."

"You don't get it. My parents' marriage was great until they had me. I drove them apart. Isabel convinced me their relationship wasn't representative of all relationships, but then I had to go and pick a stupid fight with her, and she died because of me. She wouldn't have been in that Uber, at that intersection, if I could've just pushed aside my ego for a moment. Then of all the people to start opening up to again after *four* years, I choose a girl who I know is leaving. *Every single* time I was the one responsible for the heartache I've had to go through. I'm finally accepting that I'll never be enough to keep someone who loves me in my life."

"That's not true. Olivia could be the one. I can *feel* it."

"Even if she stayed here in Roots, our relationship would only end in worse tragedy. That's just how my life goes."

"Stop it! I hate hearing you talk about yourself like that. Have you ever paused to consider all the people who love you right this very second? Me. Jack and Mandi. Olivia. Even Maverick loves you. You can't tell me that you're not worthy of love when you're surrounded by people who love you. Maybe things didn't go perfectly in your life, but when you get kicked down, you get back up. You know that." Her voice is sharp, and it stuns me.

I want to be as strong as Callie. She's the most resilient

person I know. When Isabel passed, it took her all of a week to move back to Roots. One month later, she was asking me to invest in her coffee shop.

"Rhett, I don't know what it will take to get through to you, but I promise you, one day I will. What happened to your parents wasn't your fault. They were adults who maybe weren't ready to have a child. What happened with Isabel wasn't your fault either. You're allowed to disagree with your girlfriend once in a while, and your fight had nothing to do with her getting t-boned in the Uber that night. You deserve another chance at love."

I take a step back. I've never seen Callie outraged like this. Even after Isabel's accident, she seemed pretty even keel. She'd tear up on occasion in front of me, but she always tried to suppress her emotions around me until now.

"I'm sorry," I whisper, desperate to ease the tension.

"Don't apologize. I just wish you could see yourself the way everyone else does. You're so amazing. Your parents divorced when you were little and basically disowned you just because you were following your heart and got engaged young. Then you lost your fiancé a matter of months later. Yet here you are, thriving. You've helped me with my dream of opening a café with Isabel. You do incredible work at Copper Hill. You bake the most delicious desserts. You've helped countless people around town. You were there for me when we lost Isabel even though you were hurting just as badly. You've helped Olivia in so many more ways than I think you realize. You have a beautiful heart. I believe Olivia is worthy of that heart, and I promise you that you are plenty worthy of her too. You are plenty worthy of any woman."

I'm speechless. I don't know what I expected when I showed up at Callie's door, but it wasn't this.

"Thank you."

"You're welcome." Her words still sound angry, like she's caught up in all the frustration she's probably been holding in for a couple of years now. "One more thing. If you can't give love a shot for yourself, then do it for Isabel. She would've wanted you to be happy. Sometimes I picture her watching us down here, and I think about how disappointed she must be." Tears flood her eyes, but they don't fall yet. "I just know she would've wanted you to be happy, and yes, you've done a lot of incredible things, but you've been doing them all alone. She wouldn't want that for you. She'd want you to be with someone like Olivia who lights you up inside and out. I feel like I'm not doing my job if I don't make sure you know that."

"I'm not your responsibility. You know that, right?"

"I do, but it was always about Isabel when I was growing up. Even after she's gone, it's hard to shake that." She swipes at her eyes. "My shit doesn't matter though. What *does* matter is that you deserve to be happy, and you need to recognize that you're worthy. Can you repeat that to me, please? I need you to say it and believe it."

"Are you serious?"

"Yes! Say it. 'I deserve to be happy, and I am worthy of happiness.'"

I frown and cross my arms but follow her directions anyway. "I deserve to be happy, and I am worthy of happiness."

For the first time since I showed up, she smiles. "Good! I'm going to make you keep saying that to me every day, a hundred times a day until it finally settles into that stubborn brain of yours."

"That's not—"

"I'm not letting you talk me out of this. I'm so serious

right now. Stop getting in your own dang way. Let yourself be happy."

As much as her words are opening things up for me, it's still hard to hear them after years of putting myself down and blaming myself. After years of believing I'm broken and a monster, it's crazy to hear that someone who knows the full truth about me still believes I deserve to be happy.

I pull her in for a tight squeeze. "Thank you. I needed to hear this, even if I don't fully believe it yet."

"I'll help you work on it."

"Seriously, thank you." I pull back. "One more thing."

She raises her eyebrows. "Now you're getting greedy. I only have so much wisdom to share."

"How do I go forward with Olivia? I just pulled back from a kiss tonight, and she's supposed to leave in six weeks. Is there even any chance of recovering from what I did? Wouldn't I be a fool to try to put myself out there now?"

"I'm not so sure Olivia is going to leave. I know what she said tonight, but you have to look at it from her perspective. We already know she will give up her happiness for the sake of those around her, and she values stability. She isn't just going to jump into staying in Roots until she knows she can make it happen and do so while making everyone around her happy too. Maybe if she knew she'd have the support of a man she cares about, she'd be more willing to stay." She winks.

"Okay, so I need to figure out a feasible way for her to stay here."

"Yes, but first you need to tell her the truth, even if it's little by little. I don't think you'll ever allow yourself to be all in with her until you know she accepts you. Relationships are about being vulnerable. You need to open yourself up to her if you two have any chance at being something."

Even as I recognize the truth in her words, I feel my stomach sink. *What if Callie is wrong? What if Olivia doesn't accept me for all that I am, for everything that has happened in my past? What if she still wants to leave after I open up to her? Can I even recover from that?*

Callie begins shaking her head. "I see those wheels turning. Don't get in your head. Olivia has shadows too. She will understand."

I can barely hear at this point. My mind is already going a mile a minute. I need to find a way to provide Olivia with the stability she craves in this little town.

Chapter Thirty-Five

Olivia

I twirl my spoon into my cup of ice cream and raise a melty, creamy bite of chocolate heaven to my lips. Mom and I spent the day in Fort Worth together, walking through the stockyards and popping into cute little shops. She insisted we round out our day with ice cream for dinner, and I'm honestly not mad about it.

"So, tell me more about your fundraiser. What are the latest developments? Last I heard, you had quite a few vendors who were interested in joining."

"Yeah, I got a list of a few more from Callie when I told her about the idea, and all but one agreed to join the cause. Jax said we can use the bar parking lot, which I figured would be a good central location. Plus, it's one of the few places in town that I think could actually host such a large event."

"I agree. That's part of the charm of Roots though, right?"

"Yeah, I guess so."

She gives me a satisfied smile but surprisingly doesn't say anything more. I think she's finally learning to bite her tongue, so she doesn't scare me off.

"Carol also let me completely take over the rescue's Instagram account. I can't keep up with all of the ideas I keep getting for content." I stick my spoon in my ice cream and grab my phone from my back pocket, opening up my camera roll. I have a whole album dedicated to the rescue now.

I click into the video I took a few weeks ago and sent to Rhett. "I already have a song in mind to play over this clip. It'll be super powerful to show everyone not only the volume of dogs at the shelter, but the different types of dogs. I think there's a misconception that there's only a certain type of dogs in shelters, so people who maybe don't like Pitbulls and German Shepherds just never consider adoption, but clearly, there's a lot of different types that could suit a lot of different people."

I pause the video and zoom in a bit. "See. This is Razz. He's some sort of Poodle mix and the sweetest dog ever. I told Carol she's not allowed to give him to anyone that I haven't personally vetted. Oh, and here's Penny. We aren't sure what she is, but she's adorable, and not the kind of dog I would expect to see at a rescue. She's only twenty pounds, and we don't think she's going to get any bigger. And—" Mom's laughter stops me. "What did I do?"

"Nothing. I've just never seen you so... lit up. There's no sight more beautiful than this happy and excited version of you. I can't say you've ever been this way about work. It's nice."

I drop my phone into my lap and take a bite of ice cream. "I love being around these dogs. Don't get me wrong, some days are freaking hard, like yesterday when I helped

Carol bathe one of the new dogs at the shelter. He was covered in his own poop, and his ribs were protruding so badly that I was afraid I was going to hurt him just by touching him. No animal should have to live like that. I hate seeing it, but I *love* that I get to help make these dogs' lives better.

"One of the Huskies that came to the rescue a few days before my first time at Resilient Paws was so timid around both Carol and me, but he's starting to grow his confidence with us *and* the other dogs. I had a role in that, and it's one of the most fulfilling things I've ever done with my life. Sometimes I think—" I stop dead in my tracks, knowing better than to say these words out loud with my mom. They will give her all kinds of false hope.

She places a hand on my back and rubs gently, reminding me of when I was little. I melt into her warm touch, adoring the affection that I haven't had from either of my parents in so long. Thanks to me. "What do you think?"

Her comforting motions release the words from my mouth without any more hesitation. "Sometimes I just think I wasn't put on this earth to do taxes. Every day in San Francisco, I woke up with this awful feeling of dread weighing me down, and each time I logged on, it felt like I lost another piece of myself. Since being here, that feeling of dread has gone away, and I'm making friends. It's just made me think a lot about how I wanted my job so badly coming out of college, but now, I feel a little lost. My job was all I ever wanted, and now it's... not."

There's a tightness in my chest as tears form in my eyes. "Have you ever had something that made you feel that way? Something that made your stomach sick with anxiety just by thinking about it? Something that drains you of everything you have to the point where you think you can't go on one more day? Yet I have no other choice other than to get up and do it all again. It's my job, and it's how I afford my life."

Mom's eyes are soft as she watches me intently, giving me all the room I need to keep venting to her, so I do. "Now that I'm helping with the rescue, it feels like maybe that's what I'm meant to do in my life, something with meaning, something that makes the world a better place. I've spent the last several years thinking I had to live without hope or fulfillment for the next forty years until I retire, but being here and helping Carol makes me think that there could be more. I really want more." I choke back a sob. "I know that's crazy. I know most people spend their lives hating their jobs, and they just suck it up to pay the bills. I shouldn't be so naïve and selfish."

I sniffle and Mom leans in to gently swipe a stray tear from my cheek. It reminds me of when she took me out for ice cream, sitting with me patiently, until I finally told her about how Natasha, my best friend since first grade, ditched me for her new boyfriend and spread rumors about me. My mom swiped away my tears that day the same way she does now.

Her soft voice brings me back to the present. "You should never, ever feel like you need to spend the rest of your life in misery. I don't want you waking up every day with dread. I don't want you to hate your life, and you should not have to spend every day doing something that takes away pieces of you. You have this light inside of you that shines so bright. You're kind and driven. I *know* you're meant for good things, whether that's a fancy job at the Big Four or helping the local animal rescue. It doesn't matter what anyone else thinks or what society says. At the end of the day, you're the one that has to live your life and live with your choices, so make ones that will help you be happy."

She grabs my hand gently, pulling it into her lap as her eyes bore into me, intent on making me meet her gaze. "You can always make a change, and you'll never be alone in making that change. Your dad and I are always here for you. We want you to be happy, and we will move mountains to make that happen."

I just got the tears back under control, but her words turn the gentle flow into a flood. I lean into her as I fight back another sob. "Do you think Dad would be disappointed if I left now, right before making it to senior?"

"Oh, honey." She smoothes her hand over my head in a comforting motion. "Your dad could never be disappointed in you. You're his daughter, and he loves you unconditionally. We both do. You're not responsible for righting your dad's wrongs, if you could even call them that. Yes, I think he wonders what could've been, but your dad is so happy with his life now. He wants the same for you."

"You're sure?"

"I'm positive. You need to do what's right for *you*."

"Thank you. Please don't say anything about this to Dad. I need to talk to him myself."

I swipe away a little snot with my napkin. This is not a pretty cry, this is an "I'm exhausted, and I've lost hope, but I've found hope and I want to chase after it but I'm afraid to" ugly cry. I should be embarrassed. I should close down and not let her see me like this. I've spent so long building up walls and keeping her out, but it's so hard to remember why I've done that when her warm touch feels so comforting. Her gentle words feel like home, and it's been so long since I've felt the feeling of home. God, I've missed her. I resent myself the slightest bit for keeping her at a distance for years, and I resent myself for letting the urge slowly creep in right now, but some little piece of me finds enough strength to push the urge aside and for once let my mom help me. It feels so good to be cared for, to get help.

Her voice drops down to a whisper that could be lost if the breeze caught in right. "Have you thought at all about staying here? You could make Roots your home. You know everyone would love to have you stay. You can keep helping out at the shelter, and I'll bet Rhett would be more than happy to let you continue living with him or rent out the cottage when it's ready. I know he adores having you around." She smirks. "You're also welcome with your dad and me at any time. I know it's embarrassing, or whatever, but we will always take you in if you need a place to land."

"Thank you."

She must see the hesitation on my face because she adds, "If being here doesn't make you happy, then don't stay, but you need to know that you're absolutely welcome here if that's something you want. You have options. You don't need to go back to a horrible job that sucks the life out of you and gives you so much anxiety that you have panic attacks." She's never been able to say those words out loud before, but she doesn't even blink now.

"You're right, honey. We aren't put on this earth just to work a job and get promoted. Yes, you need to make money to support yourself, but you shouldn't have to wake up dreading every day to make that money. That's not a good life. We will figure something out together. Whatever the right solution is for *you*, we will make it happen. You're not alone in this world, and I hope you never believed you were."

A wave of something unfamiliar washes over me. It's calming and cleansing. I feel so heard and understood. I've spent years thinking there was something wrong with me for believing there could be more to life than working seventy-hour weeks and breaking myself down daily. Now I finally have someone who is telling me my feelings are valid, someone to empower me to make a change. I feel lighter.

The tears that slither down my cheeks in ragged trails are no longer sad tears. They're filled with hope that maybe I finally have my mom back, and in the kind of way where I don't feel like a burden to her for the first time in a long time. Maybe I don't have to keep living my life the way I had been all this time. Maybe there is a way out.

The thought reminds me of my conversation with Rhett earlier this summer. His words echo through my mind, urging me to take this vulnerable moment to talk with my mom about all the shame and guilt I carry with me from that dreaded day all those years ago. My counselor seems to think it'd be good for me to clear the air too, but this moment is too good, and I haven't had the chance to rehearse the conversation with my counselor. My fear shuts down the thought immediately, and instead, we just quietly finish our last bites of ice cream before heading to the car.

The entire ride back to Roots, we blast Taylor Swift, screaming the lyrics at the top of our lungs. When "The Best Day" comes on, I pause the music quickly to ask, "Do you remember when I first showed you this song?"

"Of course I do. It was the first time I'd ever seen my baby's heart broken. That freaking Natasha Knight! The second she hit puberty, I knew that girl was going to be trouble." I can't help but laugh, but Mom turns serious. "I mean it. Seeing your child's heart broken, however it happens, really sticks with you. Plus, this song is just so wholesome. I love the way she talks about her relationship with her mom, and the fact that my fifteen-year-old showed it to me, telling me it reminded her of our relationship. I've never forgotten that moment."

"I always think of you when I hear the song. It's still your ringtone."

She reaches out to pat my leg briefly. "On the days when I missed you and knew you were busy in the trenches of busy season, I'd listen to this song to help make me feel closer to you."

My heart sinks as I'm once again reminded of just how much I affected my mom by keeping her out of my life. I wasn't protecting her, despite my intentions. Instead, my actions hurt us both.

"Aww, Mom!"

"It's okay. You're an adult. You have your life. I get you for five more weeks, so I'll take what I can get." She gives me a bittersweet smile.

When she presses play on the song again, she cheerily picks up her singing. Joining in, I can't help but think maybe it wouldn't be so bad if this could be my life from now on.

Chapter Thirty-Six

Olivia

You could say I've been distracted since my talk with my mom two days ago. My shift at the café today has been unproductive because I've been busy creating a checklist on my phone of things I need to accomplish in order for me to quit my job in San Francisco and stay in Roots.

I know Callie can tell something is wrong, but she's been a great friend and given me lots of space today to process my thoughts. I'm thankful for that because I don't want to tell anyone I'm thinking about staying here until I know I can make it happen.

The bell over the door jingles cheerily, but the atmosphere in the café immediately feels somber, drawing me from my thoughts and my duty of drying mugs. The second I see her face, it makes sense. I should've known it was her.

Lauren Rhodes waltzes across the room, exuding sadness. It emanates off of her like a pungent perfume. Her eyes are glossy and the bags underneath them carry their own frown. She looks like someone who is beaten down and shattered.

I give her the kindest smile I can muster and can't help the soft pity in my voice as I greet her.

To her credit, she smiles back. It almost seems genuine when she tells me she's doing well, but what gives her away is the smallest wince, as if smiling is painful.

I set the dry mug on a shelf behind the counter and move toward the register, asking what I can get for her.

"Oh, just a blueberry muffin. I don't drink coffee."

"I'm not sure I can trust you if you don't like coffee."

"I enjoy the smell, but the taste is a bit too strong for me, if that helps at all." She laughs shyly.

"How do you function without caffeine?"

She shrugs. "I don't know life any other way."

"Whoa, you must be superhuman."

She blushes as she absentmindedly plays with the zipper on her purse while I punch a few buttons into the register. I give her the total and while she taps her credit card, I swivel toward the kitchen to grab a fresh muffin for her, instead of one of the ones under the counter. She looks like she could use a pick-me-up.

"Are you hiding back here?" I ask Callie as she hands me a plate.

"No, I'm not hiding. You've got this one handled, so I figured I'd finish cleaning up. I want to leave right at close today, so I have some time to do my hair before Ladies' Night."

"You're doing your hair? Who are you trying to impress?" I tease.

She whacks me with the rag she's holding in her hand. "No one! Now get back out there. A paying customer is waiting."

I go to hand the muffin to Lauren, but something stops me halfway across the counter. She gives me a questioning look, probably wondering why I'm gatekeeping this muffin from a hungry girl. Even so, I pull the muffin back a bit, not ready to let this interaction with her be over yet.

"What are you up to today?"

Not taking her eyes off the muffin, she says, "I just have a few errands to run this afternoon. Austin has been visiting another ranch near Amarillo for a couple of days, so I need to get things ready before he gets back home tomorrow afternoon."

"Will you still be running those errands at about eight o'clock tonight?"

"No, I'll probably be curled up on the couch binge-watching Netflix by then."

"A girl after my own heart. If it wouldn't be ruining your plans, you should come to Ladies' Night at the Long Neck with us instead. Callie, my mom, Carol Greer, her sister, and I are all going to go together. I think it'd be great if you came. I'd love to get to know you a little better."

Plus, I get the sense she could use a little fun.

"I'm not sure. I haven't had a drink in a *long time*."

"That's okay. You don't have to drink at all if you don't want to. Just come dance with us and have a good time."

"Okay, yeah, I'll think about it."

"Great!" I instantly feel a wave of satisfaction wash over me, and I swear I can see the sadness start to slowly slip out of her like a ghost. "Here, give me your number so I can text you all the details after my shift."

After she punches her number into my phone, she slips back out the door, but this time, she has a smile on her face as she crosses the threshold.

The second the bell above the door jangles, Callie

comes out of the kitchen. "Are you ready for Ladies' Night? Only one more hour till we can blow this popsicle stand!"

"Popsicle stand?"

"It's an expression. I'm just excited."

I laugh. "I'm excited too. I hope you don't mind we are going to have some additional members."

"Who?"

"I invited Carol and her sister, Aimee—"

"Please don't tell me this is your way of trying to set your mom up with friends for when you leave. You're not leaving Roots. I won't let you. You can keep working at the café. I'll give you more hours if you're worried about money. We will get it sorted out. You just can't leave."

My heart warms as I hear the desperation in her voice. "Aww, I love you too, Cal." I wrap her up in a bear hug. I want to tell her my plan, but I can't until everything is perfectly in place, so instead I test the waters a little. "We've been through this already. I can't stay here, especially because I know every single one of you would do everything you could to help me make this work, and I'm not about to become someone's burden."

"You're not a burden. We love you, and we *want* to take care of you. That's what family does for one another. You're like family to me."

I bite down on my lip hard, trying not to feel the sappy emotions rising in my chest. She definitely passed the test.

"Whether I stay or not, it'd be good for my mom to have a friend. Our relationship got a little rocky when I felt like the center of her universe. It doesn't feel that way now, but I want to make sure it never does again."

"I admire that. The Greer sisters are fun. What's Carol going to do with the dogs?"

"She said Rhett was going to hang out on the property for a few hours, but she's not going to stay out very late."

Callie shakes her head. "That woman is incredible. The sacrifices she makes for those little furballs..."

"Yeah, she amazes me. Not everyone is built for that, but she does an outstanding job of handling it all. I think a night off will be good for her."

"We all need a night off once in a while."

"Which brings me to my next point. I invited Lauren too. I think she could use a night off as well."

"You invited Lauren? The Lauren that was just in here? Lauren Rhodes?"

"Yeah. What's wrong with that? She seems nice, and I just thought she could use a night of fun. She carries this sadness around with her, and I know what that's like, so I just thought—" Seeing the flames lit in Callie's eyes, I stop. "Should I not have invited her? What did I do wrong?"

She presses her thumb and forefinger to the bridge of her nose. "It's fine. Lauren seems nice enough. It's just that... everything about the Rhodes family feels off. It's a cute story and all that they've been passing down that ranch for generation after generation, but that's so much pressure, and Lauren is just Little Miss Perfect, already engaged to her high school sweetheart and ready to take over the ranch for her brother who failed to fulfill the family legacy. I just don't feel the need to get wrapped up in that dysfunctional world and whatever game she's playing trying to be the perfect child."

"That seems a little harsh. Do you even know Lauren?"

"We went to school together, and I knew Charlie."

"That's her brother who left?"

Callie winces and I immediately get the sense there's something she's not telling me, some history with the

Rhodes family that she's keeping hidden. *Why does everyone in this town seem to be keeping secrets?*

"Yeah, that's the one."

"Maybe you have a good reason for not liking her, but she looked so sad when she walked in the door today, and I just thought she could use a friend. I was trying to be like you, making sure she didn't feel alone."

Callie instantly looks guilty. That wasn't my intent.

"I guess I can give her a chance, but this is one hundred percent for you, not for her."

"Really? I'm so excited. We're all going to have a great time."

"Famous last words," she mumbles.

Chapter Thirty-Seven

Rhett

CALLIE

Repeat after me: I deserve to be happy and I'm worthy of that happiness

ME

It's been over a week Cal. Moment's over

Have you talked to Olivia yet?

I'm trying to find the right time.

Then you must not believe it enough yet.
SAY IT!

I deserve to be happy and I'm worthy of that happiness.

Very good. I'll check in again tomorrow.

———

I roll over and glance at the clock. It's after 12:30 in the morning. *Why am I being woken up right now?*

I hear drunken giggles and stomping up to my porch, so I climb out of bed and march down to the front door.

Before I get a chance to open the door, I hear Olivia's sweet voice. "Shhh! I think the front door should be open. We can just slip in and out without bothering Rhett. It's late. He's probably asleep."

"Not anymore I'm not."

I swing the door open, and Olivia's mouth gapes as I stand there in the doorway in nothing but boxers. I know she's attracted to me. I just wish I knew for sure that her feelings were enough to get her to stay here with me.

When I take her in, the world stops. Everything around me goes quiet for a moment, and all I see is Olivia. She's wearing Callie's cowgirl boots again, but this time they're paired with a white cotton dress with colorful little flowers on it that remind me a lot of the wildflowers she's come to love so much. She blinks, and her eyelids shimmer a soft pink that makes her eyes pack even more of a punch than normal when she draws them back up to meet my gaze. She's absolutely stunning.

Lauren and Callie lean into one another, giggling and watching the two of us. When Callie stage whispers, "Get a room you two," I'm drawn out of my haze.

"You girls are so damn loud!"

"Sorry, Rhett. I didn't want to bother you, but we are supposed to stay in the cottage tonight, remember? I guess I forgot my keys, so I can't get in, and—"

"I'll get my spare."

As I dig through my drawer, Maverick comes padding down the steps that lead to my room.

"Hi, Mav!" Olivia coos, crouching down to the ground

and extending her hands. "Rhett, can I bring him over to the cottage? I want him to cuddle with me tonight."

"No, there's still a couple things that haven't been finished up there, and I don't want him getting into anything. Besides, you girls are way too loud. I'm sure Maverick would prefer to have a quiet night over here."

"But Maverick's my baby. He should be with me!"

"He'll be waiting for you tomorrow."

"I want him now."

"How are you going to leave him when you go back to San Francisco in a few weeks?"

"I'm not going back if I can help it. San Francisco sucks. It's noisy and busy, and it doesn't have you."

The corners of my lips quirk, and my heart soars. *It doesn't have you.*

Callie cuts in. "What about us? Are we chopped liver?"

"That's what I mean. San Francisco doesn't have any of you." Olivia swirls her hands around to encompass the whole room. "Or my parents. Or Carol."

There goes that soaring feeling. I'm just another friend to her. "Well, this is all news to me."

She leans into my ear as if letting me in on a secret. When her lips brush against my skin, I shiver, even though it's hot as hell tonight. "No one is supposed to know I'm thinking about staying yet. If I tell everyone and can't figure out all the details, I'll just hurt people. I need to do a few things first, like talk with my dad and find a new job."

"All right, well your secret is safe with me."

She gives me a satisfied and dopey-looking smile that makes me want to wrap her up in my arms. I don't care what she says, I'm keeping her in Roots with me. Look at her! She's so cute.

"How about I let y'all in now, so you can go to sleep?"

"Oh, we aren't going to sleep yet. We have to have girl talk first," Callie insists.

"Okay, then I'll let y'all in so you can have girl talk."

I desperately wish I could be a fly on the wall in the cottage tonight. *I wonder if Olivia will talk about me. Will Callie try to play matchmaker again?* Oh god, look what she's doing to me! I'm not usually so obsessive and uncool.

They follow me over to the cottage like three drunken ducklings following their mother. I slip the key into the lock, giving it a little jiggle before swinging the door open.

"Thank you, Rhett." Olivia slips her purse off her shoulder, searching for something before popping back up with a drunken laugh. "Oh my goodness! You aren't going to believe this!" She dangles her keys out for everyone to see. "I *did* have the keys." She bursts into laughter, immediately followed by Lauren and Callie.

Holding back a smile, I close the door behind me. "You ladies have a good night and please stay out of trouble, especially you two." I point my fingers at Callie and Olivia, doing my best to look stern.

"Yes, sir." Callie salutes me as I leave. Her lips are in a straight line for all of zero seconds before she bursts into a fit of laughter.

It takes everything in me to finally close the door behind me. Something about the energy in the room suggests trouble is ahead.

Chapter Thirty-Eight

Olivia

Once the door clicks shut, Callie immediately drags Lauren and me onto the couch. "Who's up first?"

"First for what?"

"Girl talk. Which one of you is going to tell me all about your life first?"

Lauren drags one of the throw pillows in front of her, crossing her legs and remaining silent.

"How about you go first?" I offer.

"I don't have anything going on in my life, though."

"There has to be *something*."

Callie purses her lips, thinking hard. "Nope. Nothing. My life is boring. I need to bring some more excitement into it."

"Um, what do you call tonight?"

"You know what I mean. Don't worry. I had a lot of fun tonight, but I don't have a wedding coming up or a big fundraiser I'm planning and a handsome roommate I'm this close to finally getting with." She pinches her thumb and forefinger together.

"Wait, isn't there something going on with *you* and Rhett?" Lauren asks Callie. "I heard he was at your place late last week. Some ladies at Sweet Mae's Diner were talking about it the other day."

My stomach sinks. *Am I a total idiot who tried to come onto someone else's man? Not just someone else's, but Callie's!* Callie is my friend. I adore her, and I value our friendship.

Callie's brows knit together. "Oh, that's just talk. I promise you there is nothing going on with Rhett and me. Whatever someone thinks they saw, they're just plain wrong."

Relief washes over me immediately. I'm not sure what would make people spread that rumor, but I'm smart enough to know the talk around this town is never true. If Callie says nothing is going on, then I believe it. I think.

"You're sure there's nothing? I'm not stepping on any toes?"

Callie reaches across, taking my hands in hers. "I promise you there is *nothing* going on with Rhett and me. Never has been, never will be. He's so far gone for you."

I scrunch up my nose. "See I kind of thought so too, but we spent all day together last week, and he still won't completely open up to me. It doesn't matter anyway. I'm leaving soon."

"I thought you just told Rhett you wanted to stay?" Lauren pipes up.

My stomach somersaults. I was supposed to keep this a secret until I had everything figured out. This is what I get for opening my big drunk mouth.

Sighing, I tell the truth. "I *do* want to stay, but I need

to figure some things out first. I haven't wanted to tell anyone I'm thinking about it because I'm scared I won't be able to find a job here or convince my dad that it makes sense for me to quit my job in tax. I don't want to become a burden or ruin my relationship with my parents that I've started to build back up over the last couple months. There's just so much I have to work out still. You have to promise not to tell anyone I'm thinking about staying."

"We promise."

"You don't need to worry about finding a job," Callie says. "You already have a source of income from the café, and we can find you something else. The world has changed. You can work from anywhere in the world. Living in Roots won't hold you back from having whatever job you want."

"I looked at jobs this morning before I came in for my shift, but I don't even know what to look for. The accounting jobs all seem so dull. I get that same sense of dread reading the job descriptions for those roles as I do when I think about going back to my public accounting job, but I'm not qualified for anything else. I'm just so scared I won't be able to figure out how to make it work."

"What if you do figure it out? Isn't it worth trying?"

"Yes, but my life in Roots was always supposed to be temporary. What if staying here doesn't solve any of my problems? What if my anxiety comes back and I push my parents away again? What if Rhett finally realizes I'm too much of a mess to ever love?"

"You are in control of your life. It's up to you to keep getting the help you need to manage your anxiety and up to you to put in the time for your relationship with your parents. It's even up to you whether you keep trying to get through to Rhett or give up. Just don't let fear keep you from being happy."

I'm speechless. I look from Callie to Lauren, hoping she will help me.

Thankfully, she does speak up. "What brought you here?"

I explain how my coach found me at work and then how my parent's concern for me brought me to Roots during my time off.

"Have you had any panic attacks since you came here?"

"Just one, but I haven't been working, so it's not a fair comparison."

"You *have* been working. You've been planning the fundraiser, volunteering at Resilient Paws, *and* working at the café. You've been *busy*," Callie says.

"That doesn't count. I haven't been working a job that stresses me out like my job in San Francisco does. Plus, none of those would pay my bills if I moved to Roots."

"You can't tell me planning that fundraiser hasn't been stressful for you. I've seen all the hard work you've been putting into it, all the details you've had to figure out. Maybe it's not that you aren't experiencing any stress here. It's more that the stress you have now is outweighed by the support system you've created and all the beautiful things you're working toward. You're doing something you believe in. Are you passionate about taxes?"

"No."

"Maybe that's been your problem all along. You just needed to realign. You found a solution here that works for you, whether that was intentional or not. I don't think that will change if you stay. I think it'll just improve your life."

"You don't think it's me running away from everything?"

"You'd be running away if you left Roots. It's easier to stay in your old habits, but to actually have to start over and find a way to make life work in Roots, to take a shot at a relationship with Rhett, and to let your parents back into your life again, that's difficult. But I think it'd be worth it. There's something more out there for you."

I give Callie a nudge with my knee. "Thank you. Why do you have to be right all the time?"

"It's a blessing and a curse."

Laughter breaks free, and it feels good. The last several minutes have been more intense than I expected.

"Your turn!" Callie says, turning to Lauren with a smile on her face.

Lauren starts rambling, trying to evade the question and steer the conversation in another direction, but as Callie keeps prodding her, the conversation takes a turn.

Lauren chokes on a sob, and as tears stain her cheeks, she whimpers, "Am I just stupid? I thought Austin and I were meant to be. From the moment I laid eyes on him, it felt that way, and we just made sense. Both our families are ranchers. He's the perfect person to run the ranch with me. But now, it just hurts to love him. I feel like I'm clinging onto us so tight, and he's just pushing me away. I'm starting to think maybe he never even cared about me. He just cared about the ranch."

I leap up from the couch, running to grab a box of tissues, and setting it in her lap as I wrap a comforting arm around her. "Why do you think Austin just cares about the ranch?"

"You know how I said he's on a business trip right now?"

I nod.

She brings a tissue to her nose, blowing loudly. "He's

been going on a lot of these trips. He says he's building rela-tionships with other ranchers and seeing what they are doing so we can improve Copper Hill, but he's yet to come home with a new idea. He doesn't tell me much of anything about his trips, and honestly, I've felt us drifting apart for a while now."

She dabs a tissue under her eyes before continuing on. "And the worst part is, I think he's cheating on me. I haven't proved it yet, but I could've sworn he came home smelling like another woman the last couple trips. I know I'm prob-ably just being paranoid, but I can't shake the feeling."

"Never doubt your intuition. I always hated that prick," Callie says.

I give her the eye, murmuring, "Cool it," before turning back to Lauren. "I'm sure there has to be some other explana-tion. I don't know Austin well, but I'd like to think he's a good man if you saw something in him. Maybe it's just the stress of the ranch now that he realizes it's going to be his responsibili-ty." Growing more confident by the second, as I think about the ways I've previously closed people off to protect them, I add, "Yeah, that has to be it! He's probably just trying to prove that he is worthy of you and the responsibility of taking care of the ranch, so he hasn't focused on you as much. He will come around. Have you talked with him about how you're feeling?"

"Loads of times! Nothing has changed. It usually ends up with him storming out on me."

"Have you mentioned the cheating thing to him?"

"No, I want to believe in Austin." She pauses like she's plucking which parts of the truth to tell. "He was my first love, and I always pictured him being the person I grew old with. I'm trying not to let my mind get the best of me and ruin our relationship. I'm trying to give him the benefit of the doubt. We've spent eight years of our lives together. I owe it to him."

The hurt in Lauren's eyes is evident, and I'm finally understanding what has been weighing on her since the day I met her. It pains me to see that she feels so stuck. It's clear she's unhappy, but she's afraid to do something about it. I just want to fix things for her.

Then it hits me. That must be how everyone else around me feels, watching me suffer when I have the power to make a change.

Callie interrupts my thoughts as she leaps up from the couch. "We just need to get you proof! That will give you peace of mind."

I narrow my eyes at her. She didn't even want Lauren to come out with us tonight. Maybe it helped to see that "Little Miss Perfect" isn't so perfect after all.

"How would we do that?"

"I don't know. We could show up tonight and surprise him. That would either be great for your relationship as a spur of the moment little getaway together, or it would finally give you the proof you need. Do you know where he's staying?"

Panic rises inside of me. "We aren't just going to show up at his hotel room tonight. It's late, and Amarillo isn't exactly close."

"But Lauren needs to know. She deserves the truth. She can't just keep sitting around thinking her relationship is okay if it's just going to end."

The silence that falls over us is suffocating. I think of Rhett and how I've been wanting him to open up to me, but I haven't given him anything to indicate that it'll be worth it. I've always made it clear we had an expiration date. I can't blame him for not wanting to take the next step with me, or any step for that matter.

"I bet Jax would drive us." I can practically see Callie's heart pounding out of her chest. She seems way too invested in this, like maybe she's familiar with the feeling of losing someone she thought she had a future with.

"I don't think we should do anything rash tonight. Let's just sleep it off, and we can regroup in the morning. If you think there's a chance there's something going on with Austin, then we can make a plan to find out for sure. He won't be able to keep that hidden for long."

"I don't have time! We are supposed to get married in two months. I can't be planning a wedding to a man who doesn't think of me as the only woman in the world."

"And you shouldn't settle for anything less than that. I promise we will figure this out. Let's go to bed."

Callie and Lauren exchange a glance but nod somberly. The cottage is silent as we brush our teeth and wash our faces, but I swear I hear the sound of the door creaking open after I've slipped into bed.

Chapter Thirty-Nine

Rhett

Too late! How do burgers, baked beans,
and corn on the cob sound?

Fine... but I'M going to cook for YOU one
of these days

Fine by me

Fifteen minutes later, the burgers are on the grill, the beans are on the stove, and the corn is boiled. The doorknob jiggles as Olivia lets herself in, immediately making my heart hammer in my chest. I'm determined to swallow my pride and finally tell her the truth about my past. Callie was right. That's the only path forward with Olivia if there ever will be one. God, do I want there to be one. I swing the door open, and Maverick rushes in, immediately making himself comfortable. Olivia follows behind, her earth-shattering smile making me feel like I've just come home. I want to tug her into my arms and feel her warmth, let her presence seal all the cracks that have formed in my soul over the years.

"Hey, Wildflower. You're right on time."

She follows me to the back patio as I pull the burgers from the grill and turn it off. "So, are you going to fill me in on what happened with Callie and Lauren?"

"I'm not sure how much of the story I can tell you because, you know, girl code."

"Okay, then tell me what you can."

"Callie came up with a sort of sketchy plan last night. I thought I convinced her it was a bad idea, but I woke up this morning to an empty house, and now I can't get ahold of either one of them."

I reach out, running my fingertips gently across her back to soothe her. Concern is painted all over her face. "Are you worried they're in danger, or are you just upset that you don't know what's going on?"

"Maybe a little of both? Neither one of them were in any condition to drive last night. They mentioned Jax driving them, so I'm hoping he did. I'm worried about Lauren though. I don't think there's any way the situation could've ended well."

"I can try to call Callie if it'd help."

"Please!" She desperately clings to my arm.

I pull my phone out and scroll to Callie's contact. When she doesn't answer, I leave a quick voicemail and then click into the messages app.

ME

Hey! Olivia is really worried about you and Lauren. What happened last night?

"There. I sent her a text too."

"Thank you." She looks up at me through her long thick lashes. "Is your sound on?"

A chuckle escapes me as I flick the button on the side of my phone up. "It is now."

"Thank you."

"You know I'd do anything for you."

The earth-shattering smile she gifts me makes me feel on top of the world. The feeling is better than when I roped my first cow or when I finally finished writing my first song for the guitar. She feels like home, more than any other human being ever has, and it's a reminder that I'm supposed to swallow my pride and finally tell her everything about my past.

Last night, hearing her affirm exactly what Callie told me, that she wants to stay but needs security and the knowledge that she can please everyone, made me more certain this can work.

I lead us inside, and we each dish up. As we sit at the table, I can't stop thinking about what I'm going to say to Olivia when we talk. I know I should wait until after dinner, but I'm not sure if I can. The anticipation is killing me. Thankfully nothing has felt off between us since we didn't kiss a little over a week ago, but I still want to set us on the right path forward.

"So, you're trying to stay in Roots?"

Her eyes go round, and she presses her fingers to the bridge of her nose. "I guess I didn't just dream about telling you I wanted to stay then, huh?"

"Nope." Thankfully not. The memory of her lips gently brushing up against my ear last night still charges my blood. "What do we need to do to make you comfortable with the idea of staying?"

I try to act casual, but it's nearly impossible not to get my hopes up. There's still a big part of me that wonders if it's even worth putting myself out there to tell her the truth if she isn't going to stay here. I'm just warming up to the idea of a relationship in general. I'm sure as hell not ready for a long-distance relationship.

"I have a whole list of things."

"What's on that list?"

"I want to talk with my dad about what my job has been putting me through, to make sure he understands and approves before I leave."

I instantly go into protective mode. "I hope that won't be something that holds you back from going after what you want. You don't need your dad's approval to do what makes you happy."

"I know. I believe his love for me will outweigh whatever expectations he has of me, but because of the respect I have for him, I need to talk with him before I quit my job." I nod along, feeling a bit better. "I also need to find a place of my own to stay."

"You do?" There's no hiding the hurt in my voice.

"I mean aren't I going to move back into the cottage in a few days when everything is finalized? And I was only supposed to be there until the end of July, which is coming up quickly. I don't want to overstay my welcome. Plus, if we are going to try to be tog—"

She stops, pressing her lips together.

"If we are going to try to be together, you think we shouldn't start by living together?" She nods nervously. "I love having you here with me, and I honestly don't want you to go back to the cottage in a few days, but if living somewhere else is what it takes to get you to stay in Roots and give things a shot with me, then I can live with that." The concern on her face slowly morphs into joy. "You can stay in the cottage if that feels right. Stay as long as you want. I don't have any other use for it."

"Are you sure?"

"I'm positive."

She purses her lips, looking uncomfortable. "Then you'd at least need to charge me market rent."

"I don't need the money."

"Rhett, I don't care if you need the money or not. I can't just move here and live in a little fantasy world. I need this to be real life."

"Maybe you've missed the message during your time here, but people in small towns like Roots like to help each other out. It is real life in Roots to let you stay for free in a cottage I have no other use for."

Crossing her arms, she mumbles, "Fine. But I still need a job."

"What kind of work do you want to do?"

"I don't know." After a beat she adds, "I know I don't want to be in tax anymore. The insane deadlines just don't work for me, and I hate that I have to put my life on hold for almost six months out of the year."

"Okay, so we look for a job that gives you the freedom to still have your life outside of work. Anything else you want or don't want?"

"I want to do something meaningful. I've never felt as passionate about anything as I feel about helping Carol with the rescue. Even if I'm not making any money from it, it's very fulfilling. I want to continue to help her and also find that feeling in my next job."

"We can work with that."

My phone dings, and I pull it out to find a text from Callie, which I read out loud.

CALLIE

We're okay. Tell her I'll fill her in soon

————

Sitting on the back porch after dinner, we watch the sun set, lighting the horizon in oranges and pinks. Birds chirp cheerily in the trees, and Olivia sits next to me. I can't think of any place I'd rather be.

I don't want to break the peace of this moment, but I'm about to burst from holding in the story I need to tell Olivia. "I kind of had something I wanted to talk with you about too."

"Should I be worried?"

A strangled laugh slips from my throat. I'm not sure how to answer that question. "I know I've kept a lot hidden from you—"

"I'm sorry for digging so much, Rhett. I just want to get to know you and understand you, but I realized it hasn't been fair for me to keep insisting that I'm going to leave Roots and then ask you to open up to me anyway."

"I was actually thinking it's time I tell you the real reason I came to Roots."

Chapter Forty

Rhett

She does a terrible job of trying to hide the smile growing on her face, and it's so damn cute that I nearly forget what we were talking about.

"I'm not sure where to start," I say nervously.

"It's your story. Start wherever you feel is right."

I take a breath, planning on remaining calm and confident while I tell her, but as soon as I open my mouth, the words come tumbling out like an avalanche.

"As you already know, I went to college in New York. During my second semester of freshman year, I had one of my introductory business classes with this girl, Isabel. She was intelligent, funny, and absolutely radiant. I fell for her hard and fast, and somehow, I was incredibly lucky because she fell for me too. Despite all my reservations about love, she made me want to try. She made me believe that my parents, and everything in my past, had nothing to do with my future. By the end of the year, we made things official, and I just knew she was the girl I wanted to marry."

Confusion swirls in Olivia's eyes as I speak. I'm sure she is wondering why I'm telling her about how much I loved another woman. Maybe it's unfair to share that with Olivia, but my love for Isabel made me who I am today, and I can't tell my story without talking about Isabel.

"By the beginning of our senior year, we had planned out our whole lives together. I was going to move back to her hometown, Roots. We knew it'd be a great place for us to raise a family, and we knew we'd have a support system here. My relationship with my parents had never been all that great, but she had a great relationship with both her parents and her sister, Callie."

Olivia's jaw drops to the floor. "You dated Callie's sister?"

"Yeah, she was my fiancé."

Her mouth hangs open, but she remains silent, so I keep going before I lose my nerve.

"Maybe it was naïve of me, but I couldn't wait to start forever with her, so during our second semester of senior year, I proposed. Isabel said yes, and I couldn't have been happier. Of course, our parents weren't exactly thrilled about us getting engaged so young. My parents completely cut me off when they found out I had proposed to Isabel. They wouldn't return my calls and texts, and they stopped sending checks to pay for my tuition. After everything they had been through with their marriage, they thought I was making a mistake, but I didn't listen. I still haven't spoken with them since."

Olivia instinctively reaches for my hand, pity filling her eyes.

"It stung a little bit, but I was still on cloud nine because I had Isabel. I guess I've been seeking out a parental relationship in other places of my life since then, hence my close relationship with *your* parents, but it was all worth it to have Isabel by my side every day for eternity.

"About three weeks before graduation, my best friend was throwing a big party for his twenty-second birthday. Isabel and I came together, but while we were there, we got into this ridiculous fight. I honestly can't even remember what started it. I just remember it was fueled by alcohol, and it escalated quickly. Isabel stormed off, and I figured it was best to just let her have a moment to herself. I figured she'd come back to me when she was ready so we could talk things through, but instead, she decided to leave the party early without telling me."

My stomach churns, and a lump gets caught in my throat. Not only does it hurt to relive these memories, but I'm terrified of how Olivia is going to react. I know we haven't exactly started anything just yet, but this truth has the power to prevent us from ever having a future together. Not having Olivia in my life in any capacity would gut me. After just over two months, she's weaseled her way into my life and my heart, and I don't want her out.

I suck in a deep breath and force myself to go on. "Isabel died in a car crash on the way home from the party that night. Her Uber was t-boned. She was supposed to be safe with me, but instead, we got into this huge fight, and she left the world angry with me. I could handle having a terrible relationship with my parents, but Isabel leaving this world right after a fight was all I needed to realize that love was never meant for me. I convinced myself I wasn't worthy." I squeeze the hand she has wrapped around mine. "I'm working on changing those beliefs because there's someone else in my life who lights me up more than anyone ever has, and I'll live my life in regret every day if I don't at least try to give love one more chance."

The silence fills with the sound of cicadas and frogs, and I'm thankful for their steady rhythm to calm me ever so slightly.

"Is that why you showed up at the bar to drive us home and why you panicked when you didn't know where I was?"

"Yes, I wanted to make sure you two got home safely. You're two of the most important women in my life. I couldn't live with myself if something happened to you. Then when you disappeared, I was worried you were mad at me and had left."

She moves from her seat, crawling into my lap and hugging me tight. After a few moments, she draws back to look me in the eyes.

"I know this isn't the reaction you expected, but all I want to do is kiss you right now." She's right. That is not the reaction I expected at all. *What the hell?* "You're a good man, and it means so much to me that you were able to completely open up tonight. I feel like I can finally see all of you, and I adore every *single* part that I see."

She caresses my cheek, and I can't help but slightly nuzzle into her touch as her words stun me to silence. *Did she just respond to that story by saying she wants to kiss me, that she adores every part of me?* Warmth floods my chest as I process what is happening right now. *Olivia accepts me and all my flaws. She isn't turned off by the string of terrible relationships that I've left in my wake. She thinks I'm worthy of love!*

I breathe a sigh of relief and reach for her hand, tugging her out of her chair and to my chest. Gently, I whisper, "I'm sorry I didn't tell you sooner. I've been afraid that sharing my past would just scare you off, and that would only validate the fact that I don't deserve love. You make me want to believe in myself again, but it's going to take some time. I haven't trusted myself in so long, and I'm still terrified I'm not enough to keep you safe and make you happy."

"I know what it feels like to think you are doing more harm than good for the people you love, but I've learned over the last couple months that sometimes your mind lies to you. Don't let that part of you win. You're more than enough, Rhett."

"It doesn't scare you that I've had all these bad experiences with love? You don't think I'm cursed?"

"How could I possibly think that? You've been nothing short of amazing with me since I got here. Yeah, there was that one night that you yelled at me," she smirks teasingly, "but I deserved to be called out on my shit, and you only did it because you care for my parents so much. You've been there for me since I came to town, reassuring me I deserve happiness, showing me around Roots, introducing me to Callie, cooking and baking for me without expecting anything in return. You're incredible, and what happened with Isabel, or your parents, is not a reflection on you as a person in any way."

I gently brush her cheek with my hand before crashing my lips into hers. This kiss is fierce and desperate. There's an "I need to have you now" to it. With each sweep of my tongue, I hope to show her just how badly I've wanted her over these last few months and how hard I'll work to prove myself worthy of her each and every day that she lets me.

After all those passing touches that set my body on fire, this kiss sets my *soul* on fire. It's unlike anything I've ever experienced. I've never felt so made for a person as I do for Olivia. It's like our bodies and souls were made together, two halves meant to fit perfectly together to create a stronger, more beautiful whole.

Chapter Forty-One

Olivia

THE FEELING OF RHETT'S LIPS ON MINE IS ELECTRIC. His touch is simultaneously gentle but passionate. The feeling of his hands on me, one around my waist, the other in my hair, is intoxicating. We pull apart for just a second, but it's enough for reality to hit me.

Before he can lean back in, I reach a hand out to his chest, slipping out of his lap as my eyes grow round. "Oh my gosh! I'm so sorry. I shouldn't have done that."

His brow furrows, and he stands up. "*I* kissed *you*. Why are you apologizing?"

"You may have been the one to lean in, but *I* spurred this on by telling you I wanted to kiss you."

"I'm still not seeing the problem." His rich laughter makes my whole body tingle.

"I know I'm trying to stay in Roots, but I haven't checked off a single box on my to-do list yet. What if things don't work out? I couldn't bear to be responsible for breaking your heart again."

He wraps an arm around my waist and pulls me close. With my cheek against his chest, he gently cradles the back of my head. We stand there for several moments before he tilts my chin up to meet his gaze. "I'm going to ask you something, and I need you to be brutally honest."

I nod, anxiety swirling in my stomach. Its tendrils wrap around my lungs and gives them a squeeze.

"Do you want to stay in Roots? If you put me aside, put your parents and Callie aside... if you put your job in San Francisco, everyone else's opinion, and what you think is truly possible out of your mind, what do you want to do?"

"I want to stay," I mumble into his chest, barely audible. There's no hesitation. I've known I've wanted this for a while now, but I've been afraid to let myself want it. I don't want to let people down, and not being able to make it work would hurt like hell, not just for me but for all the people who care for me.

"Can you look me in the eye and say it again so that I can hear you?"

A soft smile dances on his lips as he waits for me to respond. I don't feel rushed or pressured. I just feel safe.

"I want to stay," I say, louder this time.

"That's good enough for me. If that's what you want, then you are going to get it, and we will figure it out together. You are never going to deal with hard things alone anymore."

"Thank you."

"Of course. I don't know if you've realized it, Wildflower, but I would do anything to see you happy. Yes, I selfishly want you to stay in Roots, so we can explore what this could be, but I also just want to see you find peace and experience joy and love and laughter. Your beautiful soul deserves a beautiful life, and I would go to the ends of the earth to make that happen."

My heart is pounding furiously. It feels like it's about to take flight. I have *never* in my life heard someone say such kind things to me. That's what's so incredible about Rhett. He speaks, and I know every word that comes out of his mouth is genuine. He's not saying this to manipulate me. He's saying this because he desperately wants me to know how much he cares for me and because he wants to see me happy above all else. If I told him I wanted to go back to San Francisco, I know he would support me, even if it broke his heart.

Unsure how to convey all the emotions I'm feeling, I stand on my tiptoes, sinking my fingers into the hairline at the nape of his neck as I pull him in.

Fireworks. There's no other way to describe the feeling of our lips touching. Together, we are vibrant, colorful, loud, and beautiful. It's terrifying, but I can't help the thought crossing my mind. *I want to spend forever here. I want to spend forever stringing together moments like this with Rhett by my side.*

———

Rhett absentmindedly traces circles on my leg while we lie on a blanket under the stars in the exact same spot we did over a week earlier.

"Can you answer a couple more questions for me? I'm starting to process things, and I have *a lot* to ask you."

"Go ahead."

It feels like I'm a little kid and I was just told I could have ice cream for breakfast. I've been dying to get to know

Rhett. Now that I've had a little taste, I'll never stop seeking more.

"Why did you come to Roots? I know you said you were going to come after graduation with Isabel, but—" I pause, not sure how to end my sentence.

"The circumstances changed," he offers.

"Yeah."

"I felt pretty lost after her death. I didn't know what to do. In one night, my entire plan for life after college was unraveled. Roots wasn't necessarily my first choice afterward. I didn't think I wanted to be in a place that would remind me of Isabel, even if I hadn't been there with her before. I knew I couldn't go home to my parents because they were still upset with me for proposing so young. They thought I was throwing my life away, and their lack of support didn't change after the accident. I actually think they thought her death was God's way of teaching me a lesson for being so naïve."

Immediately I reach out to grab his hand. "That's terrible."

"Yeah, I know. I'm still working on creating a different narrative to explain why something like that would happen to such a good person."

Hearing the way he speaks about her makes me a little jealous, and it doesn't feel good.

I must not do a good job of hiding it because he rolls toward me, planting a gentle kiss on my forehead, then the tip of my nose, and finally my lips. "I'm sorry for talking about her so much. She was my first love, and I can't deny that, or erase her from my past. I'll always love Isabel, but I'm not still *in* love with her." A weight lifts from my shoulders. "Our relationship was fun and uncomplicated, but I've moved on. I know it's early, but I can tell you and I have something special. We've both shared our darkness with each other, and we still want to be together. You've sort of become like my best friend over the last couple months, but I also can't keep my hands off you, and that's pretty great."

"I think so too." I give him a soft smile. "Oh, wait! You still need to finish your story. You didn't explain how you decided to come here."

"I guess I didn't know where I wanted to go after college. I didn't feel like I had a home or a family. Callie and I were there for each other a lot through the grieving process, and she became a good friend to me. She convinced me to come here. She always loved Roots, and I think she needed a friend too. She told me she could be my family, that the people of Roots would take me in too. I didn't think I had anything to lose at the point, so I came."

He continues drawing circles. It tickles ever so slightly, but I'd be upset if he stopped. I'm in love with the feeling of his touch.

"We started the café together. She and Isabel always talked about opening one someday, and when Callie came to me for help financially, I couldn't say no. I quickly fell into a good life that I was happy with."

"Did it help to have Callie around? You know, since she was someone who actually knew what happened."

"It did. Her parents moved out of Roots pretty quickly after I got into town, so we both bonded over the shared experience of losing Isabel and our parents. Callie helped me slowly realize that maybe everything that happened didn't have as much to do with me as I thought. I have her to thank for finally getting the courage to tell you everything tonight."

"What do you mean?"

"After we didn't kiss the other night, I immediately went to her place to talk with her. I told her about how I was getting in my own head, and she helped me see that I could either keep denying love and be miserable or go after what I want and maybe find happiness. She encouraged me to be open with you about what happened. She said you'd be supportive."

Realization hits me as I connect the dots. Lauren said she heard Rhett was at Callie's late the other night. *That's* why.

I roll over to lie flat on my back again, looking up at the sky. The clouds have been slowly rolling in, and it's growing darker and darker out here.

"I'm sorry the stars aren't better tonight."

"It's okay. The company is all I need."

A droplet of water splashes down on my skin. I brush it from my cheek, giggling. Another droplet falls, this time on my arm, followed by one on my lip. Rhett leans in to brush it off with his thumb. It's crazy how natural this already feels, even though this is all new to us.

"Were you afraid of me before?"

"What? You mean when you answered the door with a frying pan? Yeah."

I shake my head, laughing. "No! I just got the sense you were trying to avoid me when we first met. Things didn't feel this natural at first."

"Of course I was afraid. The slightest brush of your skin against mine was enough to power the entire state of Texas. I was terrified of what you'd do to me. I thought if I let you in too much I'd lose control, that I'd wind up letting you in and falling in love. I was right."

I blush, feeling a little guilty. "I'm—"

"Don't you dare finish that sentence. I don't want an apology. You are exactly what I needed."

Now I'm blushing for other reasons, and I don't know what to say, but I'm saved as the gentle rain quickly turns into a downpour. My clothes soak through in seconds, and my hair turns into a sopping mop.

As I leap up, shrieking, Rhett swipes the blanket from the ground and wraps an arm around me, sheltering me from the rain as we quickly wind our way down the path back to the house.

The rain continues to soak us to the point that I can feel it in my bones. I've never been in such an intense downpour. The path quickly turns into a muddy mess, and as I try to shuffle through it, my foot slips. Rhett has to grab me to keep me upright. Thunder claps overhead, shaking the ground. I've never heard, or felt, thunder like this before. I guess the saying is true. Everything truly is bigger in Texas.

As I cower, Rhett pulls me in closer. "It's okay. I've got you. We're almost back."

"I'm so glad we left Maverick at home."

"Me too."

The wind begins to pick up, swirling and howling.

"Did you know it was going to storm tonight?" I have to shout and still don't know if he can hear me.

"I had no idea. I wouldn't have brought you out here if I did."

The dim light of the house comes into sight. *Thank God.*

We hurriedly shuffle into the house, leaving a trail of mud across the back patio and into the kitchen. I close the door with a little extra effort, and Rhett flicks the locks behind me, trapping me between his broad chest and the door.

We both take a deep breath, assessing the messes that we have become from being exposed to the elements.

I finally break the silence, swiping a bit of mud off his cheek and murmuring, "You look like a monster."

Instantly, the look of concern on his face is wiped clean, and we burst into a fit of laughter.

Chapter Forty-Two

Olivia

"She's alive!" I rush over to Callie's booth, clipboard in hand. "You are so lucky I've been so busy over the last week. Between my parent's Fourth of July dinner, the annual firework show in the park yesterday, and then planning the fundraiser, I haven't even had time to breathe. Otherwise, I would've been busting yours and Lauren's doors down to find out what happened the other night."

The smile on her face is quickly erased. "I'm sorry! I—"

"It's okay. I'm disappointed I wasn't included in things, but I'm glad you helped her take some action. I hated seeing her so unhappy. I'm still a little confused though. How did you go from telling me not to invite her out with us to running off to Amarillo with her in the middle of the night like she's your best friend?"

"Alcohol?" She offers, flashing a hopeful smile. When I continue frowning, she droops her shoulders. "I had some preconceived notions about her from a long time ago. I realized she was pretty fun, and when I found out that she had some difficult things going on, I wanted to help. I've been in a relationship before where I thought we were on the same page, and it turned out we weren't. If I could've found out sooner and saved myself some of the heartbreak, I would have, so I wanted to help give her that chance."

"I'm sure Lauren appreciated it. I just wish you two would've trusted me to come along."

"Drunk me was convinced you were going to kill the plan." She chuckles.

I roll my eyes, then focus on my clipboard. "I see you have your booth number hanging up already. Here's a few maps of all the booths in case anyone asks you for one. I'll come around every hour, so I can keep a constant count of our total funds raised. I think if we are very transparent with where we are at, it will incentivize people to buy more and help us reach our goals." I take in the booth and my checklist once again. "I think that's it. Is Rhett going to help with the booth at some point, or do you need me to step in?"

"I think it's just me. Rhett said he wanted to be around to support you." She wiggles her eyebrows. "Speaking of keeping secrets, I think there's something *you* need to fill *me* in on!"

Dodging her comment, I glance around the parking lot. "I haven't seen Rhett here yet. Have you seen him?"

She softens with sympathy, and I feel oddly inclined to give her some sort of comfort. "He *did* text me this morning to wish me luck, and he left flowers and a card outside my bedroom door *very* early this morning. I'm talking before the sun was up because he somehow managed to get them there before I stepped out at 5:30."

"I *knew* it! Something happened. Finally!" She shrieks gleefully. "Tell me everything."

"I would love to, but I can't right now. I need to go check in with the rest of the booths. Just let me know if you see Rhett."

"He'll be here."

I nod, not feeling comforted. I'm so nervous about this event. I want it to go well, not even for myself, but for the dogs and Carol. The one thing that I think could calm my nerves right now is a hug from Rhett. His touch just makes everything right in the world.

I move along to the next booth, a small business that sells spices and rubs just outside of Dallas.

The man at the booth is dressed in a pearl snap shirt, jeans, boots, and a cowboy hat. I'm impressed he's not dying in this heat. We set up a bunch of tents throughout the parking lot to keep the sun off everyone, but the intense early-July humidity still makes my forehead bead with sweat.

He reaches out his hand as we exchange greetings.

"Thank you so much for coming out here. I just wanted to do a quick run-through of my checklist." I hold up my clipboard.

He nods and smiles along as I read off each of the items to him. When we are finished, he grabs my arm before I can dash off to the next booth. The sudden movement causes me to nearly jump out of my skin.

"Sorry, I didn't mean to startle you. I just wanted to let you know that the work you're doing here is really important. You should be proud of yourself. Let me know if there's anything more I can do to help out."

"I'm just trying to help the dogs. They're the real stars here."

He gives me a nod, loosening his grip.

I move toward the next booth, but I'm once again

stopped by the firm grip of a hand. This time it's wrapped around my waist. The arm swivels me around until I find myself face-to-face with Rhett. He gently brushes a strand of hair from my face, giving me a reassuring smile before he kisses me. I instantly sink into him, relief washing over me. We pull apart and he takes the opportunity to wrap me up in a bear hug. As I inhale his scent and sink into the feeling of his arms wrapped around me, I feel at peace.

"You're here."

"Of course. I wouldn't miss a second of this." He presses a kiss to my forehead. "So, what can I help with? Have you heard from Carol yet?"

"Carol has been back and forth. My parents are supposed to help her bring some of the dogs over, but maybe you should check in with them. That's the one part of our plan that was not the most ironed out."

He nods, leaning in to give me another kiss. "On it!" He salutes me with a cheesy smile and marches off, pulling his phone from his pocket.

I round the tables to find Lauren's booth, looking pristine. "Hey, Lauren! Just doing my rounds." I glance down at my clipboard. "It looks like the first item on the list is an explanation of what happened the other night. You and Callie just took off. I was worried."

She shrugs, and it's then that I see something different in her eyes. Sadness lingered like a cloud around her from the moment I met her, but that sadness is replaced with betrayal and anger. "Jax came and picked us up, and I got some answers." She grabs my arm. "I know you're busy, so I promise I'll fill you in later."

"I'm holding you to that."

"Good. I need to be held accountable."

She's smiling, but it's tightlipped. I'm tempted to just

call off all my responsibilities now, so we can ditch this place and catch up over a tub of ice cream, but the dogs need me just as much as Lauren does, if not more. So, I tell her, "I'm here for you," before I wrap up my checklist and move on.

———

The event has gone without many hiccups, although both Rhett and my parents have claimed it's no surprise considering the amount of time I dedicated to planning this.

While all the vendors take care of their booths, I'm helping manage the many dogs we brought to the parking lot. It's crucial for everyone to see exactly what they're supporting. Maybe I also thought it would help a few of these sweet angels find their forever home. Sue me for being optimistic.

A woman with thick, wavy brown locks approaches. She's dressed in a button-up blouse and striped flowy pants that look like they're worth more than everything in my closet. She crouches down to pet one of the pit bulls with a radiant smile on her face, not at all worried about creasing her trousers or getting slobber on her fancy outfit.

After giving the dog the attention he rightfully deserves, she glances up at me. "You're Olivia Parker, right? You're the one that made this whole event happen?"

"Yes, I am. And the adorable monster you're petting is Gus. He's up for adoption if you're interested."

"I'm always interested, but my husband will kill me if I bring another rescue home. We already have five." She leans in closer to me. "But maybe I can convince him we need an even number, right?"

I already like this woman. "I'm sorry, I didn't catch your name."

"Oh, of course! I'm Morgan Newton. I work with a PR firm outside of Fort Worth that helps non-profits."

I lean in closer, immediately intrigued. "Wow, that's so cool! Do you do that full-time?"

"Yup. We have some pretty generous donors that help give the firm the resources it needs. We only started a couple years back, but we are trying to grow so we can keep helping non-profits do good work like you're doing with this event today." She reaches into her pocket and pulls out a business card. "You should give me a call sometime. I'd love to take you to lunch and see if we could be a good fit for you… if you're interested."

I take the business card, unable to speak. There's no way this just fell into my lap. *This is almost exactly what I've been looking for!* I glance around to see if anyone else is here to witness this, and I lock eyes with Rhett, who's watching our exchange intently. I give him a knowing look, and he quickly refocuses his attention on the dog standing in front of him. Busted!

"Thank you so much, Morgan. I will definitely be reaching out soon. I'd love to hear more about the work you do."

"Great!" She gives me a genuine smile. Even if Rhett helped align our paths, her smile reaffirms she thinks I'd be an asset, and it feels dang good.

The second she leaves, Rhett glides to my side with a sly grin on his face. "What was that all about? Was she offering you a job?"

"Don't act innocent. I know you put her up to that. I can figure this out on my own, Rhett. I don't need everyone getting involved. I'm trying *not* to be a burden."

"I swear I didn't put her up to anything. I've never seen or heard of that woman in my life."

"Then why were you giving that look?"

"Because I want you to stay! And I could see on your face how excited you were about that job. Seeing you happy makes me happy."

"How did I go from really not liking you to turning into mush every time you speak?"

"I'll never tell my secret." He smirks.

Before I can lean into him and tease him more, a man approaches one of the German Shepherd mixes I'm holding, crouching down to give her a gentle pat. After stroking her cheeks silently, he looks up at me. "Are you Olivia Parker, the one who planned this event?"

"Yes, I am."

I glance at Rhett, and the look on his face looks guilty as hell. It's immediately clear that Morgan might've been a fluke, but whoever this man is, he is here because of Rhett.

"My name is Chance Marlowe." He reaches out his hand, and I shake it firmly. "This event is incredibly impressive. How much have you raised so far?"

I glance at the time on my phone. "I'll be announcing an updated amount in fifteen minutes. I need to start collecting tallies from the booths again, but as of the last check-in, we had collected over twenty-five hundred dollars."

He raises his eyebrows. "Like I said, impressive. I hear you work for an accounting firm now? Someone with your talent for marketing should be working for someone like us. I work for a small firm about half an hour from here. We work with a whole bunch of clients, hosting fundraisers and campaigns, but I've never seen something like this. You have a gift."

"Thank you. That means a lot."

He whips out a business card, thrusting it into my hand. "I know you're busy today, but give me a call, and we can talk more."

"Thank you."

He shakes my hand once more and keeps moving. I swivel around to Rhett. "You're meddling!"

"Haven't you learned by now you don't need to take on the world alone? Let me help."

Glancing down at the ground, I consider what my counselor and I have been working on for the last several weeks. To be honest, I don't want to figure all of this out alone. If Rhett wants to help me, is it so bad to accept that help?

"Thank you. I appreciate you."

"You're welcome. I just want you to be happy. It's a total coincidence that it would also make *me* happy if you stayed here."

"And me!" My mom calls from several feet away, apparently listening in on the whole conversation. She waltzes over to me and leans into my ear. "I don't think we are going to be watching movies this week. You have a lot to catch me up on."

"*Mom*," I grit out, hip-checking her. She bursts into laughter.

"I need to count up the money in everyone's jars, so I can announce the updated total. Can you both please behave for fifteen minutes while I'm gone? No more scheming, and no more embarrassing me."

They laugh in unison. "You two are the worst!" I huff, quickly rushing off to the next booth, but I can't help the smile playing on my lips and the fluttering in my heart. This could be my life now. Roots could be my *home*. I keep my eyes on the ground while I gather my composure again, trying to will away the tears of joy that are pooling in the corners of my eyes as I picture it. But there's still a lot of work to be done.

Chapter Forty-Three

Rhett

"Seriously, Ol, I'm so proud of you. You surpassed your goal. That's huge! And five dogs are already pending adoption. I guarantee you there's more to come." Mandi gives her daughter one last squeeze before she steps out the door to join Lauren, Callie, and me on the Parkers' front porch.

"Thanks for dinner, Mom."

"Any time. We should do this more often. It sounds like we might be able to with your *two* job offers on the table."

"They're not offers. They're just invites to talk and see if it would even be worthwhile to offer me a job."

"There's no way they could talk with you and not want you to work for them, honey."

"Your mom has a point," I say as Olivia blushes, looking flustered.

"We will just have to see. I don't want to count on anything. Please don't tell Dad. I still need to talk to him about our conversation the other day."

"My lips are sealed, but please hurry and tell him. I hate keeping secrets."

Sensing the emotions building up inside Olivia, I wrap an arm around her waist and spin her toward my truck. "Should we head home?"

She gives a nod, her eyes glazed over as the wheels in her head start turning round and round. I can practically see the steam streaming out of her ears.

Callie pulls her in for a hug. "We're getting lunch together soon, right?"

"Yeah, I don't think I can wait anymore to hear about your antics with Lauren."

Callie rolls her eyes, and Lauren goes pale. "They were hardly antics, but fine."

As she and Lauren each slip into their cars, I go around to the passenger side to open Olivia's door for her. I close it gently behind her and once I'm in the truck with my door closed and my seatbelt buckled, I turn to her. "How are you doing?"

"I'm a bit overwhelmed."

"You've had a big day. I hope you're proud of yourself though. The event is over. You can breathe easy knowing it was a success."

"Yeah, you're right." After a beat, she quickly turns to me. "I just can't stop thinking about the next event. This one was great, don't get me wrong, but I think I could do something that would bring in even more money, get the dogs more involved, and spur on some adoptions."

She's positively glowing as she speaks. Each word rolls off her tongue as she radiates more light. This is what she is meant to do. I don't even need to know Olivia to see it. It's just evident in the way she's talking right now.

"Do you think Morgan or Chance would support you if you wanted to plan another event for Resilient Paws?"

"I don't know, but I guess that should be something I ask them when we meet." She pulls her phone from her back pocket and immediately begins typing out a note.

I let her continue tapping out ideas as we drive the rest of the way home in silence. She's clearly on a roll, and I'm not about to interrupt.

When we pull into the driveway, I once again rush to open the door for her. She steps out, and I grab her, swinging her up over my shoulder as she squeals with glee. "Rhett! What are you doing? Put me down!"

"I'm taking you hostage. It's been too long since I've had you all to myself. I need to be a little selfish tonight if you'll let me. Please spend the evening with me. I'll bake you whatever you want."

"Even lava cakes?"

"Even lava cakes."

"Okay, then I'll hang out with you, but only for the cake."

"I'd expect nothing less."

————

Two and a half hours later, Olivia drills her spoon into the spongey, chocolatey goodness and moans. "This was *so* worth the wait! I forgot how good these are."

I chuckle as I spoon my own bite. "I've been thinking."

"Uh oh." She worries her lower lip.

"It's nothing bad."

"I can't think of a time that someone started a sentence with 'I've been thinking' and ended it in a good way."

"Give me a chance to be the first."

"Go ahead." She points her spoon at me before scooping into the cake again and pulling up a melty morsel. I get a little distracted as I watch her delicately take a bite and swipe her tongue across her upper lip. I remember the first time we had these cakes together and how badly I wanted to touch her, how unsettled that made me feel. Now, I get to touch her and taste her and call her mine... I think. That's what I'm trying to do at least.

"I've been thinking that I'd like to call you my girlfriend and take you out on a real date, not just kiss you and hang out with you. I want the real thing."

She tries to hide her smile, but it shines through instantly, her excitement and giddiness making me feel the same. "I guess you just proved me wrong. There is a good way to end that sentence."

"Is that a 'yes?'"

"Of course! I want that too." She leans in to nuzzle me before giving me a gentle kiss. "So, what kind of moves can I expect Rhett Lawson to break out on a first date?

"I can't tell you! Then they won't work."

"I didn't realize you needed the element of surprise on your side to successfully get the girl."

"I don't, but it doesn't hurt either."

She purses her lips. "Fair. Can you at least tell me what we are going to do?"

"I want that to be a surprise too."

"You're killing me!" she groans, her mouth full.

"I'd hardly say I'm killing you. I *did* just bake you cake."

"And I'm very grateful, but you got me all excited now. I want to know what we are going to do. When are we going to do it?"

"I have to work the next two days, and you're busy this weekend with your movie night, right? So maybe we could do something Monday evening. You don't have to work at the café on Tuesday, do you?"

She glances at her phone. "I don't, but I was going to pop over to Resilient Paws in the afternoon to help Carol put together some new crates that are supposed to come in that day."

"That's perfectly fine. I just want to make sure I don't have to rush my time with you. I want to savor every single moment."

I pull her chair toward me, tugging her until she's between my legs. I brush a strand of hair from her face and note the chocolate on the corner of her mouth. Instead of handing her a napkin like I'm afraid her touch will electrocute me, I swipe my thumb across my tongue and rub the chocolate spot off before licking it clean and tugging her chin to me to give her a long, slow kiss. When I finally pull away, I look her straight in the eyes and ask, "Will you please go on a date with me Monday night?"

"Fine," she groans, but her eyes shine with excitement.

"Oh, come on now. Don't sound so excited! I'm a good time."

"Yeah? Prove it." She quirks an eyebrow.

I immediately push out of my chair and pull her out of hers. The second she's on her feet, I twirl her around once as I lean in to turn the music up. Cody Johnson's "Give a Cowboy a Kiss" flows through the speakers.

"This isn't George Strait."

"Despite what you believe, I don't exclusively listen to his music."

"I've lived with you for two months, so I can honestly say I don't believe you."

"Just get over here." I tug her toward me and then shimmy to the upbeat tempo.

A fit of giggles pours out of her as she takes in the sight of me. "You're so ridiculous!"

"Yeah, but you're still here with me anyway."

"Because I'm ridiculous too," she says as she does her own little jig.

"You're right. You *do* look ridiculous."

In one swift step, I grab her hand and pull her onto the couch. Maverick immediately gets riled up by the excitement in the room, and I can't blame him for getting swept up in all of this. There's so much love and joy in this room right now. I have no clue what I'm doing standing on the couch with Olivia busting out the most absurd moves I've ever seen, but I want to do this for the rest of my life. That's just what being around Olivia does to me. She makes me happy and crazy and impulsive but caring and considerate and so very much in love.

———

Lying in bed with just the moonlight as her makeup, Olivia looks stunning. I watch her breathe deeply and try to memorize every sun-dusted freckle on her face and across her shoulders.

Maverick readjusts himself at the foot of the bed, and I find myself wincing, terrified he will wake her. Sure enough, she stirs and opens her beautiful eyes, peering sleepily at me. "What are you doing?"

"Just trying to make this memory permanent in my mind."

She smiles softly. "Tonight was pretty great. Thank you."

"Thank *you*."

"For what?"

"For being so incredible. For not letting me keep you at a distance and for being persistent enough to get me to open up my heart to you. For being so easy to fall in love with."

She gasps.

"Shit. Sorry. I know it's way too early to be saying things like that. It's just that I've been burying my feelings for you for months now, and I guess now that I can finally act on them, I can't get myself to stop."

"I know what you mean. It scares the hell out of me."

"Why? I never want to be a source of stress for you." I wrap my arms around her and pull her so that her back is flush with my front.

"You're not. It's just that we don't have anything figured out. It's scary to take this leap without knowing that everything is going to work out. I still need to figure out how I'm going to stay in Roots. Yes, I have those potential jobs from today, but I still have a job in San Francisco I'd have to leave and parents to appease. I don't want to leave my current job for just anything, and I don't mean to throw this in your face, but I'm just scared you're going to change your mind. You were so adamant that love wasn't meant for you, and now you're willing to try. How do I know you won't change your mind again? My mind has been swirling, to say the least."

"We will figure it out together. You don't have to be in this alone anymore. I don't know how to get that through to you, but I'm going to find a way to do it. You're... the way you make me feel... there are no words to describe it. I know you don't see it, but you have this radiance about you that's enough to make the sun jealous. I just want to be around you all the time. Being apart from you drives me wild and makes me do irrational things. Without even trying, you've made me into a better man. Each and every second I spend with you, I'm convinced I just get better because you make me want to be better. When you feel this way about some-one, you want to move mountains, and big leaps feel less scary. I'm just asking you for the chance to prove to you that I'll be there for you."

I watch her bite her lower lip as she tries to hide her cautious smile. I can feel the pounding of her heart as she's pressed against me. It's grown much quicker in the last thirty seconds. She rolls toward me and looks up at me through her beautiful lashes, and those amber eyes staring up at me melt me like an ice cream cone in the Texas heat.

Instead of speaking, she grabs my face gently in her two hands, pulling me in for a kiss that says so much more than words ever could.

She pulls away first, but it's only to ask, "What did I ever do to deserve you?"

Before I have the chance to respond, she is diving back in to press her soft lips to mine again. I can feel the warmth of her touch everywhere on my body. It warms me from the outside in, making me feel in love. *Oh my god! I haven't felt this way in so long.*

This should make me feel uncomfortable. A couple of weeks ago, this feeling would make me want to run for the hills, but now that I've had a taste of what it feels like to love Olivia, I never want to quit.

Chapter Forty-Four

Rhett

"COME ON! THAT WAS *CLEARLY* A STRIKE!" I BELLOW.

"Hey, ump! Get yourself some glasses will ya?" Jack seconds my frustration as the Astros' batter takes a base. "I am *not* about to watch the Rangers lose to the Astros! Not this year. The Astros haven't been worth spit this season."

My stomach churns. I'm not sure why I thought it was a genius idea to watch the game with Jack and *then* talk to him about dating his daughter.

I want the Rangers to win just as badly as Jack, but I have a little more riding on this than whether or not my team wins. I need Jack in a good mood. After everything Jack and Mandi have done for me, I feel like the respectable thing to do is let them know I'm going to be taking Olivia out on a date before they hear it from someone else. I already know Mandi will be supportive, and I know Jack respects me, but his opinion of me as a young man who helps them out and watches sports with him may not remain the same when I become the man dating his daughter.

The Astros' batter strikes out, ending the inning. One more to go, and the Rangers are only up one. *Come on.*

The first two pitches of the inning are strikes, and I'm hanging on the edge of my seat. I can feel Jack's temper boiling up even from my seat across the living room. The next pitch is good enough to get the batter on base. The tension in the room could be cut with a knife as we both lean in, watching the game with laser focus.

Mandi walks in, beaming. "Oh, you two are watching the game? How's it going? Are they creaming the Astros?"

"No, they're only up by one," Jack practically growls. It's amazing what sports can do to a man. Jack is otherwise a pretty kind, approachable guy, but when his team is losing, or even at the risk of losing, he scares the hell out of me.

The next batter strikes out, but the one following him gets a double, and I feel my shoulders relax just the slightest bit. *Come on. Come on.*

Strike one. Strike two. Jack's face is scrunched up into a scowl. But the batter adjusts properly, shooting the next pitch high up into the stands.

"Yeah!" Jack leaps out of his chair, jumping up and down. He takes two steps toward me to give me a high five, a huge smile lighting up his face. That's three runs for the Rangers, putting them at a four-run lead. I wish we could just call the game now.

The next batter steps up to the plate, and my phone buzzes in my back pocket. Normally, I'd let it go to voice-mail during a game, but the urgent pattern of the buzzes indicates it's Olivia, so I quickly swipe to answer. Jack glances at me with a furrowed brow as I point to my phone, standing from the couch and excusing myself to the other room.

"Hey, Wildflower."

"Thank goodness you answered."

Panic inflates my chest at the sound of desperation in her voice. "What's going on? Is everything okay?"

"I'm freaking out!"

"Why? What's wrong?"

"I followed up with Chance and Morgan after the fundraiser, and Chance just called me back to ask if I could meet him for dinner *today*."

"That's great! Why are you freaking out?"

"Because I'm so nervous. I have no time to prepare. It's been a couple years since I've had to interview for a job, and I'm so worried he's going to realize that I don't have any experience in marketing."

"Don't be ridiculous. You just planned a fantastic event, and you exceeded your goal. Plus, you've been running @Dog_Central_ since college."

She groans. "I know, but that's not enough. It's not like I'm a professional. Plus, he only reached out to me because you intervened."

"I may have reached out to him, but he didn't have to show up at the fundraiser at all. I didn't hold a gun to his head and force him to get in touch with you. He took the information I gave him and decided he wanted you all on his own. You don't need a ton of experience to excel at this job. I'm sure he just wants to make sure your personalities mesh and you have the qualities that can't be taught, which you do."

"How can you be sure I have those qualities? You've never worked with me."

"I've been around you constantly for almost over two

months. I'd have to be an idiot not to notice how kind and responsible you are. Plus, you're driven and a self-starter. You're passionate. He's going to be chomping at the bit to hire you. Just take a deep breath and go show him how incredible you are."

She lets out a deep sigh. "You're right. He would be lucky to have me."

"That's my girl!"

"But how do I show him all those sides of me just over dinner?" Again, I can hear the self-doubt in her voice, and I want nothing more than to wrap her up in my arms so she can physically feel how much I care for her, how much I think the world of her. If only she could see herself the way I see her.

"Just be yourself. Your passion, your drive, your competence, they all shine through just in the way you talk and the way you carry yourself."

"You're sure?"

"I'm positive. You're going to crush it. Believe in yourself."

"Thank you."

The second I hang up, Mandi steps into the foyer. She was definitely listening. I can see a touch of sorrow on her face. I'm sure it stings a bit to hear I was Olivia's first call and not her. That's her baby girl, her best friend.

Instantly, I try to defend Olivia. "She just called me because I helped her get in touch with Chance."

Mandi gives me a half-hearted smile, rubbing my arm. "It's okay. She would kill me for saying this, but I can tell she's falling for you. This is just how it is when your kids grow up. They start to create their own lives, their own families. I'm just happy to be included in the ways I am."

I try to push past the part where Mandi said Olivia is

falling for me because if I think about it for too long, I'm going to start dancing around with a stupid smile on my face. I can't believe I get to be the lucky one that Olivia is falling in love with.

"She adores you, Mandi. I think she's afraid to express it to you. I *know* she's been afraid of somehow being a burden. I just want you to know not to take Olivia's love for you at face value because it goes so much deeper."

"Yeah, she's been like that for a long time. I hope you'll remember that with her too. When things get hard, she tends to think she has to go through it all alone, that her struggles would cause her loved ones strife. I've failed a dozen times at weaseling my way into her life and getting her to accept my help, but maybe you can do better than me. Maybe you can be the one that she finally accepts help from."

"I should be so lucky." Again, that earns me another smile. I scratch the back of my head anxiously before asking, "Does Jack know too?"

"It's so obvious! How blind do you think we are? You two were practically drooling over each other when we played pool the other night, and I saw you holding hands during the fireworks show." She laughs, and I can immediately feel heat rising to my cheeks. "But I know it would mean the world to Jack if he heard it from you. He thinks of you as a son."

"I appreciate that. You both have been so incredible to me. You're the parents I always wanted and needed. Thank you. I'm going to do everything I can to be worthy of Olivia's love, and quite honestly, yours and Jack's."

"Oh, honey. You've always been worthy."

My heart swells. I finally have the love I've sought for so

long, from both parental figures and an amazing woman. It feels incredible.

I escape back into the living room just in time to catch the last two batters. The first strikes out, and the second makes a weak hit straight to first base. The game is over. The Astros only scored once this inning. The Rangers won, and so have I.

Jack gives me a cheerful high five, and I can't contain my secret anymore. "Jack, I need to tell you something."

"Is this about you and Olivia? I know already, son. Don't worry about it."

"I just thought—"

"There's nothing to discuss. You're a good man, and I couldn't think of someone better to date my daughter."

"Oh, okay then." *This went better than I thought.* Maybe it's because the game went our way.

"Does this mean she's going to stay in Roots?"

"That's not my place to say. I think you need to talk with Olivia."

He nods silently. Then, like the flick of a switch, his kind smile turns to a frown. "Just don't break her heart, or I'll break out my shotgun."

I really would like to believe he's joking, but there's something about the look in Jack's eyes that makes me think I better not find out.

Chapter Forty-Five

Olivia

I swipe my palms casually across the sides of my pants before shaking Chance's hand. It takes everything in me not to let my voice quake as I say, "It's a pleasure to see you again, Chance."

"Yes, it's so great to see you too, Olivia! I hope you don't mind, but I brought along a friend." He gestures to a towering woman in a pressed blouse. Her hair is graying, but it's swept up into a bun that makes her look elegant and intimidating.

After introducing the two of us, he explains, "Margaret here is my boss, but I see her as more of a mentor to me. She's part of the hiring team, so I thought it'd be good for you two to meet as well."

He seems chipper and smiley. This should ease the tension in my shoulders, but I can't take my eyes off Margaret. Her gaze is like a laser, boring a hole into my soul. I can feel her judgment as she looks me up and down. I tug anxiously at my blouse, wondering if maybe I didn't dress up enough, or are my sweaty armpits soaking through my shirt already?

We take a seat at the table Chance reserved for us an hour earlier, and we all assess the menu in silence. The contrast to the noise in my head is overwhelming. *Say something! You need to show them you have a personality, or they won't want anything to do with you.* Oh gosh, I wish Chance had given me more notice. I would've looked up him and Margaret on LinkedIn. At least then I could've come prepared with questions. This is a disaster.

"Do you two come here often? What's good here?"

"I like the cobb salad," Margaret says. A girl after my old San Franciscan heart. Now that I have the time to do things besides stand at a desk for fourteen hours a day, I prefer a meal with a little more protein.

Chance jumps in with his opinion. "The pulled pork is outstanding. You can get it as a sandwich with a side or just the meat with two sides."

"Oh, that sounds great." He looks satisfied with himself. One glance in Margaret's direction makes me think that's my first strike, as if what I order for dinner is going to dictate what kind of worker I am.

Again, I brush my clammy palms against my pants. I clasp my hands firmly in my lap, hoping that will help stop some of the shaking, but all it does is make them sweat more. *Disgusting.*

The waiter comes to take our drink order, but Margaret grabs him by the arm, insisting, "I think we are ready to order food too. We might as well do it all at once."

The waiter, who appears to be in his late teens, nods eagerly as if he too is feeling a little offput by Margaret and desperately wants to win her approval.

As he scurries away, I say, "I'd love to hear more about

the kind of work you two do at your firm. You said it's a mix of non-profit work and marketing for other businesses, right?"

"Yes, we do a wide variety of work. Margaret is more of a supervisory role, overseeing client relations. I handle some of the client relations as well in some cases, but I do a lot more of the creative side of the job, taking our client's needs and turning them into a fantastic marketing campaign."

"If I joined the team, what sort of role do you foresee me taking on?"

Margaret jumps in as if she's been waiting for this exact moment. "What sort of skills do you bring to the table? You're a tax accountant, right?"

"Yes, I work in tax at one of the big four public accounting firms in San Francisco. It's an extremely competitive process to get a job offer at one of those firms. I handle a wide variety of clients and have developed a lot of soft skills in addition to my technical skills. I'm up for promotion to senior this fall, but I've been given the privilege of acting in the senior role on about half of my clients this spring. As a result, I've learned a lot about teaching, leading, and engagement management."

"But your work is primarily tax work? You have no marketing experience?"

"Well, uh, I've run an Instagram account with dog videos since my freshman year of college. I've done affiliate marketing for several products through my page, which has taught me a lot. I also have marketing experience from hosting the fundraiser for Resilient Paws last week. I spent a couple months planning the event, and while I had some help from the owner of the rescue and a few locals, I was completely responsible for the marketing and most of the planning. I revamped the rescue's Instagram account and created a website for the rescue, which I believe could translate very well to—"

"But one successful event doesn't mean you're cut out for marketing."

The server chooses now to come out with our food, and I can't help but feel a hint of relief. I just *know* Margaret was about to tear me apart. Maybe these couple minutes will give me time to come up with a solid pitch to win her over.

The young waiter looks like he wants to run for the hills as he realizes what he walked up to, and I feel kind of bad for him, but he still manages to do a good job of calmly placing our food down and asking if we need anything else before promptly running back to the kitchen.

The second he leaves, I cut in before Margaret has a chance to discredit me. "I recognize planning one event isn't the same as having a resume filled with accolades, but I am a hard worker, a quick learner, and when I'm truly dedicated to something, like the rescue's cause, I will move mountains to get things done well."

I push my pork around on my plate. Such a shame, I was looking forward to this, but now I feel more nauseous than hungry.

"Miss Parker, I appreciate your eagerness, but I just don't see how this will be a good fit. You don't have an education in marketing. Your experience for the past two years has been in *tax*. That's a very structured job, not creative like marketing. And quite frankly, I don't think our firm has the capacity to teach you the fundamentals of the job. We need someone who already knows the basics."

"I'd like to argue I *do* know the basics, considering what I just accomplished yesterday. That has to count for something. Plus, I've done extensive research on search engine optimization and used it successfully on the social media pages for the rescue and my account from college."

There's desperation in my voice now, and it's like she feeds off of it. She gives me a smile that's more like a sneer, and I can feel sweat begin to drip down my back. *Oh god! Chance, give me some back up here! Come on!*

"I can teach myself any of the basics I still don't know outside of work. It won't cost you any time or money."

"You've already chosen your path. I'm sure you're a great accountant if you made it to the large five or whatever, but I just don't see how you'll benefit us here. You're best to just stick with what you know. It'll be easier for everyone."

My teeth are starting to chatter and my whole body is shaking as my nerves take over. I don't know what else to say to this woman. She's starting to make me doubt myself, and everything I thought could be true for me and my future. "I'm not looking for easy," I manage to squeak just before I glance to Chance for some support.

He chomps down another bite of his pulled pork sandwich and pauses briefly with his cheeks stuffed like a squirrel when he realizes Margaret and I are both looking at him. He gulps down his food just to say, "Maybe this won't be the best fit after all, but we appreciate your time, Olivia."

I look back and forth between the two of them. *Am I just supposed to leave?* We only got our food five minutes ago.

"Uh, yeah, thank you both for meeting with me. I'm sorry it didn't work out." I keep my gaze on my lap as I try to blink back tears. This went so much worse than I ever could've imagined.

Margaret reaches out a hand, giving me a dry smile. Guess that answers my question; it's time to go. I take it firmly and then turn to Chance, murmuring thank you one more time.

I walk out of the place like a dog with my tail tucked between my legs, shame radiating off me like an odor. I slunk outside, managing to barely keep it together until the doors close behind me. I choke back sobs, desperate to protect the family walking ten steps in front of me from the mess that is about to explode.

I make it to my car and slam the door shut just in time for the tears to start streaming down my cheeks. I pull out my phone desperate to call someone and be comforted. I actually have people to call now! But then it hits me. *Who am I going to talk about this with?* My mom, Rhett, Callie, Lauren, they'd all be so disappointed the meeting didn't go well. They were all counting on me to make this work so I could stay in Roots, and I blew it. I got their hopes up, but I should've known it was stupid of me to think the stars would just align and I could get a job outside of accounting just like that. That's not how the real world works. *How could I let myself be so naïve?*

My chest starts to tighten as my thoughts spiral, and I already know what is coming, but I don't make any attempts to count or breathe like my counselor taught me. I feel like I'm right back where I was before I came to this town. I keep mercilessly pummeling myself with dark thought after dark thought. *I'm so stupid! I can't believe I let my guard down and let people in. Here I am, being a burden again. I blew it. I need to learn my place. It's in tax. Even if I hate it, that's just how it is.*

My lungs grow tighter and tighter until I'm gasping for breath. Tears slither down my cheeks, and all I want to do is scream in pain. There's this awful ache inside of me for everything that could've been. *How dare I let myself believe*

I could do better? This isn't just impacting me now, I have people I've let care about me, and I'm letting them down too. I swore I'd never let that happen again, but I did.

I clutch at my chest and let myself sob until I realize just how badly I'm panting, sucking in desperate gasps for air. My natural reflexes of self-preservation finally take over and I begin the box breathing technique my counselor taught me. In... two... three... four. Hold... two... three... four. Out... two... three... four.

My body slowly returns to equilibrium, the tightness in my chest lets up little by little, the tears on my cheeks slowly dry, and I feel myself catching my breath. Even as my body physically starts to feel a little better, my mind continues to swirl, and my heart feels shattered. Where do I go from here?

Chapter Forty-Six

Olivia

THE SECOND MOM ANSWERS THE DOOR, I'M overwhelmed. She's smiling too much. Her hug is too tight. She's too happy to see me. This is all wrong. *Look what I've done.*

She pulls back, looks at my face, and frowns. "What's wrong?"

"It's nothing."

"How did your dinner go with that marketing firm? What was that guy's name? Chase?"

"It was Chance."

"Did they offer you a job on the spot?" Her proud smile crushes my heart into a thousand tiny pieces.

"They did *not* offer me a job on the spot. I'm not ready to talk about it."

She purses her lips, clearly bothered by the dark cloud of pessimism I brought with me but unsure how to deal with it or how to get the dang thing to go away.

"Have you thought about what movie you want to

watch tonight?"

"No, Mom. I've had other things on my mind."

"Would you like to talk about them? We don't have to watch a movie. We can just sit on the couch, eat ice cream, and talk. I'm good with that." Her smile is so pure. In some messed up way, I resent her for being such a good mom. She makes all of this so much harder. It was hard to keep her at a distance before, and it's going to be even harder now that we've reconnected, now that we've redeveloped a relationship that goes beyond just being mother and daughter.

"That's okay. Let's watch a movie. You can pick tonight."

"Are you sure?"

"Yes, I'm sure," I growl.

I can see the look of horror on her face, but she doesn't press me. She's making this easy and yet so dang hard all at once.

———

Swiping at a tear, Mom takes my empty ice cream bowl and says, "Gosh, that movie gets me every time, even though I know what's coming."

I give her a tight-lipped smile. The movie did nothing to quiet my mind. I can't stop thinking about how I need to protect her. I can't stay here, and I know it's going to kill her to hear it.

"Do you want more ice cream? I'm so obsessed with the Cookie Two Step."

"No, I'm okay. I should probably get going."

"But it's only nine o'clock. It's still early. Your dad won't be home for at least another hour, and I'd like to hear how your dinner went. I know you said you didn't want to talk about it, but I might have some insights that could help. I know you're always so hard on yourself. I'm sure it went bet—"

"No, it didn't. It was horrible. Okay, Mom? I know you think I'm some superstar, but I'm just a human being, a human being that picked a dead-end career path and is going to wind up stuck there forever. I don't know what I was thinking. I literally had to leave the dinner early while I fought back tears. It was *awful!* I've never felt so ashamed."

"Oh, Ol! Come here! Let me give you a hug." She pulls me in before I have time to resist, gently smoothing the top of my head. I feel some of the tension melt away for a moment. "You're not stuck. You're going to get through this. We will find you something so you can stay in Roots and be happy."

Her words are like snapping a rubber band against my skin, bringing me back to reality with a sharp sting. My lower lip begins to quiver, and I bite it hard. I can't cry. I need to be firm. If I cry, it's only going to make things worse.

"I can't stay in Roots. It was stupid of me to ever believe that it could work. I enjoyed my time here, but we all knew it was going to come to an end."

No part of me wants this, but I don't know what else to do. Today proved there's no escaping my life in San Francisco. I need to get out of here. It hurts too much to stay here and dwell on what could've been. Plus, the longer I draw out my time in this town, the harder it will be to say goodbye.

Mom's eyes are already filled with glimmering tears. "No, you can't go back! You can't give up. We will find you something. I promise. We still have time. I just want you to be happy. Are you going to be happy if you go back to your life in San Francisco?"

I take a deep breath, trying to give myself the confidence and determination I need to get this next part out in a believable manner. "I've been lying to myself this whole time. I thought staying in Roots—" I can't even finish the lie I'm about to say. "I just can't stay here, Mom. I need to go back."

"I don't believe you. You told me—"

"It doesn't matter what I said. I've woken up from the fantasy and realized I need to go back." Great, now the tears are coming. I try to bite down on my lip again, but it's no use. "I need your support right now, not you questioning me and arguing with me."

"But—"

"I should go."

She sits on the couch, watching me and looking heartbroken. It's almost enough to make me run back into her arms and tell her I'm sorry, to beg her to help me fix this mess, but I'm not her problem. I've been her problem for far too long. It's time *I* clean up my messes.

I walk out the door, making sure not to throw another glance at her because I know it will just break me down. As I cross the threshold, there's a tiny voice that asks *Clean up your own messes, huh? Is that what you call what you're doing right now?*

I shirk off the thought as I slam my car door closed and queue up some Shania Twain to blast on the five-minute drive home. Man, this town has changed me. I don't even want to listen to Taylor Swift right now. Somehow that makes me angrier.

I barrel into the driveway, hardly able to take all the emotions that are swirling inside of me like a tornado. I'm grateful to see Rhett's truck is gone. He must be meeting with Callie about the café.

I walk like a zombie across the gravel to Rhett's door, letting out a groan of frustration as I jiggle the lock up and down trying to get the damn door to open.

When it finally gives way, Maverick rushes to me, but he stops at the sight of me, his wiggling butt slowly becoming less wiggly. He looks at me with his head tilted as if he can tell something is wrong, and that look is all it takes to break my fragile heart. The dam bursts as tears flood my eyes, and I crumple to the floor. "Mav, I don't know what the hell I'm doing."

It hits me then that going back to San Francisco is going to mean I have to say goodbye to this adorable little mutt. No matter how much we've grown to love each other, or how much Rhett has insisted that Maverick is truly my dog, I know Maverick wouldn't have a good life in the city of concrete, cooped up all day in a five-hundred-square-foot apartment while I work twelve plus hours a day.

"I'm so sorry!" I wail.

He sits there for a moment, watching me with sad eyes. Then he gently lifts a paw, setting it on my leg before pressing the top of his head into my chest. Without even speaking, he tells me he loves me. He tells me it's going to be okay. He makes me cry ten times harder until my thoughts spiral to the place I don't want them to go. They settle in my lungs until I can't breathe again. Two panic attacks in one day. This hasn't happened in months.

I lean back so that my back is flat against the kitchen tile, and Maverick follows, lying down next to me with his head on my chest. "Good...boy..." I manage.

I watch his face, and I swear I can see the heartbreak in his eyes too. It's that look that pulls me back in to remember my breathing. In.... two... three... four. Hold... two... three... four. Out... two... three... four.

Chapter Forty-Seven

Rhett

I COULD SENSE SOMETHING WAS WRONG BEFORE I EVEN opened the door to the house. Olivia's car is in the driveway, but the house is dark. It's only nine thirty, so I know she hasn't gone to bed already.

When I reach the front door, it's unlocked. I swing it open, flicking a light on to find Olivia lying on the floor, clutching Maverick to her like both their lives depend on it. Her eyes are puffy and there's black underneath them like she's been crying. My stomach drops.

"Is everything okay?"

She looks up at me as if she just noticed I'm here. When her eyes latch on mine, her whole body sags and I see tears forming in her eyes. Horrified, I pull her close to me, pressing her face into my chest and holding the back of her head gently in my hands. "What's wrong?"

"I have to go, Rhett."

"Go where?"

"Back to San Francisco," she mumbles. "To stay."

Her words take the air out of my lungs. "What? Why? What's going on?"

She pulls away from me, but I hold on tight, afraid that letting her go will be the end of us, whatever we were. I guess we never really had a chance to be anything yet, but Monday was supposed to change that.

"The dinner..."

"I know you texted and said it didn't go well, but like I told you, I'm sure it wasn't as bad as you think. You don't give yourself enough credit."

"No, it really *was* horrible."

She fills me in on every horrific detail of the dinner, and I can't help it as my jaw falls to the floor.

"You're kidding! Who is this woman? I swear I'll kill her."

I hate the thought of someone tearing down Olivia, *my* Olivia.

She grabs onto my biceps. "No, you won't." She pauses to wipe the tears from her soaked cheeks. "She was right. Roots, the idea that I could find another job outside of tax, us... they were all just a fantasy. I came here knowing this was only temporary. I was always supposed to go back. It's time I get back to reality. We all know that it would just be a mistake if I stayed here. It'd be messy. I'd be in the way. I'm just ripping off the band-aid instead of delaying the inevitable."

Her voice is firm, but I can see something soft in her amber eyes. She doesn't want to believe a word of what she's saying. I can tell from that look that maybe her mind is saying all this, but her heart is begging her to stay and prove all of her biggest fears wrong.

I draw back from her enough to make her look me in the eyes. "You're not going anywhere. This is not just a fantasy.

Roots, a new job that makes you happy, and you and I together, are all within reach. You can't let that wicked woman win. You're not a burden. We want you here. Your mom, your dad, Callie, Lauren, me... we all want nothing more than for you to be here for good. And you can't try to give me some bullshit about not wanting to be here because you've told me you want to stay, and I can see it in your eyes even now. So stay. Please."

Her eyes are wide, and I can feel her heart pounding against my chest. "It's not that easy. Everyone is getting attached now, and I can't give you all what you need. I screwed up. Just let me go home before I make things worse, please."

"You *are* home. *You* are all that I need." I drop my lips to the crown of her head. "I've already told you I'll help you get settled. You're not in this alone. What else do you need from us to finally let yourself be happy?"

Her breathing has slowly been getting quicker with each second that passes, but my question triggers something in her because in an instant, she's wheezing uncontrollably. There's panic and fear in her eyes. She clutches her chest as she turns away from me and crumples to the ground.

I feel a squeezing in my chest, and an ache in my heart. I need to make this better. I want to see her happy again. I want to hear her beautiful laugh. It breaks my heart to think that I may have done this to her.

"Olivia, can you hear me?"

She nods as she continues clenching at her chest, her breathing loud and shallow.

"Can I touch you?"

She nods again.

I gently stroke her back. "Can you try to slow down your breathing? I'll breathe with you."

Maverick whimpers and rushes over to us. He sets his head in her lap as if to say *I'm here with you too.* What a good freaking dog.

"I.... can... do... it..." she says before she takes a deep breath, holding it for an extended period of time before slowly exhaling.

My eyes don't leave her for so much as a nanosecond as I inspect her to see if the breathing is helping release some of the tension in her shoulders or erase some of the panic in her eyes.

After several minutes, I finally start to think we might be in the clear. She calmed down much faster this time than the last time I was with her. When I say something about it, she nods. "The techniques I've learned in therapy have helped me feel a bit more in control."

"Are you okay?"

"Yeah."

"What can I do for you?"

"Can you keep holding me like this please?" The look in her eyes is so sad. She looks defeated.

"If you think I'm going to let go of you anytime soon, you're sorely mistaken."

She laughs. It's not her full laugh. It's a bit breathless and half-hearted, but it's something. It's a step forward from where we were a few minutes ago.

I wrap an arm around her waist, pulling her between my legs. She lets me. Then I lean her gently back so that she is lying against my chest. She feels stiff. "You can let your-self sink into me. I don't mind."

"I know I'm supposed to accept help. I've been working with my counselor on that for the last month, but it's also important for you to know that you don't have to take care of me." She sighs. "I think that's why it hurt so badly to fail when I met with Chance. I was trying to accept your help and turn it into something, so you didn't have to worry about me, but here I am, becoming a burden again." Her shoulders shrug up as she draws away from me.

"Oh no you don't, Wildflower. I'm not doing this because I *have* to. I *want* to hold you and comfort you. I want to see you at your weakest and your strongest moments. I want to be with you every second of every day. You've made it impossible not to fall in love with you, and whether you like it or not, when I love someone, I will do anything for her. I will do *anything* for *you*. I want to protect you. I want you to allow yourself to be vulnerable with me, and I hope that you'll allow me to be vulnerable with you too. Because let me tell you, I'm a mess."

She giggles. This time it sounds more like that musical joy I've heard escape her in the past when she's not trapped by her own thoughts, so I keep going. "I want to make you dinner and dessert whenever you feel like it. I want to play guitar for you just to see that look of wonder in your eyes. I want you to believe that you're strong, worthy, and loved. You're not a burden. You will never be a burden to me, or anyone else in the world, for that matter. You are Olivia *freaking* Parker. You are incredible. You light up the world with your presence. You will bring the world to its knees because you are brave and determined and destined to be happy, however that looks for you.

"And I need you to know, I'm so in love with you. Today doesn't make me think less of you. It makes me think more of you because every time you're kicked down by your anxiety, you still manage to get back up. You still manage to put on a smile. You still manage to lift other people up, to love, to experience joy, to absolutely crush every single thing you do. You amaze me."

"I don't even know what to say."

"How about *It's about damn time someone told me how amazing I am.*"

There's that beautiful laugh again. I want to keep her laughing forever.

"Or how about *Thank you, Rhett. You're right. I'm going to stay in Roots and put myself first for once.*"

"You're right. I need to get back up. I'm just so scared."

"You don't need to be afraid. I'm here with you, remember? We are going to figure this out together."

"But today just proved no one wants me. I'm only good for doing taxes."

"Today proved there are stupid people in the world, but it didn't prove no one wants you. I know you're afraid of hurting people but leaving isn't going to keep us from getting hurt."

She nods. "You're right."

"I know." I plant a kiss on her cheek. "Can we move our date up? I don't want to wait anymore."

"Move it up?"

"Yes."

"You're sure you still want to go on a date with me after seeing all of this?"

"I'm sure. Just come on the date with me, Wildflower. Let yourself be happy for a moment. We will figure everything else out from there."

She presses her lips together as she considers what to say. I try not to be hurt by the fact that her answer isn't an immediate and enthusiastic yes. She *is* still coming back from a panic attack, and I know my speech isn't going to automatically cancel out all the demons in her head.

"Let's do it," she says with a timid smile. "But there's something I have to do first."

Chapter Forty-Eight

Olivia

Even though it's early in the morning, Mom swings the door wide open within seconds of my knock. I can't help but wonder if Rhett told her I was coming. She pulls me into a hug, and I return it, squeezing her tight as if she might slip from my grasp if I don't hold her close enough to me. I don't know the last time I did that, maybe high school?

"I know you're independent, and you have your stubborn streaks, but please don't leave Roots, Ol. You belong here. I know you need a job, but we can figure that out. I just really think—"

"I love you, Mom," I blurt out, unable to watch her continue with that sad and desperate look on her face. I gently pull away. "Can I come in?"

"Of course. You never have to ask."

I march over to the couch and set myself down. Maverick trots behind me and plants himself at my feet, which I'm grateful for because my hands shake the slightest bit. I didn't think I'd be so nervous to have this conversation, but I guess I've been putting it off for so many years for a reason. "Where's Dad?"

"Out working on yet another project. You know your dad. He always has to keep himself busy." Her laugh is soft. I can tell she's nervous too, anxious to see what kind of bomb I'm going to drop on her now. I can't blame her.

"Yes, that sounds like Dad." Picking at my nail with laser focus, I say, "I talked with Rhett."

I half expect her to tell me she already knows about my panic attack and the conversation I had with Rhett, but instead, she just sits silently on the edge of her seat, watching me.

Pressing my lips together, I desperately try to hold back the words that want to flow in an overwhelming swirl of regret. I hold back for a beat before the words win out. "I'm sorry, Mom! I'm sorry for pushing you away for all these years. I'm sorry for letting you back in and then pushing you away again now. I'm sorry for not listening to you when you said we could figure something out to keep me in Roots. And I'm really freaking sorry for the way I've affected you over the years. I know dealing with my anxiety has been tough on you and Dad. I never wanted to make you worry about me or make you..." I choke on a sob, trying to keep the tears from flowing freely. "I never wanted to make you give up your dreams because of me. I never wanted to get in the way of you living your life."

With furrowed brows, Mom immediately reaches out to me, and I can't help but tense up. She's comforting me again while I'm trying to apologize to her for making her take care of me for so long. "No, Mom, I'm fine. You don't need to comfort me."

"Olivia Loraine Parker, I don't know what on earth

would make you think that you've been a burden to me or your father, but you need to get rid of those thoughts right now. I have loved being your mother, and I adore the young woman you've become. I'm so incredibly proud of you. Your anxiety has never been a burden to me, and you *certainly* never made me give up my dreams."

"But you were fired when you came to comfort me during my panic attack freshman year. That was your dream job, and you had to miss out on a huge meeting. You got fired because of *me*." Saying it out loud makes my heart crack.

"That was not your fault. I should've made sure I left the materials needed for the presentation, and I could've tried to reschedule the meeting. I had a good relationship with one of the big investors. Your panic attack opened my eyes. That job seemed like what I wanted at the time, but the second I saw you still needed me, and that I still had a role to play in your life, I realized that job wasn't what I wanted. I wanted the ability to still be there for you and spend time with my family. That job wouldn't have allowed that. It was taking over my life, late nights and working weekends to meet deadlines. You may think you ruined my plans that day, but you didn't. You saved me. Don't apologize for that. *I'm* sorry I never thanked you for what you did for me." She nudges my chin so that I'm forced to look up at her instead of my rugged cuticles. "Thank you for helping me realize what matters in life."

"Are you sure you're not just saying all this to protect me? I can take it."

"I'm positive. You've always been a ray of sunshine in my life. Yes, I worry about you with your panic attacks, but that just comes with the territory of being a mother and caring about someone." She presses a big noisy kiss on my cheek. "I love you so much. Don't you worry about me. I'm the parent. *I'm* supposed to worry about *you*. You just focus on living your own life. It's about time you finally start living it for yourself." She pulls back. "If you don't want to stay in Roots, that's fine, but I think we need to get you out of this job. I can't stop thinking about all the things you told me that day we went shopping. You should find something that doesn't make you miserable. Don't worry about your dad."

"I agree." I bite my lip, a little nervous to say the next part. "I think I want to find something in Roots, or at least near it. I really do love it here. I have you and Dad and Callie and Lauren... and Rhett."

She smirks. "I knew from the moment I laid eyes on that man that you'd fall in love with him."

"*Mom!*" I blush.

"What? It's so exciting! My little girl is in love." She sniffles. "*And* she wants to stay in Roots. I'm going to have my baby back. Minus having to share with Rhett, but lucky for you, I like that boy, so I guess I'll be okay with it."

We both laugh just as my dad barges in the back door, headphones in his ears as he blissfully whistles. He takes one look at the two of us, teary-eyed and clinging to one another, furrows his brow, pulls out an earbud, and asks, "What did I miss?"

Again, Mom and I laugh, tears still slithering down our cheeks. "I think I'm going to stay in Roots." I volunteer. "Would you be okay if I don't stay at my firm until I make senior? I don't want to disappoint you."

Dad immediately frowns. "How dare you ask such a silly question! I don't care about your job title. I just want my girl to be happy. If you told me you wanted to stay in

Roots and become a unicorn wrangler, I'd still be okay with it as long as you're happy."

Laughter slips out of me. "Well, I don't want to be a unicorn wrangler, but I don't want to do taxes anymore."

"I'm so glad to hear you're going to stay. This place is just so much brighter with you around. Plus, you're a much more worthy opponent in pool than your mom." Dad winks and pulls me in for a hug. "I mean it, Ol. I don't care about you being an accountant. I just want to see a smile on your face."

"She forgot to mention the part where she's in love!" Mom singsongs.

"I didn't say I'm in love." I rush to press my hands to my cheeks, desperate to hide the flush of color. My dad has always been so protective when it comes to boys.

Instead of teasing me or making a remark about how he's past due to clean his gun, he just walks over to me and wraps me in a bear hug. "He's a good man. Don't worry, I already gave him the talk, so you're good to go."

"*Dad!*" I laugh more out of shock than anything. "I don't know why I thought I would want to stay here. You two are always in my business." I tease.

"And you love us for it." Mom stands from the couch and pulls my dad and me into a hug, sandwiching me in the middle of it all. Maverick tries his best to weasel his way into the mix too, barking in excitement.

"Can't. Breathe."

"Just let it happen, honey. Your mom has been waiting to do this for years."

That truth bomb hits me hard, so I do as my dad says, letting the two of them smother me in love. It's nice. It feels good to allow people to care for me.

The sweet moment swiftly takes a turn as Mom asks, "So, can I expect grandbabies in the near future?"

"What?"

"I wouldn't mind having some grandkids running around the yard. Maybe they'd be the excuse I need to finally convince your mom we should get some horses. Think of all the fun they'd have here learning to ride horseback, milking the goats, and chasing the chickens around."

"I thought you'd be on my side, Dad!"

"I'm always on your side but you can't tell me it wouldn't be fun to have tiny little versions of you running around."

There's a quick flash in my mind of a little boy and a little girl, with my freckles coating their cheeks and Rhett's beautiful green eyes. They're covered in dirt and squealing with glee as Rhett chases the little girl around and my dad shows the little boy how to be gentle with the goats. The image is like a lightning bolt to the heart. I've never wanted something so badly. I've known for a little while now that I have very strong feelings for Rhett. I've known he's an incredible person and that I want to explore life with him, but it's just now hitting me that I don't just like him. I *love* Rhett, and despite not being on an official date yet, I know I want to build a life with him here in Roots.

"Oh my god."

"What's wrong, honey?"

"I love Rhett."

"I told you." My mom's face is filled with pure glee. "Go tell him. We're done here. I'll get plenty of time with you now that you're staying." Mom begins shooing me toward the door. "In fact, I can start making some calls and looking at job postings the second you leave. We are going to find you something. Don't you worry. For now, just focus on telling that man how much you care for him."

"Thanks, Mom."

I take one step out the door and then promptly swivel back around to give her one more hug. I pull away and lean in toward my dad, giving him one too. "Thank you, both."

Chapter Forty-Nine

Rhett

"I think that's all I need from you for the day. You said you had plans tonight, right? You should head out," Lauren says as she brushes her hands off.

"Are you sure?"

She nods, and I don't bother arguing with her. I need all the time I can get to prepare for my date with Olivia tonight.

When I get into my truck, and pull out my phone to play some music, I can't keep my mind from drifting back to the look of defeat on Olivia's face when she told me no one else wanted her, that she was stuck in tax. I know she's open to giving things another shot, but I want to help her. I never want to see that look on her face again.

An idea pops into my head, and before putting the truck in drive, I type a quick message to Olivia.

ME

How does 6 sound to meet for our date? I'm going to take care of something too. I will pick you up. Wear whatever you want. I don't do super fancy and you outshine anyone in anything you wear anyway xo

OLIVIA

You're so full of crap!

But yeah 6 works

I'm not full of crap. You're the most beautiful woman I've ever seen. Inside and out

You must want something

Just you

Also come hungry

Noted

Gotta go. See you at 6!

Can't wait 🤍

As I get out onto the road, it occurs to me that maybe I should call instead of just showing up uninvited, but I'm only thirty minutes away, and if I just show up, I won't be shut down before I even get a chance to sell my point, so I turn up the stereo a couple of decibels and keep driving.

———

Morgan Newton's office is impressive. I was expecting it to be a small and modest office, but this is the opposite. It's off the beaten path, but it's hardly small. The entrance hosts a crystal chandelier that shimmers in the sunlight streaming in through the large glass windows. The walls are lined with large, framed posters that advertise events. I'm sure they're all mementos from the past success of the firm.

A receptionist sits at the desk, a self-help book propped in her lap and an earbud in one ear. When I approach her desk, she doesn't look up at me right away, clearly trying to finish her paragraph as she sets her bookmark in the book but still doesn't lift her head to give me the time of day.

Finally, she slams the book shut. "How can I help you?" She gives me a warm smile. It's kind and innocent enough for me not to be irritated by the fact that she didn't immediately offer to help me.

"Is Morgan Newton in today? I'd like to see her."

"Do you have an appointment scheduled?"

"No," I admit, glancing down at my dirt-covered boots.

When I look back up at her, desperation rising inside of me, her face softens. "I'll give her a call and see if she's available. Can I give her your name and why you're visiting?"

"Rhett Lawson. I'm here to talk with her about Olivia Parker."

"Rhett Lawson. Olivia Parker. Got it."

She picks up the phone, and I try not to stare her down as anticipation fills me. I hear a click and then some murmuring on the other end before she speaks. "Hi, Miss Newton. I have a Mr. Rhett Lawson here who's hoping to speak with you. He said it's about Olivia Parker." More murmuring comes from the other end of the phone. "Okay. Yes, I will tell him. Thank you, ma'am."

I watch her carefully as she hangs up the phone. If my attention makes her uncomfortable, she doesn't show it. Maybe she can tell this has nothing to do with her and everything to do with my love for another woman.

"She says she has some time. Her office is the second

door on the left." She swivels around in her chair to point to the left wing of the hallway behind her. Swiveling back to face me, she adds, "Miss Newton likes to act very professional, but she's a big softie. Whatever you have to pitch to her, all you need to do is be raw and honest with her, and she won't be able to resist giving you what you need." She gives me a kind smile, her youthful eyes filled with hope.

"Thank you so much!" I wave a hand in her direction as I pass by her in two big steps, anxious to speak with Morgan.

I round the corner to her office and give two quick knocks. The door immediately opens to reveal Morgan with an expectant look on her face.

"Mr. Lawson." She reaches her hand out to shake mine.

I take it quickly, trying to calm my nerves. This isn't even necessarily for me, and I'm more nervous than I've ever been about anything. I just want Olivia to be happy. I'm terrified that if this doesn't work out, Olivia will be so beaten down that she won't hear me out again to stay any longer. She will pack up her things and be gone, out of my grasp for good. The thought makes my stomach roil, but I persevere because I can't take not trying.

"Feel free to take a seat. What can I help you with today?" Very professional, just like the girl at the front desk said she would be.

I take a seat across the desk from her, unable to keep from twiddling my thumbs anxiously in my lap. "I wanted to talk with you a bit about Olivia Parker. I know you spoke with her at the Resilient Paws Fundraiser she put on in Roots." I look at her, waiting for recognition to cross her face. She gives me a quick nod, so I go on. "I believe she reached out, and I haven't heard a thing about you two getting connected, so I just wanted to make sure you understand how incredible she is. If you let her pass by, you'll be making a huge mistake. Olivia is dedicated and kind. She puts her whole heart and soul into everything she does, and people love her. She'd be a huge asset to you as a marketing company because she just has this way of hooking people in. She'll be able to help you get more sponsors to keep the firm afloat. She can bring in new clients and catch people's attention with her marketing. She has a real passion for non-profit work and creating content for social media. She's even been posting content for a page all about dogs for years now, which she continued to do while working seventy hours a week for her real job. She will exceed your expectations. You just have to give her a chance. Please."

I pause, breathless. Morgan gives me a gentle smile, a knowing light in her eyes. "Can I ask what your relationship is to Olivia and why she didn't come down here herself to tell me all this?"

Shit. Did I just make things worse? "I'm her, uh, friend? More than that? I don't know yet, but I know I want to be everything to her." The words spill out quickly. "I'm sorry. I hope I didn't overstep by coming down here, but Olivia is amazing, and she has a hard time standing up for herself and fighting for the things she deserves, but she is made for more than accounting, and I *know* you could see that too based on the event she put on. Just think how much more she could do if given the chance. You have to talk with her. You'd be insane not to want her working for you."

The silence that fills the room is deafening. I squirm in my seat as I assess Morgan. Finally, she leans her forearms on the desk, gracefully lacing her fingers together. "I did see potential in Olivia, which is exactly why I gave her my card. She reached out, and I responded, but I never heard back from her. I think she could be a great fit for us here, but I'm not interested in hiring someone who doesn't want to be here."

I'm stunned. I open my mouth and then clamp it shut again. Finally, I say, "She was so excited when you came to speak with her at the fundraiser. I'm sure she wants the chance to work here. She's just afraid of being rejected. But I believe in her, and it sounds like you do too. Like I said, give her a chance."

"I'll tell you what. You go home and tell her to respond to my email. I'd like to get coffee or lunch with her and chat, see for myself that everything you said about her is true. If that's the case, there's room for her here as far as I'm concerned."

I let out a puff of air. "Thank you. Thank you! Oh my god, she's going to be so excited. I will tell her right away. Thank you!" I stand from my chair and reach my hand out to shake hers again. When she takes it, I can't help but add once more, "Thank you."

"Don't thank me yet. The ball is in Olivia's court now."

I give an eager nod, turning to walk toward the door.

"Oh, and Rhett?"

"Yeah?"

"When you have her reach out to me, please also tell her *she* gets to decide who she is and who she wants to be, not anyone else. We can all try to help her, but at the end of the day, she needs to believe in herself, or she won't get anywhere."

Chapter Fifty

Olivia

"I should head out now. Thank you so much for helping me get dressed. I don't know what I'd wear without having access to your closet all summer."

Callie scoops up the pile of discarded outfits resting on her bed. "You'd actually need to buy your own clothes. I thought your mom took you shopping a while back?"

"She did, but Rhett's already seen me in those clothes, and I want to wow him." I pause, then let out a breath and shake my hands out, groaning. "I'm nervous. Why am I so nervous? I've hung out with Rhett plenty of times before. We've kissed. We've shared a bed. This isn't exactly a monumental step to go on a date."

"I think you're just nervous because you two are finally all in. You get to tell him you love him. He's already told you. This is exciting! You know, they say being nervous and excited are the same feeling. Maybe you're not nervous at all. You're just excited."

"No, I'm definitely nervous, and you're making it worse.

I forgot about the part where I'm supposed to tell Rhett I love him. And on our first date. That seems so out of order."

"He's already told you he loves you. You don't have to worry about him not saying it back."

"He could've changed his mind."

"You're being ridiculous. You've already spent a bunch of time together. This date is just a formality. Don't get in your head."

"I'm always in my head." I flounce myself backward onto her bed with a dramatic huff.

"Don't do that. You'll mess up your hair. I spent a long time getting you those beautiful waves."

Laughter escapes me as I sit back up. "Yes, ma'am."

"Don't call me that. It makes me feel old." She scrunches her nose.

"I think the excitement of realizing I love him has worn off and now there's just nerves. This is all his fault! If he didn't make me wait the extra hour, I wouldn't be so in my head."

"Just be yourself. I think Rhett has managed to bring out the best in you in many ways. Enjoy that. Enjoy the feeling of being in love. And then hurry back and tell me all about it." She winks.

"I think I can do that."

"Good! Now get going or you're going to be late."

"Yes ma'am."

Callie grabs a pillow off her bed and swats me with it, corralling me toward the door.

"Okay, I'll take the hint. I'm going! I'm going!"

———

I pull into the driveway just as Rhett is walking out his front door, dressed in a clean pair of boots and Wranglers, which is a feat in and of itself considering he's always dirty, but the look is completed with a backward hat. He looks *damn* good.

He meets me halfway and holds out a bouquet.

"Are these the wildflowers that grow behind the house?" I gasp. "They're my favorite."

"Yeah, they are. That's why I got them."

"Thank you."

Silence falls over us, and I try to find a way to fill it. If I don't, I know I'm going to end up blurting out my feelings for him instead of picking the right moment. After all the wonderful things Rhett has done for me, I want to get this right.

"So, what are we doing for our date?"

Rhett glances down at his feet nervously, moving his palm to the back of his head. "Actually, before we go, there's something I wanted to tell you."

"Oh, okay." My stomach sinks. Something is wrong. He wants to take back what he said yesterday. He just got caught up in the moment, trying to comfort me. He doesn't really love me.

Immediately he reaches out to me, wrapping me up in his arms. "Everything is fine. I can see the concern written all over your face. You don't need to worry."

"Then what is it?"

"I spoke with Morgan Newton today."

"Oh."

He releases me. "She told me you haven't responded to her email, but she wants to give you a chance at her firm. The place seems great, and it'd be a real, secure job that would allow you to stay in Roots. So, if you're still interested in working with her, the door is open. She also told me that you need to believe in yourself and that you get to determine who you are and who you want to be, not anybody else."

Heat rises to my cheeks. "You make it sound so easy, but my meeting with Chance and Margaret showed it doesn't just take me believing in myself. I need someone to take a chance on me too. I fought for myself, and they still didn't want me."

"That's just one company. Believing in yourself means that you don't let one instance kick you down. You keep going. You keep looking into other opportunities until you find the right one."

"I guess so."

"I know so. Putting aside any of your fears, are you interested in a job with Morgan?"

"Yes," I say, hardly audible.

"Say it like you mean it."

"Yes!"

"That's better. You should email her right now. I'll wait."

He doesn't say it, but the look on his face makes it abundantly clear how much it would mean to him to see I'm making an effort to stay here.

"I can do that."

A smile blooms on his face. "I'll be right by your side through this. I'm your biggest cheerleader."

"Thank you. For everything. For helping me yesterday. For supporting me now. For supporting me all the time. I don't know what I ever did to deserve you."

"I could say the same. You're *way* out of my league."

"Shut up!" I shove his shoulder, laughter slipping from my lungs.

"Okay, email her now. I'm excited for the rest of our date, and I'm starting to get impatient."

I pull out my phone and begin typing, trying not to overthink my email. Once it's written, I hand the phone to Rhett. "How does this sound?"

He scans the screen, handing my phone back to me. "I think that's perfect." He pulls me in for a quick kiss. "I'm so proud of you."

"I couldn't do it without you."

"You could, but you don't have to." He laces his fingers in mine. "Should we get going?"

"Yes, please."

We spend the ten-minute drive teasing each other and making plans for the future. It feels amazing to finally have hope that I can have all the things I want, a job that doesn't drain me, and a slower, more intentional life filled with the people I love.

When he finally pulls off the road, I take in our surroundings, noting that I have absolutely no clue where we are right now. All I see is a vast empty field with the slow rolling river cutting through it all. "Where are we? What are we doing?" I ask eagerly.

"Just be patient. You'll see."

"Why do you keep doing this to me? Surprises don't work well for me. I like to plan, and I have *zero* patience."

"Then this will be good practice for you."

I groan as Rhett throws the truck in park and leaps out of his seat, bearing a lopsided grin. I don't know that I've ever seen him so excited and seeing that immediately makes me vibrate with energy too.

Before I can get out of the truck, he rushes around to my side, swinging my door open and reaching for my hand. *God, I'm so in love with this man.*

Once I'm safely out of the truck, Rhett opens the rear door to pull out an ice chest and a lump of foil. "I might need a little help setting up. I'm sorry. I had this planned out better, but then I got caught up with going to see Morgan."

I press a kiss to his cheek. "I don't care what we do. Nothing about this needs to be perfect. I'm just happy to be here with you."

Again, that lopsided grin of his is back. His green eyes are shining, and he's never looked more handsome than right now with all that love and joy flooding out of him. I can't hold things back anymore. I grab the ice chest and pile of tin foil from his hands and set it on the ground behind me.

"I love you, Rhett. I love you so very much."

"I lov—"

"Wait, I'm not done."

"But—"

I press a quick kiss to his lips, cutting him off again, before I continue. "You have managed to turn my life upside down and right side up again in a span of just a few months. You make me believe I'm worthy of love and anything else I could possibly want in life. You constantly push me to be a better person, and you make me feel whole. I owe you a million thanks for everything you've done for me, but one of the most important ones has to be thank you for helping me realize it's okay to accept help and for not giving up on me when I gave you plenty of reasons to."

"I'll never give up on you. Thank you for not giving up on me either."

"I will always be here for you, whether you want me to or not." I smile. Grabbing his hand, I add, "I hope, with every fiber of my being, that I can prove myself worthy of your love and make you feel worthy too. I hope I can make you feel special and loved every second of every day because you deserve that and more. There's been something between us since the moment I met you, and it's been incredible to watch it bloom. I love you, Rhett Lawson."

"Can I say it now?"

I nod.

"I love you too, Wildflower. So damn much."

When I pull him in for a kiss, it's fierce, filled with passion and desperation. It's as if knowing that we are both finally committed to being together has unlocked a new level for us. Every kiss before this has been electric, but this one is that and more. There are sparks and fireworks and lightning all at once. The chemistry and passion are enough to knock a woman out cold and yet they just light me up.

Chapter Fifty-One

Rhett

"Oh my god! This was so good. I didn't think you ate things like this in Texas." Olivia dabs her smirking lips with a napkin and tosses it on her empty plate.

"What're you talking about? It's buffalo chicken. That's Texas."

"It's on a baked sweet potato. I didn't think you ate vegetables unless they were fried."

"I had to make it a little more city for you."

"Hey! I'm turning into a true Texas girl now. I even own a pair of boots." She lifts her foot for me to see.

"You're right. You're a Texas gal through and through now." I laugh. "I might've also remembered you telling me you love sweet potatoes."

"I do. This was perfect."

"I hope you're not ready for the date to be over already. I'm not done yet."

A cautiously optimistic smile crosses her lips. "There's more?"

"Of course."

I get up from the blanket I've spread across the wild grass and move toward the truck, unlocking it and pulling my guitar from the back seat.

When I come back and sit down on the blanket across from Olivia, she's arching her brow at me.

"I've been working on this for a couple of weeks. I think I'm finally ready to share with you."

Fighting back a smile, she sits cross-legged with her hands securely in her lap. She looks like a perfect angel as she watches me expectantly. Just like that, a wave of nerves washes over me. I take in a deep breath that does little to release the tension in my chest.

"Are you okay?" Olivia's hand on my knee grounds me again.

"Uh yeah, just a little nervous. I want you to like this."

"Whatever it is, I'm going to love it because it's coming from you."

"I just want to make sure it's as good as you."

"Rhett Lawson! I've already told you you're worthy. I've told you I love you. Stop getting in your head and play me the damn song before the curiosity kills me." Her stern tone is immediately offset by her gentle laughter.

"I just want to point out the irony of *you* telling *me* that right now."

"Yes, I know, but at least I acknowledge I need to work on it, and I'm getting help."

"Touché." I let out one more deep breath and begin the first couple of chords of the song. After about five to ten seconds, I glance up at her, trying to see if recognition is crossing her face yet.

Instead of seeing her beaming like I expected, tears are filling her eyes. I instantly pause, setting the guitar aside to tug her into my lap. "Hey, what's wrong? What did I do?"

Brushing a stray tear with the back of her hand, she shakes her head. "You didn't do anything wrong. Keep going. I just can't believe you learned 'The Best Day' for me. You remembered me telling you about that song?" Her voice cracks as she finishes the question.

"I thought you knew by now that I hang onto every single word you say. I cherish every little detail you share with me."

"I knew you listened to me, but I still didn't think you'd care all that much about a story I told you from my childhood."

"I could tell this song, and the memory it brings with it, was important to you, so it's important to me. Don't you get it by now? The things that you care about are the things that I care about. The things that you love are the things I love, even if that thing is a damn Taylor Swift song." I smirk.

Her jaw drops open, but she quickly clamps it shut, biting her lip to hide a smile. "You take that back!"

I plant a soft kiss on her cheek and work my way down to her neck, just barely dusting it with my lips. "I love you."

"I love you too." She returns my affection with kisses of her own. Desire overtakes me, but she cuts me off when she innocently asks, "Will you finish the song, please? I promise I won't cry anymore."

A puff of air escapes my nostrils. "You can cry if you want to as long as they're happy tears."

"Okay, I promise. Just play it, please."

She draws away from where she was leaning against my chest, and I selfishly want to pull her back to me. Feeling her peel away from me feels like losing a limb. She's a part of me now. I'm not whole without her. But instead of being selfish, I let her sit across from me and pull my guitar back into my lap, starting the song over from the beginning again.

She sits there, watching me with a soft look in her eyes for the entire four minutes that I play the song. When it's done, she claps for me, making my cheeks flush. "Oh, jeez. Don't clap for me."

"But it was so good. I'm tempted to ask you to play it again."

"I can if you want me to, but I have one more song to play you first."

Her brows knit together. "Okay. Is it another one I'll recognize?"

"I don't think so. It's kind of a Rhett original."

"I get my own Rhett song?"

"You'll probably end up with several, the way you've been inspiring me lately. I've always wanted to write music, but I've never really had much inspiration. The pain of losing Isabel inspired me enough for one song, but once I was done, I couldn't get anything else right again. But now, with you, the ideas won't stop coming. You've opened the floodgates."

"Rhett, that's amazing!"

"You're the one who's inspiring me."

"But you're the one writing the songs."

"And I wouldn't be writing them without you."

"Just take the credit while I'm giving it to you."

I scrunch my face up at her. "Fine."

"Is it just the guitar or do I get to hear you sing again too?"

"You don't want to hear me sing. I sound like a dying whale when I sing."

"You do *not!* I'm such a sucker for that raspy voice you have. And I'm not just saying that because I love you. You genuinely have an incredible voice. I can't believe you've never tried to pursue a career in music."

I just shrug. "I love music, but I also love working on the ranch. I think this is a gift I'd like to keep private, just as a hobby. I don't need to ruin it by turning it into something for money. I just want to write songs for my beautiful girlfriend."

"I think I can live with that."

I let out a sharp exhale. "Here goes nothing, I guess."

I strum the first few chords, and watch as she becomes instantly entranced, unable to take her eyes off me. That feeling is more than mutual. I look deep into those beautiful amber eyes that drive me absolutely wild as I strum a song about how she opened up my whole world.

Chapter Fifty-Two

Olivia

I set down my turkey, bacon, and avocado sandwich. "So, let me get this straight, you two drunkenly convinced Jax to drive you all the way to Amarillo so you could track down Austin, *and* you caught him with another woman? You're *sure* it was romantically?"

Callie nods emphatically, her eyes practically popping out of her head.

"Yeah, I'm sure of it," Lauren says. "She was naked in his hotel bed. I swear it was like something you only see in the movies. He couldn't even try to deny it."

"What happens now?"

Lauren winces. "I called off the wedding, obviously, and he's moving out. He says he's going to live with his parents temporarily, but I hope he just moves to Amarillo to be with that girl. I don't really want to see him everywhere in town now, and it'd somehow make me feel better if there's at least some real feelings there. After being together for almost eight-years, I'd prefer he cheated on me because he found the real love of his life, not just because he's a horny dude, or, I don't know, that I just wasn't enough for him anymore."

"Lauren, no!" Callie bellows. The elderly couple at the table to our left pause their conversation to eye her. "Sorry, Mr. and Mrs. Colt. Please enjoy your meal." She gives a cheesy grin and a wave before leaning in toward Lauren, lowering her voice. "Don't you dare think for one second that this is your fault or that you weren't enough for him. If anything, he wasn't enough for you. He just proved that with his actions."

"Thanks, Callie."

"I just can't believe someone would do that to another human, especially a human as sweet as you."

Callie waves down the waitress, turning to Lauren and adding, "I know what will cheer you up." She orders us something called a gooey cookie.

"This might not be all that helpful yet since things are still fresh, but I think this could be good for you," I say.

Lauren arches a brow, forcing me to explain myself. "When I asked you to come out with us the other night, you tried to tell me you had to get things ready for Austin to come home. Then a little bit before you and Callie left, you were talking about how you felt like you two had just been living parallel lives. It just seems to me like this can be an opportunity for you to live life on your own terms, not for anyone else. As someone who was constantly trying to satisfy other people all the time, I can tell you it's exhausting, and it's really freeing to finally escape that."

She nods. I'm sure it's a little early for her to hear all of this, but it's evident she's at least trying to give my words some thought.

Unable to tame my curiosity, I change the subject. "So, how did you convince Jax to drive you two all the way to

Amarillo? If you left after his shift, it must have been at least two-thirty in the morning."

"You should've seen it! Lauren has some sort of magical powers or something because she just batted her eyelashes at Jax, and he was like putty in her hands. I've never seen that flirt look so uncool. It was amazing!"

"Whoa." I quirk a brow, turning to Lauren. "Don't think I didn't notice the way he teased you at the bar the other night, and he has a nickname for you."

"Oh, stop! Jax is Charlie's best friend. He's always thought of me as an annoying little sister, and he only calls me Freckles because he knows I've always hated my freckles. He does look out for me when I need it though, especially with Charlie being in Los Angeles now. Hence him taking us to Amarillo."

She flips her napkin inside out as she watches the waitress bring out the gooey cookie, which is a chocolate chip cookie served in a warm skillet and covered in a mountain of vanilla ice cream.

"I don't even want to think about another guy right now. I'm still kind of getting over my last relationship. Besides, it's going to take me a little while to trust my judgment again. I really thought Austin was *the one*. I pictured having babies together and taking care of Copper Hill together. I saw it all with him, and it came crashing down in just a couple of months."

Callie covers her mouth with a napkin to hide the fact that she just took a giant bite of cookie. "You're going to be okay. You've got us."

"Yeah, and as long as I can help it, I'm not going anywhere, well except to get my stuff in San Francisco, but otherwise, you're stuck with me."

"Thank you." Lauren forces a smile on her face.

"Enough of that sappy talk. You *have* to explain what's going on between you and Rhett. I saw him hanging all over you at the fundraiser, and I heard you two were out late in some field near Copper Hill last night."

I want to keep comforting her, but I can tell from the look in her eyes she's desperate for a change of subject.

Callie leans her elbows on the table, placing her chin in her hands and watching me intently. Picking up on what Callie is doing, Lauren joins in, innocently batting her eyes at me, waiting for me to fill them in. Unwilling to play into their hand, I spoon a melty bite of cookie, careful to get a good ratio of ice cream in the bite as well.

"What do you want me to say?"

"For starters, have you two kissed?"

"Yes."

Callie lets out a shriek that makes Mrs. Colt turn toward us again. In an effort to appease her, Callie just waves cheerfully as she spoons another big bite of the delicious dessert.

"Wasn't that obvious?" I ask.

"Yeah, but we still had to make you say it," Lauren teases.

"I've decided I actually hate you two."

They both laugh in unison, and I can't help but join in. I haven't had friends like this since—I don't know how long it's been. I don't know if I've ever connected with other girls my age in the same way that I have with Callie and Lauren, not even Anna from college. They've just embraced me immediately, making me feel loved and free to be myself. I've been open with them about my anxiety and panic attacks, and never once have they made me feel ashamed. Instead, they just lift me up and tell me about their own scars too. It feels so good to have real friendship like this.

"How did it happen?"

I fill them in on how Rhett opened up to me. I'm careful not to get too detailed, even though Callie knows all about Rhett's past. As far as I know, Lauren doesn't, and that's Rhett's story to share. "Anyway, after he told me some personal things about himself, I let it slip that his honesty made me really want to kiss him. Next thing I know, he was pulling me in for the best kiss of my life. I'm telling you I thought Brady Mitchell from sophomore year of college was a good kisser. I was wrong. Rhett puts that boy to shame."

"Oh my god! Oh my god! Oh my god!" Callie cries. I can't help but laugh. She already knows most of this, but she is still genuinely acting giddy over hearing it all again.

"Have you said the "L" word to one another yet?" Lauren asks.

"Maybe."

"I *knew* it! Oh my gosh! This is so great! So now what? Have you figured out the job thing yet? Are you going to keep living with him?"

"Rhett and my parents have both been super support-ive. Rhett talked to someone on my behalf about a job and has offered for me to stay in the big house or the guest house, my choice. The cottage is ready, but I still haven't been able to bring myself to move out of Rhett's guest bedroom. I love being there with him. I can't picture moving out." The girls return my answer with more squeals. "All of this is sort of freaking me out though. I've spent my life trying to keep from being a burden, and here I am letting someone else try to take care of me again."

"That's not being a burden. Rhett *wants* to do that for you. It's very clear from the way he looks at you, and the fact that he told you he loves you, that he wants you around for the long haul. Accepting help from other people doesn't make you a burden."

"Thanks, Lauren."

"You will *never* be a burden to any of us," Callie chimes in. "It's best you learn that before you move here. We are all family, and we take care of each other."

I give a soft smile, not knowing what else to say. I want that so badly, but I'm worried I don't know how to get it. I've never had so many people caring for me and accepting me as I do right now. What if I mess it all up?

We finish the gooey cookie, scraping the bottom of the skillet for every last bit of chocolate, and pay. As we shuffle out of Sweet Mae's Diner, I give Lauren a tight squeeze, and she rushes off, explaining, "I promised my dad I'd help him move the cattle into a new pasture this afternoon. With Austin leaving, we are a little short-handed."

"We totally understand. Go. Get out of here. And tell Austin he can go to Hell!" Callie calls after her.

Lauren gives a shy smirk before turning to her truck, getting in, and speeding off out of the parking lot.

"That girl is always in a hurry," Callie notes, a hint of affection in her voice. She turns back to me, and her smile falters. "Are you okay?"

"Yeah, I just don't get how you went from not liking her to treating her like she's actually your friend."

My words wipe the smile off her face. She chews on her lower lip before finally admitting, "I used to date her brother, Charlie. We started dating junior year of high school. He went to college in L.A., and I stayed in Texas for school. We did long distance for a whole year, and I thought the plan was for him to get his adventures outside of this little town and then come back, but after a year there, he decided he actually wanted nothing to do with this town...

or me. It sucked, and I wanted someone else to blame. Lauren always seemed perfect. She had the perfect grades, the perfect boyfriend. She had it all, and she just swooped right in to clean up his mess when he left, so she was an easy person to blame. I never wanted to believe that it was just that he left because I wasn't enough. Because then my parents left me too, and it was all just too much. I realize now it was dumb, but that's why I didn't like her before."

"Aww, Callie!" I pull her in for a hug. "He doesn't know what he's missing. Your parents too. You're absolutely enough."

"Thank you." She gives me a soft smile as she returns my hug. "I hope you know you're doing okay. I know it's scary to let people in and accept change, but you're finding your way. You've got an incredible man who adores you, a loving family that has welcomed you here with open arms, and the best friends a girl could ask for." She winks. "The rest will come, but you've built all of this on your own. You know what you're doing. Don't let yourself overthink things."

A swell of pride rises in my chest. I'm doing pretty well. Three months ago, I never in my wildest dreams could've pictured this is what my life would look like, that I'd feel so happy and loved here in Roots, that I'd grow to tolerate the humidity and appreciate the flat plains of Texas, but here I am. I guess we all surprise ourselves sometimes.

When I get in my car, I pull out my phone and find an email notification. It's from Morgan. I swallow my nerves and open it up.

Chapter Fifty-Three

Rhett

I SIT OUTSIDE SOME TRENDY RESTAURANT NEAR FORT Worth, eagerly waiting for Olivia to finish her lunch with Morgan. If it were up to me, I'd be sitting right next to her, holding her hand through the whole thing, but I know she's an adult and can handle things herself. I have to let her spread her wings on her own. So instead of sitting by her side through this, I sit in my truck with Maverick, the air conditioning cranked to full blast, strumming on my guitar as I create my third song since I started writing again.

But it's damn near impossible to focus when I know how nervous she was beforehand. She talked through things with her friends and her therapist, and she's doing a much better job of unapologetically believing in herself and her bright future, but I know she still had that small amount of doubt in the back of her mind. I hate just sitting here, unable to know what's going on, unable to make sure she's being protected. Meanwhile, I still have immense hope and more than enough faith in Olivia to believe she's going to come out of this meeting with great news.

I play the first couple chords of the song again. It sounds good, really good, possibly the best I've come up with so far. I'm so excited about this one, and yet I can't bring myself to get out of my head enough to keep going.

Maverick starts whimpering in the back seat, and I turn to soothe him, but I can tell he doesn't want attention from me. His eyes are laser-focused on Olivia walking out of the restaurant. I watch her smile and give Morgan a handshake before they split off in opposite directions.

The second Morgan's back is turned to me, I shoot out of the truck. I rush to Olivia's side, swooping her off her feet and into my arms. As I carefully assess her face, desperate to gauge how things went, I finally ask, "How'd it go?"

She looks somber for a brief moment, but it lasts for all of two seconds before her face splits into a grin. She tries to bite back her smile, but it's no use.

"Don't you dare try playing tricks on me. I can already tell you're trying to hide a smile. It went well then?"

"It was great. She offered me a job on the spot. I still need to see the official offer, but it sounds like the pay should be good, and they'll have benefits like health insurance and a retirement plan. She wants me to bring in some of my own clients, so I can create a portfolio of causes that *I* actually care about." She's absolutely glowing. "I can keep helping Carol out with the rescue in a volunteer and marketing capacity, *and* I get to help *more* non-profits."

"That's amazing! I'm so happy for you. When do you start?"

"I told her I'd get back to her by tomorrow."

The smile I was wearing a second ago is wiped off my

face. "What do you mean? I thought this was all good news? What do you have to consider? If it's about tying up loose ends in San Francisco, you already know your parents, Callie, Lauren, and I have all volunteered to come help you move. So, what's wrong?"

She grabs onto my hand, stroking her thumb across my skin gently. "Nothing is wrong. I wanted to talk through things with you since you're a part of my future, and I want to make sure I'm not just leaping into this because I want to stay in Roots or be out of my old job. You and Morgan were right. *I* get to decide who I am and who I want to be, so I just want to make sure I'm not leaping into the job because they're the first firm to give me a chance. I know my worth, and I'm going to make sure this is the right fit. If it's not, then I'm ready to quit my job in San Francisco and keep looking *here* in Roots." She places a kiss on my cheek. "Don't worry. There's no place I'd rather be than here with you. I'm not going anywhere."

My shoulders slowly release. "Thank God!" I can't help but laugh, feeling a little silly. "I think that sounds very rational. Look how far you've come."

I open Olivia's door for her but pull her to me so that we're chest to chest. I look her in the eyes and say, "I am so damn proud of you for taking charge of your life, for deciding you weren't living the life you wanted, and recognizing you have the power to change that. And I hope you already know this, but I'm going to say it anyway, I'm here for you. I'll help you move out of your apartment. I'll talk through pros and cons of taking the job with Morgan. I'll be by your side when you put in your notice. Whatever you need, I'm here for you. I love you, Wildflower."

"I love you too, Rhett."

"I told you this town makes people want to stay." I smirk.

"You were right. I hate it when you're right." She presses a kiss to my cheek as a dopey smile lands on her face.

Epilogue

One Year Later

Olivia

"Mᴀʏ I ʜᴀᴠᴇ ᴛʜɪꜱ ᴅᴀɴᴄᴇ?" Rʜᴇᴛᴛ ᴀꜱᴋꜱ, ʜᴏʟᴅɪɴɢ ᴏᴜᴛ a hand to me as a Kane Brown song comes on over the speakers.

"Yes, please." I giggle, my second drink starting to get to me.

He keeps my hand locked in his and moves his other hand to my waist, drawing me into him. I take advantage of the closeness and gently whisper, "How are you doing?"

"I'm actually doing okay."

"Are you sure?" Concern lines my brow. He's been out with me three times now since he told me the truth about why he doesn't come to bars anymore. Tonight is his first time having a drink. He's on his second beer, which he's been nursing for an hour, but that's still a feat in and of itself. He's been out on the dance floor line dancing with Lauren, Callie, and me. He's better at it than me, which is *so* annoying. *Why does he have to be good at everything?* I'm telling myself his background with the guitar helps his sense of rhythm.

"I'm with you, how could I not be okay?"

My cheeks flush. Even after being officially together for a year now, he still gets to me. His touch still sets me on fire. His words still take my breath away. He still makes me believe in myself and makes me feel cherished, never like a burden.

"Just tell me if you want to leave, okay? And you don't have to finish your beer. You can take things slow. I'm just proud of you for trusting yourself enough to let loose even a little bit when you want to." I nuzzle into his chest.

He draws out from me to look me in the eyes. "I'm okay. I promise. In fact, I've never been better."

"Yeah?"

"Yes." He gnaws on his lower lip.

"What's going through that head of yours?"

"Come with me." He tugs me toward the front door of the bar.

"Where are we going? Callie and Lauren are still inside. We can't just leave them."

"We aren't leaving them. Don't worry."

We step out into the cool night air, and he continues to pull me along. We round the corner of the building where Callie and Lauren are hunched over something looking like a couple of deer caught in the headlights.

"Rhett! What are you doing? You're early. You're ruining it." Callie gives him a very meaningful look.

I glance between the two of them and then down at Callie and Lauren's feet. There's a tangle of string lights, an absurd amount of wildflowers, and a tiny to-go box like the one Rhett brought lava cakes in when I first came to town. I turn back to Rhett for an explanation, and he's down on one knee, wielding a ring with a dainty circular diamond and a tiny diamond accent on either side. When Callie and Lauren manage to plug in the string lights behind me, it shimmers in the light. It's perfect.

"Rhett, are you—" My voice comes out shaky.

Rhett's eyes are watery. "Yes." His words send chills across my body despite the fact that it's easily eighty degrees outside.

"I love you with every fiber of my being, and you have continued to challenge me and make me into a better version of myself than I could ever be on my own. You've supported me and pushed me to believe that I am a good person who is worthy of love, and I hope to spend the rest of my days doing that for you." He swipes a tear from his cheek. "I couldn't resist you from the moment you rolled into town, and our connection has only gotten stronger and stronger. Now that you've settled into the job with Morgan, and we've lived together for longer than we've been dating, I have this knowing in my heart that I'm ready for the next step with you. I want to create a life with you. I want to raise beautiful babies with you. I want to grow old with you. I want everything with you. Will you marry me, Wildflower?"

Lauren and Callie each let out shrieks, and I swear I can hear some sniffles behind me, but I'm only focused on the man I love kneeling in front of me. "Yes! Yes! I want all of that with you. Yes! Please!"

He jolts upright, wrapping his muscular arms around me tight and crashing his lips into mine. It's a messy kiss, mixed with tears and made difficult by each of our insistence on bearing huge smiles. When we pull back from one another, I find a swarm of the people I love all around me. Rhett. Callie and Lauren. My parents. Carol. Everyone is here, snapping photos, taking videos, and giving hugs and words of congratulations.

A year ago, I rolled into this town only focused on getting through the three months I *had* to be here, desperate to keep people at a distance. Now, I have a whole swarm of people who love me, and I'm putting down roots in the place I least expected. Yet, I wouldn't want my life to be any other way. I finally get to live life on my terms with the people I love.

Author's Note

The idea for my debut novel came to me in a dream, but if I'm being honest, I don't even know exactly how the idea for *Putting Down Roots* developed. It almost feels as if it just flowed from my fingertips without any conscious thought.

I wrote the book at one of the darkest times in my life. I felt alone. I felt stuck. I felt consumed by my anxiety, and I was having panic attacks that mirrored those Olivia experiences in the book.

Writing *Putting Down Roots* became my outlet, a therapeutic way for me to create a reality where a girl could leave the big city, quit the corporate job that didn't fit her, and make friends and family a priority again. Eventually, I made this *my* reality too.

Now, *Putting Down Roots* is my way of sharing with the world the lessons that I learned from all my struggles. After reading this novel, I hope you believe that even when you find yourself in a dark place, you can find your way out. You will find people who love you at your worst. You can make changes, even when people tell you you can't. You don't need to fit the mold everyone else expects you to fit into.

Move to the new city. Leave the job that crushes your soul. Make time for the people you love. Life is too short not to create one that makes you happy.

While this book is meant to be like a warm hug for anyone who has been in that place— lost, hopeless, or consumed by anxiety— I also want to take a moment to acknowledge how proud I am of myself for deciding that the life I was living wasn't enough and then striving for more. I am proud of myself for not only finishing this story when I thought it was no good, but for also turning it into something that I am so incredibly proud of.

I hope with all my heart that you can't relate to the dark side of Olivia's story. But if you can, just know you are not alone, and it doesn't last forever. Thank you for reading this story. It means the world to me.

Just like all the books I write, I hope you were able to find something within the pages of *Putting Down Roots* that gave you hope and made you feel a little less alone in this great big world.

Acknowledgments

Mom, Dad, and Jeffrey, thank you for your endless support. I don't know too many people whose families would agree to road trip across Texas with them just to do research for a book, but you did. Thank you for willingly taking detours so I could take pictures and videos. Thank you for stopping into Buc-ee's with me at 9:30 at night so we could pick up a couple pints of ice cream that I researched online and put in my book. Most of all, thank you for building memories with me that I will cherish forever. I love you all so much!

Mom, thank you for being the only one to read *Putting Down Roots* before I finished edits. I can't begin to describe how much I appreciate your willingness to always make time for me. You are the greatest mom a girl could ask for. When I wrote this book, I knew I wanted to create a special mother-daughter bond between my characters, and while I had to complicate Mandi and Olivia's relationship for the sake of the plot, I pulled all the wonderful parts of their relationship from my relationship with you. I love you, and I am so grateful to call you my best friend.

Patrick, thank you for always being my shoulder to cry on, holding me through the tough moments, and showing me that I don't need to be perfect to be loved. Thank you for always listening to my ramblings when I was nervous, excited, or stressed about this book. Your intentional support throughout this process meant the world to me.

Kinsley, thank you for being my number one fan! Every time you commented on my posts telling me how much you loved *Where the Sun Lights the Shadows*, and how excited you were for *Putting Down Roots*, it instilled me with new confidence, which I so desperately needed. Your endless support reminded me why I do this, and I can never thank you enough.

Caitlin, thank you for pushing me to make this into a better book, for hopping on calls with me to brainstorm, and for giving me patience and grace when I struggled with the editing process.

Kimberly, thank you for the role you played in building my confidence back up. You didn't even know I needed it, but your encouragement and support helped me believe in myself again. Coming to you was the best decision I could've made for this book. I love the author-editor relationship we are building.

Melissa, thank you for putting up with all my chaos. You have been such a pleasure to work with, and you truly brought my vision for the *Putting Down Roots* cover to life. I cannot wait to see what we can create together for the next couple books in the series!

To my ARC readers, thank you so much! There are a million little things that go into publishing a book, and as an indie author, I tackle a lot of them on my own, but ARC reading is an essential part of the process that I get to share. I am so grateful you decided to be a part of this journey with me. Thank you for all your reviews and edits. Thank you for sharing your excitement about this book. And thank you for helping me not only reach the goals I set myself, but surpass them.

Thank YOU, reader, for choosing to pick up my book

out of the millions you could choose to read. I've dreamed of being an author and sharing the stories swirling inside my head since I was seven years old. That dream is now a reality because of people like you.

About the Author

Jenna Rogers loves crafting heartfelt, closed-door contemporary romance stories. When she's not writing, you can find her curled up with a good book, baking something sweet, or pumping iron at the gym. Jenna calls the Pacific Northwest her home and enjoys all the beautiful sunrises and sunsets the region has to offer. Her debut novel, *Where the Sun Lights the Shadows*, marked the start of her professional writing journey, but Jenna started writing when she was seven years old. Even then, she was captivated by love, writing a story about cows falling in love and another with a romantic plot set along the Oregon Trail. You can find her on her website at www.jennarogersbooks.com, where you can buy signed copies of her book and sign up for her email list. She is also found on the following social media platforms:

instagram.com/jennarogersbooks

threads.net/@jennarogersbooks

tiktok.com/@jennarogersbooks

goodreads.com/jennarogers

Also by Jenna Rogers

Where the Sun Lights the Shadows

Roots Series Book #2 - Coming Late 2025

Roots Series Book #3 - Coming 2026